Let Love
Find You

JOHANNA LINDSEY

Let Love
Find You

G

Gallery Books

New York   London   Toronto   Sydney   New Delhi

G

Gallery Books
A Division of Simon & Schuster, Inc.
1230 Avenue of the Americas
New York, NY 10020

This Gallery Books export edition June 2012

GALLERY BOOKS and colophon are registered trademarks of
Simon & Schuster, Inc.

For information about special discounts for bulk purchases,
please contact Simon & Schuster Special Sales at 1-866-506-1949
or business@simonandschuster.com.

The Simon & Schuster Speakers Bureau can bring authors to your live event.
For more information or to book an event contact the Simon & Schuster Speakers
Bureau at 1-866-248-3049 or visit our website at www.simonspeakers.com.

Manufactured in the United States of America

10 9 8 7 6 5 4 3 2 1

ISBN 978-1-4516-8959-4
ISBN 978-1-4516-3329-0 (ebook)

Let Love Find You

Prologue

THE BOY STOOD AT his bedroom window, watching the falling snow. It was sticking to the street and might stay around this time. It was cold enough to. He liked snow. It made the street look so bright and clean, especially at night with the streetlamps shining down on it. His bedroom faced the street. He often stood there and watched the fancy coaches driving past during the day. Occasionally, when he couldn't get right to sleep, or he woke up for some reason, he'd stand there at night as well. And that's when he'd see one coach in particular stop in front of the town house he lived in with his mother, Elaine, as it did now. The coach never came during the day, only late at night.

The tall man stepped out of it, his greatcoat swirling around him as he turned to close the door and say something to the driver before the coach drove off. The man hurried inside. He had his own key. For as long as the boy could remember, this man had been coming to his home.

It had seemed like a normal London household he was growing up in. They had a few servants. His mum was always available to him during the day. And for the longest time, he went to bed early enough not to know she wouldn't be available to him at night.

He had just turned six, but couldn't remember how old he'd been when he'd asked his mum who the man was. He just knew it was long ago. She'd seemed surprised that day that he even knew about the man.

"Lord Wolseley is our landlord, is all. He comes to make sure his house is in good repair."

"So often?"

"Well, we actually became friends, good friends. He's not a happy man and I've got a good shoulder to cry on." She patted her shoulder with a grin. "You know it well, you've done all your crying on it, haven't you?"

He remembered that he'd felt embarrassed that day. She was talking about all his hurts and bruises that he *wouldn't* have cried over if she didn't always gather him into her arms to coddle him. He tried to picture that tall man crying on her shoulder but couldn't.

He'd been told his own father was dead, had died when he was still a baby, though his mother refused to say much more than that. "It makes me cry, those memories," she would say. "Someday I'll tell you all about him, just not now."

But she'd never told him more. The only time he could remember his mum being sharp with him was when he persisted with questions about his father. And the last time he asked, she did get tears in her eyes. He never asked again.

But the landlord continued to visit late at night, and the boy would hear the door to his mother's room quietly open and close. Sometimes he'd go out in the corridor and could hear her laughter on the other side of her bedroom door. If the man made her happy, why didn't they marry so he could share in that happiness, too?

Earlier this year, his curiosity took a new turn and he asked his mother, "Is he going to be my father?"

She'd gathered him close and said, "Whatever can you be thinking, darling? Lawrence has his own family, a wife and children. He's just a friend. I get lonely, you know. It's nice to have someone like him to talk to."

Soon thereafter the boy began to think Lord Lawrence Wolseley was his real father. Once the notion took hold, it wouldn't let go. He was afraid to ask his mother, though. She didn't want to talk about this landlord of theirs and didn't want to talk about his "dead father." It hurt to think she'd lied to him. He hoped he was wrong, but he had to find out for sure.

So tonight he went out in the corridor. His mother's bedroom door was closed as usual. He didn't knock. He heard the laughter, then voices talking so quietly he couldn't make out what they were saying. He didn't put his ear to the door, he just sat down in the corridor, crossed his legs, and waited.

It was a long wait. He almost fell asleep there. But finally the door opened. He jumped up immediately before he got stepped on. He'd never seen this man up close before. He was taller than the boy had thought, handsome, well dressed, with hair as dark as his own. His greatcoat was draped over his arm, and a jewel-crested ring on his finger flashed in the light.

The boy asked his question before he lost his nerve. "Are you my father?"

The man, who hadn't yet noticed him, glanced down at him now. A scowl formed on the man's face. "You should be abed. Go!"

Frightened by the man's harsh tone, the boy couldn't move,

but the man walked off briskly down the corridor. The door to his mother's room was still open. The boy peeked inside to make sure his mother was all right. She was sitting at her vanity across the room admiring a necklace he'd never seen her wear before.

The boy hurried back to his room, confused and scared, hoping the man wouldn't tell her about the question he'd asked—which hadn't been answered.

Later that week, his mother summoned him downstairs to the foyer. Just inside the door stood a man he'd never before seen. Hat in hand, big, he had blond hair and blue eyes like the boy's mother. And she appeared angry. With him? Or with the stranger she was glaring at?

She looked down at him and said, "This is your uncle Donald, my brother. We haven't talked for a good number of years, but Donald would like you to stay with him for a while on his horse farm in the country. You'll love it there."

The boy's eyes widened. He didn't know his mother had a brother! More afraid than ever before in his life, he turned and wrapped his arms tightly around her waist. He was being sent away? He didn't understand!

"No, please!" he cried. "I'll never ask questions again, I promise!"

She hugged him tightly to her. "Hush, darling, I'll visit you soon. You're going to have so much fun in the country, you won't even miss me."

"No! I want to stay here with you!"

She pushed him toward his uncle. "Now, before I cry!" she shouted at Donald.

The boy was dragged screaming out of the only home he'd

ever known. He tried to get out of the waiting coach. When his uncle prevented that, he hung out the window instead, calling to his mother, tears streaming down his cheeks. He could still see his mother standing on the stoop, waving at him.

But his mum had been right. Although he missed her terribly, as the months passed, he found himself enjoying living with his aunt and uncle in Lancashire on their large country estate. Because of the puppy his aunt gave him for his very own, and so many others always underfoot in the big house. Because he made his first real friend, one of the workers' sons, and they became inseparable. Because there was so much more to do there than in the city. But mainly, because of the horses. There were so many of them! He was allowed to help care for them. Soon he excelled at grooming and feeding them and progressed to training the newborns.

He never saw his mother again. Not alive. The day his aunt and uncle came to tell him that she'd died of pneumonia, all the pain of her abandoning him returned. He was going to turn eight that year, and he was still too young to know how to hold back the tears that streamed down his face.

"She wanted you to have this."

He looked down at the porcelain horse Donald placed in his hand. His mother had taken her love from him, abandoned him, never even visited him once since she had sent him away. He wanted *nothing* from her now, and in a burst of heartbroken rage, he raised his arm to throw the figurine against the wall to smash it as she'd smashed his hopes that they would be together again someday. She'd died instead, making sure that would never happen.

But Donald stopped him. "Don't, lad. She wanted you to

keep it. She said that one day you'd understand and realize how much she loved you."

Lies! She was gone! He'd never see her again, never feel her arms around him again. And the tears wouldn't stop that day, or the next, or the next when his mother's body was brought home to Lancashire to be buried where she'd grown up. The pain he felt was overwhelming as he watched her being lowered into the ground. It hurt so much he dropped to his knees. His aunt knelt beside him and held him.

Late that night, he snuck out of the house and ran to the small graveyard. He'd brought the porcelain horse with him. He would have buried it today with his mother if he didn't think his uncle would have stopped him. He buried it now beside her grave, but the pain was somehow worse now, he could barely see through his tears. He wouldn't keep the stupid horse! He wanted nothing of hers, nothing to remind him that his own mother didn't want him.

He swore to himself that night that he'd never cry again . . . or love anyone again. It hurt too much.

Chapter One

LADY AMANDA LOCKE SIGHED as she gazed at her reflection in the oval mirror. Sitting at the vanity in the comfortable room she'd been given at her cousin Rupert's house in London, she imagined she saw a wrinkle at the corner of one eye. She gasped. Did she? She leaned closer. No, just her imagination and the light, but it wouldn't be long before it wasn't. She had just turned twenty! The *ton* would be calling her an old maid soon—if they weren't already.

She sighed again. Her maid, Alice, pretended not to notice as she pinned the last blond lock of Amanda's coiffure into place. That wouldn't have stopped Amanda if she felt like being vocal about her melancholy tonight, but she didn't. Alice had heard it all and heard it often. Amanda's whole family had heard it all, and she had a large family. But she *was* tired of complaining about such a sorry state of affairs, she just couldn't help it sometimes.

Her first London Season shouldn't have been such a disaster. It was supposed to be a roaring success. She had expected no less. Her family had expected no less. She was a beauty, after all, even quite fashionable with her blond hair and powder-blue eyes, and she also had the aristocratic bones that ran in her family. She was *also* the only daughter of Preston Locke, the 10th Duke of Norford. That alone should have had the proposals streaming in. And no one had doubted that she would outshine all the other debutantes that Season two years ago, herself included. But then no one had been prepared for the infamous Ophelia Reid, who had debuted that same year, and no one, not even Amanda, could compare to Ophelia's dazzling beauty.

It was almost funny, Amanda thought as she looked back on it, how jealous she'd been of Ophelia, so jealous that she'd spent most of that first Season stewing about it and thus ignoring the young men who had tried to get to know her. So really, she could blame that disaster on herself. But of course her emotions got out of hand, especially when she found out her own brother, Raphael, was also falling under the ice queen's spell.

Ophelia hadn't even been likable back then! Amanda recalled wondering how her brother could be so dense just because Ophelia was a raving beauty! Ophelia was manipulative, a liar, and spiteful to boot. Anyone with two eyes could see it, which meant every man in London that year wasn't utilizing both of his eyes, Amanda's brother included!

Rafe did fall in love with Ophelia, he did marry her, and he did tame the shrew. There was nothing *not* to like about the Ophelia her brother had married.

That had all been part of Amanda's first disastrous Season in London. Last year she'd tried to take her brother's advice to heart and just let love find her. She'd had fun doing so, maybe too much fun. Relaxing, just enjoying herself and the many entertainments, she'd found that she actually liked some of her beaus, could even call them friends now, but not one had ever pulled at her heartstrings. So before she knew it, her second London Season was over and she still hadn't found a husband.

Now, at the beginning of her third Season in London, she was quite desperate. *Something* needed to change this year because she obviously wasn't going about husband hunting the right way. She wasn't as silly and flighty as people thought, but even she knew that she gave that impression sometimes.

"You're bored already this Season, aren't you?" Alice said as she stood behind her.

Amanda frowned as she met the maid's eyes in the mirror. Was the problem that simple? Bored all day long, and then when she finally had something to do in the evenings, she was so pleased she overreacted, behaving a bit more effervescently than she ought to?

She didn't try to deny it. "It's different here, not a'tall like at home in the country, where I've got so much to occupy me."

"Your aunt made a suggestion the other day. Why didn't you agree?"

Amanda rolled her eyes. "Help with that sewing class her friend started? I love needlepoint, but not enough to teach it to little girls who'd rather be out fishing."

Alice couldn't hold back her laughter. "I really don't think most little girls have fishing on their minds like *you* used to. But you should find something to do while we're in London instead of counting the minutes until the next party. Going from utter boredom to utter excitement isn't a good balance under any circumstances."

Amanda managed *not* to sigh again, but of course she was ready to leave the house and was already beginning to feel the excitement. Tonight could be the night she met her future husband. Well, it *could* happen. So she merely nodded to her maid and decided that thinking up a project to occupy her during the day could wait until tomorrow when she felt bored again.

She had to admit she was nicely decked out for not one but two parties tonight. Amanda did one last twirl in front of the full-length mirror to make sure nothing was out of place. It wasn't. Her maid was superb in that regard. The pale pink of the new evening gown highly suited her and was perfect for her mother's rubies at her neck and ears.

She didn't look any different from how she had during her first Season, when she'd thought she'd be the first among her friends to get engaged and she hadn't ended up engaged a'tall. *Let love find you, it will, you know,* Ophelia had assured her. Yes, but when? How long was she supposed to wait for that magical moment to happen?

Amanda went downstairs to see if her cousin Avery had arrived yet. The second of Aunt Julie's three sons, Avery had his own flat in London now, but Amanda had sent him a note in the afternoon, informing him that she was in need of a chaperone tonight, since Aunt Julie's oldest son, Rupert, and his new bride, Rebecca, hadn't yet returned from Norford as Amanda had hoped they would. And Aunt Julie's third son, Owen, was too young at sixteen to be anyone's escort.

Amanda had stayed at the St. John household last year for the Season as well, since her father didn't own a town house in London. And she could depend on two of her St. John cousins as well as their mother to serve as her escorts, even if none of them were ideal. But now her old friend Rebecca Marshall was part of the household, too, having recently married Rupert St. John, and *she* was ideal.

Amanda had been delighted by the news of Rebecca and Rupert's marriage. Rebecca would make a perfect chaperone because Amanda could actually have fun with her. But Becky had surprised Amanda by flatly refusing at first, claiming it didn't seem right because she was several years younger than Amanda. But Amanda's stubbornness had kicked in—she could be quite tenacious without even realizing it—and she'd convinced Becky to agree. But then Becky had hied off to the country without a by-your-leave, putting Amanda back at square one with her old choices.

She so hoped her old friend had returned by now. She wasn't worried that Rupert would want to tag along. He'd had his fill of balls and parties. He'd been Amanda's escort in the past and never failed to cause a stir, as handsome and flirtatious as he was, which tended to make every other gentleman present quite jealous, and jealous men didn't want to dance. That was why she only asked Rupert to chaperone her as a last resort.

His mother, Julie, was just as bad! She'd raised her three boys on her own after her husband, the last Marquis of Rochwood, had died, and she tried to be both mother and father to them, which, unfortunately, had turned her into somewhat of a bully. As Amanda had told Rebecca recently when she'd been trying to talk her into being her chaperone, "While Aunt Julie will agree to accompany me to parties, she'll also spend the entire night grumbling. And believe me, there aren't very many men who don't quickly retreat after receiving one of her scowls."

Rebecca had made a good point though: if Amanda's beaus could so easily be intimidated by her aunt, then they weren't for her. Amanda had to admit she'd been glad when a few of the more obnoxious ones had been scared off by Aunt Julie.

Amanda had almost reached the bottom of the stairs when

her steps slowed. She wondered if Avery had arrived yet. While he never minded escorting her—at least he never complained about it—he usually had to cancel his own plans to do so, which made her feel bad. Occasionally, he wasn't available because he was out of town.

She supposed she should have waited to dress for the evening until she had received confirmation that he was coming. Now she started to panic. Aunt Julie would be furious if she had to dress at the last minute to join her. But Amanda had already canceled two engagements because of Becky's absence. She simply couldn't cancel the two tonight, not when one party was being given by one of her closer friends, and the other by her sister-in-law, so Amanda had decided to attend them both—but not without an escort!

It wasn't Avery who appeared in the parlor doorway, drawn out by her loud sigh, but the man standing before her made her forget every one of her woes.

"Father!" She flew into Preston Locke's open arms. "What are *you* doing here? You never come to London except on business."

He gave her a brief hug before he set her back to explain, "I consider this business, family business. I came to find out what your cousin Rupert was doing here while his new bride was in Norford. You do know they didn't even bother to inform me of their marriage?"

Amanda winced for her cousin's sake. Her brother, Rafe, had done the same thing, married Ophelia Reid on the fly, as it were, without telling the family first, and their father had been quite put out about it.

"Well, that would explain why Rue left so suddenly today," Amanda said, giving her father a knowing grin. She could just imagine how that conversation between annoyed uncle and

LET LOVE FIND YOU

admonished nephew had gone. "So he'll be bringing Becky back to London, d'you think?"

"I would imagine."

"Soon, I hope? Perhaps even tonight?"

"I highly doubt it."

Amanda sighed.

Preston chucked her chin. "What?"

"I was looking forward to having Becky as my chaperone tonight. Now I'm stuck with Avery again."

Preston frowned thoughtfully. "Isn't Becky a bit young for that—?"

"No, no," Amanda quickly interrupted. "She's *married*! You know that makes it quite acceptable."

Preston gave her a doubtful frown, which started her squirming. He was a big man, tall, strapping. She and her brother, Rafe, both got their blond hair and blue eyes from him, though Preston had a little gray at his temples, which quite annoyed him. But he rarely lost his temper, didn't even appear to have one. He could exert such a calming influence on friend and foe alike that it was quite difficult to maintain a temper in his presence. He didn't argue his points, he got them across in a reasonable manner, and if he was proven wrong, he'd merely laugh about it and go on from there. The only exception was how he dealt with his siblings. Where his sisters were concerned, he enjoyed pulling their cords, was quite the tease in that regard. Her brother had gotten *that* from their father, too, much to her annoyance.

Before her father actually forbade her to rely on Rebecca as her chaperone just because she was a few years younger than Amanda, she said, "You did know that Becky was a maid of honor, right up till she married Rue? That's where he met her, at the palace. But having served in the royal court, she's more a stickler for proper etiquette than anyone I know."

"No, I didn't know, on either count. Your aunt Julie is still your best—"

"She doesn't like going to these parties. She'll go, of course, but you know how she is when she doesn't like something," she mumbled.

Preston sighed. "I wish she had remarried instead of practicing being a curmudgeon."

"She wishes the same thing about you," Amanda said, then sputtered, "Not the curmudgeon part!"

Was that actually a blush climbing his cheeks? Surely not. It wasn't as if the family didn't know why he chose to stay single after his wife had died. He'd loved her too much. He'd preferred to honor that love and not try to replace it. Actually, she and Rafe had concluded that their father didn't want to be disappointed in a second wife after having been so happy with the first. They could hardly disagree. They didn't want their mother to be replaced either. But they did want their father to be happy, so if he did find someone who could make him that happy, they certainly wouldn't object. He just wasn't looking. He already knew all the unattached ladies at home and wasn't interested in any of them, and he rarely came to London, where he might meet someone new.

But he was here now. She wondered . . .

"By the by, I sent Avery home," Preston said matter-of-factly. "I'll be your escort tonight, m'dear. I want to see for m'self the current crop of eligibles and what's taking you so long to make up your mind."

Although it was quite hard to utter a delighted squeal and a groan in the same breath, Amanda managed it just fine.

Chapter Two

"TWO PARTIES IN ONE night, is that normal these days?" Preston asked curiously.

Raphael laughed at his father. "Is that why you and Mandy showed up so late? Went to another party first?"

Preston made a face. "Your sister insisted she couldn't miss either one, so, yes. The other was at an old school chum's house just down the street. Wouldn't even call it a party, so few were in attendance."

Raphael was keeping his father company on the edge of the large ballroom where Ophelia's guests were gathered that evening. Thankfully, no one there was likely to recognize Preston, he so rarely came to London, and never for social events unless at the queen's request. So they didn't know that the Duke of Norford was present. If they did, they'd be lining up to make his acquaintance.

At least Raphael's father was used to social gatherings in the country these days, thanks to Ophelia. Preston's five sisters used to entertain at Norford Hall frequently, but that was so long ago Mandy hadn't even been born yet. And after the last of the five had married and moved elsewhere, Norford Hall remained quiet. Their mother preferred it that way, and after she died, Preston had become somewhat of a recluse. He wouldn't even entertain for Amanda's first come-out, had simply sent her off to London where she could be guaranteed her pick of the most eligible bachelors of the realm. It was the bane of the family that she hadn't picked one yet.

As for his father's curiosity, Rafe said, "No, two parties in one night isn't normal a'tall and is probably Phelia's fault. This party was rather impromptu. She only sent out the invitations for this one this morning."

Preston was amazed. "And this many showed up last minute, as it were?"

Raphael chuckled. "Becoming the premier hostess in the realm used to be Ophelia's heart's desire. Got the idea from her mum, who thrived on entertaining."

"Such a trifling thing."

"Not to the ladies it isn't!" Raphael laughed. "But she gave up that goal after we married. It was no longer the least bit important to her after Chandra was born."

"Yet it happened anyway?"

"'Course it did, simply because of who she is. She's too beautiful, too controversial, is still to this day talked about much more'n she ought to be, and to add to that, she's now the daughter-in-law of the reclusive Duke of Norford."

Preston snorted at being described that way. "How can I be reclusive when Ophelia entertains so much at Norford Hall every time you two stay with me?"

Raphael said, "Yes, but she only invites the neighbors in the country, no one you don't already know. Here in London is quite a different matter, and I can't count how many strangers show up here because she doesn't just invite friends and mere acquaintances, but also anyone she finds interesting, anyone the *ton* finds interesting, and of course the current crop of debutantes to help their cause."

Preston frowned. "She hasn't taken up matchmaking, has she?"

"No, of course not, she leaves that to the old dames, like those two over there, Gertrude Allen and Mabel Collicott." Raphael nodded toward the two oldest women in the room, across from them. "Look at them, you can just hear the wheels turning in their heads, trying to match up every unmarried person their eyes clap on." Then he teased his father, "You better hope they don't glance *your* way!"

Preston actually laughed. "I think I'm safe in that regard. I know Gertrude. Sweet old bird who cornered me years ago to see if I was interested in marrying again. I set her straight on that."

"Well, those two matchmakers should be quite happy tonight, since Phelia does make a point of finding out who all the new debutantes are and including a few of them at each of her parties."

"You don't mind so much entertaining?"

"Not really. She enjoys it. And it's bloody hard not to want to make her happy, as much as I love her."

"Mandy didn't mention this was a ball," Preston said, glancing about the ballroom.

Raphael chuckled. "It's not! Ophelia would have entertained in the parlor for what she considered merely a soiree, but as frequently happens at her parties, double the number invited usually show up."

"It sounds like you need a sterner butler at the door," Preston said in disapproval.

"It's not party crashers. It's friends and extra escorts of those who *are* invited, and Phelia hates to turn anyone away, so she simply adjusts and makes sure she always has extra food on hand. The simple fact is, no one wants to miss one of her entertainments, and they *do* cancel other engagements to come to hers instead, which is probably why there were so few guests at your first party tonight. Most hostesses make sure they pick nights Phelia isn't entertaining. They'll even confer with her about it! But occasionally she will throw an impromptu event like this one, especially when we've only just come to town."

Preston's eyes lit on Amanda in the center of the room. Raphael followed his gaze. His sister was laughing delightedly with four young gentlemen surrounding her, each vying to entertain her, and apparently, one of them had succeeded. That was encouraging.

Preston must not have thought so. He actually sighed before he remarked, "They flock to her, but I can see why she's having a hard time at this husband-hunting business, if this is the best out for the Season."

They still flocked to Raphael's wife, too, much to his chagrin, even though she was married now! But he spared a glance at the four young hopefuls surrounding Amanda and had to agree with his father. Rather plain looking, the lot of them, not that his sister would snub a man just because he wasn't handsome, but she wasn't likely to fall in love with someone who wasn't at least interesting. And she was holding out for love, not title, not wealth, just love. He'd heard it *so* many times, that love was the only thing that could make for a happy marriage. He used to scoff at that, but how could he now when, because of love, his marriage was so happy?

"What about your friends?" Preston added. "Has she met them all? None you could recommend?"

Raphael nearly choked. "Gad, no! The few who wanted to marry did so before Mandy came of age. The rest I wouldn't let anywhere near my sister, rakehells the lot of them. But I highly doubt this is a good assortment of the current batch of young men wife-shopping this Season. It wasn't intended to be that sort of event. A good half of the guests are married. Unfortunately, I've noticed two of those couples are Mandy's old friends."

"Unfortunately?"

"Bound to bring back her melancholy once she happens to notice them," Raphael guessed. "But she did complain to m'wife a few days ago that all of her friends are now either married or engaged, so not likely to show up at any gatherings this year, which would have been why Phelia invited a few of them here tonight, just for Mandy's sake. Wish she'd told me first so I could have explained she *shouldn't* invite them—for Mandy's sake."

"Nonsense. I know my darling girl isn't happy that she's still not married. I am, if you must know." At Raphael's raised brow, Preston added, "I'll miss her terribly once she moves to her own household, though don't ever tell her I said that. Don't want her to have even more to worry about. But she can't be upset just because her friends married before she did."

"Can't she? No one enjoys being last in line. And she's mentioned it to me, if not to you."

"Well, she seems just fine tonight, as effervescent as usual—

and enjoying herself. Actually, I can see she's chattering too much."

"When doesn't she?" Raphael said with a laugh, then glanced at his sister again. *She* was doing the entertaining just then and not giving those four young hopefuls a chance to get a word in edgewise. "She's talking their bloody ears off, but she's too beautiful for that to put them off. It does appear that tonight is a wasted effort though. I'll have a talk with Phelia to make sure her other parties this Season include *all* of the most eligible bachelors making the rounds. If this really is the lot, we're doomed to never hear the end of Mandy's old-maid complaints."

Preston snorted. "She's *not* an old maid by any stretch of the imagination."

"Try to convince her of that. Once she gets a notion, you know it's nigh impossible to shake her loose from it."

"Did *she* mention it?"

"No, but if she doesn't spot her future husband in the next couple of weeks, I don't doubt it will occur to her," Raphael said. "I'm surprised speculation about her lack of success in that regard isn't already a juicy tidbit in the gossip mills. Actually, for all I know, it might be, just no one would dare mention it to me."

"Perhaps it's time I stepped in to do something about this," Preston said thoughtfully.

"And buy her a husband? Gad, no, don't even try. It's love or nothing for her. I promise you, she'll settle for nothing else."

Preston tsked. "No, I didn't mean anything as old-fashioned as arranging a marriage for Mandy. I know very well how much that would upset her. But I've been rather selfish, hoping she'd take her time at this, when three Seasons at it may have unwanted consequences, as you say."

"The title of *old maid*?"

"Indeed. Beyond silly, but I'll agree it wouldn't be to her. No, I was thinking more along the lines of having a little chat with my old friend Gertrude Allen."

Raphael chuckled as he glanced at the two matchmakers again. "I suppose it couldn't hurt at this point. Should have thought of it m'self."

"Exactly. And then I'll feel that I've done something to help her with this husband hunt that's so important to her."

A bit of commotion at the door drew their attention along with everyone else's, as two late arrivals stepped into the ballroom. The shorter of the two men looked vaguely familiar to Raphael, but the other man, probably in his midtwenties, was tall and handsome, had a strapping body, black hair a bit longer than the current fashion, and a dangerous air about him that made him seem quite out of place at first glance, even though he was properly dressed. A bit too muscular, he reminded Rafe of a bloody bruiser or worse.

"Who is that?" Preston asked with interest. "Is *he* part of the current crop of eligibles?"

Raphael's protective instincts shot to the fore. "I don't know who he is, but I don't want him going anywhere near my sister."

Preston raised a brow at him. "Why?"

Raphael groaned inwardly. Pure instinct had made him say that, and something that strong was hard to ignore. Was he the only one who sensed that this newcomer was dangerous?

He hedged, "A little rough around the edges, don't you think?"

"So's your good friend Duncan MacTavish."

"Duncan has an excuse. He was raised in the Scottish Highlands."

"Maybe you should find out who this big fellow is before you discount him just because he looks a little out of place here."

So his father at least noticed that? But the chap wasn't a complete stranger to the *ton*. Some of the guests tonight obviously knew him because a young, engaged couple hurried toward him and greeted him effusively. Perhaps Raphael was wrong. Perhaps the man was perfectly harmless and only appeared dangerous because he was so big.

"M'lord Duke?"

Preston coughed over being called that, and Raphael turned to see a middle-aged gentleman extending a hand to Preston. They'd found him out! That got Raphael's mind off the newcomer for a moment and he almost laughed, imagining a line of guests forming to meet the reclusive Duke of Norford.

"Deny it," Raphael whispered to his father with a grin.

"Don't be absurd," Preston shot back, and accepted the fellow's hand.

Raphael saw another couple heading eagerly toward his father and said in an amused aside, "You asked for it."

He heard Preston sigh before Raphael left him there and went off to find Ophelia. *She* had to know who that bruiser was.

Chapter Three

"I HAVE NO IDEA WHO he is and haven't had time yet to find out," Ophelia said. "We only just got to town, so I'm not yet abreast of the current gossip. But I did hear a few people calling him Cupid. Quite interesting, that."

Raphael tamped down the pang of jealousy he felt at Ophelia's finding the chap interesting and waited for her to finish giving the servant instructions to take to the cook. Of course she'd want to know who was at her party. She always made sure to find out who the uninvited guests were before they left in case she should want to include them on the guest list of her next party.

"Now, where were we?" she asked, turning back to give Rafe one of her stunning smiles.

God, she was beautiful, he thought. White-blond hair, blue eyes, ivory skin, features so exquisite they dazzled all who gazed at her. That little dent she'd got high on her cheek when a horse had trampled her didn't detract from her looks one tiny bit. He would have wished it did if it wouldn't have upset her. No one should be *this* beautiful. He did wish he didn't still get jealous occasionally when he saw her talking to other men. He bloody well had no control of it when it snuck up on him, even when he *knew* he had no cause. But then no one had ever compared to her in beauty and probably never would.

"We were discussing your handsome uninvited guest," he reminded her.

"Ah, yes. I did invite his friend the Honorable William Pace, because he's got a sister having a come-out this year and I couldn't remember her name. I thought he'd bring her, but I suppose she was otherwise engaged."

"Pace, of course, now I remember him. Good chap. Lost both his parents recently. Don't think I've met his sister, though. . . . Cupid, eh?" Glancing again at the pair across the room, Raphael rolled his eyes. *Exactly* how rumors and inaccurate gossip got started, when people didn't know all the details of a subject and elaborated on their own. "That's probably a rumor gone awry, since it would otherwise suggest he's a matchmaker."

Ophelia chuckled. "I quite agree. I'm sure only women dabble in that. But there must be something that's making him a bit of a sensation for me to have heard the name Cupid at least three times before he even arrived, and quite a few more times after he appeared. But before I could ask why, I was asked about your father. Someone has recognized him, so everyone is curious now to know why he's come out of hibernation, as it were."

"For Mandy, of course. You'd think they'd draw that conclusion and let it go at that."

She disagreed. "Not a'tall, when she's had two Seasons without his chaperonage."

They both glanced toward Amanda, but Raphael frowned, noticing the one chap in her group who hadn't been there earlier. "What the deuce is Exter doing here? That blighter is a known fortune hunter."

"He's staying with Lord and Lady Durrant. I didn't know that until they arrived with him in tow. Besides, Mandy won't be fooled by the likes of him. She may like to pretend otherwise, but she is a smart girl."

"I love her to pieces, but you're talking about *my* sister. She can be the veriest scatterbrain and—"

Ophelia poked his chest. "She's nothing of the sort. She's just easily excitable. Nothing wrong with that. I doubt she'll have trouble a'tall figuring out which of her beaus are in love with her and which are in love with her father"—Ophelia paused long enough for Raphael to burst out laughing—"er, her father's title."

He put his arm around his wife's shoulders. "I know, I'm probably worrying for nothing." He tapped his chest. "I just feel it here, Mandy's unhappiness with the difficulty she's been having. She shouldn't *be* having such a hard time of it. Look at her, she's adorable, she *is* a prime catch. What the deuce is taking these young men so long to win her?"

"Because none of them have been quite right for her, of course. Rotten timing has been the problem. You can't force love. It just hasn't happened for her yet. But there's a new crop of gentlemen come to town this year. New choices, new chances. We can hope this year love will find her."

They both ended up staring at the new arrival again, the tall, handsome one. Having seen him laugh with the young, engaged couple, Raphael didn't think the man seemed quite as menacing as he had at first glance. And perhaps Raphael ought to be sociable and make his acquaintance to find out for himself if his first instinct had been accurate.

Ophelia was thinking something else entirely. Cupid? Only someone successful at matchmaking could earn a nickname like that, surely. Unless it was just a joke, which it could certainly be. No man would *want* to be likened to a cherub, would he? In either case, she ought to find out for sure.

Across the room, as soon as Sir Henry and Elizabeth Malcort finished chatting with them and moved off, William Pace assured his best friend, "I told you you'd fit right in *and* know some of the guests."

Devin Baldwin laughed because they both knew the first part of that statement wasn't the least bit true. Devin was too big, too tanned from spending every day outdoors, and too abrasive because he didn't mince words and never would, no matter what company he was in. He might have been schooled in how to be a gentleman, but he'd found those lessons to be useless, either absurdly amusing—or hypocritical.

William had been trying to get him to come to parties like this one for years, but Devin had only recently seen a benefit to doing so. Not that he hadn't begun socializing this year when he found the time. But the invitations he'd received from his clients had been to lesser affairs, which he considered business, nothing as fancy as this one, where every guest bore a title of some sort. Yet now he was receiving invitations from titled nobles he'd never even met, all because he'd helped a few of his clients with matters that had nothing to do with the horses he bred.

He'd ignored the fancy invites so far—until tonight. He didn't exactly like these rich London nabobs—unless they were his clients. But even then, he found them to be a silly, frivolous bunch mostly concerned with trifles and entertainments rather than real life. They reminded him too much of the father he hated. They reminded him of the mother who had turned her back on her family so she could enjoy the sins of London. He was more used to country gentry anyway, lords who actually ran their own estates instead of turning them over to factors, men he could respect because they weren't afraid to get their hands dirty.

"Fascinating, isn't she?" William remarked.

Devin shifted his gaze to the ballroom's ornately carved fireplace before he said, "Which one?"

William laughed at him. "Well, our hostess is married and, by all accounts, blissfully so. But you know I was talking about Little Miss Sunshine."

"I'm trying not to notice her."

"Why?"

"You're the one looking for a rich wife, not I," Devin replied. And that little chatterbox his eyes kept returning to was too pretty by half. The last thing he needed was to get tempted by a woman he could never have.

"Good of you to bow out on this one for my sake, old chap, but I'm not a complete blockhead," William said. "Don't stand a chance with a prime chit like that."

"Nonsense—"

William cut Devin off with a chuckle. "Very well, I'll own up to it, I gave it my best shot last Season. Didn't know yet that her father's a duke. Didn't care after I found out. But she couldn't even remember my name! Deuced hard on the ego, that, so I gave up. But you, big, handsome, they don't even care that you're a little rough around the edges."

That produced the laugh William had intended to elicit from his friend, even if it was quite true. "I may have revitalized the home farm, but I don't actually consider that *my* income.

And the title that used to be in my family trotted off centuries ago through a daughter instead of being passed down to distant cousins. You do realize Little Miss Sunshine's family would require at least one of those attributes, if not both?"

"You'd think so," William said thoughtfully. "Yes, yes, you *do* think so, but some families are so rich and lofty, normal expectations simply don't apply."

"Or they're even more important."

William shrugged. "Who knows? But I'll shut up—mind you, only because you insist you're not interested in a wife yet. Just think you should keep an open mind in case one happens to fall into your lap—"

"Thought you were shutting up?"

William grinned, but then his eyes suddenly flared and he said, "Uh-oh, brace yourself, your competition is bearing down on you."

"My what?"

Devin turned to see the two old ladies approaching him. The one in the lead was plump and gray-haired and looked angry enough to spit. The other was shapely, still had blond hair mixed with her gray, and looked embarrassed as she tagged along behind the stouter dame.

"Young man, I've a bone to pick with you!" the old dame in the lead snapped at Devin.

"Madam, adjust your tone or take your bone elsewhere," he replied just as directly.

She was rendered speechless for a moment. William took that opportunity to jump in with quick introductions. The second lady, Gertrude Allen, even seemed surprised at hearing Devin's full name.

"You wouldn't happen to be related to Lydia Baldwin, would you?" Gertrude asked him.

Devin spared a smile the for soft-spoken woman. "Indeed, she's my aunt."

"Oh, my, I know your family quite well. My late husband used to travel all the way to Lancashire just to replenish his stable from them. Wonderful horse breeders. An old family tradition, eh? Your grandparents were still alive then as I recall. And more recently your aunt helped my Fluffy after she and your uncle moved to London. What a superb dog trainer she is. After only a week with your aunt, my Fluffy came home and never chewed on another table leg again! Mabel, I told you about—"

The older dame had recovered by then and cut in, "He can breed all the horses he likes, but he should keep his nose out of what he can't possibly know anything about. Listen here, *Cupid*," Mabel said in a derogatory tone, using the nickname that Devin had recently earned, "you might be something of a sensation right now because you've had a bit of luck at matchmaking, but it's absurdly presumptuous of you to even try your hand at it when you're a newcomer to town and—"

"I'm not new to London," Devin said.

"'Course you are. Who has ever heard of you before this Season?"

William tried to deflate the old bird, but he was sounding a bit annoyed himself now on Devin's behalf. "Wouldn't call m'self a nobody, Lady Mabel. Devin's my best friend, as it happens. He and I went to school together. He was even born in London, if you must know. He's merely been up north revitalizing his family's horse farm since we got out of school, so he's been too busy to come to town to socialize these last years. But he's bought a property near London in order to be closer to his clients, so you'll be seeing a lot more of him now."

The old bird wasn't deflated in the least, merely spared William a glare to say, "That is *not* good news, William Pace." Then she actually wagged her finger at Devin. "You've been lucky so far, but it's a serious business you're tampering with, and people will get hurt if you steer them wrong. This is just a lark for you, isn't it? Just an amusing pastime?"

Devin shrugged. "Can't deny it's amusing, but it's not something I set out to do. It just fell in my lap. But there's no luck about it, it's simple animal magnetism that makes for a good match. A man and a woman have got to want to rut, but after the rutting, they've got to have something in common or their happily ever after falls apart."

"How . . . how dare you!" Mabel sputtered.

"Think about it, old girl, and you'll realize I'm right. How many of your happy matches are still happy? Or are the husbands already keeping mistresses on the side?"

William was coughing, having choked on a half laugh, half groan. Gertrude was staring down at her feet. Mabel was speechless again and so red in the face she looked as if she might burst. Even Devin knew he'd just gone beyond the pale, but he simply didn't care. Damned jealous old biddy had no call to upbraid him for commonsense methods that worked.

Their hostess took that moment to make her presence known, and to go by her expression, she seemed quite amused over what she'd just overheard. And now Devin was blushing! Bloody hell.

Ophelia put her hand gently on Mabel's arm. "There's no reason to be upset, m'dear. A little outspokenness is refreshing from time to time. Imagine what would happen if all artists wanted to paint the same way? Our walls would be nothing but boring."

"Hardly relevant," Mabel mumbled, her cheeks beginning to cool.

"Perhaps, but no one is stealing your thunder. The tried-and-true methods always work, yet there is room for innovation, yes? But goodness, I haven't even met this guest of mine yet." Ophelia cast a brilliant smile at the two men. "I'm Ophelia Locke. So good of you to join us this evening. Oh, and, William, good to see you as always."

Mabel actually chuckled at that point. "You really shouldn't do that, Phelia."

"What?" Ophelia asked with an innocent grin.

"You know very well you've just dazzled the speech right out of both of them. Serves 'em right." Mabel marched off, dragging Gertrude with her.

"I think you'll survive on all accounts, won't you, gentlemen? But tell me, Devin Baldwin, do you mind being likened to a cherub, or do you merely find it amusing?"

William was still staring at her agog. It took Devin a few moments to actually *hear* the question. He'd already thought this woman was the most beautiful he'd ever seen in his life, but bloody hell, her smile was lethal. He pitied her husband—like hell he did, he almost laughed to himself.

"As the myth goes, Cupid is also the god of love, as well as the son of Venus."

Her eyes flared. "Good grief, I never realized they were calling you a god!"

He laughed. "Which is about as silly as it gets, so, yes, I find it quite amusing."

"The matchmaking methods you were discussing are quite interesting. Has that approach helped you to find a wife yet?"

"I've no time for a wife."

William piped in, "Dev is working toward producing racers now on his new farm just outside of London, north of the racetrack."

"Yes," Devin said, "I've changed the focus my family has always favored. It's a long process, but I'll know come spring if it's working or not."

"Do you have any fast mounts for sale? My husband's birthday is approaching and I thought about buying him a new horse."

Devin grinned. "Possibly faster than he's used to."

"Splendid! Now *that* will be a worthy surprise for him. I look forward to doing business with you."

Chapter Four

"AND THERE WE WERE, my lovely boat heading straight for this rock sticking out of the water that I swear wasn't there moments before," Oliver Norse was telling the group surrounding Amanda. "The sailboat was brand-new! I was horrified it was going to shatter into pieces."

"Did it?" asked Farrell Exter, the only one in the group who hadn't heard the story yet.

"Oliver told us to jump ship and we did," John Trask said with an engaging grin. He'd actually been on the boat with Oliver that day.

"But I went down with the ship!" Oliver bragged.

"He means to say he got tossed off it when it tilted to the side and got quite beached on the bit of land surrounding that rock."

Farrell laughed. Amanda had laughed, too, the first time she'd heard the tale last Season. She managed a polite grin now, despite feeling terribly bored.

She should have realized that with Ophelia and her brother

Rafe's only just coming to town, her sister-in-law wouldn't yet be au courant with all of the newcomers this Season. Ophelia had merely invited a few of the young men she knew from last year who weren't married yet. But Amanda already knew them as well and wasn't the least bit interested in them other than as friends. *She* was having to do most of the talking tonight or her little group would fall painfully silent as it had before Oliver had jumped in with a story he'd told many times before. But unlike her beaus, she had a wealth of stories to tell, mostly about her brother, who'd led a much more exciting life than they had.

"It's time to share, gentlemen," Phoebe Gibbs said as she arrived and slipped an arm through Amanda's to pull her away from the young men who were staunchly refusing to leave her side tonight. "I haven't seen Mandy all week, so do excuse us for a while."

Amanda was grateful for the rescue. Phoebe was one of her school chums who had married last year. Amanda had caught a glimpse of another one who was also married. She had nothing in common with her old friends anymore so she hadn't approached either one, at least that was the excuse she'd given herself. The truth was, they just made her feel even more disheartened over her predicament, being last in line to find happiness.

But Phoebe was the worst gossiper of her old group of friends, loved to hear it, loved to pass it on, so Amanda wouldn't be surprised if she had some juicy *on-dits* she was dying to share, and Amanda was right.

"The Earl of Manford, I really thought he'd be here tonight," Phoebe said.

"Who's that?"

"A *good* question. Got his title as a child, losing both parents, poor boy. He's just come of age, but no one I know has clapped eyes on him yet. I thought surely if anything could lure him to town, it would be one of Lady O's parties."

Amanda's interest perked up. A young man she hadn't met yet? She grinned. "He needs to be lured?"

"Apparently," Phoebe huffed. "By all accounts, he's not ready to marry so he won't bother coming to London yet. Too busy chasing down fast horses."

Amanda instantly lost interest. If the young earl wasn't interested in marriage, then she had no interest in meeting him. But she politely pretended otherwise to her friend. "Another horse breeder?"

"No, he just acquires them for his collection. Avid horseman. Only time I've heard his name mentioned is when fast horses get mentioned."

Amanda shuddered. She didn't like horses—well, unless she was watching them from afar at the racetrack and betting on which one might win. But she'd taken a bad fall as a child not long after her riding lessons had begun, and she'd been afraid to get back on a horse after that and never did again.

Phoebe sighed now. "Obviously you've already heard about the horse breeder who's here tonight?"

Amanda managed not to snort. How could she not hear about the man whose name was on everyone's tongue? She'd noticed him immediately when he arrived. Handsome in a rough, overly masculine sort of way, but that's exactly why she'd dismissed him out of hand. *Too* brutish looking by far.

"Such a silly nickname they've given him, Cupid!" Phoebe giggled. "Yet so apt! Imagine someone like him being a successful matchmaker."

Amanda did snort this time. "Exactly. I'm not convinced he belongs here for any reason when he looks like a thug."

Phoebe's eyes lit up. "Then you *haven't* heard it all! The Baldwins are gentry from Lancashire. There was even an earl in their family tree a while back. But they've always dabbled in horse breeding, which might account for this Baldwin's being a bit more . . . more—what the deuce is the word I'm looking for?"

"Brutish?"

Phoebe frowned. "No, that wasn't—oh, *earthy*! That's the word that eluded me."

Brutish was more apt, Amanda mumbled to herself. And she wasn't going to politely lead this topic any further. In fact, she sent Lord Oliver a smile, urging him to return to her side, and he complied immediately.

Phoebe wasn't pleased to have her gossip cut short and said so, "Really, Oliver, I was *only* going to keep her for a few minutes."

"One minute away from Amanda is like an eternity, dear lady," Oliver replied gallantly.

Phoebe tsked, but then grinned. "Hard to argue with that, I suppose, and I do see my husband waving at me. I'll talk to you later, Mandy."

Amanda almost laughed as she was surrounded by her beaus again. Now she was back to being bored! So she began the story about the wonderful painter Rafe had discovered on the Continent and had sponsored *after* he'd fished him out of a river. She soon had her audience laughing, but she was keeping her eye on her father across the room. As soon as he finished his conversation, she was going to suggest they leave.

Devin was more than ready to leave the party. He'd had a long day, spending most of it at the racetrack because he'd had a chance to buy one of the horses listed and wanted to see first-hand if the stallion was worth adding to his breeding stock. The stallion had come in third, better than he'd hoped, but not high enough to affect the price he was willing to pay.

But he'd met most of the guests tonight and had accomplished what he'd come for—to find out if it would be worth his time to start coming to upper-crust parties like this one where he could meet the richer lords in London who might want to buy his horses. Indeed it was. He even had two possible sales lined up. So he was glad that William had joined him at the races today and talked him into coming along tonight, but he didn't think staying any longer would be useful. And he was annoyed with himself. His eyes kept returning to Little Miss Sunshine. The chit wouldn't close her mouth long enough to let her admirers say a single word to her! How the deuce did she expect to win one of them?

"Bloody rotten luck that Blythe had to get the sniffles yesterday and reddened her nose so much she refused to leave her room today," William complained beside him, gazing in the same direction as Devin. "Lady Amanda doesn't appear the least bit interested in those young bucks surrounding her. My sister could have had her pick of them."

"She'll meet them soon enough."

"Yes, I know, I just never expected that *I'd* be the one having to make sure she marries well. My mum was so looking forward to this." William sighed. "I miss them terribly."

Devin was uncomfortable with his friend's grief. "Buck up, old boy. We'll have her married in no time!"

Devin hadn't said *we* just out of sympathy for his old friend. Devin had already assured William that he'd help any way he could, short of marrying Blythe himself. Even *she* knew she could do better than him. The fact was, the Paces, brother and sister, were quite pinched in the pocket these days, the deaths of their parents having left them with a pile of debts and no way to dig their way out of it other than through marriage. Work was out of the question. They were aristocrats, after all, and if not from the upper reaches, their father had been a lord and their uncle was an earl. But the plan was to get Blythe married first, then William could stop worrying about her and concentrate on finding a spouse for himself. Pace financial woes would be fixed nicely and everyone would be happy.

Devin wished he could map out his own life so easily, but he knew a wife wouldn't be part of it, at least not one he might meet socializing with the *ton*. They might accept him for whatever reason, but they wouldn't let their daughters marry him, not when the truth about him was revealed, and that wasn't something he could withhold in good conscience from a potential wife or her family. But, in the meantime, he didn't mind using these people to promote his new farm or to profit from the sideline that had fallen into his lap and was turning out to be surprisingly lucrative.

No matter how he looked at it, that sideline was funny as hell. Matchmaking, and they paid him for it! Just because he found people so easy to read, particularly young people who talked too much when they were nervous. He'd even met the perfect match for William a couple of weeks ago, felt it in his gut that they'd fall head over heels for each other, and was just waiting until William's sister was settled to introduce them. But this sideline had caused the invitations to elite parties to roll in, ever since Sir Henry and Elizabeth Malcort had announced their engagement and claimed that Devin had helped them find each other.

The *ton* considered him a curiosity, and because of that, they wanted him at their parties. He actually didn't care why as long as it brought him business for either of his endeavors. But he wished to hell he could keep his eyes off Little Miss Sunshine, yet once William moved off for some refreshments, it was impossible to do so.

She really did sparkle, and it had nothing to do with the expensive jewels she was wearing. Vivacious. Effervescent. When she smiled and laughed, she seemed to light up the room, she was so beautiful. He'd love to know what she was talking about to keep her young admirers so raptly attentive. Actually, they might not even care what she was saying, they could merely be delighted to be in her company.

"I think you better get your eyes off my sister until I know your intentions."

Devin glanced to his side. At a few inches over six feet, he was used to towering over other men, but that wasn't the case with this chap he hadn't yet met. Blond, blue-eyed, the man was as tall as Devin and was staring at the center of the room where Devin's eyes had been, not necessarily at the same young woman, but that would be a good guess. While the animosity of the man's statement wasn't revealed in his expression, a strong note of warning was in the tone of his voice.

"I have no intentions," Devin replied. "I was just wondering how she can look like she's having a good time, yet be bored to tears."

The man frowned slightly, still staring at his sister, then said, "Bloody hell, hadn't noticed that. You *do* read people very well, don't you?"

Devin shrugged. "It's a knack."

The animosity was still present in the man's tone. Why? Was

the brother so protective of his sister that he didn't even like that Devin had "wondered" about her? Possibly, and that would be a clear indication the fellow didn't think Devin was good enough for his sister. Devin knew he wasn't, but no one else knew why he'd be the first to agree. Ordinarily, reactions like this didn't bother him in the least. Tonight it did, and he wasn't sure why.

"Are you married?"

"No," Devin said tersely, about to walk away.

The man was still frowning when he remarked, "Deuced odd, then."

Devin raised a brow. "What is?"

"That you're not drooling over my sister like the rest of these young bucks." The man paused. "Unless you're a confirmed bachelor?"

Devin just smiled, but that caused the man to rock back on his heels for a moment, and the animosity was suddenly gone. "Well, that explains it. Understand perfectly. Was one m'self until I met my wife. By the by, I'm Raphael Locke, Rafe to my friends. And you're Devin Baldwin, from the Lancashire Baldwins, titles distributed elsewhere, gentry nonetheless."

Now the man gets around to introducing himself? "It sounds like the gossip mill has been busy tonight," Devin said.

Raphael chuckled. "Can't stand gossip m'self. No, m'wife just makes it a point of finding out who shows up at her parties, in case she'd like to invite them again."

This was who was married to their ethereal hostess? William had forgotten to mention the family ties when he'd admitted he'd tried his hand at winning the duke's daughter. "Lucky fellow."

"Oh, indeed, don't I know it," Raphael said. "Surprised we've never met before, though I still spend most of the year in the country with my family. So this amusing matchmaking oc-cupation of yours has brought you to town?"

"I don't consider that an occupation. Horse breeding is my occupation and my passion. That's what keeps me busy, espe-cially since I'm trying my hand at producing racers now, instead of just quality mounts. And my aunt and uncle who moved to London suggested I bring my efforts closer to them, since I was never finding time to visit. So I bought the old Harksten place just outside of town, close enough that I can live with them again, which makes them happy."

"Humph, I guess Phelia forgot to mention that part! Racers, eh? I just might have to visit your farm."

Now that was funny. Devin supposed he ought to tell Lady Ophelia that if she didn't buy her husband's birthday present soon, she'd have to find something else to buy him. But he didn't see the lady anywhere nearby, and he wasn't about to go searching for her when he'd rather just leave. He did spot Wil-liam looking bored with the conversation he was having across the room and, catching his eye, nodded toward the exit. His friend grinned his agreement, so Devin bid his host good night and started across the room—which took him right past Little Miss Sunshine.

He should have resisted. Really. But if the girl had been on the marriage mart since last year, which was when William had said he'd met her, then she ought to know by now what she was doing wrong.

Devin paused and leaned close enough so his whisper didn't reach any ears but hers and advised, "How are your beaus sup-posed to woo you if you won't keep quiet long enough to let them?"

Chapter Five

It was a wonder Amanda had got to sleep at all last night she'd gone to bed so furious. The nerve of that odious man to say something so outrageous to her and then leave the party before she'd recovered enough to give him the sharp side of her tongue. They hadn't even been introduced yet!

But she slept off the worst of her anger and the next day was merely annoyed at the man's presumption to give her advice when he didn't know anything about her.

Who was Devin Baldwin really? A thug, as she'd thought, or just a country clod lacking in manners and refinement? That would certainly account for such audacity, but she should know that for certain by now because they'd spent hours at the same party! He should have had someone introduce him to her at some point last night so she could have found out more about him other than the gossip, which might not be accurate. Why the deuce hadn't he?

She'd almost seen to the matter herself after her little chat with Phoebe, which had piqued her curiosity a bit despite her certainty that he didn't really belong there. She'd considered introducing herself when she saw her brother talking to him later in the evening. With Baldwin standing next to Rafe, it was like looking at night and day side by side. Rafe was blond and fair. The brute was so darkly tanned, yet she couldn't help noticing again how handsome he actually was with his raven hair and— were his eyes actually amber? She hadn't got close enough to him to be sure. He was certainly old enough that this wasn't *his* first Season in London by any means.

Where had he been hiding himself? He was so mysterious! No one really knew anything about him or his family other than they hailed from Lancashire and were long-standing horse breeders, so the rumors that were circulating about him might not be true a'tall. A matchmaker? How absurd to attribute something like that to him when all he'd done was introduce a few friends who ended up liking each other enough to want to marry. She'd done exactly the same thing herself her first Season, but no one was calling *her* a matchmaker. But she knew how the *ton* were. They'd latch onto anything worth gossiping about, even something as silly as a horse-breeding matchmaker! Well, that *was* a bizarre mix, wasn't it? And exactly why it would be so interesting—if it was true. And exactly why her own curiosity was piqued.

She'd almost barged in on her brother's conversation with Baldwin, had been getting up the nerve to do so. And what had that been about? Nervous? Her? She was *never* overcome with shyness like that! But Baldwin certainly wasn't the sort of gentleman she was accustomed to—if he could even be called a gentleman. And it was a good thing she did hesitate. The few words he'd said to her had confirmed that her first impression of him had been accurate. He was nothing but a rude, presumptuous country clod, and he'd better hope she never saw him again or she'd tell him so!

Ophelia came by early that morning to invite her on an outing. "Where are we going?" Amanda asked when she came downstairs to join Ophelia and her maid, Sadie O'Donald, in the parlor, where they'd been waiting for her. "Am I dressed appropriately?"

Both women stood up to put their coats back on. Amanda had brought a fur-trimmed pelisse with her, but kept it over her arm, not sure if she needed it. It was late autumn, but not quite cold enough yet for more than the heavier clothing and extra petticoats favored at that time of year. Amanda's pale blue–and-white walking dress was made out of thick brocade, and the matching jacket that ended at her waist was likely all she'd need to keep warm.

"You look perfect, m'dear, as always." Ophelia hooked her arm through Amanda's to lead her back to the foyer. "We're going shopping. I thought you might like to get out of the house, and I need to pick out your brother's birthday present."

"And you need my advice on what he might like?"

"Actually, no. But come along, I'll explain on the way."

Ophelia wasn't quite sure how to broach the subject, or even if she should yet. She'd made a bold decision to hire Devin Baldwin to help Amanda, despite Rafe's initial distrust of the man. In fact, she was acting against his wishes. She'd spoken to Rafe about it last night after the party, teasingly suggesting that Cupid might be able to figure out Amanda's problem. Rafe had rejected the idea out of hand, said he wasn't quite sure what to make of the man after talking to him, but until he could put his finger on why he still had misgivings, he'd rather Amanda not become acquainted with the chap for any reason.

Ophelia didn't always agree with her husband. This was definitely one of those times. After being intrigued by Cupid's more modern approach to matchmaking last night, and having spoken with the couple he'd already helped and heard from them about some of his other successes, she'd been convinced that Cupid was just what Amanda needed.

She'd never gone against Rafe's wishes, though. But if this worked out as she hoped, then everyone would be happy, and Rafe didn't even have to know that she'd played a part in it. But that was if Devin would even take the job. He might already have too many clients. He might simply not have the time, since his horse farm was apparently his first priority. She had to find that out first. So there was no point in jumping the gun and telling Amanda about it until the man had actually committed to helping her.

"Shopping outside of London?" Amanda said when she noticed they were on a country road.

"Yes, your brother mentioned a few months ago that his stallion is getting old, so I thought a new one would be a nice surprise for his birthday. And an actual horse farm will have a good selection to choose from. But I invited you along because, honestly, m'dear, I know you don't like to ride and why, but don't you think it's time you gave it a try again? We could get you a mount today, too."

"No," Amanda said immediately.

"But it's such fun and a very social activity, too, you know. And riding in one of the parks while you're staying in town, there's no telling who you might meet. It will also give you something to do during the day, since you discourage your young beaus from calling on you at Julie's—do you still discourage them? Or was that just last year?"

Amanda rolled her eyes. "I see too much of them as it is, when none of them really interest me." Then she grinned. "And Aunt Julie is such a perfect excuse to use. Once they've met her, they readily believe that she doesn't like men cluttering up her parlor. The ladies still call, of course, but that doesn't take up all morning and afternoon."

"No, of course not," Ophelia agreed. "Which is why I thought you might want to try riding again. It would be a good way to fill in some of those idle hours."

Amanda actually bit her lip for a moment. "I am hoping to find something interesting and fun to occupy me while I'm in town, but it *won't* be riding. Really, Phelia, I did try it again— well, I was going to, but I just . . . no, riding just isn't for me."

Ophelia didn't press it. That had been a long shot anyway. Raphael had told her about the fall Amanda had been injured in when she was a child, and that it had left her afraid to get back on a horse. Ophelia had hoped enough time had passed that Amanda might have outgrown that fear, but apparently not.

"Well, that was just a thought anyway," Ophelia said. "You can still help me pick out a horse for your brother. I'm sure it won't take long."

But a few minutes later she amended that statement. Laughing at herself after glancing out the window, Ophelia said, "Oh, my, I can't imagine why I was expecting all the horses to be inside a single stable. I had no idea this farm was this big."

As her driver helped them out of the coach, Ophelia was forced to conclude that Devin Baldwin was definitely not just a dabbler at horse breeding like so many aristocrats who tried their hand at it, loving horses as they all did. She had no idea where they might find him. She had thought he'd probably be in the stable, but there were three of them! And a barn. It was definitely a decent-size property for a horse farm.

"Well, since no one is rushing out here to help us, Paul, you try the left stable, Mandy, you check the center one, and I'll check in the one on the right."

"What are we looking for?" Amanda asked.

"The factor or owner, or anyone who can show us the horses that are currently for sale."

Chapter Six

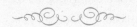

AMANDA WAS IMPRESSED. SHE'D been driven past many horse farms in the country, but she'd never seen one on such a grand scale as this. In addition to the three stables, there was a barn and a rather rundown two-story house. So many horses were grazing in the fenced-in fields that she didn't even try to count them. There was even a riding track! It looked like a smaller version of the racetrack to the south that she'd attended with her aunt, but it didn't have any stands or other accommodations for spectators, so she doubted any races were actually held here.

Amanda struggled to open the regular-size door of the middle stable where Ophelia had directed her to look for the owner. The large double doors of all three stables were closed, no doubt to retain any heat inside during the cooler months.

But she encountered *much* more heat than she was expecting when she finally got the door open. Good grief, it felt like a hothouse in here. Lanterns hung from numerous posts, and she counted three large braziers that gave off light as well as heat. A wagon filled with hay stood in one aisle. Horse stalls lined the sides of the cavernous space, which accommodated a third set of stalls down the center. Walking down the aisle on the right, she saw a horse in every stall she passed.

She wasn't quite sure, but most of the horses appeared to be in the latter stage of pregnancy. This didn't surprise her. Aunt Julie had told her during one of their visits to the racetrack that racehorses were usually mated during the spring and summer months because it took a mare nearly a year to produce a foal. This timing ensured that two-year-old foals would be ready to be tested in the late spring when the racing season began. Races took place throughout the year, weather permitting, but the races during the prime season were the most exciting and the best attended because racegoers got a chance to witness new champions in the making.

Amanda passed a worker who was grooming a mare in one of the stalls. She was about to question him when she realized he wasn't wearing a shirt. Unaccustomed to speaking with bare-chested men, she moved on. One of the double doors at the back of the stable was opening, letting in more light, and she saw a man on a horse silhouetted against the bright light of day. Shielding her eyes, she called, "Hello! Is the owner about? My sister-in-law is here to buy a horse."

Having got the horse inside, the man was closing the door again. Had he even heard her?

"Lady Amanda, isn't it?"

She gasped and swung around to see Devin Baldwin poking his head out of the stall she'd just passed. There was that deep voice again, that same voice that had insulted her last night. She opened her mouth to give him the belated tongue-lashing he deserved, but the words didn't come. He'd brought the rest of his body out of the stall and closed the stall door behind him. He shouldn't have done that. He was half-naked!

Amanda didn't look away as she ought to. The thought never even occurred to her. Nothing could have got her eyes off his tall form in such virile disarray. Muscles bunching in his arms, a mat of dark hair covering his wide chest, which was glistening with sweat, his trousers tucked into a pair of old work boots caked with dried mud and who knew what else. His brow was sweaty, too, which he wiped now with the short towel that had hung over one of his shoulders.

Being confronted with someone who was exposing more skin than was proper wouldn't ordinarily have bothered her. She would have just tsked daintily and quickly averted her eyes. It wasn't as if she'd never seen male servants before who had adjusted their attire because of the heat. In the summer on the way to town she'd passed bare-chested gardeners working under the hot sun, not that the Norford Hall gardeners stripped down that way. The employees of a duke had to maintain decorum at all times, no matter how hot the sun—or overheated the stables.

She was just having that thought when *he* seemed to realize the inappropriateness of his attire, or lack of attire, in her presence and reached for the shirt hanging on a stall rail. But then he swore and reached for a bucket of water instead.

Amanda gasped again as he bent forward and poured water over his head, splashing her boots and the hem of her dress. This was the man who was the *ton*'s latest sensation, the matchmaker called Cupid? How dare he treat her like this! He was nothing more than a boorish brute!

"Sorry." He rubbed the towel over his head and chest. "We keep it hot in here because I don't want any of these ladies catching a draft. I've got a good horse doctor for them who lives nearby, and even he tells me I pamper them too much. But pampering doesn't hurt. I haven't lost a foal yet."

She just stared at him wide-eyed, prompting him to guess, "You don't remember me? I'm Devin Baldwin. We met last night at—"

"No, we did not!" she cut in, finally finding her voice. "You didn't bother to introduce yourself to me properly before you insulted me with your misplaced advice. One goes before the other, in case you don't know."

"I'm aware of what goes where," he said with some amusement.

"And I certainly don't need advice from the likes of you!" she huffed. "You don't know a thing about me. How can you possibly presume to—"

"I know you chatter too much. You're doing it right now. But last night at your sister-in-law's party, you didn't give those poor boys a chance to say a bloody thing to you. How's a man to flatter you if you won't keep quiet long enough to hear his compliments?"

Amanda's eyes narrowed in a scowl. "Did it never occur to you that those young men aren't new acquaintances of mine? That I've known them a long time? That they've already given me every conceivable compliment they can think of?"

"Name me one."

"What?"

He snorted. "As I thought, you heard them but you didn't *really* listen to them. Now I understand. Really, Lady Amanda, why waste your time if you're not interested in these gentlemen?"

"Maybe because unlike you I'm not *rude*?"

He raised a brow. "You don't think it's rude to keep them

dangling like that? Young men actually hopeful of finding wives? If you don't want to marry any of them, send them on their way so they can find women who are willing."

Beyond enraged, Amanda yelled, "I give them no encouragement a'tall!"

"No, you just like that they all flock to you whether they stand a chance at winning you or not. But I realize it's *who* you are that is the problem. They're not going to stop trying for a duke's daughter until she's no longer available. So pick one of them and put the rest out of their misery."

She was speechless. That was absolutely his worst insult yet, saying that her beaus only danced attendance on her because of who her father was. He might as well have said no one could find her attractive or like her for herself.

But then Devin Baldwin's eyes passed over her from head to foot, slowly, too slowly—even *that* was an insult—and he added grudgingly, "You're pretty enough. It's too bad you haven't figured out how to utilize that instead of monopolizing conversations and—"

"Good Lord," she cut in furiously, refusing to hear another word. "I cannot believe you're doing it again. I do *not* want your advice, *Cupid*!" She heaped as much scorn as she could muster into the moniker the *ton* had given him. "You, sir, are intolerable!" Amanda turned and stomped out of the stable.

Chapter Seven

DEVIN WATCHED THE LADY stomp out of his stable. Not so sunshiny today, was she? And what the devil was she even doing here? Wait, she'd started to mention her sister-in-law before he caught her attention. He quickly finished dressing and went off to find Ophelia Locke.

"What on earth did you say to Mandy?" Ophelia Locke asked him. "She's out front snarling at the grass."

Devin laughed. "Is she? Funny thing about free advice, it tends to be ignored or scoffed at if it doesn't come from family or a friend. But pay for it and you think you've got your money's worth."

With perfect timing, Reed Dutton joined them. Devin's best friend from childhood before he'd gone off to school and met William, Reed and Devin were still close, and if not for Reed, whom Devin trusted enough to leave in charge of the Lancashire farm, he would never have moved his base of operations near London, where he felt free to deviate from his uncle's breeding program to concentrate on racers instead. Reed still brought down the Baldwin horses that were ready for sale, since Devin's uncle had actually had more clients from the south than near home, and whenever it slowed down on the northern farm, Reed would help Devin on the new one.

Devin introduced Ophelia to Reed, explaining, "Reed will bring some horses for you to choose from to the track. I assume you know your husband's preferences? Some men actually like the power of a stallion and even enjoy the challenge of handling one—a kind of battle of the wills. Others just want the speed without the occasional difficulties."

"Rafe's current mount is a stallion, he even bred him from his very first horse. Sentimental you might say."

Devin grinned. "I still have the offspring of my very first mare, as well. She's not good for anything except looking pretty these days, but I won't let her go."

"Too old to be ridden?"

"No, just too gentle for my current goals. She's got the stamina, she'll just never have the speed, and all her offspring pull toward her temperament, so I've stopped breeding her." Then to his friend he said, "Reed, bring the animals we discussed to the track so the lady can see if we have what she's looking for."

As they walked down to the racetrack, Ophelia confessed, "I was actually hoping to buy a horse for Amanda today, too, one like you just described, but she still refuses to ride. Had a fall when she was young and was afraid to get back on a horse after that."

"Fear can be easily overcome with the right guidance and instruction."

"I know, but she doesn't really have a reason to want to try. By the by, I did still have another reason for coming here today. I was quite impressed with your matchmaking theories last night and would like to hire you for someone who could definitely use some help in that regard—that's if you don't have too many clients already?"

"Not a'tall, but I'm not actually for hire in the usual sense. I do, however, agree to help certain individuals in regard to matrimony as a favor."

"But surely you charge for it?"

"No. But this farm is still being developed, so I don't turn down gratitude in monetary form. No one feels indebted then for a mere favor, and anything I make off of those efforts, I put into this farm."

She smiled. "I quite see your point. And I'm so glad you do favors of that sort. I meant to ask you last night, how did that come about?"

He shrugged. "Quite by accident, as it happens. When I changed over to breeding Thoroughbreds just for racers, I spent a lot of time at the track just south of here to test out my stock or acquire new studs. I've met a lot of people there, other horse fanciers. Some of them were fathers hoping to get their offspring married. Some of those fathers brought their sons with them. I'm not even sure why I asked one of those sons to describe what he was looking for in a wife. Just making conversation, really, since the boy didn't want to talk about horses. But oddly enough, I'd just met a young woman through William's sister who perfectly fit the young man's expectations, and I introduced the two of them. They were married last spring. And suddenly, out of the blue, other fathers started approaching me and offering me money to get their children married. It certainly wasn't a hard task, and since I could use the money to improve my breeding stock, I didn't refuse."

"How many have you helped?"

"Just four couples so far, though I did find a perfect match for William. I'm just not going to mention that to him yet, since he wants to get his sister married off first, before he looks for a wife."

"What *is* his sister's name? I thought he'd bring her to the soiree last night, but I couldn't remember her name to put it on the invitation."

Devin chuckled. "Her name is Blythe Pace. She'll be delighted if you keep her in mind for any other parties this year."

"Are you matchmaking for her, too?"

"No, she hasn't run into difficulty yet, having only just turned eighteen. I'm merely keeping my eyes open for her, but she doesn't give me much to work with. I've known her for years, yet all I've ever gathered about her is that she's happy running a household. No other interests to speak of, at least none that she'll talk about. Mere attraction isn't enough to make a truly happy marriage." He grinned. "Though it's enough to get the ball rolling. More is needed for a lasting relationship."

"That's a good point, and yet surely you've encountered exceptions to your theory?"

He laughed. "Of course, there are exceptions in any situation. But you'd be amazed how many young people don't have a clue as to what they really want for themselves, let alone what they want in a spouse. Yet most of them think they have to get married, at least the young women think so, and they foolishly think everything else will just fall naturally into place after that."

Ophelia gave him a curious look. "You might be viewing marriage from only the male perspective. You men have so many interests, do you really think a woman needs as many?"

He smiled. "'Course not. And you're about to tell me that

some women are blissfully happy just being a wife and a mother, that they don't need a single other thing to feel everything is right in their world."

She coughed delicately. "Yes, I was."

"And, yes, that is often the case. But what about the husbands in those marriages? Do you really think they will remain blissfully happy when they have nothing in common with their wives other than the children they produce together? Or is that why they keep mistresses on the side? Because they bloody well aren't satisfied with their wives?"

He was appalled to hear the bitterness that had just snuck into his tone, and the lady didn't miss it, either. She was giving him a wide-eyed look. Her maid was doing more than that. She was glowering at him for introducing a subject unfit for her lady's ears.

Annoyed with himself, he added curtly, "Sorry, I've seen it happen. No one's happy in situations like that. There's guilt, shame, and a multitude of other nasty emotions that affect everyone involved. And that's why I feel more is needed in a marriage for both spouses, and they need to know it before they marry, not afterwards when it's too late."

Ophelia nodded, mulling that over for a moment. "I must say, you're sounding more like a guardian angel than a Cupid."

He burst out laughing. He would never have taken that view, but he knew well that women did *not* think the way men did.

"Oh, my." She'd noticed Reed on his way back to the stable with a string of horses behind him. "How did he collect them so quickly?"

"We train them as well as breed them. He'll get them saddled before he brings them down here."

Chapter Eight

Amanda tried waiting in the coach while Ophelia finished her business, but she couldn't do it. She was still too angry to sit still for more than a moment. Instead she tried walking off her anger, but that didn't seem to help either. She was still so furious at Devin Baldwin that she wanted to scream. No one had *ever* talked to her like that before. No one!

She was amazed that the man owned this impressive horse farm. He must have other people who handled the business aspects for him or he'd have no clients a'tall. Who would deal with someone as arrogant and condescending as he was? She had a good mind to fetch Ophelia before he ended up insulting her, too. They could go to another horse farm to buy Rafe's birthday gift.

She passed several benches but ignored them, still feeling too agitated to sit. She kicked several clumps of grass before she realized she'd made a full circuit of the three stables. The second time around she saw where Ophelia had gone, over to the track behind the stables. Three horses had just been led inside it. And *he* was there. It was a wonder hailstones weren't falling from the sky on his head, she was glaring at him so furiously.

"Insufferable cad," she said.

"What's a cad?"

Amanda swung around with a gasp and saw a little girl standing there, holding the reins of a pony and gazing at her curiously. About five or six years of age, she had a pretty, freckled face and red pigtails. What on earth was a child doing on this farm?

Goodness, Amanda didn't realize she'd spoken aloud. In response to the girl, she said, "A cad is no one you'd ever want to meet."

"Oh." The girl looked puzzled. But then she smiled, revealing a missing tooth. "Do you want to meet me? I'm Amelia Dutton."

Despite her foul mood, Amanda couldn't help but smile. "Yes, I am delighted to meet you, Amelia. I'm Amanda. Do you live here?"

"No, I live with my parents in Lancashire at Uncle Devin's other horse farm, but my father brings horses here sometimes. Mum and I don't usually come with him, but Uncle Devin had this present for me." Amelia stroked the pony's mane. "So I got to come this time. He's wonderful, isn't he?"

Amanda was startled to hear the word *wonderful* right after Devin's name, but then she almost laughed, realizing the child was talking about her pony.

"Yes, that's a wonderful pony you have."

"You like horses, too?"

"Well, I used to, when I was your age, but I don't so much anymore."

"How can you not like horses?" Amelia asked in wide-eyed amazement.

Amanda wasn't about to frighten the child by mentioning the terrible accident she'd had falling from a horse when she was Amelia's age, which was why she'd never got back on a horse again. Instead she asked, "So you're related to Devin Baldwin?"

Another missing-tooth smile lit up Amelia's face. "I wish I was, he's so nice and funny, always making me laugh. But Mum said I should call him uncle since he's my father's best friend. That's my father with him now."

Amanda looked back at the fenced-in track where she saw two men racing their mounts. The demonstration was for Ophelia, who must not have decided yet which horse to buy for Rafe. Devin, on a black stallion, was slightly in the lead. Amanda would have picked the white horse Amelia's father was riding, but only because she remembered seeing not long ago in Hyde Park an acquaintance trot past her carriage on a sleek white mare and thinking that she'd look splendid riding a white horse herself. She'd even had a spark of courage that day and had thought she should try riding again. The thought had been there and gone before she got home.

Apparently, Ophelia had made her decision because she was waving at Devin and pointing at his mount. Amanda wasn't surprised. Even she was impressed by how graceful and commanding Devin looked on the horse. He had such presence that she suspected he could even make a nag salable. Had she been too harsh in her judgment of him? Even this child adored him, and children could be uncannily perceptive.

Having just had that thought, Amanda was taken aback when she heard the little girl say, "You don't hate horses enough to hurt them, do you?"

She glanced down to see Amelia frowning at her. "I don't

hate them a'tall, I just don't like to ride them. But what makes you think I'd want to hurt them?"

"I heard my father talking about it."

"About *me*?"

Amelia shook her head. "No, he was telling my mum about the rotten hay that made some of the horses sick, and my mum said the horses would have turned up their noses at rotten hay, so it had to be something else that hurt them."

Amanda understood now. Of course the child would take note of something that sounded mysterious and scary and build it up in her mind.

Hoping to ease the child's worries, Amanda reminded her, "From what you've told me, your uncle Devin sounds too nice to have enemies."

"I didn't think anyone was trying to hurt him, just the horses."

Amanda chided herself for giving Amelia even more to fret over, so she chuckled to make light of it. "I'm sure Devin isn't going to let anything bad happen to his horses. Now I must rejoin my brother's wife, since it appears she's picked out the horse she wants to buy. It was nice to meet you, Amelia."

Amanda hurried back to the front of the stables. Having calmed down after talking with the little girl, she realized she was a bit chilled after being outside for so long. She stepped into the stable to warm up for a few minutes, and when she heard Ophelia's voice coming from the back of the building, she headed that way.

"—so I'll take him."

"A good choice," Devin said. "My current stud was sired by him, which is the only reason I'm willing to let him go. But don't you want to know his price first?"

"When it comes to pleasing my husband, price is irrelevant. And that goes for his family, too."

Amanda came around the corner in time to see Ophelia hand Devin a heavy purse. "This is for your matchmaking abilities," Ophelia added. "I'll double that when you're successful."

"And who is it you want me to help?"

"My husband's sister. She's having a deuced hard time finding love and she won't settle for anything less. And after three Seasons trying, well, the whole family feels her plight. You're just what's needed to turn this situation around, and I'm delighted you've agreed to help."

Amanda stopped cold in her tracks, mortified that Ophelia would do something like this without even discussing it with her. And to make it sound as if she were in dire need?! To tell *him* that!

She didn't even notice that Devin had begun to frown halfway through Ophelia's explanation, but heard him ask, "I don't suppose your husband has more than one sister?"

"No, just Amanda."

Devin handed the purse back to Ophelia with a rude snort. "Forget it. If a duke's daughter can't make a match in three Seasons, she doesn't need my help, she needs a miracle, and I'll even tell you why, free of charge. She talks too much, is too vain to listen to anyone tell her what she's doing wrong, and by all accounts, she'd much rather run up a tally on how many men she can keep dangling before they get a clue that—"

"How *dare* you!" Amanda cut in, marching forward. "You're the one without a clue, you obnoxious clod!"

Devin stiffened, but all he said was "That might have been a bit too blunt, what you just heard, but I didn't anticipate a young lady would be sneaking around my stables eavesdropping. Not that I'm in the habit of wrapping up the truth prettily for any reason."

Amanda gasped, even more hot color reddening her cheeks. "No, you're just in the habit of being an arrogant boor." But she was even more enraged at Ophelia and dismissed Devin completely to turn her heated glare on her. "Pheli, how could you do this?! Hire him behind my back? *Him?* I could be drowning and I wouldn't accept *his* help!"

Ophelia winced. "Mandy—"

"No, not in front of him. Not another word in front of him!" Amanda hissed.

She lifted her skirt and ran back the way she'd come, afraid she was going to burst into tears at any moment. She could barely breathe she was so choked with emotion. She'd never been so humiliated, but she'd never behaved like such a shrew, either. My God, she didn't know what was worse, what she'd heard or how she'd reacted to it!

Pushing open the stable door, she ran out and immediately collided with someone. She would have lost her balance completely if a pair of hands hadn't quickly come to her shoulders to steady her. She glanced up to apologize for the near accident, but no words came out. She was looking at the amiable countenance of one of the most dashing gentlemen she'd ever seen.

"Hello," he said in a deep voice. "That was clumsy of me. I didn't hurt you, did I?"

"No, I—" She found herself completely tongue-tied. He was so handsome! Curly, light brown hair, beautiful green eyes, nearly six feet tall.

"Let's sit you down for a moment to make sure you're all right." He led her to the bench under the lone tree in front of the stables. "Please allow me the liberty of introducing myself.

Lord Kendall Goswick, my lady, at your service. May I beg your name?"

Blushing, she said, "Amanda."

"You *are* all right? Please, assure me."

"Truly, I'm fine. The fault was mine, I wasn't watching my step."

With a boyish grin he said, "I consider that my good fortune. Are you here buying a new mount? Baldwin has remarkable stock."

"Yes, for my brother's birthday."

"Then you must love horses as much as I do!"

"Well, actually, it was my sister-in-law's idea, but, yes, certainly, what isn't there to love about horses?" Amanda smiled at him but she groaned inside. She couldn't believe she'd just said that!

Chapter Nine

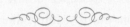

DEVIN STARED AT THE chit as she ran away and in that direction after she was gone from sight. Twice now she'd stalked off in a rage. Amanda Locke, all fire and brimstone, was definitely a sight to behold. Blue eyes flashing, fists clenched, trim little body bristling, she was too angry to even listen to Ophelia's explanation. He didn't know too many ladies who would actually lose their decorum like that for any reason—no, scratch that, he couldn't think of a single one.

After a few moments Ophelia actually snapped her fingers in front of his face to get his attention. He started to laugh at himself, but cut it off and glanced at her instead. She didn't look too pleased either and appeared to be filled with annoyed chagrin.

"You probably should have warned her," he said with an amused grin.

"No, I wanted to make sure you were available before I broached the subject with her."

He shrugged. "Well, you see what I mean? Instead of

admitting she's going about this husband hunt all wrong, she takes offense."

Ophelia tsked at him. "Anyone would have taken offense at what you just said."

"I'll be the first to admit she shouldn't have heard that, but the truth isn't always pretty."

"The truth could be broached in any number of ways that don't include derision, but first impressions aren't always accurate, and from the sound of it, you've misjudged Mandy out of hand. I would think that you of all people wouldn't jump to conclusions like that."

The lady was scolding him? He did laugh this time. "She doesn't want my help and I don't feel like leading any men to the slaughter today. So why don't we scratch this matchmaking mission up as not doable."

"You make it sound like you think she's a lost cause. She's not, you know. She just hasn't met the right man yet. But that's where you would have come in, to find that right man for her. So why don't you keep this." Ophelia slapped the purse against his chest. "And simply give it some thought. If after a week or two you can't think of a single man she might like that she hasn't met yet, then no harm done."

Amanda Locke was going to need a lot more help than that, but Devin had already said as much. If the lady still wanted to squander her money on a lost cause, he wasn't going to throw away a gift horse twice.

"Very well," he said.

"Oh, and if you should meet my husband again, please don't mention that I've hired you."

"As it happens, he said he was going to come by for a new horse, so you might want to take your stallion home today and give him his present early. But why don't you want him to know about this other business?"

She sighed. "I broached the subject of hiring you to help Mandy with him last night. He was appalled by the notion, told me to bite my tongue and not give it another thought. He thought his sister would be horrified if she found out about it, and he was right about that, as you just witnessed."

"He forbade you to arrange this, didn't he?"

She nodded with a slight wince. "And he'll think I'll abide by that."

"You don't think his sister will tell him, as angry as she is?"

"I'm going to do my best to convince her that wouldn't be a good idea."

"But you're not really worried about deceiving him?" Devin guessed.

She blinked. "I'm doing nothing of the sort—oh, wait, you think his dictate is the final word in the matter?" She almost laughed, he could tell she was fighting it. "No indeed. We have a marriage of the sort you try to arrange, blissful in every way. I'm trying to help his sister. He would have done the same if he didn't think Mandy would hold it against him. But even their father has concluded that a new plan of action is needed at this point and last night spoke to one of the old matchmakers he is acquainted with."

Devin laughed. "Then you don't need me."

"On the contrary, I don't know what came of the duke's conversation with the matchmaker, but I don't really think she can help. I *do* think you can or I wouldn't have asked. Your approach is innovative. You go beyond what's clearly on the surface to make sure a match will be lasting."

He gave her a skeptical look as he led her into his office

at the back of the stable to conclude their first business. "Do you want me to deliver the stallion today to your London residence?"

"No, we celebrate all birthdays at Norford Hall, and Rafe's isn't until next month. The whole family will adjourn to the country for the celebration." She jotted down the location and the date for Devin. "I'll think of something to make sure Rafe holds off buying a mount for himself in the meantime."

"As you wish."

Devin waited until she'd put the bill of sale away and they were walking toward the front of the stable before he reminded her, "You know I gave your sister-in-law good advice. She took offense and, as you said, was out there snarling at the grass because of it. Now, after what she heard, she'd sooner spit at me than work with me toward her goal."

"She's simply touchy about her situation, and that's quite understandable. All of her friends have found husbands. She's the only one who hasn't."

"Which proves she's too bloody particular," he said under his breath as he opened the stable door for Lady Ophelia.

"I heard you, but I disagree. You said it yourself, attraction must come first and—" She paused as she looked outside. "Oh, my, I think that requirement has been met. Who is that handsome young man sitting next to Amanda, enthusiastically talking her ear off? She seems quite enthralled by him."

"Kendall Goswick, the Earl of Manford," Devin answered, surprised to see Kendall there. "He's been a client of mine ever since he came of age last year and shook off his guardians. Quite the horse fancier he is. If you can't get Amanda back on a horse, he's not for her."

"Really?"

"Really. The man spends most of his days in the saddle when he doesn't have to! He doesn't just love horses, he's a bit obsessive about them and thinks nothing of hying off to other countries to track down new mounts for his stable, now that he has control of his purse strings. He must have just returned from Ireland. He went there a few weeks ago to buy a mare he heard about."

They'd been noticed. Kendall gave Devin a jaunty hail and came over to meet Ophelia. Devin introduced them. Amanda wasn't looking the least bit furious as she joined them. She couldn't seem to take her eyes off the young man.

"Was your trip successful?" Devin asked Kendall.

"Indeed! You're going to be amazed when you see this mare, Devin, and, yes, you can still have the first filly. I'll bring her round in the spring to—er—"

"Of course," Devin said to spare the lad more blushing over mentioning Devin's stud service in mixed company.

Kendall said to Ophelia, "You must be Lady Amanda's chaperone? I was just about to ask her if she would be agreeable to my accompanying her for a ride some morning in the city, perhaps in Hyde Park? I've heard they have extensive riding paths there, though I haven't been to the city yet to find out. Would that be permissible, Lady Ophelia?"

The smile disappeared from Amanda's face. Devin noticed that she cringed slightly at the idea. Of course she couldn't say yes when she didn't ride!

But before the young man noticed Amanda's reaction, Ophelia quickly said, "Why don't you come for tea this week and we can discuss it. I'm sure her brother, Rafe, would like to meet you."

"Of course, what a dunce I am, first things first!" Lord Kendall eagerly agreed.

They spoke a bit more, directions were given to Ophelia's town house, and the young man actually bent to kiss Amanda's hand as they parted, leaving her blushing and smiling again.

Back in the coach, Ophelia said triumphantly, "See, I knew Devin Baldwin would be able to help!"

"*He* didn't arrange that meeting," Amanda began sharply, then sighed. "Thank you for that rescue. I simply couldn't think of what to say to Lord Kendall when he mentioned riding."

"That might be a problem," Ophelia said carefully. "Or was I merely imagining that you seemed to like the young earl?"

Amanda grinned. "Was it that obvious? What wasn't there to like about him? Handsome *and* charming!"

"But he's an avid horse fancier and rider."

"Is he?"

"Yes, according to Devin, extremely so. So I'm not surprised that instead of asking to call on you, he asked to ride with you. You do realize what that suggests, don't you?"

"What?"

"That he wants to be sure you love riding as much as he does. That he could well consider it a mandatory requirement— for a wife."

Amanda slumped in her seat.

Ophelia scolded lightly, "Don't give up! I was assured today that with the right guidance and instruction, you can be back on a horse *and* enjoy it. We'll have you riding with the earl in Hyde Park in no time!"

But Amanda's fear had kicked in and she said hopefully, "Perhaps that isn't mandatory a'tall. It might be helpful to find that out before I risk breaking my neck again."

Ophelia tsked. "That would be putting off an opportunity

to see the Earl of Manford again soon, or when he comes for tea will we have to decline his invitation because you didn't start your lessons immediately? You might never see him again if I have to tell him that." Amanda chewed her lip, prompting Ophelia to add, "Really, Mandy, there won't be any neck breaking with the right guidance."

"Baldwin you mean?" Reminded of him, Amanda said again, "Pheli, you never should have tried to hire him, and it's a good thing he declined."

Ophelia refrained from mentioning that he hadn't declined after all. There was no point in discussing that when it looked as if it might not even be necessary now! So she merely said, "I was just trying to help. The man has clients from all over England, men you might never meet otherwise yet could be just what you've been waiting for. Like Lord Kendall. Who would have guessed we'd meet someone like him there today? Are you going to cross him off because of a simple little fear that you could easily conquer? Most men love to ride. Most husbands enjoy riding with their wives. You know, I ride with Rafe every morning when we're in the country. It's fun, it's exhilarating, and occasionally we even race, though I probably won't be winning any more of those races after I give him his new stallion!"

"Did Baldwin agree to teach me to ride?"

"No, but I'm sure he can be persuaded. *He* was the one who said it would be easy."

Chapter Ten

"Forgot to mention yesterday when we arrived that Miss Hilary is getting married."

Devin glanced up to see Reed leaning against a post, watching him saddle his stallion for the ride back to London. "I haven't heard that name in ages," Devin replied. "I'm surprised she's waited this long. It's been nearly two years since I left Lancashire."

Reed sighed in relief. "So it doesn't disturb you? I thought it might, since you seemed to be courting her—unofficially, of course."

Devin shook his head. "I wasn't courting her, merely enjoyed her company on occasion."

He had been attracted to Hilary, though. He just didn't love her and couldn't have married her even if he'd wanted to. He'd tried to make it clear to her that they could never be anything other than friends. But he was afraid that she'd held out hope anyway that they could be more, and that was why she'd waited so long to accept a proposal of marriage from another man. He hoped she'd be happy now. She would never have been happy with him once she learned the truth about him.

To prove he wasn't harboring any regrets, Devin added in a lighthearted tone, "Her mother's cook was the best in the county! Truly, that was what really lured me to her house."

Reed laughed and remarked with a teasing light in his eyes, "Well, those were certainly lovely ladies who visited this morning, beautiful enough to make a man forget every other woman he's ever met!"

Devin chuckled. "You noticed that, did you?"

"Knocked me on my arse, the married one. Can't remember ever being that stunned by a woman's beauty."

"Lady Ophelia seems to have that effect on most men—at least at first sight. But it was definitely a profitable visit. Even Lord Goswick talked me out of another yearling before he left."

"Sounds like your luck is finally turning," Reed said with a grin.

"I'm inclined to agree. In fact, I'm feeling damned good about today. I'd been beginning to wonder, after those setbacks we had. One oddity was bad enough, but two in the span of a few weeks?"

Reed's humor vanished. "I know. I'm still not convinced losing three foals plus a mare to a farmer's carelessness was what happened that day. The stallion, though, falling over dead in the middle of a race, well, incidents like that *do* happen. But bad hay that could have wiped out all of your mares? That wouldn't have been just rotten luck, it would have put an end to this farm."

"At least you were on hand that day to realize something was wrong."

It had been a mad dash to pull back the hay that was being

distributed in all three stables. The first mare to eat it had died, her foal expiring with her. The others had rallied, but both had mis carried the next day. The farmer who'd delivered the hay had sworn he'd never seen the like. Neither had Devin. But the hay had had a slightly odd smell to it, so obviously something had contaminated it before it had arrived, but no one could figure out what.

"But that promising stallion, I'd only just bought him!" Devin said angrily, still disturbed about that death. "He'd still be alive if I hadn't been so eager to test him in that minor race last week."

"It wasn't your fault. He was unproven, you had to test him before putting him to stud."

"He was in the lead, you know, could have won easily. Did I mention that?"

But then the absurd had happened—the animal had simply fallen over, dead. His heart had given out, was the general opinion. It was not unheard of, though rare with horses that young. Rotten luck, again. But at least the rider had survived the fall.

"I've been keeping a close eye on the lads here—just in case," Reed assured Devin. "But they all seem to be honest hard workers."

"I wouldn't have suspected otherwise, but you're right, it doesn't hurt to look under every rock and into every cranny— just in case. I'm glad you've agreed to extend your stay here this trip. I appreciate it more than you know."

Reed laughed. "Can't get Amelia off that pony long enough to take them home! And my wife doesn't mind. In fact, she's delighted to have enough time on this trip to get that old house cleaned from top to bottom."

Devin chuckled. "The bloody thing is falling apart."

"But at least it will be a clean shambles!"

Good friends were a blessing, Devin thought as he rode back to London. But today was definitely a turning point as luck went. He hadn't just sold a couple horses, he'd made another two hundred pounds for doing absolutely nothing—yet. But he could buy prime horse stock for much less than that, or finally, the champion Thoroughbred, this one already well proven, he'd thought he'd never save up enough money to buy. Or he could finally fix up the house that had come with the property. And another four hundred pounds had been promised if he actually got that temperamental minx married.

That certainly wasn't a foregone conclusion. It could have been. If Amanda Locke were a horsewoman, it would have been the easiest six hundred pounds he'd ever earned. And he'd even had a more in-depth talk with Kendall today to see if he had any other interests besides horses. He didn't. But Devin had already guessed as much. So despite Amanda's apparent interest in the young lord, that wasn't going to work out a'tall if she didn't get her arse back on a horse.

But he still felt good about being hired by the next Duchess of Norford. That was either going to be an incredible piece of luck, if he was successful, or it could backfire on him if he wasn't. The backfiring part did worry him a bit. It could put an end to his profitable new sideline. This matchmaking business he'd fallen into had turned out to be a boon that was helping him to finance his breeding farm. And now, with London's richest hiring him, too, it could well turn out to be more profitable than the farm had been thus far.

He'd rather not see his sideline shut down. What he'd started with his new farm was far more exciting and challenging than running the already established farm in Lancashire for his uncle, and it gave him a greater sense of purpose. Not that he wouldn't have been happy working up in Lancashire, considering how much he loved horses. But it just wasn't the same there after Donald and Lydia had moved to London.

He hadn't known they'd been planning to do that for quite a while and had only waited until he finished school to tell him about their plans.

"I don't want you to think we're abandoning you, far from it," Donald had told him a few weeks after he'd come home from school. Waving his hand to encompass the estate, he'd said, "All this will be yours one day, since you're my heir. Now that you've finished school, you're old enough to take over here."

Donald had actually adopted him after Devin's mother had died so Devin could carry on the family name. How ironic, when he'd wondered more than once if he would ever even have met these only surviving members of his family if his father hadn't wanted him gone from the house Devin had lived in as a child. His mother certainly hadn't ever mentioned that she had a brother until the day she kicked him out of her life.

Devin had never spoken of these things with his uncle. After his mother died, he couldn't bring himself to talk about her at all. He'd hated her for dying. And then he'd been sent off to school, a fancy one, and all the questions that had been too painful to ask got buried.

Until that day when Donald had told him he was giving him the farm and had added, "Your mother would have been so proud of you."

The mention of his mother opened the floodgates. "You disowned her, didn't you? Is that why she never told me about you until the day you collected me from London?"

"No, we'd just had a falling-out is all. It doesn't matter now."

Obviously his uncle didn't want to talk about it even then. But Devin's bitterness had returned, and all those old questions he had never asked were resurfacing.

"Don't you think I'm old enough to hear it, that I'm a bastard?"

"Of course you're not!" Donald tried to insist, but the color drained from his face and he couldn't look Devin in the eye when he reiterated, "She married your father. He just died when you were a baby."

"A man whose name I can't even remember because she refused to ever speak of him? Was he her creation? Or yours?"

Donald sighed, sat back, and closed his eyes. He was in his midfifties then, though he looked older. Blond hair thoroughly peppered with gray, blue eyes so like his sister's, weathered skin, stooped shoulders. He hadn't just bred horses all his life, he'd trained them, he'd groomed them, he'd fed them, he'd treated them as if they were the children he'd never had himself. And he'd imparted all his knowledge and love of horses to the boy he'd taken in all those years ago.

Devin didn't think his uncle was going to say another word, he looked so pained. Devin would have let the matter go because of that. He loved his uncle. The man had been nothing but good and kind to him.

"My sister had such good prospects," Donald finally said with a touch of some old bitterness. "Three proposals before she was even of age, one from a viscount. But she fell in love with a man from London she couldn't have, and you were the result. When she wouldn't come home, I said some harsh things she never forgave me for. I let pride come before love, and I've regretted that to this day. Yes, I let it be known that she'd married and her husband died just after you were born. She was so angry at me that she wouldn't use the name I created for him, though she did use the story, merely telling people she preferred her maiden name since she hadn't been married long."

His uncle's words stirred a memory that Devin had long forgotten. "She told me once, 'You don't know what it's like to love like this. I hope you never find out.' I'd asked about my father that day. That was her excuse for not wanting to talk about him. But she was talking about my real father, wasn't she?"

"I honestly don't know, Dev. I don't doubt she loved him. I think that's why she wouldn't come home. She wanted to be near him even if he wouldn't—couldn't marry her."

"Lord Wolseley, the bloody landlord?"

Donald's eyes snapped open, hearing the hatred in Devin's voice. "Wolseley? He was a friend of your mother's, yes, but he wasn't her landlord. She owned that house. Your father gave that to her."

"Then why would she say—never mind, just a lie, obviously, to explain his many visits late of a night. He *was* her lover! She sent me away because of him!"

"Devin, no, that wasn't it. She sent you away because you were starting to ask questions and she felt you were too young to hear the answers. When she asked me to come get you, she told me what you mistakenly thought, and that when you were older, she would explain to you about your real father. I don't know if she loved Wolseley, but I'm sure she loved your father. She never would tell me who he was. She was afraid I'd try to kill him and I probably would have. He paid for your schooling, you know. I could have done so. I almost threw away that anonymous missive that arrived, telling me your entire education was already paid for and the name of the school that was expecting you."

"Why didn't you?"

"Because I wasn't going to spite you just because I hated him. And your aunt convinced me that it was the best thing for you. What you learned there and the contacts you made would allow you to move in the highest echelons of society. And to be honest, I felt he owed you that, at least, since he otherwise didn't want to be part of your life."

Devin still didn't believe it, that Lawrence Wolseley wasn't his father. His mother had lied to him. Why wouldn't she have lied to her brother, too? All to protect that bastard that she loved so much she'd abandoned her family for him, her *entire* family. Someday he was going to confront Wolseley about it. But he wasn't going to upset his uncle further over a subject that had no resolution—yet.

For five years he got so involved in the day-to-day running of Donald's large estate that there wasn't much time to think of unresolved issues. Donald didn't just turn it all over to him, he and Lydia were leaving Lancashire for good! They wanted to do some traveling before they got any older, and they were gone for three years doing that. But Lydia also wanted to live again in the city she'd been born and raised in, London. All her old friends were still there and had begged her over the years to bring her talents back to them. She had mostly bred dogs in the country, but she actually excelled at training them as well, and her skills were quite in demand now in London. And Donald had taken up painting, of all things!

His aunt and uncle had lived in London for four years now—Devin had only been there half as long—and they were happy there, especially now that Devin pretty much lived with them again. That was the real reason he hadn't fixed up the house on the farm yet.

His uncle's town house was nicely located on the west end of Jermyn Street, not far from St. James Square and just south of Piccadilly, which connected to Bond Street, so his daily ride to and from the farm wasn't long.

He left his horse at the stable on the corner himself, rather than have one of Donald's servants see to it. It was such a quiet, pleasant street that he actually enjoyed the short walk, even when the trees lining the street were bare, as they were now.

He stopped on the steps leading to the house's main entrance, looking toward the next block, where his mother's old town house was, thinking of her again. He'd never stepped foot in that house again, didn't want to. All the furniture had been sold, his mother's personal effects packed up and stored in the attic in Lancashire. He'd never looked through those trunks either. She'd only been twenty-six years of age when she'd died, his beautiful mother. She *could* have still married and actually lived a normal life. But she didn't, not as long as she still loved that bastard Lawrence Wolseley. Still to this day, Devin didn't understand why. Love, her excuse, was not a good reason to ruin your life. Perhaps it was simply because Wolseley had supported her in fine style. She'd had servants, fancy clothes, jewelry. She'd even had quite a tidy savings that Donald had turned over to him. He hadn't refused that. It had allowed him to start the new farm, which was paying for itself now. And he had an abundance of stock now that was his own. He didn't *have* to keep them all for breeding, so he was finally seeing some profits. And he had a new windfall in the form of Ophelia Locke.

Devin found his aunt in the parlor. She was a good ten years younger than Donald, still trim of figure, no gray yet in her black hair. She had two guests, though one was probably a client, he surmised, since the woman held a dog in her arms and seemed hesitant to set it down with so many other dogs in the room. Lydia might have other pastimes, but training and breeding dogs was her favorite, and at least a half dozen dogs and puppies always littered the house. Three of them were lying at her feet, another was curled into the corner of the sofa, and two young ones were fighting over a scrap of lace they'd found somewhere in the house. The other guest, a younger woman, was bent down laughing at the puppies' antics.

Lydia stood up. "Devin, allow me to introduce Lady Brown and her daughter Jacinda. They were just leaving, though Jacinda mentioned knowing you."

Devin didn't recognize the young woman, but didn't embarrass her by saying so. "A pleasure, ladies," he said with a slight bow.

Jacinda had straightened and now gave him a slow smile. Taller than her mother, lithe, she was quite pretty with her blond hair and brown eyes, so he knew he wouldn't have forgotten her if they had actually met before. Young enough to be one of the *ton*'s debutantes this season, she had an intriguing, sensual glint in her eyes as she looked him over. He wouldn't have expected a debutante to look at a man that way.

Her mother was eager to leave and said as she started for the door, "Thank you again, Lydia. I will remember to trim her nails more often now."

Devin was disconcerted until he realized the woman was talking about her dog, not her daughter!

The girl walked past him a little too closely as she followed her mother. "A shame you didn't return home sooner," she whispered in a pouting tone.

He always tried to be polite to his aunt's clients, but this might have to be an exception. This girl was obviously trouble, the sort he steered clear of.

"Where do you know me from?" he asked bluntly.

"I don't. But I've heard so much about the infamous Cupid, it seems like we've already met!"

"Jacinda, come along," Lady Brown called from the hall.

Jacinda sighed. "I hope I'll see you at the Hammonds' upcoming ball. I will reserve more'n one dance for you so we can . . . get acquainted."

That pause was a little too long. Devin shook his head. "I highly doubt that's going to happen. Run along, your mother is waiting."

She smiled, then sauntered out of the room with a sexy swaying of her hips. Devin rolled his eyes.

Lydia returned a moment later to complain with a laugh, "Lady Brown thought I was a dog doctor! But I was still able to help. Her poor dog was limping because she's never once trimmed its nails. Oh, before I forget, the front door was quite busy today, much much more than usual."

"I noticed the stack of invitations in the hall has doubled in size."

Lydia gave him a lovely smile. "I'm not surprised. Look how handsome you turned out. Hostesses in this town must love you. Meeting anyone I should know about?"

Devin almost laughed. His aunt would be pleased if he married and gave her some babies to fuss over. Oddly enough, she didn't view his illegitimacy as an obstacle, but then she was quite certain it would never come to light. She and Donald had made sure of that. But they didn't know that while he didn't care what most people thought, he couldn't take that cavalier attitude into a marriage. Yet they did expect him to marry to carry on the family name. He couldn't do it, not unless he could find a woman who wouldn't care what his mother had been.

"It's Cupid who's getting all those invitations, Aunt Lydia."

She rolled her eyes at him. His aunt and uncle had both laughed uproariously when he'd told them about the nickname he'd garnered. "Don't you believe it," she said. "You're an eligible bachelor, *that's* getting you invites. And I hope you took my advice and remembered to order some formal attire for this Season. Two of those invitations in that pile are to upcoming balls."

Bloody hell, he'd forgot. He didn't own a single set of fancy evening clothes. "I've been busy. 'Fraid it slipped my mind."

She gasped. "Devin!"

Chapter Eleven

AMANDA WAS PRACTICALLY TIPTOEING out of the house. Her father *would* have to pick that exact moment to leave his study and notice her making her way to the front door.

"Where are you off to, m'dear?"

She couldn't tell him! If she failed at her mission, she'd have to admit it, and that wouldn't do a'tall. So without actually lying, she mentioned the other things on her agenda that she did plan to do later that day.

"A walk while the sun is out. A quick visit to Lilly's house to let Rebecca and Rue know I've come home for a few days. And I'll probably stop in Norford Town. But I'll be back in time for luncheon."

"Invite them to dinner then."

"A good idea!"

She waved and slipped out the door before he offered to come with her. The ducal mansion spread out so widely, it was quite a trek to the stable, so she hadn't lied about taking a walk! Her mother's touch was still evident in every room of Norford

Hall. She'd redecorated the entire house before she died, and no one wanted to change a single thing. The mansion was so large, it was quite easy for guests to get lost in it. Each of the three separate wings on the ground floor contained three parlors.

Norford Hall. This was home, the one place that could fill her with peace and a sense of well-being. Family, servants she'd grown up with who were like family, so many memories. Rafe and Ophelia still lived here most of the year. And Amanda's grandmother Agatha lived here, too, though she rarely left her suite of rooms. Most of the family dreaded visiting her upstairs because she kept those rooms so hot, but everyone did nonetheless. Agatha also couldn't remember anyone's name anymore, she was so advanced in years. She always mistook Amanda for one of her many daughters. Amanda didn't mind, she just went along with it, which was much easier than trying to correct Agatha.

When Amanda reached the stable, she walked through it and found old Herbert where she'd asked him to meet her. She was still amazed she was going to do this. But she had to!

On the way back from Devin Baldwin's horse farm the other day, Ophelia had taken Amanda straight to Bond Street to order a few riding habits. Amanda hadn't agreed to any lessons yet! She was still mulling that over and resisting the idea. It wasn't as if she hadn't tried to get back on a horse after she'd mended from the accident. She could still remember the fear that had overcome her. But perhaps it had just been too soon, with that horrible pain still too fresh in her mind. So she didn't decline Ophelia's offer to set her up in advance with the proper clothes—just in case.

She was still quite excited over her meeting with Kendall Goswick. He was the first young man in a long while whom she was actually attracted to. A lot! She wasn't about to cross him off, as Ophelia had put it, just because she was afraid to ride. Surely that couldn't be a real detriment to a budding romance. But what if it was? Dare she take that chance?

By the end of that day she'd worried herself into a frazzle over it and finally concluded that she ought to at least *try* to get back on a horse. But she wasn't going to ask that infuriating horse breeder for help. No and no again! So she decided to return to Norford Hall with her father the next morning. Spending a few days in the country with family and friends was sure to bolster her courage. And she'd sent a message to the old groom who'd given her riding lessons when she was a child that she was ready to try it again. If anyone could get her back on a horse, Herbert could. He'd been nothing but kind and patient with her.

Herbert was waiting for her behind the stable. The horse he'd brought for her looked as old as he was. Amanda had managed to keep her fear blocked away—until she actually stood next to the horse. With the moment at hand, the memories of her accident, the pain, so much pain, all came back to her. . . .

"We'll take this very slow, m'lady," Herbert said, sensing her anxiety. "There is no hurry."

She didn't answer him, so he stood silently while she stared at the mount he'd saddled for her. And stared. And stared. And broke out in a sweat.

Finally he said, "Don't worry about it, m'lady. Riding isn't for everyone."

She sighed and walked away. No, it wasn't for everyone. She'd have to tell Kendall Goswick that. And if he lost interest in her, well, too bad for him. The Season had barely begun! Lord Goswick certainly wasn't going to be the only new face in London this year, although it hadn't sounded as if he was even going to take part in the Season. But if he wanted to see her again, other than on a horse, he might. Besides, she still simply couldn't believe that he'd base matrimony on a silly requirement such as a woman's enjoying riding. Ophelia had merely thrown out the worst conclusion possible; that didn't mean she was right.

In much better spirits, Amanda returned to London with her cousin Rupert and his wife, Rebecca. They had stayed in the country a few extra days to visit with Rebecca's mother, Lilly. Amanda was even able to talk them into escorting her to her second ball of the Season tonight. And her friend Larissa Morrise stopped by that afternoon to visit while Amanda was preparing for the Hammonds' ball, to fill her in on what she'd missed the last few days.

Like most of Amanda's school chums, Larissa had already married. She was also quite enceinte, five months so, and avoided evening entertainments because of it. But she still made daily calls to her friends who were in town, and like Phoebe, she loved to gossip. Devin Baldwin's name was still on the tip of everyone's tongue, apparently, though Larissa was the first to mention that a few of the younger debutantes had set their caps for him.

"Jacinda Brown, in particular, is bragging that she's going to win him."

Amanda stared at her friend incredulously for a moment before she scoffed, "But he's a horse breeder." She could have added, *And utterly lacking in refinement and rude to boot,* but then her friend would ask her why she thought so, and she'd rather not talk about her encounter with him at his horse farm.

Larissa giggled. "So? Nothing out of the ordinary in that, when so many nobles take up that interest. Horses, dogs, if it can race, it's something they'll bet on and get involved with!"

"And who is Jacinda Brown?"

"One of the debutantes this year, and a little too bold, if you ask me. She pretends to be more sophisticated than she can possibly be. But the latest *on-dit* is Viscount Altone, who will be making his very first appearance in London at tonight's ball. They are saying he's going to be *the* prime catch this year."

"Why?"

"Well, he's handsome *and* already titled. And his father's a marquess, *and* rich."

"Are you sure?"

"About what?"

"That he's handsome?"

Larissa giggled again. "No, not sure a'tall, since I haven't met him to verify that part. I'm just repeating what I heard yesterday. But there's usually some truth to the gossip making the rounds."

"Or none a'tall. And I've never heard of him before—" Amanda stopped and suddenly grinned. "Or have I? His name wouldn't be Kendall Goswick, would it?"

Larissa shook her heard. "No, Robert Brigston is his name, but who's Kendall Goswick?"

"A charming young man I met a few days ago."

"Why haven't *I* heard of him?"

"I don't think he's been to London yet. He just came back from Ireland, where he went to buy a horse. He told me all about it."

And not much more, Amanda realized. That *was* all he'd talked about when they met. She groaned inwardly. She was probably going to have to forget about him—no, that hadn't been determined yet.

Amanda said, "But I've never heard of Robert Brigston before."

Larissa shrugged. "Neither had I, but that's probably because his family lives in the north. Where was it?" She frowned, then brightened. "Essex, I think. No, it might've been Kent, or—never mind, it will give you something to ask him when you meet him, won't it? But this is his first time in London, as far as anyone knows."

Amanda frowned. "Not fresh out of the schoolroom, is he? That would make him younger than I am!"

Larissa made a face. "That's quite possible, but *he* won't know that. But perhaps he's not. He could have been taking the tour of the Continent and only just returned. So many men do, before they start looking for a wife. But the moment I heard of him, I thought of you."

Amanda sighed. Every single one of her friends had expected her to marry before them. Every single one of them, after she was married or engaged, had taken a turn at matchmaking for her, with a cousin or a brother, even a young uncle! Or like Larissa, just by letting her know whom to keep an eye out for. She knew they were only trying to help, and she loved them for it. But it only reinforced her feeling that she couldn't manage finding a husband for herself on her own. She was a failure. Soon she was going to be an old maid. Was she being a little too critical of herself?

It was quite possible. After all, until she'd met Kendall Goswick, the only man these last two years who had sparked her interest even a little had been the Scotsman Duncan MacTavish, and *he'd* been engaged to Ophelia. They'd had an on-and-off engagement that had never progressed to marriage because he'd gone and fallen in love with Sabrina Lambert while he and Ophelia had been figuring out that they just didn't suit. All the other men that Amanda had met hadn't been interesting a'tall—no, that wasn't quite right, either. Some had been handsome, such as John Trask and Farrell Exter. Quite a few had been funny, making her laugh a lot, such as Oliver Norse. Oliver had been so friendly that she was still friends with him. But not one had drawn her eyes to him repeatedly or tugged at her heartstrings.

It *was* her fault! Was she too picky? Were her expectations too high? Well, she'd have to turn *that* about and right quickly. And yet, love was supposed to just happen, wasn't it? She'd always thought that she'd know the very moment she saw *him* that she was in love. But if that was so, *he* was taking his bloody time making an appearance.

She glanced back at her friend suddenly and asked, "Did love show up for you instantly?"

Larissa laughed. "Goodness, no, it just sort of snuck up on me."

"Then when did you know?"

"When that first Season of ours was over and I'd gone back home to Kent—and was missing Lord Henry so much I could barely stand it."

"That's right, you met him again in the spring, didn't you?"

"Yes, at a country gathering. He proposed before it was over." Larissa grinned. "He'd been missing me, too, something fierce."

Amanda sighed to herself. That was likely the problem right there. She'd been expecting love at first sight, to simply know immediately when it happened, and because that didn't happen, she'd given up on all those young men who might have suited her just fine—eventually. And all because she didn't fall in love with any of them on a fantasized time schedule!

Chapter Twelve

DEVIN GLANCED AROUND THE ballroom, taking note of the people he already knew. He spotted a few clients and was surprised to see Owen Culley. Not exactly where Devin would expect to find the elderly nobleman, although Mabel Collicott and Gertrude Allen, who were also up there in years, were in attendance. But he knew why *they* were attending this ball and every other major social event this Season. He hoped they'd steer clear of Blythe. The girl was anxious enough without having to deal with someone as bullish as Mabel.

"Don't fidget, it makes you appear nervous," Blythe scolded in a whisper.

He almost laughed. Blythe was the one who was nervous, her terse tones a dead giveaway. It was the only time she wasn't a pleasure to be around. But Devin wasn't about to point that out to her or her cheeks would turn red. He did want her to shine tonight, but not with embarrassment.

He knew why she was nervous. The invitation to this fancy ball had been sent to him, not her, and it was the first invitation that had actually specified that he could bring only one guest. If not for that, he would have asked William along as well, though his friend claimed to have another engagement tonight that couldn't be put off and had even asked if he could borrow Donald's coach for it, since Devin and Blythe would be using the grand old Pace family coach tonight.

Thank goodness Blythe had been prepared and didn't have to scramble at the last moment for a ball gown, as *he'd* had to do for his fancy duds. He'd never use *that* tailor again. But Blythe already had her wardrobe for the Season, which William was now in debt for. "Bloody expensive, getting a sister married off," Will had complained more than once in the last months.

"It's these new clothes," Devin said, explaining his fidgeting. "They're uncomfortable, stiff, scratchy."

Blythe's green eyes briefly moved over his black attire, broadcloth with velvet lapels. "They don't look uncomfortable and they do fit you nicely."

"The tailor lined them with wool! Raved about women having their petticoats made that way, so why shouldn't men get an extra layer for the cold season, too. Bloody idiot."

It was his own fault for having to find a new tailor who would work overtime when his regular man wouldn't, and since he was already paying him extra for the rush, he didn't want to spring for the extra expense of soft wool. But his exaggerated complaints did what he'd intended. Blythe looked much more relaxed now, even seemed to be holding back a laugh.

He added, "And might I say, you look quite fetching tonight." She was done up grandly for the night in her pink-and-white ball gown. Blond hair, green eyes, plump in the right places, good bones, she wasn't a beauty by any means, but she was pretty nonetheless, far more so than some of the other young debutantes present. A little short, perhaps, but so were many of the men in attendance.

A slight blush touched Blythe's cheeks. "You've already said, but thank you again."

"And what's that you were given at the door when we arrived?"

She showed him the little leather-bound booklet with their host's crest on the front that she'd already attached to her wrist. "I know this is your first ball just as it is mine, but surely you learned about dance cards when you were taught to dance?"

Devin chuckled. "One of those classes I barely paid attention to."

She gasped. "You *can* dance, can't you?"

"I think I can manage that."

"Well, the dance card includes a list of all the music that will be played by the orchestra tonight. There's even a pencil attached. Go ahead, put your name next to one of the dances. That will reserve it for you."

He felt like groaning as he did so. One more thing for him to worry about: Blythe's getting her dance card filled. The problem was, this was a ball for debutantes and Blythe hadn't been to enough parties yet to know even half the people in attendance. Devin was seeing a lot of new faces tonight as well. At first, he'd thought that Ophelia Locke had arranged this invite, which would mean Amanda would be attending, but the room was already quite full and the musicians were tuning up their instruments and he hadn't caught sight of her, so possibly not.

The young men had been making the rounds, signing dance cards, but with the music about to start, they rushed at it now. Two of them whom Devin had already met stopped by with a greeting. Devin immediately introduced them to Blythe. They signed her card, and moments later five more men came by to sign it as well. Well, that was a relief.

He grinned at her and teasingly checked her card again. Oliver Norse had even signed it twice. What had Norse's interests been? Devin had met so many new people this week, he was going to have to start taking notes. Boating! That was it.

"Two dances for Lord Oliver? You might mention sailing to him while you're twirling about the dance floor," Devin suggested. "His family owns several yachts. He's overly fond of the subject."

Blythe's eyes actually lit up, making Devin wonder aloud, "Do *you* like boating?"

She laughed. "I don't know! But I've always wanted to find out. I tried to talk Father into buying us a little sailboat when I was younger, but he called it a frivolous expense and didn't want to hear another word about it. So I saved and saved to get one of my own, but then our parents died and I knew Will was counting every copper, so I gave up on the idea."

"So you *do* have other interests? Why did you never say?"

"I like gardening, too, but as for boating, what's the point of mentioning things that I never expected to come to pass?"

Devin rolled his eyes. "Who says they won't? And who says you won't marry a man who likes doing exactly what you like doing?"

"Do you like boating?"

He didn't hear the question. The first song had begun and the dance floor was now filled with waltzing couples. Amanda Locke chose that moment to step into the ballroom with her escort, a young man of exceptional good looks.

Devin hoped he was another member of her family. The chap was *too* handsome. What lady wouldn't set her cap for him if he wasn't a relative? But Devin's concern was merely the thought of losing the rest of Ophelia's "gratitude" if Amanda had already made her choice without his recommendation.

He intended to try to talk to her tonight, to see if it was possible to even have a conversation with her without her temper flaring up. A ball was a perfect place for it, on the dance floor, temporarily alone, without her beaus surrounding her. He needed to find out if she was going to cooperate and take up riding again so she could be a suitable match for Goswick. If not, then Devin was going to have to find out a lot more about her before he could make any other recommendations for her.

But someone else had come with Amanda and the handsome chap, another young woman who was entering the ballroom now, hooking one of her arms around Amanda's and the other around the handsome chap's before leading them farther into the room. Immediately, every man there who was not currently dancing raced toward Amanda. Bloody hell, was he going to have to stand in line to sign *her* card?

Chapter Thirteen

REBECCA ST. JOHN BURST out laughing. "I knew we should have stayed home tonight. Arriving at a party late is permissible occasionally when a young lady is striving to make a grand entrance, but it is never, ever done at a ball when dance cards must be filled out before the dancing begins."

Amanda's eyes widened as she saw what Rebecca saw: men racing toward Amanda from all sides of the ballroom, a few even pushing past the couples on the dance floor to reach her more quickly. No greetings first, no time for it! For the next several minutes, Amanda's wrist was pulled this way and that as the young bucks quickly jotted their names on her dance card, then got out of the way before the first waltz ended and the next group hurried toward her.

"This is normal for Mandy, m'dear," Rupert told his wife. "Would have happened no matter if we were on time. You forget, I've been her escort before."

"I'm afraid as a maid of honor I never had a normal Season.

You wouldn't find anyone at the palace rushing like this. Ever. Did you behave like this when you were younger?"

"Didn't need to. The chits came to me."

Amanda heard that and tried not to laugh. Her cousin Rue *wasn't* exaggerating. Rebecca just rolled her eyes at him.

Lord Oliver was the only one who tried to engage Amanda in conversation during that mad rush, since he'd managed to sign first and refused to move away. So she didn't actually see half the men surrounding her and could only wonder if Robert Brigston had been one of them.

Was he even at the ball? She made an effort to find out once she was on the dance floor, casually casting her eyes about the room as Lord Oliver waxed on about how spiffy she looked in her pale aqua gown, how the color made her eyes bluer, how she was the most beautiful woman he'd ever had the pleasure of . . .

She didn't hear the rest, her eyes having passed over Devin Baldwin and shot right back to him. *He* was here? Well, yes, why not? The *ton* found him so fascinating he was still in the current gossip mill, and thus on everyone's guest list.

He wasn't dancing. Amanda almost smirked, thinking a brute specimen such as him probably didn't know how to dance. And then she was annoyed at herself for even thinking about that rude man, especially now that she had Lord Brigston to think about instead. And who was that young woman Devin was standing with?

"Met him at a country party in Yorkshire last year. Nice chap, if a bit quiet."

Her eyes snapped back to Oliver. "Who?"

He nodded to the other side of the room. "Lord Brigston. He just arrived."

She glanced toward the entrance, but it was already empty. And she recognized everyone even remotely near it. Where had the viscount disappeared to so quickly? Then the music ended and Lord Oliver escorted her back to her cousin and hurried off to find his next partner.

Amanda had a moment to open her dance card to make sure she had an open space or two for Lord Robert to sign when he got around to signing. She didn't look any further than the first page, her eyes stopping on Devin's name next to the fifth dance. So he did dance? Or was he going to murder her feet trying? And how the deuce had she missed *him* signing her card, as big as he was? He must have signed her card while standing behind her and Oliver had been monopolizing her attention.

John Trask bowed formally over her hand when he arrived to dance with her, then gave her a cheeky grin that made her laugh as he led her out to the dance floor. She'd met John last Season, they must have conversed a dozen times, yet what, really, did she know about him? Or any of these young men for that matter? She really had been counting on love at first sight to settle the matter of a husband for her, and because it hadn't happened yet, she'd discounted all of these fine chaps. She might have two exciting prospects right now, but one might trot off because she wasn't a horsewoman, and she hadn't even met the other yet. And what if neither of them would do? She'd have to start over, wouldn't she? What a daunting thought!

She decided to give Lord John her full attention. She did recall that he had a good sense of humor. Like Oliver, John was one of her beaus who could easily make her laugh. But she couldn't remember a single other thing about him, so she spent the entire dance asking him questions she'd probably asked him before! Hopefully he wouldn't point that out.

An earl's son, but third born, John wasn't in line for his father's title. He enjoyed betting on the races. Who didn't? But once horses were mentioned, he didn't want to talk about anything else. Another horse enthusiast? John was one of her more handsome admirers with dark brown hair and eyes, tall, strapping, though not nearly as muscular as . . . she cut short that thought. Whyever was she comparing him to Devin Baldwin?

The dance ended and her next partner was already waiting for her, chatting with her cousin, though he broke that off the moment she arrived. But Amanda couldn't concentrate on him a'tall, not when the very next dance had been claimed by Devin Baldwin.

She'd have to tell him she wouldn't dance with him. But what if he took offense and embarrassed her over it, outspoken as he was? She didn't doubt he would, too, that brute. Very well, she'd dance with him, but only to find out why he even wanted to dance with her. Just to insult her some more? She was afraid he was going to say something to infuriate her again and she'd end up making a scene she'd never live down. Could she control her temper long enough to get through one dance? She could, of course she could, she'd bite her tongue if she had to.

He looked so handsome tonight in his formal togs, quite the most handsome man in attendance—well, unmarried man anyway. It *was* hard to find a more handsome man than her own cousin Rupert St. John. But she could see why some of the debs were fascinated by Devin as Larissa had mentioned, though they probably hadn't actually spoken to him yet and found out how rude he actually was! And where the deuce was Lord Robert? He was supposed to be handsome, too, but she still hadn't spotted him. She'd seen Devin during each of the last three dances, and he hadn't been dancing, not even with his companion, who had danced the last two sets.

Then the moment arrived. Devin stood before her and bowed politely. At least he didn't drag her straight off to the dance floor. He gave her a moment to introduce him to her chaperones.

"The infamous Cupid?" Rupert said, and laughed. "Good God, man, I expected to see a short, chubby little fellow, not a bloody Corinthian."

"Be nice, Rue," Rebecca scolded.

"I'm always nice," Rupert rejoined, and kissed Rebecca's cheek. "Anyone brave enough to give Mabel Collicott a setback is a man after my own heart. He knows I'm teasing."

"You heard about that?" Devin said with a grin.

"Phelia overheard it. She is a member of the family, you know."

"Yes, Lady Amanda's family is quite large."

The music hadn't started yet, but Devin held out his arm to Amanda and walked her to the front of the crowd circling the dance floor. She was surprised at how well behaved he'd been with her family, but she braced herself, expecting the worst now that he'd taken her away from them, only to find it was to meet his companion!

"Be polite," he whispered in an aside to Amanda before he said to his friend, "Blythe, I don't believe you've met Lady Amanda Locke yet. Your brother and I went to a party at her sister-in-law's house earlier in the week." And to Amanda: "You're acquainted with Blythe's brother, the Honorable William Pace."

Amanda was too incredulous for words and barely heard the

rest of what he'd said. He hadn't *really* just whispered "Be *polite*" to her, had he? She *had* to have misheard him.

Blythe smiled. "A pleasure, my lady. Is this your first Season in London, too?"

Amanda saw the way the girl had looked at Devin with adoration in her eyes before she glanced at Amanda. Another debutante who'd set her cap for him? But then the girl's question registered with her and Amanda stiffened. Did the young woman know it wasn't her first Season or was she just being sociable in asking? Whom was she kidding? *Everyone* knew by now that Amanda was on her third Season. That was quite a catty remark Blythe Pace had just made.

Hate at first sight, now *that* wasn't hard to achieve a'tall.

Chapter Fourteen

THE MUSIC HAD STARTED up again, Lord Oliver arrived to escort Blythe to the dance floor, and then Devin said to Amanda, "Shall we?"

Amanda understood now. He was Blythe's chaperone, so he would have to attend her when she wasn't dancing. But why him instead of Blythe's brother?

But the thought went out of her head as Devin Baldwin's hand clasped hers for the waltz and the fingers of his other hand, which should only have barely touched her waist, gripped her quite firmly. She was too close to him! Even at the permissible distance, which wasn't really close a'tall, it felt too close. With him. It took her a moment to realize it must be because his chest and shoulders were much wider than those of the men with whom she was accustomed to dancing. That width plus his height made it seem as if he were surrounding her.

"You don't remember meeting my best friend, do you?" Devin asked.

"Who?"

He chuckled. "Exactly."

Her lips tightened. "No. Who are we even talking about? Blythe's brother?"

"Yes. He was with me the other night. You met him last year."

She shrugged. "He looked vaguely familiar, but, no, I don't remember ever meeting the chap who was with you at Phelia's party."

"Perhaps that's part of your problem. You—"

She stiffened. "I don't have a problem, and if I did, I wouldn't be discussing it with you." She might as well have saved her breath for he continued on as if she hadn't interrupted him.

"—meet all these men, then promptly forget them. Why is that?"

She had to bite her tongue and count to ten before she could say, "Maybe because I've met too many people? I've been at this for three years, *as you well know*. Why don't you ask your friend if she can remember everyone she's met so far."

"She probably can, but then this is her first Season of husband shopping, so I concede the point."

It almost sounded as if they were having a normal conversation, but they weren't, of course. He was conceding? One little point? What about all his other nasty remarks that had been based on mere assumptions? And what about his own flagrant flouting of the rules in escorting a young woman who wasn't a relative of his?

She wasn't going to mention how Blythe had looked at him when Amanda had only assumed it was a look of adoration, which made it highly inappropriate for him to be her chaperone. The girl could have been thinking about some other man she was in love with and Devin had just got in the way of those pleasant thoughts when he drew Blythe's eyes to him to introduce her to Amanda.

But after all the insults he'd dealt her, Amanda jumped at the chance to criticize him, saying, "You shouldn't be Miss Pace's chaperone. A proper escort for a young debutante is another woman, a relative, or her fiancé."

His lips turned up slightly. He found that amusing, did he? Or just that she should mention it? A man as rude as he'd been to her wouldn't care about proper etiquette. Actually, he probably didn't know any better.

"Well, it's true I'm none of those," he said. "Though it does feel like she's a sister to me as I've known her for many years. And besides, tonight I'm just filling in for her brother, who was otherwise engaged this evening. They have no other relatives to call on."

"So you're just doing her a favor?"

"Exactly. All aboveboard. Her maid is even waiting in the coach. So you might want to add a trusted, long-standing friend of the family to that list of yours."

She conceded that point with a nod. When she had to scramble for her own chaperones even with a *big* family, she couldn't imagine what it would be like to have only one family member to depend on. Trusted friends would have to do in that case—no, actually, that still wouldn't do a'tall! It would have to be a married woman friend. Amanda had chosen that option herself when she'd begged Rebecca to escort her to the first ball of the Season because she'd thought it would be much more fun to be accompanied by an old friend. But a male friend would never do. And certainly not one as young and handsome as Devin Baldwin. *That* was still highly irregular.

She said as much. "If her brother couldn't attend, she should have asked a female friend of the family. Have they none?"

He chuckled. "You *are* persistent, aren't you? If you must know, the invitation was mine. She's here as my guest. Otherwise, she wouldn't be here a'tall. Her brother thought it a splendid opportunity for her to meet some new marriageable chaps, and so it is."

Amanda could feel the blush rising and looked away, hoping he wouldn't notice. Yes, that did make a difference, but she wasn't going to say so. And why were they even dancing? Just so he could criticize her again? He'd started to, but she'd stopped him by offering an explanation, and he'd conceded. She could explain away his other negative assumptions about her, too, but she wouldn't. She could not care less what he thought—as long as he kept it to himself.

She glanced at him again. "Did you ask me to dance to apologize? If not, I think you should take me back to my cousins. You and I have nothing—"

"The truth isn't always pleasant. But what I told your sister-in-law wasn't for your ears, and I might have been exaggerating a bit to make a point. Didn't expect you to be eavesdropping."

Color rose in her cheeks again, due to anger this time. That was supposed to be an apology? No, it was nothing of the sort.

Stiffly she said, "So that was your roundabout way of telling her you weren't up for the job?"

He raised a dark brow. "Prevaricate instead of tossing out a simple no? Hell no, that's not my style."

Her eyes narrowed on him suspiciously. "You don't still think you've been hired to play Cupid for me, do you?"

"You don't think I might want to help someone as desperate as you out of the goodness of my heart?"

She snorted over such a failed attempt at being amusing. "After what you said? No, I do not! Besides, I don't think you have a heart."

"I notice you didn't deny that you're desperate."

She gasped and took her hand from his, turning to leave. He actually grabbed her hand and pulled her back to him, tightening his grip on her hand and waist. She couldn't believe it! What if someone saw that! Good Lord, she'd *known* she'd end up making a scene if she got near this exasperating man again!

"Let go of me!" she insisted.

"We're not done—dancing. So your temper is yet another problem?"

"I don't have a temper—unless I'm around arrogant brutes like you!"

"You don't deal well with criticism, do you? No matter how well-intentioned?"

"Well-intentioned insults, now I've heard everything," she said scathingly.

"Nothing was said to insult you, you're just too touchy to admit you've been going about this all wrong—unless you don't actually want to get married for some reason? That would certainly explain your resistance to good advice."

She clamped her mouth shut. She glared at him. She was close to screaming in exasperation. He was going to be the ruin of her if he didn't shut up!

"I didn't think so," he said with a nod. "So I'm going to help you despite yourself. Let's call it a good deed."

"Oh, I see, taking your *god* of love nickname a little too seriously, are you?" she said, sarcasm dripping from her every word. "You actually think you're capable of producing *miracles*?"

He actually laughed. "*That* was the exaggeration. So which

is it to be? Lord Goswick and riding lessons, or we find out who you're compatible with and go from there?"

It was on the tip of her tongue to tell him, We *aren't finding out anything together,* but his mention of Kendall made her say indignantly, "I can win Kendall Goswick without anyone's help, thank you very much."

He shook his head. "That's too bad. It actually looked like you fancied him, but I must have been mistaken."

"I did. I do." But then her brows snapped together. "Stop it. I have dozens of other things to recommend me—"

"Won't matter a jot once he finds out you don't like horses."

"I love horses. Love to see them race. Love to have fast ones hitched to my carriage. Who wouldn't love something that useful?"

"You know I was talking about riding. I know Goswick very well. He doesn't have parents to nag him about getting married. He doesn't give a fig about socializing, so don't look for him to show up at these affairs. You're probably the first lady he's shown the least bit of interest in since he came of age."

That was thrilling to hear and erased her anger for the moment. "Did he say something about me?"

"Yes, actually. He said he looked forward to riding with you. But when that doesn't happen, you'll never hear from him again."

"Nonsense. Love transcends *requirements*."

Devin chuckled. "Are we back to talking about gods?"

"You know what I meant," she huffed.

"Yes, of course, you think love can surmount all obstacles. In some rare cases it might. But you won't even get to that point with Goswick. He's not going to have a chance to fall in love with you if you never see him again. And as soon as he finds out you're afraid to get on a horse, I guarantee you'll never see him again."

Chapter Fifteen

WITH THE DANCE *FINALLY* over, Amanda would have rushed away from Devin, but he still wasn't letting go of her. He hooked her arm through his and walked her back to her cousins. Very well, another few moments and she'd *never* have to talk to him again.

But as if their conversation hadn't ended, he said in an aside to her before he let her go, "Isn't there some unwritten rule that the offspring of dukes have to be courageous?"

How ridiculous! But he walked away before she could tell him so. And it only took her a moment to realize he'd just called her a coward! She couldn't let *that* remark go unchallenged! But when she tried to see where he'd gone, she finally spotted him back on the dance floor, with Blythe Pace this time.

Blasted man. How dare he challenge her to get back on a horse? And, of course, the only way she could prove him wrong was to actually get back on one. But she'd tried that when she went home with her father! Did she really? No, actually, old

Herbert had just helped her to give up by not giving her any encouragement at all.

She chewed at her lower lip. Despite Ophelia's telling her horse riding would be a prerequisite for a match with Kendall Goswick, she'd still been hopeful about furthering her acquaintance with him. But now Devin was telling her the same thing, and her hope just evaporated. Despondency was sneaking back up on her. She'd *really* enjoyed having two prospects for the Season—and where the deuce was the other one? She still hadn't even clapped eyes on Robert Brigston.

"Is something wrong?" Rebecca asked her in a whisper so Rupert wouldn't hear.

"No, why?"

"You were frowning."

Amanda sighed. "I have so many, too many really, choices of men to pick from. It's just becoming a bit difficult to sort them all out."

"Is it really?"

Amanda laughed. Rebecca had been her best friend when they were children and knew her too well.

"It's that the one I favor the most is an avid horseman. Phelia doesn't think he'll court me if he finds out I don't ride."

"You still don't? I know you refused to try after that fall put in you bed for a whole summer, but I thought by now—"

"I drive my own carriage instead. I never thought I would actually *need* to ride a horse. Now I do, and I *will*, but, what if I can't?"

Rebecca laughed. "Gumption and doubts in the same breath, only you could pull that off with such flair. If you want my advice, don't put the cart before the horse. Find a good teacher and give it a try first, before you fret over—"

"There you are, gel," Mabel Collicott said to Amanda. "What the deuce were you doing, dancing with that horse breeder? Stick to your own kind, a nice chap like Farrell Exter—"

Considering Mabel had just barged in on her conversation, Amanda had no trouble interrupting, "Excuse me, ladies, but I only have a few minutes left on this break to get some refreshment before the next dance. I'll be right back, Becca."

Amanda hurried away, not sure what about that old dame annoyed her. But really, Amanda already knew Farrell, considered him somewhat a friend, but for a matchmaker to recommend to her a second son with no prospects? The woman had to be going batty in her advanced years.

On the long walk to the refreshments table at the other side of the room, Amanda skirted the back of the crowd so she wouldn't get stopped by anyone she knew. She was still stopped. Actually, her dance card was pulled right off her wrist!

She swung about to upbraid the fellow for not simply asking her to wait. The words never came out. The young man was of average height, had blond hair, blue eyes, and was handsome! This had to be Robert Brigston, Viscount Altone. And here he was, signing her card and grinning while he did so.

When he looked her in the eye as he handed the little booklet back to her, the grin left his face. He actually looked surprised as his eyes moved over her face, then briefly lower. "My, oh, my. I'll admit you looked pretty from afar, but seeing you close up bowls me over. You're a raving beauty, ain't you?"

She didn't know what to say to that. Compliments before introductions? She'd at least like to know for sure who was complimenting her before she responded with more than a blush.

But he wasn't finished! "I wasn't going to marry, no need to yet, but now that I've met you, I must. Do say yes."

She simply couldn't help the giggle that produced, though she quickly cut it off. How outrageous he was! But she didn't really mind silliness of that sort a'tall. Grinning, she replied, "I'll say nothing of the sort. And you haven't introduced yourself to me yet."

He laughed, a little too loudly, drawing attention their way. "You so dazzle me, my manners flew right out the door. Robert Brigston, your servant, your slave—I'll take whatever I can get. And you must be the incomparable Amanda Locke?"

She was mindful she shouldn't be talking to him without her chaperones close by, at least not until they danced. She hoped he'd signed more than one line in her card. She definitely wanted to find out more about him! But for the moment, she needed to end this first encounter or steer it toward greater propriety.

She nodded. "I was getting some refreshment before rejoining my cousins. Perhaps you'd like to come by and meet them?"

"I'll pass on that opportunity, lovely lady. Relatives are so boring. Until our dance?"

He kissed her hand! And not the polite barely touching of lips to skin, either, but a firm kiss. Then he just strolled off, leaving her surprised and quite disappointed that he hadn't wanted to extend their encounter by walking her back to her cousins.

But, at least, now she had a dance with Lord Robert to look forward to tonight. That nipped that bit of despondency in the bud and filled her with a bubbly excitement as she returned to Rebecca and Rue, completely forgetting about the refreshment she'd gone for.

During her next six dances, she couldn't concentrate on her partners at all! She noticed now where Lord Robert was, dancing with other debutantes. And each time their eyes met, he'd wink at her, giving her the urge to giggle again. This was so exciting! So this was what she'd been missing her first two Seasons, actually being attracted to a man. And this year, there was not just one but two men! Would she actually have a hard time deciding which one she liked better? What a wonderful thought! But that was *if* she accepted Devin's dare . . .

Then Robert whispered by her ear, "Finally, I get to touch you."

She drew in her breath sharply. No one had ever said anything that risqué to her before. She swung about. He was grinning at her as he took her hand to lead her onto the dance floor. He wasn't supposed to be touching her hand yet, not until they were actually on the dance floor. Perhaps he'd missed that lesson in etiquette.

When Robert turned to draw her into position for the dance, he actually pulled her hand behind him so she got much too close to him. Her breasts even touched his chest! But he quickly corrected the "accident," stepping back to begin the dance in the proper position. Had he done that deliberately? Surely not.

A few twirls into the dance, he bent his head forward to say in a husky tone, "You smell divine."

She blinked. That was definitely not a proper compliment. But he was young. Perhaps he didn't know any better.

"I think you must have been tardy in attending some of your etiquette classes," she scolded lightly.

He laughed. "It's just you, sweet Amanda. You quite make me forget m'self."

His words thrilled her and brought forth a pretty blush. But she made an effort to steer the conversation to acceptable subjects—and find out more about him. "I've heard this is your first time to London. Are you just back from the Continent? Or—too busy at home to venture forth?"

She'd almost said *just out of the schoolroom*! Goodness, he rattled her so much she wasn't thinking straight. That would have embarrassed both of them. She really hoped he wasn't eighteen. He didn't look it. He could have been hiding himself at one of the universities young lords favored for higher learning.

"Dying of curiosity about me, are you?"

Of course she was, but she certainly wasn't going to admit it. "University then?"

He laughed at her evasion. "Does it matter where I've been? All that matters is I'm here now—with you."

There was that bubbly feeling again. Where had these exciting men been two years ago? She supposed it was all right if he wanted to remain mysterious for now. *Someone* would ferret out more information about him and get it on the gossip mill. That was inevitable.

A few moments later he said, "This dance will end soon. I must tell you, I already can't wait until we meet again."

She smiled. "I'm sure we will. It's more'n likely you will receive the same invitations as I."

"I was thinking of something less social."

He wanted to court her! "I'm staying with my aunt Julie St. John while in town." She gave him the address on Arlington Street. "You are welcome to call."

He made a sound of impatience. "I don't want to get to know your relatives, dear girl, I want to get to know *you* better."

She frowned, not understanding. "Privacy before an engagement is simply not allowed, and what, pray tell, did you have in mind?"

"You're going to make me steal a kiss right here on the floor, aren't you?"

She gasped and drew back from him.

He chuckled. "Does no one ever tease you? A walk in the park would be nice. Bring your maid along as a chaperone, of course."

Chapter Sixteen

DEVIN KNEW THAT DARING Amanda to tackle riding lessons had been a long shot. A man would accept the challenge, a woman would find numerous excuses to decline it. Obviously Lady Ophelia hadn't talked the girl around to letting him help her with riding lessons *or* finding her other candidates for marriage. She didn't even know he'd agreed to do Ophelia this favor after all. Apparently, it *was* going to have to be other candidates for the girl.

What had started out as a lark for Devin was definitely beginning to feel like a bloody job—well, at least in Amanda's case. The trouble was, she had too many admirers. He supposed he ought to simply ask her which ones *she* favored, aside from Goswick, to narrow down that list, but he didn't think she'd tell him. Still crackling with ire over what she'd overheard him saying to her sister-in-law, it was a wonder she'd even danced with him, much less talked to him tonight. If *he* didn't feel the thrill of a challenge now, he'd send a note round to Ophelia that Amanda really was a lost cause and let it go at that.

That *was* still a possibility. Two Seasons wasted, the third under way. Was she too particular? Looking for something specific in a man that she hadn't yet found? It could simply be a matter of titles, her father having such a lofty one. Good God, she wasn't looking for another duke, was she?

A ball was absolutely not the place to further his investigation of Amanda's flock of beaus, nor which gentlemen might fit well with Blythe. Two-thirds of the former Devin had already met and spoken with, but Amanda had danced with quite a few young men tonight that he was seeing for the first time. Finding those chaps off the dance floor while Blythe was on it, which was the only time she wasn't at his side, was proving quite difficult.

He gave it another shot and checked the refreshment table, but only a few couples were standing near it. He glanced out in the hall. Empty. He headed for the balcony. It was too cold for the doors to be kept wide-open, but he'd seen people stepping out there to briefly cool off from their exertions on the dance floor. Well, bloody hell, the balcony was empty, too. Was everyone dancing but him?

"I have a feeling you're waiting for me."

Devin swung around to find Jacinda Brown sauntering toward him. He'd seen her across the room earlier but hadn't approached her. The girl was much too forward for his tastes. He didn't mind a dalliance now and then, but he drew the line at pursuing married women and innocents. If he'd learned anything from his acquaintance with Hilary, it was that innocents read more into simple friendship than he could offer.

"Actually, I'd hoped for a moment alone," he replied.

She didn't take the hint and stopped much too close to him.

"I've been trying to get my mum to hire Cupid to help me this Season." She gave him a sultry look.

When she went straight for what she wanted? Devin felt like laughing. "You're probably the very last chit here who would need help."

She blushed prettily, taking that as a compliment. "But I don't want to wait until the end of the Season to find my man. Besides, it would be fun to work with you. Don't you think so?"

He was trying not to hurt her feelings with his bluntness, but he had no time for silly flirtations like this. "What I do isn't fun. Now if you'll excu—"

"I'm cold!" She even shivered.

"Then go back inside."

"But you could warm me. Just for a moment."

She actually wrapped her arms around him and pressed her body close to his. He was surprised enough by her audacity that he didn't react as quickly as he should have. Which was why Mabel Collicott looked scandalized when she took that moment to close the balcony doors against the draft and saw them standing there in what appeared to be a lovers' embrace.

But before the old dame could voice her errant conclusions, Devin called out, "Miss Collicott, what perfect timing!" He dragged Jacinda to Mabel's side. "Jacinda confessed she's looking to hire a matchmaker for the Season. I was about to recommend you for the job when she took a chill. I'll leave her in your good hands."

Devin escaped, but not before he heard Mabel say, "Has that boy actually come to his senses? I'll speak to your mother, gel. I know just . . ."

He didn't hear any more, didn't need to. Jacinda's ploy had

just backfired on her, and hopefully, *that* would end her pursuit of him. Relieved, he returned to the edge of the crowd where Blythe expected to find him, and just in time, too. Lord Carlton Webb returned her to Devin's side with a formal nod. But Blythe sighed as the young man moved off.

Devin glanced down at her. "What? Step on your feet, did he?" he teased.

"No. All he did was grouse about Viscount Altone the entire dance. While I wouldn't have minded—Lord Robert is exceedingly handsome, after all—Lord Carlton had nothing good to say about him."

Devin raised a brow, but Blythe's next partner arrived and whisked her away. He did spot Carlton still weaving his way through the crowd and followed him, hoping he wasn't heading toward *his* next dance partner. He wasn't. He'd headed straight for the refreshments to grab a glass of champagne. Devin joined him and struck up a conversation.

The other two fellows Devin had talked to tonight had revealed nothing about themselves and, like Carlton Webb apparently, had only been interested in gossiping about Robert Brigston. This was not surprising. The chap was the current favorite *on-dit*, though the gossip had gone from mere curiosity prior to tonight to something entirely different now.

Jealousy and resentment were apparently running rampant in the room. Brigston was too handsome not to have the young debutantes tittering about him, but that was not why he was infuriating so many of the young gentlemen tonight. They were all here looking for wives this Season, but the new rumor circulating about the young viscount was that he wasn't actually interested in matrimony and had merely come to London to have some fun. That was all well and good, but Devin would have to agree that a ball for debutantes wasn't the right place for a young man to attempt to have fun. He ought to find out if this new gossip about Brigston was true, especially since he'd seen Amanda dancing with the chap.

But that was not why he followed Carlton. He actually hoped Webb had complained enough to Blythe that he was ready to converse about a new subject—himself. Devin should have known better.

"Never heard anything so preposterous," Carlton said right off. "Brigston's here to win Lady Amanda when he doesn't even want her!"

"Lord Robert Brigston?" Devin clarified.

"Where have you been, old chap? Of course Brigston, the bloody man of the hour."

Devin kept his expression neutral. "What gave you the impression he doesn't want to marry?"

"Ain't a guess. He told me himself!"

"Tonight?"

"'Course tonight. Never clapped eyes on him before and hope to never again. And I *hope* Lady Amanda ain't fooled, but she probably will be. He's turned all the ladies' heads, as handsome as he is. And if he don't want to get married, what's he doing charming them all, eh?"

Devin almost laughed. "Let me hazard a guess, perhaps because he *is* charming?"

Carlton snorted. "If you ask me, he just wants to play the rake, racking up conquests, but his father nipped that in the bud by ordering him to win Norford's daughter."

Now that wasn't amusing at all. "Groundless speculation, Webb, that you should keep to yourself."

Carlton huffed and moved away. Devin didn't know what

to think now about the man of the hour. Probably half the men there would rather remain bachelors for a while, simply have some fun before settling down, but had joined the marriage mart at their parents' behest. Dutiful sons, they'd do as told whether they liked it or not. Was Brigston only pretending to be dutiful? He hadn't been told to marry, he'd been told to marry specifically one woman, Amanda Locke. If he subtly sabotaged his own chances with her, then he could honestly tell his father he'd failed and would win a reprieve from marriage.

That was if Webb could be believed, but the young man had been too worked up about it, *and* had tried to spread mere speculation, so really, everything he'd said had to be taken with a grain of salt. Especially since he was so obviously green with jealousy because he was sure he no longer stood a chance with Amanda, now that Brigston was on the scene. Devin wouldn't even be surprised if the new gossip was solely Carlton's spiteful doing.

On his way back to the edge of the dance floor where he would await Blythe, Devin caught sight of the man everyone was talking about—blond hair trimmed short, blue eyes, casually slouched posture. He stood alone watching the dancers, a glass of champagne in hand, a pensive look on his face. Perhaps he was foxed. That might explain some of the new gossip.

Devin stopped next to the young man, towering over him quite a bit. He didn't say anything. He waited to see if Lord Robert would.

"A nice crop of lovelies to choose from, eh?" Robert Brigston said nonchalantly, casting a nod at the couples dancing past them. "Even your friend is quite a looker. Private stock?"

"Private stock?"

"Yours?" Robert said.

"Would you like to step outside?"

The young lord laughed, but it actually had an exaggerated sound to it. "Private stock it is! No need to get in a snit over it."

Devin, knowing the young lord was deliberately trying to provoke him, said in a thoughtful tone, "You know, if you really don't want to marry yet, behaving in a manner that blackens your name isn't the way to go about it. Why don't you just be honest with your father?"

Robert sighed. "I was. Didn't do any good. Good God, man, I'm barely nineteen. Why the devil would I want to be leg-shackled? I'd never be faithful to a wife, it's too bloody soon. I'd just make her as miserable as I am."

"Which is a very good reason not to marry. But we're not just talking about any wife, are we?"

"No," Robert said bitterly. "I was supposed to have a good taste of life first. My father was in complete agreement with that, which makes this a double blow. Now he's obsessed and has been from the moment he found out the Duke of Norford's daughter was still on the marriage mart. Wants her in the family no matter what."

"What if you fall in love with another woman?"

Robert rolled his eyes. "I think I'm in love with every pretty chit that smiles at me. What the deuce do I know about love?"

"That's lust."

"They're not the same?"

Devin chuckled. "Not even close."

Amanda glided past them on the dance floor just then, catching both their eyes. Bad timing.

"She's a rare beauty," Robert said with another sigh. "Can't deny that. I suppose if I *have* to marry, I'll at least get some enjoyment out of it with her."

Devin was no longer amused. The boy was talking about bedding Amanda, and Devin had the urge to pound him to pulp for even having the thought. What the hell? Was he suddenly her guardian angel? But Brigston obviously wasn't for her. The young lord didn't know what he wanted out of life, he just knew a wife wasn't it. And he'd make Devin's job a lot harder if he caught Amanda's fancy.

"I think you had the right idea to begin with," Devin remarked.

"What's that?"

"Blacken your name. If you really don't have the guts to stand up to your father, then that's an ingenious solution to your dilemma. Because the lady in question has relatives who will tear you apart if you trifle with her feelings."

Devin had no idea what Amanda's relatives would do. That threat had actually been from him.

Chapter Seventeen

AMANDA DIDN'T REALIZE HER foot was tapping impatiently. The music had started a few moments ago and her next dance partner was late. Who was daring to keep her waiting? She gave up wondering and opened her dance card to take a peek. Devin. He'd signed twice!

She leaned up on her tiptoes to see if he and his companion were standing where they'd been earlier in the evening. They weren't there, but she did catch sight of Blythe Pace being led out to the floor, but not by Devin. She sighed to herself. She should just suggest to Rebecca and Rupert that they all go home already. It had been a long night. The ball was almost over anyway. She'd pretty much decided to accept Devin's dare, which she would probably end up regretting, so she ought to take more time to think about it instead of telling him tonight. But she had so hoped to have one more chance to talk to Robert before the night was over.

She'd heard the new gossip about him, of course. Her dance partners, each of them, had made a point of telling her the viscount hadn't come to London to marry like the rest of them. Not that that would make any difference once he fell in love with her. The men in her family had all been confirmed bachelors until they'd fallen in love with the women who would become their wives. But she wasn't accustomed to a gentleman being as boldly risqué as Robert had been, and while she'd assumed he'd just been teasing, what if he hadn't been? That type of boldness was characteristic of a rake. But surely Robert was too young to be dissolute. Yet all rakes had to start somewhere, didn't they?

His invitation for a private walk in the park had prompted her to give those thoughts more credence than she might otherwise have. A ride, as Kendall had suggested, with a footman or Ophelia along, was perfectly in order. But while a maid was an acceptable chaperone for most outings, that wasn't the case for a meeting with a man. After all, a trusted maid would keep secrets if asked to, and a private walk with just a maid trailing behind was an opportunity for a gentleman to steal kisses! Robert had even mentioned doing so!

Yes, he was delightfully handsome *and* exciting, but he'd actually made her uncomfortable a few times, too, and she didn't like that. Another talk with him could easily clear all that up, so she certainly wasn't scratching him off as a contender for her heart. But in the meantime, her unease with the matter made Kendall the more preferable of the two. He was handsome, charming, *and* a perfect gentleman, and she didn't doubt her family would approve of him. She couldn't say the same about Robert—yet.

Devin finally arrived and extended his bent arm to her so she could lightly place her hand on it. When she didn't do so immediately, he grinned, making her realize he was even turning another dance with him into a dare.

He might be able to help her to get back on a horse, but that would mean more contact with him, and more to the point, was it even possible to deal with him without losing her temper? Right now was a good time to find out, so she didn't mention his tardiness and even gave him a slight smile before placing her fingertips on his arm.

Her tolerance was put to the test the moment he took her hand on the floor and began waltzing with her. "Why hasn't your father arranged a marriage for you?"

The question was far too personal, so she just answered neutrally, "Because he promised he wouldn't."

"Yes, but why?"

And he'd called *her* persistent? But she was supposed to be practicing patience, a means to an end, so instead of telling him to mind his own business, she decided to simply tell him the truth.

"A few times over the last two years I actually wished he didn't make that promise, though that was just my impatience kicking in because it was taking so long for love to find me. But my father married for love and he wanted nothing less for me and Rafe. Of course he won't allow me to pick someone completely unsuitable, but he's never once worried that I might. He trusted my brother, and he trusts me to make the right choice."

"And you can't make up your mind."

She could feel her hackles rising. "That's not it a'tall. My first Season was a complete waste of time in finding a husband because I spent it being so jealous of Ophelia, who'd had her come-out that Season as well, that I was positive every single man that year was already in love with her. So I ignored them all."

"And last year?"

She pursed her lips. "Last year I took my brother's advice to relax and just enjoy myself. A little too literally perhaps. Before I knew it, the Season was over and I still wasn't in love yet."

Devin gave her a thoughtful look. "So you're saying this is the first Season you're actually going to take this business of getting married seriously?"

"Well, I wouldn't put it that way, but—yes. And I don't need your help in *that* regard, so you can forget about spending your good deeds on me. But I am curious. How d'you go about it, being Cupid?"

He chuckled. "Not by shooting any arrows!"

To her utter amazement, she actually laughed. "No? And here I thought you must have your bow hidden in the room somewhere. But, seriously, how d'you figure out who is suited to whom?"

"Methodically. To begin with, I need to know the interests of both parties. Let's take yourself for example—"

"No, let's not. But what has that to do with anything? Or did you mean what I, or rather, your other female clients, find interesting about these young lords?"

"No, I meant *your* interests. What you enjoy doing. What you don't like. And then I'll find out which of your beaus have the same interests."

"Stop using me as an example. Besides, I highly doubt any of these young men like needlepoint!"

"Actually . . ."

He was just teasing. The amusement in his eyes and his

smile told her so, and she actually found herself laughing again. "I don't believe it!"

"What else besides needlepoint?"

She didn't remind him this time that he wasn't her matchmaker, she was merely annoyed with herself for drawing a blank at a simple question like that. "I'd have to give that some thought—if we were actually discussing me."

"No, you don't. For instance, you like dancing."

"I don't, actually."

He raised a brow. "Then what are you doing here?"

She grinned. "Are you joking? This *is* the marriage mart, on a grand scale."

"Touché. Croquet?"

"I love it—well, I love beating my brother at it."

"Then you're competitive?"

"No, not really, just with him."

"Sibling rivalry?" He shook his head. "Not exactly a typical interest, so let's move on—"

"Stop right there." She gave him a reproving look. "Really, I do not make a good example, and you've already satisfied my curiosity."

"You know, Amanda, you can't actually remove yourself from being the recipient of a good deed just by saying so. I've already taken you under my wing, which means you get my help regardless of your druthers."

"The devil you have!"

"So you might as well tell me if any of these men here tonight strike your fancy—or if Lord Goswick is still your prime candidate?"

She clamped her mouth shut. He raised a brow at her, but then he grinned, drawing his own conclusions. "Goswick it is, then, and you know where my farm is. You'll laugh at yourself for even hesitating, once I get you back in the saddle."

"I am considering that."

"I had a feeling you might."

She ground her teeth at his smug tone. He knew she would because he'd made it a *dare*. She couldn't resist adding, "I said considering, not that I've made up my mind about it yet. It's not as if I've ever regretted not riding. My father keeps a lot of carriages and coaches at Norford Hall, so I much prefer to do my riding with a comfortable seat beneath me. But you've made your . . ." Her words trailed off.

His amber eyes suddenly turned lambent, a slow smile curving his lips. His hands even tightened slightly at her palm and her waist. She drew in her breath sharply, her pulse beginning to race. What the deuce was that feeling suddenly flipping about inside her? Her face and neck even felt flushed with heat when she wasn't embarrassed over anything.

She tore her eyes off him. What just happened? *Think! No, don't think of that, think of something else.*

"I've made what?" he said.

She latched onto his question almost desperately, but she kept her eyes averted from his as she replied, "You've made your case to give it a try. But how's that going to work then, when they're saying you just breed racehorses, which won't do a'tall? I might like betting on the races, but I'm not about to try riding a horse that fast."

He didn't answer immediately, which brought her eyes back to his to see that she'd actually surprised him. "You go to the races?"

She didn't mind answering, since she enjoyed it. "Yes, with my Aunt Julie when I'm in town."

He gave her a skeptical look. "I've never seen you there and I miss very few races."

"Well, of course you wouldn't notice us. We watch from the comfort of my aunt's coach, and she sends a footman off to place our bets. It's the only thing she loves to gamble on, and I quite agree, it's very thrilling when our picks win."

"D'you often pick accurately?"

"More'n I lose!"

"You've amazed me. That's one interest I wouldn't have expected of a young lady."

"Whyever not? We gamble at whist, we gamble at croquet, though that's not nearly as much fun as winning at the races. But you know, I never would have thought of that as an interest of mine, probably because I'd never been to the races prior to my first Season in London. Now about my concern, *do* you have a suitable mount for lessons?"

"Already taken care of. I've had an ideal mount brought down from Lancashire."

That rubbed her the wrong way. He'd been so sure she'd come to him for lessons that he'd arranged a mount in advance? "Well, if it doesn't work out, at least Robert Brigston gained my notice tonight. And *he* doesn't require me to ride a horse."

His disapproval was immediate. She actually felt him tense. But he said rather tepidly. "He looks as young as he is, fresh out of school. Are you sure you want to further that acquaintance?"

"Well, he's very handsome."

"That's an important criterion for you?"

"Not really, it just means I won't be indifferent while getting to know him."

"Has that been part of your problem? Most of your beaus bore you?"

He was a little too good at figuring things out. He'd nailed that one right on the head. No, Robert hadn't bored her, neither did Kendall. For that matter, she hadn't spent a single bored moment in Devin's presence, either, though *he* certainly wasn't in the running, so what difference did that make?

She tsked. "Are you still working on your good deed? Don't expect me to cooperate when I've asked you not to."

"I can tell you already that Brigston won't suit you."

"You've been listening to gossip, haven't you?" she guessed. "You know he's too young to be a rake yet, but even if that's his goal, it's not a good reason to discount him—yet."

"Of course it is."

She chuckled. "No, it's not. I'm quite familiar with rakes, have them in my family—well, I did. My own brother, Rafe, was definitely giving it a try before he married. And my cousin Rupert, there was no trying about him! Such a skirt chaser he was, but he's settled into marriage, too, just this year. That just leaves his brother Avery, though actually, I'm really not sure if he's trying to follow in his brother's footsteps. It's not exactly a proper subject to discuss with one's cousin."

"But perfectly fine to discuss with me?"

She managed not to blush. "I'm telling you why I'm familiar with rakes and why I don't think Lord Robert is one. If anything, he's just pulling the proverbial leg, to give himself a little risqué allure. The rest of the gossip is just jealousy gone awry tonight."

"Whether he's working toward becoming a rake or merely trying to impress the ladies with some bold behavior, the fact is the boy doesn't want to marry and intends to do whatever it takes to avoid it. Do you really want to get tarred with his feather?"

The dance ended. Apparently, Devin didn't want an answer to his last question, which was still on his mind, to go by his parting warning when he left her with her cousins.

"Brigston is heading for scandal and he'll drag you down with him if you don't keep your distance. D'you really want your father to pull in the reins and yank you back home when the Season's barely begun?"

Amanda gasped, her face flaming with color. She didn't doubt he'd said that loudly enough for Rupert to hear!

Chapter Eighteen

At the end of the long evening, Devin truly hoped he wouldn't have to attend any more balls before he found Amanda and Blythe their perfect husbands.

"Tired?" he asked Blythe on the way home.

"Not a'tall!" she replied excitedly. "That was such fun tonight. D'you think Lord Oliver found me attractive?"

"Like him, do you?"

She grinned. "I do. Once we started talking, we couldn't stop. I'm just worried he might not be rich enough to satisfy my brother's hopes for me. Is he? D'you know?"

"The Norse family is quite plump in the pockets, yes. Rest assured, William will be pleased as long as *you* are. Your happiness still comes first with him."

"Then Oliver is perfect! I can't wait to get home and tell Will about him."

It sounded as if Oliver Norse was now the prime candidate for Blythe, though the man was currently hoping to win Amanda. But then all those young bucks were interested in

Amanda right now, and only one might be lucky enough to win her, which would leave the rest disappointed, but still available.

He should have told Amanda that Brigston had revealed that his father had ordered him to marry her, but he was afraid she might find it encouraging. She probably would, too, the silly chit. Look how quickly she'd defended Brigston, scoffing at the malicious turn the gossip had taken.

She was holding out for love, so she was obviously a romantic. She seemed to think that love could conquer all, including confirmed bachelors of the rakish sort. That was all well and good, and who was to say Robert Brigston couldn't fall in love with her? But the boy *did* want to experience more of life, and eventually, he'd get around to doing so, whether he had a wife or not. And there would go Amanda's happy marriage down the drain. Why court inevitable disaster when Goswick would make her a fine husband, she already fancied him, and she merely had to develop a love for riding to win his heart? Simple, guaranteed, and no unnecessary scandal getting attached to her name.

No, Devin didn't feel the least pang of guilt for making sure Amanda's family would step in and warn her off Robert Brigston. To go by the frown on Rupert St. John's face when Devin returned her to her chaperones, she'd be getting warned off tonight. Just to make absolutely sure, he'd jot a note to Lady Ophelia tomorrow as well, warning her that Amanda's interest might be turning in a dangerous direction.

Better she hear it from her family than from him. He was going to have a difficult enough time dealing with her when she refused to cooperate. He didn't want her thinking *he'd* joined the pack of jealous men.

Of course, he wasn't jealous. Granted, he'd felt a brief moment of attraction to her while they'd danced due to her careless words. *I prefer to do my riding with a comfortable seat beneath me.* Did she have *any* idea of the image those words would conjure up in a man's mind? Of course she didn't. She was an innocent, and it wouldn't be the first time he'd wanted a woman he couldn't have.

Dropping Blythe and her maid at her house, he went inside to have a few words with William before he headed home. But even at that late hour Will hadn't returned from his appointment. So Devin merely reminded Blythe to have her brother take her to join the promenade in Hyde Park tomorrow. An excellent opportunity for her to further some of the acquaintances she'd made tonight and possibly see Oliver Norse again so love could naturally bloom between those two without any help from Cupid.

The Pace driver returned Devin to Jermyn Street in quick order as there was barely any traffic at that hour. But as Devin stepped out of the coach, the man shouted down at him, "Careful, sir, something's blocking the path to your door."

Devin saw the obstruction and shook his head. At first glance, it looked like a rather large pile of rubbish, but then he noticed the leg sticking out. A drunk? Choosing to pass out in front of the Baldwin house? He moved to investigate. The driver asked if he needed help.

Devin bent down and turned the drunk over, then sucked in his breath. Without looking back at the driver, he yelled, "Fetch a doctor, the Pace doctor if you know who he is, or *any* doctor. Just hurry!"

Devin barely recognized his friend, he was beaten so badly. Blood was caked on his face and spattered over his jacket and overcoat. "Will!" Devin said, gently shaking his friend's shoulder. "Will, what in God's name happened?" But William didn't answer. Devin placed his hand on William's chest and was somewhat relieved when he felt his heart beating. Where the hell was Devin's uncle's coach that William had borrowed tonight? Surely Donald's driver hadn't left William here like this.

Devin carefully picked up William, afraid he might have broken bones, and carried him inside the house. The servants were abed at that hour, so he had no help carrying him upstairs. But he knew the servants would be stirring soon because Lydia's dogs had noticed his return and were actually barking instead of just greeting him. He didn't notice he was leaving a trail of blood behind him, but the dogs did.

Passing his aunt and uncle's door, he shouted, "Uncle, I need your help!"

Devin took William to the spare bedroom and placed him on the bed, then turned to light a lamp. Lydia came in mumbling, still putting on her robe, but she gasped as light filled the room and she could see who lay on the bed.

She rushed forward, then drew back with another gasp. "Is that really your friend William?" she said incredulously. "Good Lord, someone tried to kill him?"

Donald entered the room. "What's happened?"

"I don't know." Devin shook his head. "I found him lying near the steps in a crumpled heap, and there's no sign of your coach. He did take it tonight, didn't he?"

"Yes, he left not long after his sister dropped him off here and you departed with her."

"Then he could have been lying out there all night, for all we know!"

"Actually, I did hear the dogs barking about a half hour ago," Donald said. "Didn't see anything though, when I looked out the window, but I confess, I was looking for a coach, not anyone at the front door."

Lydia was worried about Devin's frantic, increasingly furious tone and assured him, "He'll be fine. He's still breathing," but glanced again at William to make sure. "Yes, he is."

"He couldn't even make it to the damn door!"

Lydia hurried around the bed and put her arms around Devin, hugging him. "I know he's your friend and you love him like a brother. We'll find out tomorrow what happened, but right now I think we need a doctor—"

"Already sent for."

"Then let's clean him up while we wait. You and Donald get his coat off while I fetch some water."

They only got William's arms out of the greatcoat and left him lying on it because he had groaned painfully when they moved him. The jacket was a much tighter fit, so they left it alone.

"I think we should cut off the rest of his clothing, otherwise we won't know the extent of his injuries," Lydia said cautiously as she returned with fresh water. "I've got scissors in my room, I'll be right back."

Devin said nothing. He was staring at what his aunt and his uncle hadn't yet noticed—the wet, dark stain on the lower right side of William's jacket. Devin had nearly missed it, too, on the black cloth of the jacket.

As soon as Lydia left the room, he ripped open William's shirt and pulled it aside. Two wounds were low on his side, as if someone had come up behind him and stabbed him with a knife. Now Devin was afraid to move William at all, even to see if more wounds were on his back. Good God, William had never hurt anyone in his life. Who could have done this to him?

"That doesn't look good," Donald said as he stood beside Devin.

Lydia came back in, saying, "I think I heard a coach arriving out front."

Devin didn't glance up at her when he said, "I found two stab wounds, there could be more."

She turned around immediately. "I'll rush the doctor up here."

The physician, who only lived a couple blocks away, didn't know William; he'd merely been the closest the driver knew of. He seemed competent enough, but his manner was more suited to a mortician than a healer. He spent nearly two hours cleaning, setting, sewing, and bandaging William's wounds and wasn't optimistic when he finished.

"No broken bones, but he has lost a good deal of blood. If he survives the night, he might live. Just pray no fever develops. If an infection sets in, you might as well bid him good-bye."

If Devin had said anything to the man right then, it wouldn't have been nice. Donald gathered as much and quickly ushered the doctor out of the house. When Devin sent for Blythe in the morning, he would tell her to bring their family physician with her.

"I'll sit with him if you want," Lydia said from the doorway.

"No, you can spell me in the morning, or Blythe can. She's going to be very upset when she sees him."

"Did you send her word?"

"She had an exhausting evening and is probably fast asleep. There's nothing she can do here tonight."

Lydia nodded, but came in long enough to give Devin

another hug as he sat wearily in the chair he'd pulled up to the bed where William lay. "He's going to be fine. He's a healthy boy. There's no reason he can't recover, now that the doctor has fixed him up."

What had happened, and why? Devin wondered grimly. What the hell had Will got himself mixed up with?

Chapter Nineteen

"How was the ball?"

Devin blinked and sat forward abruptly. His friend had one eye open, at least half-open, and was staring at him. The other eye had needed a couple stitches at the corner, so it had been covered with an eye patch to hold down a bandage.

Shaking off sleep, Devin said incredulously, "You nearly die and all you ask about is a bloody ball?"

"I must look a mess, but I wasn't dying. Hurts like hell, though."

"You lost a lot of blood."

"From what?" William said, fingering the patch over his eye. "It was just a beating. Wasn't expecting it, but the bloody sod said he had to make a point."

"What point?"

"That paying my debt on time was the only way to pay it. He pounded me a bit so I wouldn't forget again."

"You were nearly killed because of a debt?" Devin exclaimed. "Who the hell did you borrow from?"

William sighed. "The same chap I borrowed from at the end of the summer for Blythe's wardrobe. Got his name from my footman, who said the bloke wouldn't need collateral like my bank wanted, and he was right. I had no trouble with that debt. I was paying it off nicely. So last month before the Season got under way I went back to the bloke to borrow a few more pounds for Blythe's dowry. But then one of his thugs came by the house yesterday demanding a payment on that loan. Not even a month had passed yet! But he claimed I was told that a larger debt would require more money to be paid back on it and sooner. Bloody well don't remember being told that."

"A setup? Are they crooks?"

"I'm beginning to wonder that m'self. But what's the bloody point of borrowing money if I have to pay it right back? Had I known, I wouldn't have signed another note."

Devin lifted William's head to get a few sips of red wine down his throat before he sat again. "You should have come to me first. You never should have gone to an under-the-table moneylender who doesn't make his terms clear."

"You don't have that kind of blunt, not without selling off half of your breeding stock, which would cripple your new farm, and I wasn't about to borrow from your uncle."

"I'm not that pinched, Will. I've got assets other than my farm."

"Assets that you never mentioned?"

Devin shrugged. "I had a small inheritance from my mum that I mostly used to start the new farm—"

"Yes, I know."

"But there was a house, too, that I don't want. I just haven't got around to disposing of it yet."

"Ah, your mum," William said carefully. "You don't still hate her for dying on you, do you? A natural reaction for a youngun, but you should have outgrown—"

"I barely remember her."

That was a lie, but Devin had never talked about his mother with anyone other than his uncle, and he wasn't going to start now. Besides, he didn't think Will would understand. The kind of pain-induced rage he felt when he thought about his mother—what she had done and what had been done to her—couldn't be outgrown. It certainly hadn't gone away, it seemed to be embedded in his soul.

But William was an understanding chap and didn't press. Instead, he said, "Well, you won't be selling anything on *my* account. Besides, this was my problem and only a temporary one. Once Blythe is well married, I'll borrow from her husband and pay him back as soon as I find a rich wife for m'self."

"Which you should have done to begin with, instead of trying to get her married off first."

"It's the bloody timing, Devin. I *was* looking before she turned eighteen and simply had no luck. Should've asked you for help with *that*, but I didn't think it was going to be so hard to find a rich wife I wanted. Met a few ladies I would have been honored to wed, one I even liked a little too much, but they were just as poor as I am."

"I *do* know someone who I think you'll like," Devin said. "Should have introduced you sooner, but you seemed so determined to get Blythe shackled first that I was afraid you'd let the opportunity slide by."

"You're probably right. But now that Blythe is eighteen, I can't ask her to sit back and wait. You know it makes no difference how old we men are when we wed, but it's a bloody big thing to a young woman. She just doesn't know how pinched we really are, and I don't want her to know. I don't want her accepting the first proposal she receives just to help me out, when she might not even like the chap. Would you do that to your sister if you had one?"

"You borrowed to get her decked out for the Season. The invites are coming in for her. Your plan was already in motion. Why did you make it worse by borrowing even more?"

"We needed a dowry for her. Can't have her going into a marriage with nothing."

"Many do exactly that these days. Dowries lost their importance at about the same time arranged marriages did. It's what these Seasons are all about, a means to get young people together so they can make their own choices."

"I can't deny her a dowry, even if it isn't de rigueur. She has to feel she brings *some* worth to the table."

It was hard to argue with simple pride. "How much did you borrow?"

"Not much, just a few hundred pounds."

Devin shook his head. "You'll have to give it back. Nothing is worth dealing with people who could do something like this to you."

William closed the one eye with a sigh. "I agree. Really didn't see this coming."

"So when did you get stabbed? Before or after your face was kicked in?"

"Stabbed?" The little color that had returned to William's cheeks after drinking the wine drained away. "I don't recall that, but it couldn't have been while I was being pummeled. There's no reason for them to try to kill me. They won't be getting their money back that way."

"Yet you were stabbed twice in the lower right side of your abdomen, and by the looks of it, from behind."

"The lender's bruiser never got behind me other than when he tossed me out into the street."

"Could you have been hurting too much to even feel it?" Devin asked.

"Could prob'bly have got run over by a team of horses and wouldn't have felt any worse than I already did. I'm not sure what the devil happened after I told the driver to get us the hell out of that neighborhood. I remember tumbling over face-first to the floor of the coach, and I must have been out cold because the next thing I knew I was lying on the cold ground somewhere. I remember getting up and walking dizzily through empty streets for a time, and then I must have blacked out again. I suppose a thief from that area could have seen me leaving the moneylender's house and thought my pockets would be full. Or I just appeared to be an easy mark, as beat up as I already was."

"But where was Donald's driver when all of this was happening? How did you get back here? Did you walk? And where is the coach now?"

William shook his head. "Don't know, but I don't doubt things like that happen all the time in that seedy part of town."

"*Were* you robbed?"

William sounded as if he were trying to laugh but quickly cut it off. "Of what? My pockets were already empty. I gave everything I had on me to the lender. So I get stabbed for some coin and the thug gets none? Is that a bright side I should be looking on? Yes, I suppose it is."

Devin wouldn't call it a bright side, but an attempted

robbery was the only thing that made any sense. A fancy, crested coach in an area riddled with thieves. Any one of them could have jumped on the back of the coach and waited until the driver turned onto a deserted street before getting rid of the driver, then entering the coach to find William unconscious on the floor. Anger at finding Will's pockets empty could have caused the blackguard to stab Will and toss him out of the vehicle before driving off with it.

Donald's driver pretty much confirmed that scenario when he returned to the house soon after dawn. He told Devin and Donald he'd been surprised from behind and kicked off his perch, cracking his head in the fall, so he'd spent most of the night passed out at the side of the road. But at least he'd found Donald's coach on the way back. It had been abandoned in a better part of town, which was probably the only reason no one else had hied off with it. *That*, Devin thought, was the only bright side to the night.

Chapter Twenty

THE DAY AFTER THE Hammonds' ball Amanda was still furious at Devin Baldwin and his loose tongue. That had been a short truce, if it could even be called that. She didn't have to listen to just one lecture because of what he had said within earshot of her cousin at the end of the ball, she'd had to sit through four! He'd had no right to utter that warning about Robert Brigston's dragging her into a scandal simply because she'd scoffed at his advice.

Rupert delivered his lecture on the way home that night. "I'll allow that you might not have heard the gossip before you danced with Brigston, but for Cupid to warn you off, you must not have been paying attention."

"He's got a name, it's not Cupid," Amanda mumbled under her breath.

"Don't change the subject, puss. You *did* see that Lord Robert was asked to leave the ball? How often does someone get kicked out of a ball, eh? I'll warrant you've never seen it happen before."

"I didn't see it happen this time either," she was quick to point out.

"I did," Rupert said. "And it implies that what was flying through the gossip mill tonight has some basis in fact."

"It implies nothing of the sort. Maybe a message arrived that summoned him home for some reason and our hosts merely delivered it to him. Or maybe he got a little too foxed before the end of the evening. I have seen men asked to leave for *that* reason before."

"Don't make excuses for this boy. He caused a major stir. It was all anyone was talking about. And if he has no intention of marrying yet, then he shouldn't have been trying to charm every deb in sight tonight. He's not for you and you know it. Even if none of it's true, he's now got a scandal attached to him. So you'll be keeping your distance until that goes away—if it goes away."

"That's not fair!" Amanda looked to Rebecca for some help, but her old friend was giving her a stern look, too, so she obviously agreed with her husband. Very well, so it looked bad for Robert Brigston, and Amanda couldn't blame them for their concern, but it still wasn't the least bit fair!

"Perhaps not," Rupert allowed, "but that's what Uncle Preston will want to know about."

"Rue, don't you dare!" she gasped.

But his lips were set mulishly. She knew he would tell her father, that nothing she could say would deter Rupert, because it didn't even matter if that gossip was true, it only mattered that Lord Robert had a scandal brewing about him. Which for the time being made him absolutely unsuitable for her.

Then her brother arrived today, just in time to prevent her

from leaving for the promenade in Hyde Park and making sure she missed it completely. And *he* was furious.

"Have you taken leave of your senses?" Raphael shouted the moment he walked into her bedroom. She was surprised he even knocked first and waited until she called out that he could enter. She was already dressed for the park and was about to put on her coat and gloves. His face was red with anger, and he only had to look at Alice once to get the maid to hurry out of the room.

"I didn't do anything except dance once with the man!" Amanda shouted back.

"So you know exactly why I'm here? 'Course you do. Well, that will save time, won't it? Don't ever speak to Brigston again."

"We could discuss this reasonably if you'd stop shouting. I thought you, at least, would keep an open mind, particularly when nothing has been proven yet."

"The fool proposed to three young women last night just to seduce them. That's something that doesn't make the rounds without some substance." Raphael paused when he noticed the blush climbing her cheeks. "Good God, you, too? I think I need to kill him."

"You don't need to do anything of the sort. They were also saying he doesn't want to marry a'tall."

But Raphael continued to grouse as if he hadn't heard her. "*Were* you the third? Bloody hell, I'll wager you were a fourth proposal, weren't you, that no one has heard about yet? Admit it."

Amanda started to laugh. "Will you listen to yourself? Which is it, he doesn't want to marry or he wants to marry everyone in sight? Those are contradictory rumors, Rafe, which just proves there's not much substance there. You more'n anyone should know how gossip can get out of hand."

"What I know is that scandal attaches by association, truth or no truth."

She didn't miss his point, it just infuriated her that he was making it. "Am I the only one to realize Brigston was just teasing? Good grief, how could those silly girls think he was serious? How could *you* think it was anything other than harmless flirtation? Have you never made some outlandish statement to a woman—prior to Ophelia, of course—that was just an exaggeration intended to be amusing? And it *did* make me laugh."

"Beside the point."

"There's no scandal yet, Rafe, but what is scandalous is how he's being slandered like this, all because he's a prime catch and the rest of the young lords are green with jealousy. There wasn't any real competition until he showed up. And they're trying to make sure it remains that way by blackening his name before he even gets his foot in the door. Until everyone actually got a look at him last night, the gossip about him wasn't the least bit nasty, just the opposite. That alone supports that jealousy turned it bad."

"Why do you defend him? I swear, Mandy, if you think *he's* the man you've been waiting three Seasons for, you will put that notion out of your head *right* now."

There was no talking to him when he took this brotherly protective stance, so she tried to assure him in another way. "I don't think that. In fact, Larissa and I finally figured out what my difficulty has been."

"Pray tell?"

"Love at first sight. Don't laugh, but that's what I was

expecting to happen. And when it didn't happen with all of the young men I'd met so far, I just assumed none of them would do."

"You aren't joking, are you?"

"No, I wish I was. Look at how much time I've wasted just because I was under such a wrong assumption. For instance, Lord Peter last year, he was adorable, but—"

"Mandy, a word of advice. Don't *ever* tell a man he's adorable."

She rolled her eyes. "I didn't. I wouldn't. But my point was, he was very pleasing to look at, yet I ignored him because I didn't fall head over heels for him immediately. But if I had pretended interest long enough to get to know him a little better, then I might not have found him to be so boring after all and could have slowly fallen in love as I should. But of course it's too late now, he married someone else that very Season."

Raphael rolled his eyes now. "Don't take this new notion of yours too much in the reverse. Don't try to pretend something is there when it really ain't."

"Then what should I be looking for?" When he glanced down and even looked a little embarrassed, she added, "That was a serious question, Rafe. Pretend I'm not your baby sister for a moment and just answer me."

"It's not the same for a man," he hedged. "You should be discussing this with a woman who's found love and can give you the right perspective on it."

"I already did that, with Larissa yesterday. But all she said was that she was missing her husband terribly—well, before he was her husband—but that's how she knew she was in love with him."

"An excellent point! I miss Pheli the moment I leave her sight."

Mandy giggled. "Do you really?"

"'Course I do."

"Did Ophelia come with you today?"

"No, but I'll send her—"

"I don't want to wait when we're already having this discussion. You came here today to warn me off one of the few men I've actually found interesting."

"That *is* a good basis to start with, just not with this scandalous chap." Raphael raised a golden brow. "A few men? Ah, that's right! Pheli mentioned that chap you need to ride a horse for. D'you want me to arrange riding lessons for you?"

She grit her teeth. "Already arranged."

"Excellent. Concentrate on that, m'dear, then I won't feel this need to kill someone."

She narrowed her eyes on him. "Don't change the subject, Rafe. Being eager to see a man can't be the only clue I should be looking for."

"Stop looking for clues and just enjoy—"

"*Don't* tell me that again. I tried that last year and it didn't help a'tall."

He made a sound of exasperation. "Yes, but last year you were still just looking for love at first sight. *Now* you know better, as you say."

She sighed. "It wasn't at first sight for you, either, was it?"

"It was *something* at first sight, but we're not discussing that."

She perked up. "What?"

"Mandy . . ." he said warningly.

"You have to tell me!"

He crossed his arms over his chest and said sternly, "I don't have to do anything of the sort."

Her brows knit thoughtfully. "Are you talking about attraction? That you were attracted to Pheli from the first moment you saw her? But who wasn't? She was and still is the most beautiful woman in all of England. So is that *really* a good indication?"

He sighed now. "Better'n most. Without that at least, you'd just be having a mundane marriage you'll be very dissatisfied with. Just *don't* mistake attraction for love. It ain't the same thing a'tall."

She nodded, but her thoughts were already ticking away. There were two men she found exceptionally handsome, so she was attracted to both of them, and since she couldn't fall in love with both—that wasn't possible, was it?—she could agree with her brother that attraction and love weren't the same thing. But her family wanted her to ignore one of those men. She knew she should, but she'd had no choices to pick from until now, and after being at this husband-hunting business for so long, it thrilled her to actually have more'n one choice to consider.

She would keep her family's concerns in mind, but she was still going to talk to Robert again to find out for herself if it was more than just the jealousy of his competitors that had stirred up the pot. She just wouldn't go on a private walk with him in the park. That wasn't a good idea a'tall. But at the moment, all she wanted to do was give Devin Baldwin a piece of her mind for causing her family to worry needlessly.

Chapter Twenty-One

AMANDA WAS AMAZED SHE'D managed to get out of the house with only her maid in tow. But she had been holding one of her two new riding habits in the box it had been delivered in, and she'd showed it to her aunt, saying, "I think they've mixed up my fittings with someone else's because this don't fit a'tall, so I'm taking it back to find out why. I won't be long—unless some new material catches my eye."

Julie had already added her wisdom to the tally yesterday afternoon after Raphael had gone back home. At least her aunt's lecture hadn't been as daunting or as long as Rupert's and Raphael's had been, probably because Amanda decided not to defend Lord Robert anymore and just agreed with everything her aunt had to say on the matter.

"It's times like these that you need to be more circumspect than usual," her aunt told her. "You can't have your name linked to this foolish boy's in any way a'tall. Can't talk to him, don't want to even be in the same room with him."

With Amanda just nodding, Julie didn't have too much

more to say. "Bless your brother, I knew he could make you see reason."

Yet the fourth lecture showed up before dinner last night. Well, maybe it wasn't really a lecture, but it ensured that no more lectures would have to be given—her father had come back to town and was staying for the Season.

"I didn't come to hear excuses," Preston told her as he sauntered into the room. "I came to make sure you won't need to give any."

Amanda wasn't displeased with her father's arrival, for whatever the reason. Since her first Season, she'd hoped that he would come to town with her, but he never did because they had so many relatives who already lived in London that he didn't need to chaperone her. So she'd never tried to talk him into it because the whole family knew he didn't like staying in London for any length of time.

So her laugh was happy as she jumped up from the sofa to hug him. "Rafe already beat my brow."

"Brothers are good for something, aren't they?" Preston teased.

At least her father wasn't angry about being forced to stay in London just to keep an eye on her. But he did intend to accompany her everywhere now—except to Bond Street. He drew the line at that.

He said the last time he went shopping with her mother, he almost strangled her before she was done. He was joking, of course, but added, "I swore I'd never go through that again and I won't. But I'll send my man with you if you haven't had your fill of shopping yet this year."

Which caused Amanda quite a dilemma. If she told anyone in her family where she was really going and why, she didn't doubt that Julie would insist she take one of the men in the family with her, since they were all familiar with horses and she wasn't. She wouldn't mind that a'tall, just not for her first lesson. If she couldn't manage to get on a horse today, then there wouldn't be any more lessons, so there was no point in telling anyone in advance that she was going to try, only to have to later admit failure. Besides, she was going to give Devin Baldwin a piece of her mind the moment she saw him today, and she wanted some privacy for that.

Her father didn't elect to stay with his sister during this longer trip to town, since the house on Arlington Street was already crowded with Julie, her two sons, her new daughter-in-law *and* Amanda. He was going to stay at Raphael's town house instead and even told Amanda to consider doing the same, now that he wasn't leaving London until the Season was over or she got engaged, whichever came first. She would probably change households—after she was done sneaking off for this first visit to Devin's farm. And her father hadn't sent his man over yet, so this morning was probably the only opportunity she'd get to go out for a few hours with just her maid.

Julie just waved Amanda off, believing her tale. Alice did nothing but complain in Amanda's room before they left and started complaining again the moment they got into the coach because she knew exactly where they were going.

Alice had been Amanda's maid for more years than Amanda could remember. A plain-looking woman of middle years, she hadn't been dismissed when Amanda first went off to school; she'd always been right there to resume her job whenever Amanda came home to Norford Hall. She was an excellent maid, but due to their long years of close association she did take certain liberties such as never holding her tongue when she had something to say.

"You didn't have to lie about it," Alice said as soon as she lowered the shades on the coach windows and started helping Amanda to change into the riding habit, which fit her perfectly well. "Lying just leads to more lying, and soon you won't know what's true and what ain't. It never serves any good purpose and will just make you feel guilty for doing it."

Amanda sighed, already feeling that guilt more deeply than she cared to admit. She'd barely been able to say those words to her aunt when not one of them was true.

But the reason for lying was still a more powerful motivator, and she shared that with her maid. "What if I can't do this? Baldwin made it sound so easy, yet he also pretty much dared me to try it, so I have a feeling even he doesn't think I can do it."

"Then don't do it," Alice said stubbornly. "It's not worth deceiving your family—"

"Will you stop? If I can get back on a horse today, I'll crow to everyone about it, but I don't want *any*one to know until I actually succeed in doing it. You know how sympathetic my family is. They'll drown me in it if they know I tried this and it didn't work out."

"And what will they drown you in if they find out you're sneaking off for this first lesson?"

Amanda winced. "I like him, Alice! You do realize how long I've waited to be able to say even that about a man?"

Alice gasped. "The horse breeder?"

Amanda blinked, then snorted. "Don't be absurd, I can barely tolerate *him*. You know very well I meant Lord Kendall.

I would *not* be doing this if I hadn't been assured this was the only way to his heart."

"I think *that's* silly."

"So do I, but some men can be silly in their requirements for a wife. Once I'm riding again, I probably won't think it's silly a'tall. Who knows, I might even love riding and have to have my very own mount. Weren't you telling me just last week that I need something to occupy my time while I'm in town? If I can get back on a horse, I'm going to need quite a few lessons. I didn't pay the least bit attention to the first ones I had because I'd caught a big fish that week and all I could think about was going fishing with Rafe again."

"And that's probably why you took that fall."

"Yes, it probably is. So a little encouragement would be helpful, instead of all this fussing, Alice. Today is *so* important. What I do today is going to win me a husband!"

Chapter Twenty-Two

Bᴇᴄᴀᴜsᴇ sʜᴇ ʜᴀᴅɴ'ᴛ ᴛʜᴏᴜɢʜᴛ far enough ahead—deception just wasn't her cup of tea—Amanda realized too late that she didn't want the St. John coach replete with family crest to be seen leaving London or passing by the racetrack when no races were scheduled today. So she went to Bond Street first after all. She stopped in at Ophelia's favorite seamstress shop, which already had her measurements, just long enough to order two more riding habits, then hurried down the street with Alice to hire a hack for the ride out of town. Dealing with the seamstress even made her explanation to Aunt Julie a tad more true. And she would need more habits if she succeeded today. There, a positive thought!

Alice continued to mumble her complaints though, particularly after Amanda told the St. John driver to take a few hours off for himself because she'd need at least that much time to finish her shopping. Yet another fib, Alice pointed out, but Amanda had stopped listening to her. She had to muster her courage for the riding lesson, and that took concentration. But it helped that she knew she looked fetching in the new pale green velvet riding habit, her blond hair tucked neatly under a jaunty hat. She was wearing a matching jacket for a little extra warmth, which she probably didn't need today because the weather was only a little chilly.

The ride to Devin's horse farm wasn't long, and halfway there she started to feel some excitement, though she wasn't sure why, when she'd expected to feel nothing but dread over today's endeavor. It had to be that remark she'd made to Alice. Today really could result in a major turning point in her life. She just had to master one tiny fear. . . .

Arriving at the farm, she left the hired coach in front of the center stable, the three buildings not being that far apart, and warned Alice to stay in the vehicle to keep warm. She was actually worried that the driver might get tired of waiting for them and drive off, leaving them stranded, but he wouldn't do that as long as his coach was still occupied.

A worker came around a corner, saw her standing by the coach, and asked her business, then pointed her toward the stable on the right. Was Devin grooming his horses again? She hoped he was more decently dressed this time! She supposed she was lucky he was even there. She hadn't thought to ask if he came here every day or just stopped by a few times a week. It would be highly annoying to have gone through all that subterfuge this morning and find it was a wasted effort.

She remembered the heat inside the other stable she'd visited. This one was very warm, too, she noticed as she closed the door behind her. It felt good only for a few moments. Yes, Devin definitely spoiled his horses. She was sure they would be quite comfortable out in one of his many fields, at least until the snow came.

She saw Devin immediately this time, pitching hay from a pile that had been dumped in the aisle. No jacket again, but at least he hadn't discarded his shirt yet. He'd rolled up his sleeves, though, exposing his muscular forearms. The loose white shirt, which was tucked into dark gray pants, was unbuttoned halfway down his chest, far more than was proper. He was such a handsome man, it was impossible not to find him attractive. Was that why her heart picked up its beat at the sight of him? Or was she just preparing for battle? He *did* challenge her, more than any other man ever had.

When he saw her approaching, he set the pitchfork aside and began buttoning his shirt up to his neck. As her eyes swept over his body, she noted he was wearing fancy riding boots today, instead of the muddy work boots he'd worn before.

She'd heard he was staying with his relatives in London, so she'd assumed he merely rode out here to see to his farm, but perhaps he actually lived in that run-down house on the property. Either that or he must keep extra clothes here. She couldn't imagine him riding in London in those work boots he'd worn the other day.

She slowed her step as she reached him. He was putting on his jacket, which had been draped over a railing. He'd taken a step closer to her to reach for it. She saw now that it wasn't just the subdued lantern light casting his face in shadow; stubble was on his cheeks. He must not don the mantle of a gentleman unless he was actually in London.

But here, working alongside his employees, he blended in amazingly well. Did he do it deliberately to put his men at ease? Some servants tended to get overly stiff in the presence of their employers. Yet why did Devin even pitch in here, when he seemed to have more than enough men in his employ to do the work for him? Did he just enjoy working with horses himself? And why the deuce were all these questions about him occurring to her?

Finally recalling how angry she'd been with him and why, she said, "I've a bone to pick with you."

"It's a wonder I have any left, so many have been picked from me lately. Why don't you leave the rest alone and let's just get down to business."

As if he hadn't said a word, she railed, "You have *no* idea how many lectures I had to sit through because of that last remark you made about Lord Robert in front of my cousin. That was—"

"Good."

She blinked. "Good?!"

"And we're not discussing that boy anymore. Or do you just want to be a mother instead of a wife?"

She gasped. A few years difference in age was so irrelevant. Why would he even stress that point? But when she opened her mouth to tell him so, she ended up gasping again. He'd closed the distance between them and was towering over her. She thought he was actually going to touch her or shake her, he looked so annoyed.

"Not one more word from you about it," he said coldly. "If for some reason Brigston buckles under and courts you all the way to the altar, it won't be only your bed he sleeps in thereafter. He has no intention of settling down with just one woman, wife or no."

Wide-eyed, she wondered if it was the setting and his work attire that made him say things so unfit for innocent ears. She was already acquainted with his bluntness even in a social setting, but he'd just gone far beyond that. He'd looked like a stableman, earthy, too masculine by half, not the owner of this farm, before he put on his finely tailored jacket. Did that make him forget, however briefly, that she was a lady and that he ought to guard his words around her?

Then, as if he hadn't just growled at her, he added in a normal tone, "But you're smart enough to realize Lord Kendall is the better choice for you, or you wouldn't be here today. Correct?"

She was *not* conceding he was correct about Robert. However, she was definitely done discussing the matter with *him* after he'd just intimidated her to silence. What a churlish brute, to use his size to win an argument!

So she nodded, albeit stiffly. But just so he knew it wasn't his advice she was following, she added, "Besides, my brother has already assured me he'll kill Lord Robert if I even glance at him again."

Devin stepped back, then actually laughed. "I knew I liked your brother."

Chapter Twenty-Three

"I WAS HOPING LORD Kendall would be here today," Amanda remarked casually as Devin led her out of the stable and into the center one where he was keeping the horse he'd arranged for her.

"Be glad he's not. I've bought you some time."

"What d'you mean by that?"

"Did you want him stopping by for tea with your sister-in-law this week, forcing her to tell him you're not ready for a ride in the park—and why? No, I didn't think so. So I let him know about an exceptional Thoroughbred stallion in France that I heard about, and he's hied off to buy him. That should give you a week or two to master this."

"Was it true, about the horse?"

"Yes, I was considering buying him m'self."

Another good deed on her behalf? This one she could at least thank him for and did.

He opened a stall to show her a sorrel mare, sleek compared to the other horses in the stables. He even began saddling it, telling her, "I had to borrow this sidesaddle from a neighbor. You're the first lady who's been to my farm that's had a reason to want to ride here."

She waved a hand to encompass everything she'd seen. "Why did you buy all this, when your family already owns a farm in Lancashire?"

"I didn't buy it all. Just the house and one stable was here, along with the fenced pastures. The house was in a sorry state, which was why the property was being sold at such a ridiculously low price. I added the rest."

He didn't actually answer her question, but another one occurred to her. "Didn't want to fix up the house?"

"What for? I don't plan to live in it."

"But why two farms?"

Though he wasn't looking at her, she couldn't help noticing the grin on his face when he answered, "Baldwins have kept horse farms running up in Lancashire for generations, producing excellent riding mounts and carriage horses. Most of my ancestors just left the handling of the horses and the breeding decisions to trainers."

"But not you?"

"No. My uncle Donald didn't either. Like him, I find that I love working with the horses m'self. But my aunt and uncle, who raised me, were just waiting for me to finish school to turn the farm over to me so they could retire to London. It only took me a few years to get the operation running so smoothly it wasn't taking up much of my time anymore. And they ended up missing me. It was actually their idea to start up this farm. My uncle knew the previous owner and that it could be had for a pittance, and it's close enough to London so I can live with them again. But like you, I didn't see a need for two farms producing the same kind of horses. Then my uncle mentioned the racetrack nearby. That was like a magical word to a young man my age and settled the matter instantly."

She'd been watching the way the muscles in his leg moved as he bent to strap on the saddle, and she wished his pants didn't stretch so tightly on his legs when he did so, but his remark snapped her eyes back to his face. "Ah, so that's why." She laughed. "The two farms are completely different."

He nodded. "Donald bred fine riding mounts, not racers. My goal is to breed the finest racers London has ever seen, *and* race them."

He was actually easy to talk to—when he wasn't trying to tell her what to do. But she actually found this subject exciting. "Have you succeeded?"

He led the mare out of the stall. "Not yet, at least not to first place, but then I knew it would take time because I was going to tackle a completely different breeding program. I even devoted six months just to testing all the stock, which is why I built that track out back."

"For speed?"

"Not just speed, endurance, too. A good racer has to maintain the speed to the finish, not just give a good burst of it at the start. The mares all have what's needed, I just haven't found the perfect proven champion yet to complement them—well, I have, but his damned owner keeps raising his price on me."

"A champion stallion? You don't see too many of those on the track." Not when mares raced, too, but that was an indelicate subject she couldn't mention. But she knew of at least one stallion that raced—and won every time. The owner had even joined her and Julie in Julie's coach one day at the racetrack because he was an old friend of her aunt's.

Devin chuckled, agreeing with her. "Takes a *very* good rider to control one, but then if the racer was gelded, I wouldn't want him."

He held out his hand to her. It took her a moment to realize he wanted to help her up onto the horse. She took a step backward. It wasn't a small mare standing there. She wasn't ready! Did she even remember how to sit on a sidesaddle?

He waited, but when she still wouldn't take his hand, he led the horse to the back of the stable and opened one of the tall double doors, saying, "I thought we would ride over to the track, but we can walk instead."

She could breathe again. A reprieve. But what the devil? If she still couldn't get on a horse, this was never going to work! She followed him quickly, taking deep breaths. She could do this, she had to do this, *everyone* did this, she told herself.

A few more saddled mounts were tied off at the back of the stable, and he'd grabbed one of those as well. She almost had to run to catch up with him as he headed for the small racetrack.

"She's very gentle and well tempered, my Sarah," Devin was saying about the mount Amanda was to ride. "If you fall, I highly doubt it will be her fault."

Amanda snorted under her breath, hearing the amusement in his tone as he said that. He was trying to put her at ease, but she didn't appreciate his idea of what might do so.

"*Your* Sarah?"

"Her mother was my first horse when I was a child, so I'm very fond of her. They were both good producers of mounts suitable for children—or beginners like you. Do you remember any of your riding lessons?"

He glanced back at her as he asked that. She was still

smarting over being given a horse even a child could ride, even though she knew she should be grateful instead. Was she so nervous she was going to take offense at everything he said today?

"I was too busy thinking about going fishing when I had those lessons," she mumbled. "So, no, I didn't pay much attention to them."

He actually turned about to face her, taking a few steps backward. "Fishing? *You?*"

She lifted her chin. "Why not me?"

He grinned. "I just can't picture you putting worms on hooks. So you like to fish, do you?"

It took a moment, but she grinned as well. "Yes, Rafe taught me how. I used to fish with him, or with my friend Becky, all the time when we were children."

"Do you still?"

She smiled. "It's odd. I never minded searching for bait when I was a child. Rafe and I would get up in the middle of the night and go outside to turn over rocks just to find the worms. But now . . ." She shuddered delicately. "No, I haven't been fishing in ages."

"But you'd still like to fish if you didn't have to catch the worms?"

"Of course I would, it was such fun."

"So, another interest you didn't know you had. I'm sure Kendall wouldn't mind baiting hooks for you."

He'd turned back around, facing forward. She thought she heard him add, "Neither would I," but she was probably mistaken, since he began giving her some pointers about how to control a horse, what to do in different situations, glancing back at her every few moments to make sure she was listening.

He finally admitted, "I've never tried to teach anyone how

to ride, but there's really not much to it, all things considered. It will probably all come back to you once you give it a try."

He'd led the two horses inside the fenced-in track to the grassy area at the center. The track was smoothly surfaced, hard-packed dirt, if a little muddy from the last rain. It really was a miniature racetrack. Devin was holding out his hand to her again. She stared at it. And stared. This was the telling moment. He'd dared her to do this. Where was her indignation at that to spur her into taking his hand? She couldn't feel any indignation because fear was rooting her to the spot. She couldn't move!

Chapter Twenty-Four

"**Y**OU CAN OPEN YOUR eyes now."

No, she couldn't, he had her on the bloody horse! Not the gentle mare, but the other horse he'd brought along, the one with the normal saddle, and she was sitting sideways in his lap as he rode around the track.

"You can't fall with me holding you."

Those words penetrated Amanda's panic. She could feel his strong arms tight around her, cocooning her in safety. That *was* reassuring, more than she could have thought possible. But despite her being cradled in such capable arms, the fear still wouldn't let go of her, not completely. But at least it wasn't as overwhelming as it had been.

"Talk to me," Devin said softly. "Tell me, what did this to you? It might actually help."

He didn't say any more, just kept riding round and round that racetrack. After a while, she felt so comfortable she almost snuggled against him! But this sense of security he was giving her was false. She wasn't doing the riding, he was. If she were alone in the saddle, she'd still be terrified instead of being lulled into feeling fully protected. Protected? Yes, he *did* make her feel that way.

She opened her eyes and glanced up at him. He was staring down at her, his expression inscrutable, still waiting for her to say something.

She looked away. "It wasn't the pain from breaking my leg in the fall. It was bad, that's all I recall. It wasn't even the pain when the bones were set, which was so much worse. I remember screaming, but I fainted before the doctor was done."

"How old were you?"

"Eight."

"That should just be a vague memory by now. Why isn't it?"

"The doctor said I might never walk right again. For four months they wouldn't let me stand on that leg. For four months I cried myself to sleep every night."

"But you don't have a limp. Why the hell would a doctor tell a child that?"

"He didn't. I awoke sooner than they expected and heard the doctor telling my father about that possibility. No one ever said it to me, but I knew, and I lived with such dread for months!"

"They should have gotten you back on a horse as soon as you mended, instead of letting you build up this unnatural fear."

Was that anger in his tone on her behalf? But he didn't understand. No one was going to push her to do anything that year. They'd been a house in deepest mourning.

In a small voice she said, "I lost my mother that year. We were all still grieving."

"I'm sorry."

She felt his arms tighten around her as he said it. Did his cheek touch her head briefly? She was surprised by his sympathy. She wouldn't have expected such a response from a—she couldn't manage to think of him as a brute just then.

"But I don't think my father would have insisted that I get back on a horse anyway," she said. "It's not as if riding was something I *had* to do. I've gotten along just fine all these years using coaches—until now."

Devin rode back to the grass at the center of the track before he stopped the horse and lowered Amanda carefully to the ground, then dismounted. "A fall from a horse is a rare occurrence, Amanda. And most falls don't end in broken bones. Really they don't. But riding isn't something you *need* to do now, either."

"Yes, it is." Her chin suddenly shot up. Her stubbornness was kicking in. She'd just been on a horse and hadn't fainted. Talking about it must indeed have helped. And while she was having that courageous thought, she held out *her* hand so he could help her up onto the mare.

Devin just stared at her hand for a moment, then locked eyes with her for several more. But finally he took her hand and drew her in front of him. She would have had to look up to see his face, she was so close, but she kept her eyes averted. She gasped softly as she felt his hands clasp her waist, nearly circling it, his fingers were so long. He just held her like that for a moment. She glanced up, wondering why, only to meet his amber eyes bright with something that took her breath away. Her heart started racing, and it wasn't from fear!

"Hook your right knee over the saddle horn immediately," he said as he lifted her and deposited her in the saddle. "That will anchor you in place."

Then he adjusted the stirrup for her left foot and even made sure her boot was firmly in it. But she only felt his doing all that because as she sat alone on the saddle, gripping the saddle horn for dear life, her eyes were squeezed tightly shut.

He must have noticed because she heard him say, "You want Goswick this much?"

She gritted out, "I'm doing this . . . to show you . . . I'm not a coward."

"Lord love you, Mandy, I knew you weren't." He chuckled. "You're too hot-tempered to be a coward."

Her eyes snapped open and she saw him grinning at her. She was tempted to grin back. Good Lord, the man had actually put her at ease. Looking down, she saw the ground wasn't all that far away either, nothing like what she remembered from when she was a child! And he was still by her side. Even if she inadvertently slid off the horse, he was close enough to catch her.

Confidence suddenly soaring, she positioned her hips facing forward—she did remember that much, after all, from her old lessons. The mare cooperated by not moving at all.

"I'll lead you for a bit." Devin gathered the mare's reins.

Amanda nodded, and as he walked her a full circle around the track, he instructed her, "When you pull back on the reins to stop her, do it slowly. She's not skittish. She won't rear up on you if you yank back abruptly, but there's rarely a need to do that. And remember, you're using a sidesaddle, so don't try to put your weight in the single stirrup. Just keep it slow and easy. You don't want to give Sarah mixed signals either. She needs to know you're in control. If you're nervous, she may well sense it, so remember to relax and just enjoy the ride."

But when he started to round the track with her a second time, she began to feel like a cosseted child. She recalled Amelia, so happy with her pony. Six years old and no one had been walking *her* around a track. And she was nicely balanced on the mare, had a comfortable perch, had been assured the horse was too gentle to bolt. She was ready to move on to the next part of the lesson: controlling the animal on her own.

"Let me try it."

He stopped and the horse stopped with him. Before he handed the reins over to her, he teased, "You promise to keep your eyes open?"

She laughed. "As long as you promise to catch me if I fall."

"That will cost you extra."

The banter left her smiling as she flicked the reins, but nothing happened. She tried a more aggressive flick and even scooted forward and back in the saddle, as if that might get the mare going. Suddenly it did, a little too much, a bloody trot! Breath caught, heart suddenly pounding in her ears, panic soaring, she had no idea how she managed to stay on the horse with her arse slamming down in the saddle with each bounce. And she couldn't figure out how to get the mare to change her gait to something slower and smoother.

She was too busy keeping her seat to even notice she'd made it halfway around the track and was nearly to the half circle at the other end of it. She had to glance back to see where she'd left Devin. He was actually racing after her. Thank God! If she could slow the animal just a little, he could catch up and get the horse to stop!

She tried pulling back on the reins slowly, as he'd said, but she had to lean too far back, and she was in such a panic, it didn't occur to her to gather the reins closer to her first. Instead she tried to stand up in the stirrup to tighten the reins. Too late, she forgot she wasn't supposed to do that!

Her eyes flared wide. The saddle started to slide to the left off the mare's back, with her in it! The ground was getting closer, the saddle was completely crooked now, and as she tried to straighten herself, she pushed the saddle even farther to the side.

It was happening again! History was repeating itself. . . .

Chapter Twenty-Five

Her scream was still ringing in her ears. Hitting the ground had cut it off abruptly when she lost her breath for a moment from the impact. Amanda was afraid to move. She felt the pain, the same pain, in the same place as before. History really did repeat itself, she thought as tears stung her eyes.

Devin hadn't been able to reach her in time, but he stirred dust in her face as he came to a skidding halt on his knees beside her. She was terrified he was going to touch her and make the pain worse. She remembered the agony of being moved all those years ago. They'd carried her to the house and it had been so painful she'd fainted, which had been a blessing—until she woke.

"Are you hurt?" Devin asked frantically. "Tell me where." But he saw her tears and swore.

She would probably have blushed, hearing his words, if she didn't feel like swearing, too. She was still too afraid to move, even to lean up to look at him. And the tears wouldn't stop because of it. She knew she was going to have to move, but the dread of what it was going to feel like was paralyzing her.

"*Where* are you hurt?" he repeated, more insistently this time.

"My left leg."

"Anywhere else?"

"I don't know. I'm afraid to find out."

"Let me help you sit up so we—"

"No!" she shouted. "Don't touch me!"

The hysterical note was probably what had him say, "Don't you think you're overreacting a bit? We don't even know if anything is broken. Or is this just because of what happened before? Was there more to that old accident than what you told me? Or are you just being missish about this because you're a woman?"

"Don't you dare—!"

"That's better. Anger comes in handy sometimes."

He did that deliberately? She realized it had worked, the terrified panic was gone. She wished the pain had gone along with it, though she realized even that was lessening. Of course she hadn't moved a speck yet. The moment she did, she was sure the pain would overwhelm her again.

"Are you ready to get out of the cold?"

"No." In case he thought she was still overreacting, she added, "I'm not the least bit cold."

That wasn't exactly true. She didn't usually mind brisk weather like this as long as she was moving about in it. But lying so still, she could feel the bite of the late-autumn weather on her cheeks and gloveless hands. She'd be shivering soon. That might hurt!

"Very well, we'll give it a few minutes, but let's at least get your face out of the dirt."

He actually lay down next to her on the ground so he could

slip his arm under her head, just enough for her to rest her cheek on his forearm without moving any other part of her body. That was rather gallant of him. And it hadn't hurt to move her neck. *Was* she overreacting?

Amanda could see the concern on his face now. He hadn't sounded worried, but he looked it, and that just stoked her fear.

But he said soothingly, "We have to find out where the break is, if there is a break. If you'll point to where it hurts—"

"No. I don't want to know—I'm afraid to know. You don't understand. This is too similar to my first riding accident."

"Are you sure? You said you fainted before. You haven't fainted here."

That was true. This pain wasn't as bad either, and as long as she didn't move her left leg, it didn't hurt. If she'd broken her leg again as she feared, could it just be turning numb?

"Let me tell you how we're going to do this," he continued in that same soothing tone. "I'm going to pick you up and carry you back to the stable. I'm going to be very gentle, and you're going to grit your teeth and manage not to scream in my ear. We know how brave you are, Mandy. You can get through this. Are you ready?"

"No," she whimpered.

He waited a few minutes before he asked again, "Are you ready now?"

She was starting to feel a little chilled. She nodded and squeezed her eyes shut and gritted her teeth as he suggested, waiting for that jolt of pain that would probably make her faint. He didn't draw out the suspense. He lifted her off the ground quickly. The pain was bad. It flew up her leg and seemed to go right to her head, but that could have been from the quick change of position. She didn't faint, but the pain was briefly excruciating. She bit back the urge to scream. But Devin was walking at such a steady gait that she barely felt him move, and once again the pain receded. Or was she just too aware of being cradled in his arms to feel anything other than him?

She felt surrounded by his warmth. He even put his chin to the top of her head to help keep her still, probably denting her little hat. The chill definitely departed! Then the warmth of the stable washed over her. She heard him send a worker after their horses, but in another few moments he entered a small office at the back, keeping the door to the stable open. Amanda saw an old desk, a couple of wooden chairs, and a narrow cot on which he gently laid her. She only groaned slightly when her leg touched the cot.

He straightened and looked down at her. He smiled slightly and ran a finger across her cheek, then showed it to her. "Dust and tears, not the best mix. Let me get some water. Don't go anywhere."

Was he joking? Where was she going with a broken leg? But the moment he left the room, she leaned up on one elbow and looked down at her legs, which were covered by her riding skirt and her boots. She was getting up the nerve to raise the riding skirt so she could see the damage when Devin came back in with a bucket of water. Another moment and she would have been blushing.

He set the bucket on the floor beside the cot. "I should get a cabinet for all this stuff, but there isn't enough room in here for more furniture."

Suddenly he was leaning over her to reach the shelf on the wall above the cot. Her eyes flared wide as the length of his body stretched across her view, but he was just getting a small towel off the shelf. Then he sat down next to her. He had barely any room to do so, but she was still afraid to move any part of her lower body, even to make room for him.

First he untied her little hat and tossed it on his desk, then he dipped an edge of the towel into the water and began to dab at her cheeks with it. Treating her like a child again? "I can do that."

"Be still." He continued washing her face. "You'll just miss something, then be annoyed at yourself later when you have a look in a mirror."

She managed not to snort at him. He was being helpful. Even if she'd rather he not be this helpful, she shouldn't complain. But he was taking a deuced long time wiping her face, and being so careful it almost felt as if he were caressing, rather than washing, her face. She was starting to feel she wasn't sure what, but his undivided attention was disturbing her in some way.

To get her mind off what he was doing, she said, "What stuff?"

His eyes met hers, but he looked confused. "What?"

He was so distracted he didn't recall what he'd just said? "You said—"

"Oh, just the stuff we keep around for the horses— liniments, tinctures, and such. Occasionally I come in and find a bottle has fallen from the shelf to the cot because the bloody shelf's so old it's tilted."

Was he trying to make her laugh? "You do realize a simple nail might fix that?"

"Do I look like a carpenter?"

No, Amanda thought, you look like a man far too handsome and virile to be sitting so close to me on a bed!

Chapter Twenty-Six

"THERE," DEVIN SAID MATTER-OF-FACTLY. "All cleaned up and ready for what you've been dreading. I'm going to have to have a look at your leg, Amanda."

"No, you don't have to do anything of the sort," she said, alarmed. "If you could fetch a doctor, I'd be much obliged."

He raised a brow as he stood up. "When we don't yet know if one is needed? There's no doctor nearby that I know of. Of course, I'll send a man to London to fetch one, but let's see first if there's a reason to do so. Which leg is it, your left? Actually, just sit up and point to where it hurts. Give me your hand, I'll help you. If we're very slow about it, it won't hurt a'tall."

She believed him. She'd leaned up earlier without making the pain flare up. As long as she didn't move anything below her hips . . .

Sitting, with her legs stretched out on the cot in front of her, she was able to put her finger directly over the area on her left calf that hurt, without actually touching it.

He seemed surprised by the location. "Not the ankle?

Good, I can't tell you how much I wasn't looking forward to your screams if I had to pull your boot off. You probably would have frightened every horse in the stable into breaking out of their stalls." But then he pretended to look appalled. "Just don't tell me you wear knee-high boots!"

She glared up at him, quite aware he was exaggerating. Provoking beneficial anger again? He even smiled to prove it. But as he carefully lifted the hem of her skirt by her left leg, tugging it out from under the leg, she gasped as she felt that horrible pain again.

"Stop!" she cried.

He didn't and soothingly said, "We haven't even seen it yet, just another moment. . . ."

Her eyes flared when she saw her swollen calf, but she started whimpering when his fingers approached it. Even to her ears, she sounded like a wounded animal.

"Shh," he soothed. "I think I can fix this."

She looked horrified by the thought, remembering the last time her bones had been shoved back into place. "You're going to make that pain worse!"

"Only briefly, then you'll be good as new again."

Good as new? He was spouting nonsense when she was on the edge of hysteria! She slowly shook her head at him and said in a small voice, "Now might be a good time for one of your miracles, Cupid, because this can't be fixed without one."

"Yes, I can see that," he said solemnly. "Very well, one miracle coming right up."

He went over to his desk. She heard him opening drawers, but she wasn't watching him, she was still staring in horror at the swollen part of her leg, which she feared was proof that she'd broken a bone again.

Returning to stand beside the cot again, he handed her a glass filled nearly to the brim with a dark, amber-colored liquid. "Drink this."

She frowned. "What sort of miracle is that?"

"One you'll thank me for. So drink it. And straight down before you can taste it. It will steady you—and make you laugh off your fears."

She didn't believe a word of that and her look must have said so. Was he trying to give her horse medicine? When she still wouldn't take the glass, he drank a little more than half of the liquid in it himself to prove it was harmless, then handed her the glass again.

She took it this time and even followed his instructions, gulped the liquid he'd left in the glass straight down. But she didn't even have a chance to lower the glass from her lips before she was sputtering and coughing. Tears came to her eyes. Her throat was on fire!

"That was hard spirits!" she accused shrilly.

He nodded unrepentantly. "And occasionally they can work wonders—in situations like this."

As he said that, he sat on the end of the bed. He had enough room to do so without having to put her feet in his lap. The cot was much longer than any she'd ever before seen. Designed for his long length? Good Lord, she wasn't actually in his bed, was she?

That thought had an odd effect on her, or was it the whiskey? That foul-tasting liquid did seem to be rushing straight through her, turning her muscles to mush, leaving her limbs *too* relaxed.

"The good news is, you haven't broken any bones."

She felt so relieved she almost giggled, until her eyes again landed on that swollen part of her leg. "Then what is *that*?" She pointed an accusing finger at her calf.

"My guess would be, just a muscle spasm. I've seen muscle spasms lay a horse low. No actual damage, but it hurts like hell. And it can be massaged away."

"And if you're wrong?"

"If the muscle was torn, my ears would be suffering by now, because you would have been screaming all this time. So lean back, grit your teeth if you have to, and let me work out this knot, and the pain will go away with it."

She couldn't follow his directions completely, she was too tense over what was about to happen. She merely leaned back on her elbows and prepared to watch him and stop him if she couldn't bear the pain. He put his hands under her calf first and slowly worked his fingers toward the inflammation. The pain was minimal. She barely felt it at first, then felt too much! But the worst of it was brief and she continued to follow his instruction and grit her teeth, continuing to hope he was right, that it would soon be gone completely.

The pain lessened, and she grew more and more relaxed as it dissipated. Before long all she felt was Devin's fingers gently massaging her leg, and she was amazed by how nice that felt. No man had ever touched her like that before. She knew he was only doing it to help her, yet it felt so sensual she gasped more than once. She couldn't take her eyes off him. His touch got gentler and was more of a caress now, and suddenly their eyes locked. His seemed to be aflame, they were so bright. She sucked in her breath, her belly all aflutter. What on earth had that whiskey done to her?

"Better?" he said in a deep tone.

She didn't think she could find her voice at that moment,

it was almost as if she were transfixed. Then she felt an urge to giggle! No wonder women weren't allowed to drink hard spirits!

Trying to shake off whatever effects had just taken control of her, she sat up again and lightly teased, "You're not a carpenter, but a horse breeder, a matchmaker, a riding instructor, *and* a superb doctor. Anything else you could teach me that I might benefit from?"

"How are you at kissing?"

"I don't know."

"Then we should find out."

The moment it registered, that he was offering to show her how to go about kissing, something indescribable happened to her. Before clarity of thought might intrude, he leaned toward her and put his mouth gently to hers. This was actually her very first kiss because she'd never encouraged a man enough for him to try stealing kisses from her. Yet she'd waited in curiosity a long time to find out about it, so she wasn't about to stop him, not yet. . . .

His hand slipped behind her neck as he leaned even closer and laid her back gently on the cot. Suddenly his chest was pressed to hers. But she didn't want to stop him.

His lips parted, slanted across hers, urging her to open hers as well. Nothing about his kiss was tepid, and she was quickly overwhelmed by what it made her feel. A fluttering sensation was deep inside her, swirling about in an exciting way. Her breath was suspended. Then his tongue actually slipped into her mouth! She started to draw back at such an unusual sensation, but his hold tightened just enough to let her know he wasn't done with her.

He was so close, so handsome, so exciting! She could feel so much of him—his mouth capturing hers, his strong hands caressing her, his chest pressed against her breasts. This was her introduction to passion. Amanda couldn't think beyond that, she could only feel, absorbing everything, marveling at so many new sensations that she didn't even know she was capable of experiencing.

His hand moved along her cheek and neck, causing shivers to shoot down her back. The stubble on his chin seemed to be abrading her, but she didn't care. She heard him groan, the sound seeming to reverberate through her—or was it just so thrilling to her ears that she ended up trembling all over? She couldn't tell! So many sensations, all new, all thrilling. Even her breasts tingled, pressed so tightly to his chest.

But the wonderful moment ended abruptly, too abruptly, when Devin shot to his feet. Panting, wishing the kiss had lasted longer, she looked up at him reprovingly. If she'd been thinking at all, she wouldn't have let her curiosity get out of hand. But then she would never have provoked him to kiss her to begin with, either. Good Lord, what had she done?!

"Stop it," he said, seeing her blush. "That was a very strong drink I gave you to help you deal with the pain. The side effect is that it impairs your judgment, clouds your thoughts, and makes you do things you wouldn't ordinarily do. Now how's that leg?"

As soon as her head stopped spinning from all that he'd said, Amanda sat up and put her feet on the floor. More gallantry on his part? Passing the blame for what had just happened between them to the drink? Well, if he didn't want to discuss that any further, she would be grateful for that as well.

"It's fine, as you well know. Thank you. Now I really should be going."

She stood up, perhaps a little too fast. Her legs were so

wobbly she was surprised they didn't crumble under her. Her hair felt as if it was in disarray. She could see a single, long lock dangling below her breast. Her cheeks and her chin felt as if they'd been abraded, and her lips felt a little swollen. Now he was standing so close that he was towering over her again, making her think of that kiss when she knew she had to put it out of her mind.

But *he* helped with that. Suddenly the brute was front and center again, saying in an adamant tone, "Don't think your lessons are over. You're getting back on a horse today, not to ride, but to take command of your fears. And we'll do it the right way this time."

She sat back on the cot abruptly. "There's only one way and it didn't work."

"The first round was a blunder, but it was my blunder. I'm not going to be responsible for your not getting your heart's desire. You *will* get back on a horse today, Mandy, like it or not."

"What blunder?"

"I never should have started you off on a damned sidesaddle. So let me show you what I'm talking about."

He grabbed her hand and led her out of the office and down the aisle to his working horse, which one of the workers had tethered to a post. Without warning, he simply tossed her up into the saddle. She tried to hook her leg over the horn, but it was a man's saddle and Devin gently pushed her right leg over the saddle so that it dangled on the other side.

Amanda gasped, trying to shove her skirt back down over her exposed legs. But she couldn't do it with a horse between her legs! "Get me down! I can't sit on a horse like this!"

"Of course you can. You already are."

"But this is indecent!"

"I've already seen your leg," he said, his eyes locked on hers.

"That's beside the—"

"Sit up straight," he cut in sharply. "Use your legs, girl. Grip the animal's sides. That's your courage. That's your control. That's how you'll stay in the bloody seat. If you'd pause a moment in your ranting to take notice, you'll see how natural that feels."

Did he *have* to be right? She grumbled, "I still can't ride like this."

"Of course you won't, not without proper clothes. This was just a demonstration for you. But if you still want to become a horsewoman after today, you're going to master riding astride first, before you attempt to master a sidesaddle again. So borrow a pair of your brother's breeches or get a skirt made for riding."

"I'm already wearing a skirt made just for riding," she huffed.

"No, I'm talking about a pair of breeches that looks like a skirt. I've only seen a couple of women wearing this type of garment, but off the horse, it looked like a skirt. Yet when the woman was sitting astride a horse, it fully covered her legs. All very proper. Talk to your seamstress. I'm sure she can figure out something like that for you."

That sounded interesting. She could even envision what he was talking about. And she didn't feel afraid sitting on the horse like this, not with her legs giving her such firm purchase. Though that could just be because of that horrid drink he'd given her, but it was still worth a try.

"Very well. But do get me down before someone walks in and—"

She didn't have to finish, he was already holding up his arms to her. She leaned to the side, reaching for his shoulders, but didn't quite get that far before he pulled her off the horse much too fast. She slammed right into his chest! He quickly put his arms around her to steady her, though she was steady—until she caught the look in his eyes. Oh, my! His amber eyes were looking right into hers, and they had that glow of passion in them again. She shivered deliciously. But he let go. Gasping, flustered yet *again*, she stepped back to make sure her skirt had settled into place properly.

"Bring a chaperone with you next time," she heard him say in a distinctly annoyed tone.

Her eyes flew up to him. "I have one, she's—"

"I mean a man. Preferably a relative of yours who might have some input about your riding—and will prevent you from taking on more lessons than you can handle in one day."

She stiffened. So that drink had affected his judgment as well, and now he regretted giving her that lesson in kissing? He obviously wanted to make sure it didn't happen again, by insisting she bring a relative with her next time. No wonder he sounded so sharp. How embarrassing.

He grasped her elbow and escorted her out of the stable, adding, "But don't bring your brother, or you may end up ruining Lady Ophelia's surprise for him."

He took her straight out to the hired coach and helped her into it. She would have said a proper good-bye, might even have thanked him for his efforts today on her behalf, but his parting words just before he shut the door and gave the driver the signal to head out left her speechless.

"By the way, you've got nice legs."

Chapter Twenty-Seven

Amanda couldn't believe he did that! For the second time, Devin had said something in front of one of her chaperones that was going to get her reprimanded.

It would have been nice if Alice had nodded off while waiting for her because then she wouldn't have heard Devin's scandalous remark, but no such luck. The maid was staring at her now with eyes as wide as saucers.

Amanda tried to escape this lecture by saying, "He was just joking."

"Joking? When there's evidence on your chin and lips that says otherwise? You better hope that abrasion fades from your face before we get home, or I won't be the only one telling you that you stepped so far over the line it's a wonder you ain't still tumbling down the hill!"

Amanda winced. She didn't want to discuss that kiss when merely thinking about it stirred her pulse again. So she explained about the fall, assured Alice she didn't break anything, but then lied, "His face must have scraped against mine when he carried me back to the stable."

Amanda wasn't worried about the evidence of the kissing lesson Devin had given her until Alice mentioned it, but since they weren't going directly home and still had to stop back on Bond Street to collect the St. John coach, she decided to go to the seamstress shop again and order a couple of those special riding skirts Devin had told her about so she could ride astride. By the time she and Alice were riding home in the St. John coach, enough time had passed for that slight redness from Devin's rough face rubbing against hers to fade. And a good thing. Her father was there at Julie's house waiting for her.

Julie, Preston, and Rebecca were in the dining room for luncheon. Amanda called out her greetings as she joined them, then hugged her father's neck from behind before she took the seat next to him.

"I understand you're leaving us today," Julie said right off. "I'll have your trunks sent over to Rafe's house this afternoon."

Amanda grinned. "So Father told you that he's going to be in town for the duration?"

"Yes, that news nearly knocked me on my arse," Julie said in exaggeration.

Preston chuckled at his sister. "I don't know why you think I'm a bloody recluse. Just because I love Norford Hall and prefer my comforts there doesn't mean I can't enjoy the festivities in London for a Season—for a good cause. And my daughter is an exceptionally good cause."

"'Course she is."

But he turned to Amanda to say, "But as it happens, Phelia wants to drag us all back home for Rafe's birthday."

"But we always celebrate birthdays there," Amanda reminded him.

He nodded. "I know, but she's making plans for a grand party, an actual weeklong affair that warrants a long guest list, apparently, so she'd like your help with that."

Amanda squealed with delight. "She's throwing a country party? You actually agreed?"

"Yes, because it's for a dual purpose. She's going to be inviting all the young eligibles and I'm adding several names to the guest list m'self, young men that come highly recommended, so you might want to pay a little attention to them."

She raised a brow. "Recommended by whom?"

"A friend of a friend" was all he said.

Before she could wonder about that cryptic response, Julie asked her, "Did you get that mishap straightened out with the seamstress?"

"Yes, but I had a wonderful idea while I was there, and she was intrigued enough to try it for me. A skirt with legs." Julie just raised a brow, making Amanda giggle and jump back up to stretch her legs as far apart as her current skirt allowed. "Really, imagine it, Aunt Julie, it will look like a skirt unless I stand like this. Only then would you be able to tell it's actually *very* baggy pants."

"Pants?" Rebecca chuckled.

"No pants," Preston said adamantly, and continued to eat his lunch.

"I assume you mean for riding?" Julie said.

"Of course for riding, I wouldn't need them for anything else."

Preston turned to face her, his sudden concern obvious. "When did you start riding?"

"I haven't yet, but I want to try it again," she admitted hesitantly.

"I'd rather you didn't" was all her father said, but that said so much.

Amanda knew he was remembering how much pain she'd suffered from her fall, and the horrible worry he'd had that she might never walk right again because of it. Of course he preferred that she never get on a horse again. She'd even agreed with him, until now.

She put her hand over her father's. "This is something I really want to tackle. If I end up hating it, then that will be the end of it. But it's a skill I've always regretted not developing. So I at least want to give it one last try. I did recently, you know."

There, she'd done it. There was no going back. Now that her family knew she was attempting to ride again, she *had* to succeed.

"Yes, Herbert told me you'd changed your mind," Preston replied.

"I couldn't even bring myself to get on the horse he brought out for me."

"Then why are we even discussing this?"

"Because I hadn't been challenged yet to succeed. And I hadn't been told yet how easy it *could* be under the right circumstances. And because I've met a man I'm quite interested in," she ended with a slight blush.

"Who?" they all said at once.

"Kendall Goswick, the Earl of Manford. He's not even in town for the Season. I met him when I went with Phelia to a horse farm to pick out Rafe's birthday present. He was so handsome and charming, he quite stole my breath away! He's the first man I actually want to see more of."

"That's wonderful, Mandy," Rebecca said, beaming at her.

"When do we get to meet him?" Preston queried.

"Soon, I hope."

"And what's he got to do with your suddenly wanting to take up horse riding?" Preston asked.

Amanda grinned. "Because I'm thinking ahead, all the way to marriage. Lord Kendall is an avid horseman. In fact, he loves horses so much he's chasing down another one in France right now to add to his stable. If we do get married, how will it work if I hate something my husband loves so much? I'd feel terrible about it! He'd be miserable about it. He might not even want to marry me if he finds out I don't ride."

"Nonsense."

"Absurd."

"Never heard of anything so silly."

Amanda bit her lip. They sounded so certain. No, they scoffed because they loved her. *She* would rather not put it to the test with Kendall. Besides, learning to ride was still something she wanted to accomplish, Kendall or no. And spending time with Devin was exciting! Even though he was impossible and not quite of her social circle, she couldn't deny, at least to herself, that she found him intriguing. He was so unlike any other man she'd ever met. She couldn't tell when he was teasing her and when he was serious. And she could learn a lot more from him than just riding. . . .

She nearly gasped at the thought that he wouldn't hesitate to answer her questions about men, unlike her brother. She could take advantage of Devin's bluntness in that regard. She might well learn things from him that would assure her success with her husband hunt. But she couldn't tell her family any of that!

But she *was* feeling much better about getting the hang of

riding, now that Devin had pointed out one of the difficulties she'd faced, how to feel comfortable and in control while sitting on a saddle.

She explained that to her father. "It's not just Lord Kendall and how riding might make for a happy marriage with him—if we progress that far. It's something I've always missed out on, anything to do with horses, and I've regretted that. I let fear persuade me that I didn't *need* to ride, but some of that fear was because I never felt secure on a horse. But I'm convinced now that *that* was the fault of the saddle. That's one thing I do remember about my first lessons, that I was so nervous each time because it felt so awkward. It's like sitting only halfway on a horse!"

"Couldn't have said it better," Julie agreed. "Nasty contraptions, sidesaddles."

Grateful for her aunt's support, Amanda continued, "I'm going to take lessons again, of course. If I still don't like riding after that, then I will feel good about having at least tried. And I've been told riding astride is so much easier, which is why I'm having the special skirt made for it. I'll worry about riding like a lady afterward."

"No fussing about this, Preston," Julie added gruffly. "You know very well I rode with britches under my skirts at Norford. The gel needs to feel comfortable in the saddle. She's got enough to overcome without adding a precarious seat into the mix. Besides, you know how stubborn she can be when she gets an idea set in her head."

Preston sighed. "Then by all means . . ."

Chapter Twenty-Eight

"HOW IS CUPID DOING?" Owen asked. "Any more matches we'll be hearing about soon?"

Devin took a break from training the two mares he'd decided to sell and joined Lord Culley at the fence, where he'd been waiting for Devin. He'd met the white-haired, old gentleman at the races last year and quite a few times after that. Then Owen came to him last year for a new carriage horse. He had insisted he wanted one of Devin's fast Thoroughbreds despite Devin's trying to talk him out of it. Owen had returned the racer a week later. Devin had had a feeling he would, and had already had one of Donald's geldings brought down from Lancashire waiting for the old gent.

After that, Owen Culley had got in the habit of stopping by the farm on his trips to and from London. Just for chats. Devin had a feeling the old man was lonely, so he never ignored him or brushed him off on those brief visits, and eventually they'd developed an unlikely friendship.

"I'm having trouble with my current client," Devin admitted, though he never mentioned names. "Temperamental chit. Beautiful, but I'm not sure that's enough to compensate for her hot temper."

"'Course it is," Owen said with a chuckle. "Keep a woman happy, she has no reason to lose her temper."

"I suppose, though it's getting to the happy part that worries me. I can't think of any man who wouldn't back off if she turned her temper on him."

"Would you?"

Devin laughed. He liked Owen, but more, he respected him because he wasn't afraid to admit when he was wrong. Owen had wanted to relive his youth with a fast carriage ride, had insisted he was up to it, but his old bones weren't. How many other lords would admit defeat like that and laugh about it afterward? With his advanced years, he looked at life differently, so Devin enjoyed their talks.

"I'm not in the running, so it doesn't matter if I can handle her or not."

"So you can handle her?" Owen guessed. "Well, give the candidates for her heart a little more credit. Love has a way of accepting the good with the bad."

Devin wondered why he was suddenly having doubts about Kendall's ability to withstand one of Amanda's tantrums. Because he had a feeling she'd be the boss in that relationship and he didn't think she'd actually like that? Even something so simple as a riding lesson she had to turn into a major catastrophe. But that had actually been his fault. Damned sidesaddles. Heaven forbid a woman actually gripped a horse with her legs the way a horse was supposed to be ridden. Instead a woman had to contort her body in a ridiculous position so she could sit on a horse *daintily* without showing any leg.

Owen's last remark suddenly sank in. *Was* she already in love with the boy? She was putting herself through what was obviously hell for her, just to win a man who would always pay more attention to his stable than to his wife. Of course she didn't know that, and it didn't mean Goswick wouldn't make a good and loving husband, merely that his wife wouldn't be his first priority. But if Amanda did end up sharing Goswick's one and only interest, they could end up being happy as larks. Yet she shouldn't *have* to master something she found so daunting just to win a husband. That was what was bothering Devin now, and that *he'd* set that in motion. But he'd had no idea just how traumatic it was going to be for her. It could still work out, but in the meantime, he shouldn't close his mind to other possibilities—nor should she.

He didn't like having doubts so he tried to put them aside and grinned at Owen. "It's too bad there isn't a younger version of you walking around. This minx is going to need patience like—bloody hell, I'm sorry, Owen. I forgot—"

"Don't give it another thought. My grandchildren died long ago."

The old man smiled to put Devin at ease. While it wouldn't be the first time he'd noticed a sad expression on Owen's face— it couldn't be easy surviving your whole family—today wasn't one of them.

"I'll take a dram of whiskey before I head out, though. For the chill," Owen added with a grin.

Devin nodded and opened the gate to walk up to the stable with Owen, but the mention of whiskey reminded him of what shouldn't have happened in his office that morning. But that and everything else went out of his mind when a bullet struck the dirt at his feet.

"Good Lord!" Owen exclaimed, as Devin instinctively grabbed the older man's arm and quickly led him back toward the stable. "Poachers misfiring this close to a farm?"

Devin blanched as he realized what could have just happened. Owen could have been hit, or Reed. Amelia was in the house now with her mother so she wasn't endangered, but this could have happened while Amanda had still been here. She could have been shot!

"Not after I get my hands on him," Devin snarled, turning and gazing at the woods that bordered the farm. "Let me get you inside the stable, then—"

"No, go on, these old legs still know how to hurry. I'll be fine. Find whoever was this careless, before he runs off."

Devin nodded and ran back to the fence. He untied his mount and leapt onto it. He debated grabbing a rifle from the stable, but Owen was right. He'd lose the miscreant if he gave him enough time to slip away. Reed raced toward him before he reached the woods, having also heard the shot. Devin directed him to ride north so they could cover more area at once, then glanced back to see some of the workers mounting up, too. They'd find him. . . .

They didn't. The woods surrounding his property were thick and a hunter wasn't likely to have a mount with him. He'd managed to hide or run off quickly. Devin and his men spent most of the afternoon searching for the poacher before Devin tracked down a magistrate and reported the incident. Poachers had never come near his property before. The man had to be an absolute fool to hunt that close to a farm. Just one more thing for Devin to worry about now.

Actually, before the day was over, he had yet another worry. Now that William was out of danger, Blythe had moved him back to their home. But it would take a couple of weeks for him to recover sufficiently to take over as his sister's escort, so Devin took her to the party she'd been invited to that night. Like most of the other guests, he couldn't help but notice when Robert Brigston walked in. Devin hadn't thought the boy would receive any more invitations after his behavior at the ball the other night. Suddenly he was on everyone's lips again.

"Behaved like an arse because he was foxed, is what I heard."

"So that's why he flirted with every skirt in sight? Have a problem with that m'self when I drink too much."

"Understandable."

"Delighted to hear that's all it was. My sister's set her cap for him."

"Prime catch once again—what rotten luck."

"Enough jealousy, boy, Lord Robert can't have 'em all. There'll be plenty of gels left for you to choose from."

Devin snorted at the turn the gossip had taken in regard to Brigston. Had the boy turned the tide, or had his father? What a paltry excuse to use to dig Robert out of that scandal he'd created the other night. Yet, apparently, it was working. But Devin wasn't fooled and would make sure Blythe didn't get her head turned by Robert Brigston. He wasn't worried that Amanda might still be susceptible to the boy's blandishments. According to her, her brother would shoot the lad if he got anywhere near her. If Rafe didn't, Devin might.

Chapter Twenty-Nine

DEVIN OVERSLEPT, SOMETHING HE rarely ever did. He wasn't surprised, considering all that had been on his mind when he'd gone to bed after such an eventful day. But the late hour had him racing to the farm. If Amanda was coming for a lesson today, she'd probably be there already. But when he arrived, she wasn't there and, according to Reed, hadn't been there earlier. He ought to set up an actual schedule with her *if* she was coming back for more riding lessons. She might not after that last crack he'd made about her legs—and everything else that had occurred while she'd been at the farm yesterday.

He definitely hadn't expected her riding lesson to turn out as it did, with blunder after blunder on his part. What the deuce had made him think that someone who hadn't ridden in years, and was fearful of doing so, could master an infernal contraption like a sidesaddle? And he'd been out of his depth dealing with fear of that sort—or a slightly foxed duke's daughter.

Bloody hell, what had possessed him? Drinking half of that glass of whiskey himself was no excuse. But because of it he now knew how sweet she tasted, how delightful she smelled up close, how damned quickly she could heat his blood. But that was all he was ever going to know about her. She was so far out of his league it was laughable.

The last time he'd thought that about a woman, he'd shrugged it off. This time he couldn't. He'd actually tasted forbidden fruit, what he couldn't have—because of his mother. Because of that bastard who'd ruined her, and him, and had never felt the least bit of remorse for it. So many times Devin had thought about confronting him, but he'd been afraid he wouldn't be able to control himself long enough to tell the bastard off. He was afraid he might kill him instead because the mere thought of him brought forth such rage.

When he noticed he'd crushed Amanda's hat in his hands while sitting at his desk thinking about his father, he threw it across the room. It didn't go far because the room was so small, but he still winced over what he'd done. She wasn't whom he was angry at, and he should probably return the little hat to her before he ruined it any further. He owed her an apology anyway for letting things get so out of hand. He might even have to face complaints about his behavior from an angry father.

So he grabbed up the hat again, stuffed it in his pocket, and headed back to London. He had to pick up an order from his tailor anyway, and he couldn't do that if he spent all day every day on the farm. A good excuse. He almost laughed at himself when he went straight to the St. John residence.

It was late morning, an acceptable time to call on any ladies of the house. But the last thing he expected to see was Robert Brigston coming down the steps. The door was closing behind him. Turned away? Or just leaving after a visit? Devin decided to find out and blocked the boy's path to the curb.

"Oh, I say, Cupid, ain't it?" Robert even smiled. "I think you're the only chap I met the other night who didn't give me the cold shoulder."

"That's right, we didn't actually introduce ourselves, did we? I prefer Devin Baldwin to that silly nickname, and what are you doing here, Robert?"

"Calling on my soon-to-be-wife."

"I'm going to assume that's just wishful thinking on your part. Last I heard, her family was going to shoot you if you got anywhere near her."

Robert winced. "I did muck it up pretty badly, didn't I? But it's getting turned round nicely now."

Devin raised a brow, remembering the gossip he'd heard last night. "Foxed? You and I both know you weren't the least bit foxed at that ball."

Robert shrugged. "My father's suggestion, and he's having the word spread through the more vocal gossipmongers. Seems to be working to quiet things down."

"But is that what *you* want now?"

Robert chuckled. "Ah, yes, I did say a bit more to you than I should have, didn't I? I was bloody miserable that night. I guess I needed a shoulder to cry on."

"So you're buckling under to your father's dictates?" Devin guessed.

"No choice now," Robert admitted with a sigh. "The old man summoned me home. Didn't know he was keeping tabs on me, but I should have. Never seen him so furious. He's going to disown me if I don't see this through."

If Amanda wasn't involved, Devin could almost pity the young lord. "If she marries someone else, that should let you off the hook."

"Right you are, except what's the chance of that, eh? I can't *not* court her now. I *have* to make the effort. My bloody inheritance depends on it." Then Robert whispered, "My father's man is waiting in my coach. He's got *his* orders, too, to make sure I start courting the chit proper."

"Did they even let you in the house?" Devin asked curiously, nodding at the door behind the boy.

"Oh, you think she hasn't heard the new gossip yet that forgives my behavior? Quite possible. But she ain't here. The butler said she changed residences yesterday afternoon. She's moved away."

Amanda had left town? Devin felt his heart sink. This had to be his fault. But at least that put her out of Robert's reach, too. It wasn't that he didn't like the boy, but he didn't like the reasons behind his pursuit of Amanda. She deserved better. Brigston might be able to overcome his bad start and actually be allowed to court Amanda. Unfortunately, Devin didn't think for a moment that she would be able to see through the subterfuge to Brigston's real motives. No, she was likely to conclude that Robert Brigston would be much preferable to her than riding lessons.

"Do yourself a favor," Devin suggested casually. "If you feel you have to go through with this, do it tepidly."

"You mean only give the appearance of being in hot pursuit of Lady Amanda, so my father thinks I gave it my best effort?"

"Exactly."

Robert gave that a moment's thought before he frowned. "But how would that work, when she's bound to fall in love with me?"

Devin refrained from laughing. "Perhaps by not sounding quite sincere to her? Or you could seem a little bored with her company? Or you could simply let her know you've been ordered to court her."

Robert looked appalled. "I can't risk telling her the truth! That could get back to my father."

"Then I repeat, keep it tepid. The girl's not stupid. If she senses you're not really interested, then she's not going to accept a proposal, when you're not the only prime catch of the Season who she's met. As long as she leans toward the other, you'll be safe."

"I have competition?" Robert sounded worried, but then Devin noticed a glint of excitement in the boy's eyes.

Devin groaned to himself. What the hell had he just done? But Robert hurried off before Devin could say anything more. He still had a hat to return, so he stuffed the little hat in his pocket and decided to pay Amanda's aunt a visit to find out where she'd run off to.

The butler led him straight to the parlor.

Julie St. John glanced up at him from the book she was reading. Her brows snapped together before she lashed, "Do I need to fire my butler? I hope you know you wouldn't have got your foot in the door, young man, if you'd asked to see Amanda."

Devin almost winced. Amanda had spilled the beans obviously. "Yes, I know she's moved—"

"That's not why you would have been turned away. She doesn't allow her beaus to call on her, hasn't since last Season, so you might as well wait until you find her at a social. You'll be turned away at her brother's door, too."

She hadn't left town? And he wasn't being called on the carpet by her aunt for his improper behavior with Amanda? Then why did the woman sound as if she'd like to be breathing fire at him?

He carefully tested the waters, grinning. "Is that so?"

Her golden brow went up at a sharp angle. "You find that amusing, do you? Why?"

"Possibly because I'm not one of her beaus? I'm Devin Baldwin—"

Julie snorted. "Should have said so. According to my son Rupert, we have you to thank for warning us about that rake sniffing at Mandy's heels. Rue spoke highly of you—despite your nickname that he finds so amusing."

Devin choked back a laugh, her manner was so quarrelsome. "I take it you disapprove of my matchmaking as much as the grand dame Mabel Collicott does?"

"Mabel! There's nothing grand about her! That old biddy doesn't have a lick of sense when it comes to *anything*. Caught her spreading rumors about my son during his rakehell days that weren't the least bit true. Have been feuding with her ever since. In fact, if I hadn't decided to hire you to look after Amanda's romantic interests this Season, I'd hire you instead to put Mabel Collicott out of business."

Devin was incredulous. Yet another member of Amanda's family was trying to hire him? He couldn't confess that he was already working for Lady Ophelia when she'd sworn him to secrecy.

"I will be happy to keep an eye out for good prospects for your niece. You don't need to hire me to do that."

"Nonsense, can't have you working on our behalf with no compensation. Succeed and you will be pleasantly surprised."

Devin gave up trying to talk the lady out of it. She was much too bullish to accept a refusal. He wouldn't take her money, though. He would leave it to Ophelia to confess the matter if he was successful. And he would be, if Amanda continued her riding lessons, which meant he was going to have to keep their relationship strictly professional henceforth.

Not until he got home did he realize he'd forgotten to return the bloody hat, which was still in his pocket. But Amanda could collect it at the farm. He just wished he wasn't looking forward to her next visit so much.

Chapter Thirty

OPHELIA HAD KEPT AMANDA so busy yesterday, she hadn't felt like going to any of the parties she'd been asked to attend last night and had simply gone to bed early. Her new riding ensemble had arrived late in the afternoon, and she was feeling much better about her next riding lesson. Dare she say she was even looking forward to it, now that she was so sure the biggest hurdle was out of the way? But she didn't fall right to sleep.

She'd tried to imagine Kendall and herself riding in the park together, pictured herself on a lovely white mare that she was able to handle exceptionally well thanks to Devin. But she kept seeing Devin riding beside her instead. Well, she could blame that on her lessons, which had barely begun. She was taking one too many steps ahead, placing Kendall beside her before she mastered riding. Just thinking she could ride didn't make it so.

But then the memory of that kiss snuck up on her and wouldn't go away. Again, she tried to pretend it was Kendall doing the kissing. That would have made it so much more exciting, she was sure. Yet, that actual kiss had been the most exciting thing she'd ever experienced with a man. While she assured herself Kendall would do even better, she kept seeing amber eyes looking deeply into hers. How aggravating! Obviously, she needed to actually kiss Kendall to make sure he followed her into her dreams instead of Devin. With a low growl, she put her pillow over her head and started counting sheep.

But this morning she was in a chipper mood. Optimism was an amazing thing, brightening the day and putting a smile on her face. Suddenly, once again, she had two men to choose from! Robert Brigston had been forgiven for his less than circumspect behavior the other night. His scandal had died a quick death. Larissa had jotted her a note all about it, but the note had been delivered to the wrong house yesterday, so Amanda didn't receive it until this morning.

It occurred to her that she could forgo any more riding lessons and simply concentrate on Robert, but she put that thought aside. Now that she felt riding was something she *could* accomplish, she wanted to see it through for herself, not just for Kendall—even if it meant she had to continue dealing with Devin.

When she arrived at the farm a little later that morning, she stood in the open doorway of Devin's little office for a few moments before Devin noticed her arrival. He was sitting at the desk, slowly pounding his fist on something flat and circular. She couldn't imagine what it was, but he seemed to be trying to flatten it. No, actually, he didn't really seem to be paying attention to what he was doing, looking quite pensive, even brooding. Was this his typical demeanor when he was alone? She wasn't going to let his dour disposition ruin her splendid mood.

"Hello!" she said cheerily.

He glanced up. "I was expecting you yesterday," he said in a grouchy tone. "When you didn't show, I figured you were going to abandon this project."

"Not a'tall. It just took some time to get this skirt made."

She didn't spread her legs as she'd done in the demonstration for her family, but she pulled the brown velvet material to the side so he could see she wasn't wearing a skirt. She thought that would get a smile out of him. It *was* his idea, after all.

But all she got was a nod and a mumbled "Perfect" as he stood up.

"And besides," she continued, having trouble maintaining a perky tone now, though she still tried, "Pheli pinned me down yesterday to help with the big party she's having at Norford Hall in a couple of weeks."

"I received an invitation. It doesn't sound like it's just for your brother's birthday."

"No, it's going to be a typical country party with all sorts of fun things to do! And there will be a ball to finish it off. D'you think you can have me ready for the party?"

"Can horses fly?"

She laughed and lightly scolded, "Oh, come now, it's not that far-fetched. I'm feeling much better about it now, thanks to you and this newfangled riding habit."

"Glad to hear it." He raised a brow. "Is that gathering at Norford also an occasion to present all the best eligibles for you?"

"Of course! D'you think Lord Kendall will be back from France in time? Pheli found out his address and sent him an invitation, of course."

"So he's still at the top of your list? No new callers lately you're considering instead?"

He sounded a little too curious, as if he was waiting with bated breath for her answer. Was he still considering her his good deed? Still intended to meddle in her affairs? After she'd made it perfectly clear she didn't want his help? Well, not in *that* regard. She did want his help with her riding lessons, and maybe some advice about men if she could get up the nerve to ask him.

She gave him the simple truth. "I don't receive callers other than my friends, haven't since my first Season. And before you make some snide remark about that being responsible for my unmarried state, I'm sure I told you that I don't encourage men I'm simply not interested in. *Kendall* will be allowed to call when he returns. And—" She snapped her mouth shut, deciding not to mention Lord Robert, when all they'd done was argue about him before.

But Devin wasn't letting that by. "And?"

She tsked. "I'm sure you've heard that the truth came out about Robert Brigston, that he'd merely imbibed too much at the ball because of his nervousness, resulting in his overexuberance with the ladies, and his saying things he doesn't even remember saying."

"Your brother bought that nonsense, I suppose?" Devin asked brusquely.

"Why wouldn't Rafe be understanding about it? He's done some foolish things when he's been foxed, too."

"That is the nature of drink. But—never mind. Why don't you just trust me on this: that boy isn't for you. I'd recommend that fortune hunter Farrell Exter before I would Brigston. At least Exter would worship you for what you could bring to his impoverished family."

"Then it's a good thing I'm not taking your recommendations! Besides, the Exters aren't impoverished, Farrell simply isn't in line for the title or the wealth, so of course he's looking for a rich wife and is honest enough to make no bones about it.

Now *why* are you so dead set against Robert?! Just because *you* didn't pick him for me?"

"Of course. That's the only reason."

She narrowed her eyes at his quick agreement, not believing him for a minute. But she noticed his hand was pressing down on that flat thing he'd been pounding, as if he was trying to hide it now. She suddenly recognized its color.

She gasped. "Is that my *hat*?"

"I'm afraid I sat on it."

She turned wide eyes on him. He ought to be blushing but he wasn't. If anything, he looked defensive.

"One of the men must have cleaned off my desk and knocked it on my chair, then forgot to put it back."

"And you decided it wasn't flat enough so you had to pound on it, too?"

The blush she'd expected showed up, but it was so slight, she barely noticed it with his dark tan. "Of course not."

So he had just been distractedly pounding on her hat without realizing it. No matter. She wasn't about to argue with him about a silly hat. To prove it, she smiled and remarked, "Poor hat, it deserves a burial at the very least. Now, shall we get to my lessons?"

He abruptly took her elbow and led her around to the middle aisle. "Where's your chaperone?"

"He got distracted by your horses as we drove up and walked down to the left field for a closer look at some of them."

Devin sighed. "I warned you not to bring your brother."

"I didn't." She kept the smirk to herself.

But she almost laughed at Devin's expression when her chaperone came up the aisle to join them. He'd wanted her to bring a male relative along, but he obviously wasn't expecting it to be the Duke of Norford.

Chapter Thirty-One

DEVIN DIDN'T LIKE SURPRISES of this sort, but he recovered quickly enough, thanks to Preston Locke's friendly and easy-going manner. And the man wanted to talk horses! That put Devin even more at ease. Yet he didn't doubt for a moment that the minx had done this deliberately to discomfit him. Dragging such an important personage along to something so trivial as a riding lesson? When she had an abundance of male relatives of less stature?

So when he got her on the track with her father leaning on the fence rail some distance away watching them, he told her, "No screaming, no fainting, and since you brought your esteemed father to watch, no falling off Sarah today."

He tossed her up into the saddle. She looked down at him to demand, "And what's that got to do with him?"

"It will reflect badly on me, not you."

She snorted delicately but said no more.

Despite her bravado, he could still sense her nervousness, but it wasn't nearly as extreme as what she'd felt the other day.

So most of his brusque sarcasm was intended to help her keep her fears at bay.

As he handed her the reins, he unbent enough to say, "I left orders for Sarah to be exercised daily, so she's no longer eager for a brisk run. Pace yourself and she'll accommodate. Don't worry, you're going to shine."

"I have to, with him watching."

So that's why she'd brought her father today? He provided incentive for her to excel? Devin chided himself for thinking her motive had had anything to do with him. The girl probably didn't give him a thought once he was out of her sight. Why should she? She had so many men ready to hand her their hearts she couldn't keep track of them all—first sons titled or in line to be titled, even second and third sons hoping to get lucky—and none of them illegitimate.

But he didn't have the luxury to forget about her once she was out of sight because she was a job to him. He assured himself that was the only reason she filled his thoughts when he wasn't with her.

"I've been meaning to discuss something with you," she said in a low, secretive tone. "I have no trouble telling if a man finds me attractive enough to, well, you know, but is there something obvious I should be aware of that can help me determine which ones I feel the same about—other than finding them pleasing to the eyes?"

Devin stiffened. Was she serious? Her innocent, curious look said she was.

"Does your heart quicken?" he asked.

"You mean like now? That's just nervousness!"

"I'm talking about how you feel when you're around these men you find attractive. Do you want to get close enough to them to touch them? Are you eager to see them again? Do you think about them constantly?"

Eyes wide, she said, "Thank you! That does clear it up a bit, and why the deuce couldn't my brother tell me that?"

Devin laughed. "You're his baby sister. He's not going to discuss desire with you."

His blunt words left her blushing. If any other woman had asked him that question, he would have thought she was just being flirtatious, but not Amanda. He actually knew more about her now than she'd been willing to volunteer, and now he could add curious to the list. He knew that she was persistent, tenacious, that she wouldn't drop a subject she'd sunk her teeth into. And she was courageous, exceptionally so. But she was hot-tempered, too, at least with him she was. She *might* still like fishing. He could offer to take her fishing to find out for sure. He enjoyed the pastime himself. And she liked to gamble on horses, but not at cards. He'd have to keep all of this in mind.

The session went exceptionally well. Amanda obviously thought so, too, because she chattered nonstop as they walked back to the stable, laughing with her father, effervescence bubbling over, Little Miss Sunshine again.

Before she and her father left, she told Devin, "I think after a few more lessons I will be at the point where I will have to decide if I'm going to take up riding seriously enough to warrant having my own mount. I'll want a white mare if it comes to that. Have you any I can purchase?"

"Why white?"

"Because the only other time I thought about riding again was when I admired an acquaintance on a white horse. I determined that if I ever rode, it would have to be on a magnificent animal like hers."

"They aren't all that common, you know. And the few I have are definitely too fast for you—at this point. They'll demand a hard gallop the moment you mount them. I'm not saying the day won't come when you'll be up for that, but I certainly wouldn't recommend it now."

Her lips turned down in an adorable pout. "Well, that's disappointing."

"Buck up, m'dear," Preston said, and chucked her chin. "You're going to want a gentle animal like the one you're learning on. Don't make me worry about this endeavor by buying a horse you can't easily handle."

"Then I'll let you find me one," she said, grinning at her father. "But it must be white!"

Both men rolled their eyes at her, but Devin stared after the coach as they drove off. He'd actually, for that briefest moment between Preston's suggestion and Amanda's declining it, had the notion to present Amanda with Sarah when she finished her lessons. But since he'd rather not part with Sarah, he wondered why he'd even had the thought! Simply because he'd thought she might appreciate the gesture? An idea designed to please her? Bloody hell, what was wrong with him?

His mood turned sour after that near blunder, though if he admitted it, it was partially because he didn't have the kind of mount Amanda wanted. But with his disposition on a downslide, it was probably an excellent time to visit William's moneylender to take care of that nasty business for his friend.

He wanted to check on Will anyway, to make sure he was still mending well at home, and to pick up the money he was returning to cancel Will's debt. If Blythe *did* still need a dowry,

Devin would sell that town house he had no use for and just wouldn't mention it to Will. But he didn't think he'd have to, especially if Lord Oliver opened his eyes wide enough to see what a gem Blythe was. Devin had caught them twice now deep in conversation and laughter at social events, so he had a feeling that had already happened.

Before long he was heading to the seedier side of town. He had the lender's name, Nathaniel Gator, and his address. It still took awhile to find the place since Devin had never been to that part of London before.

He didn't realize it was a private residence he was entering when he simply opened the door and walked in. A knock might have been appropriate, but then he wasn't there to be appropriate. But he did interrupt a couple of men who were talking in the large foyer.

"Yet another bleedin' nabob?" the bigger of the two men said with a derogatory glance. "Wot are ye gents doing? Passin' my boss's name around at yer fancy parties?"

The other man, tall, lean, and finely clothed, swung around and looked a bit shaken when Devin met his eyes. Embarrassed, no doubt, to be found by someone he knew in a sordid place like this.

Devin wasn't going to pretend he didn't recognize him. He nodded at the young man. "Lord Trask."

"You in debt, too, old chap?" John Trask asked, his tone actually sounding hopeful.

Devin supposed it would make the fellow feel less embarrassed if they were both in the same dire straits. Devin had heard that Trask had gambling debts, apparently too many if he had to come to a lender like this to get them paid off. Devin should

216 ~~ JOHANNA LINDSEY

warn him about the underhanded dealings that occurred here and probably would—once he was done with his task.

"No, I'm here for payback of a different sort," Devin said as he moved closer to the two men. And to the bruiser, he said, "You Gator's strong-arm?"

"Wot if I am?"

"Your boss picked the wrong man for one of his lessons, a friend of mine," Devin explained. "I'm here to make sure it never happens again."

He slammed his fist against the man's cheek, but it barely moved the brute. Devin grinned, anticipating a good workout now. One of the nonmandatory classes at his school had been fisticuffs. Unlike his performance in the etiquette classes, he'd excelled in the ring, not by brute force, but from the skills he was taught. So even a bruiser such as Gator's strong-arm was bound to go down—eventually. It did take about ten minutes though.

Trask didn't stick around to watch. Devin didn't even notice that the lord slipped out while he was busy getting a few bruised ribs himself.

With the bruiser barely conscious on the floor, Devin leaned over to pat his cheeks. "Where's your boss?"

The man pointed down the hall. Devin headed that way and opened a few doors before he found Gator behind one. Sleeping. In the chair behind the desk. Devin didn't believe it.

"Really? Pretending to sleep through that racket?"

The man didn't stir. He was middle-aged, nearly bald, and corpulent. A rather large tray containing empty plates lay on the desk. Devin supposed a heavy meal could have put the man to sleep. Not that it mattered. He shoved the desk toward Gator, ramming it against his chest. That got results.

"What?" Nathaniel Gator said groggily, then straightened in his chair, wide-awake at the sight of Devin. "Who the hell are you and how did—?"

"Let's not waste time," Devin said, tossing the bag of money on the desk. "That's to pay off William Pace's loan." He took the note out of his pocket and ripped it up, then tossed the pieces on the desk, too. "You should have made your terms clear to him. Let me make mine clear to you. You will never send anyone to his home again. If you ever lay a hand on him again, I will kill you."

Having just been paid off, the lender didn't seem inclined to take that threat seriously. "I only sent word that he needed to increase his payments. Two loans to the same bloke is risky, you know."

"That's not *all* you did."

The man actually shrugged. "So my man beat him up a little. It's his job to make sure the recipients of my largess pay me back in a timely manner."

"Pace is bedridden. He nearly died!"

Gator paled. "How can that be? D'you think I'm crazy? That would be like burning my money!"

"Then maybe you should find a new strong-arm. Two stab wounds to the back is attempted murder."

"No!" Gator shot to his feet. "I swear to you Pace was just beat up a little and tossed out, lesson learned. My man came immediately to me to say so and was with me the rest of the evening. If someone took a knife to your friend, it didn't happen here. Bloody thieves! I knew I should have moved to a better part of town now that I can afford it."

"Remember, stay away from Lord Pace." Devin gazed at the lender menacingly. As he walked out of the unsavory den, his thoughts were racing. Devin hadn't really thought Gator could be stupid enough to kill off one of his clients. Street thieves must have attacked Will, as Devin and Will had concluded. The only other possibility would be an enemy who was deliberately trying to kill William, but his friend didn't have enemies, and neither did Donald, whose coach might have been recognized that night. No, Devin was sure it had been desperate thieves.

Chapter Thirty-Two

THE YOUNG MAN SLUMPED into the overstuffed chair in the grand sitting room. His mother, Marianne, raised her eyes from the book in her lap. She didn't raise her head. He hated when she did that. It gave the impression that she couldn't be bothered to give him her full attention.

She glittered with jewels as usual. Even when she didn't leave her suite of rooms in the ancestral mansion, she would still adorn herself with jewels. Of course those jewels were the only thing keeping him out of debtors' prison. But she didn't like giving them to him and had grown more and more angry over the years each time she was forced to part with one of her precious baubles to pay off his debts—until in a fit of pique she'd told him the truth one day, and how he could benefit from it.

The truth had devastated him. Yet she'd discussed it without embarrassment, as if it were nothing out of the ordinary.

"I had an indiscretion ten years after your brother was born," she'd told him that day.

"I'm ten years younger than my brother" was all he could think to say, he was so shocked.

"Exactly. But this can now be to your benefit. I've recently learned that your real father is dying. He's younger than I am! But he led a very dissolute life and is now paying the price for it. Ironically, he's outlived his entire family—all but you."

"How could you!"

She'd merely shrugged. "These things happen. Your father— er, the earl that is, he knew of my indiscretion, of course, and forgave me."

It was more than he could take in all at once. The man he'd believed his whole life to be his father was not truly his father? The older brother whom he adored and had never begrudged anything was only his half brother? And Marianne's husband, the earl, had known all along? It was a wonder the earl had never treated him harshly over the years. Or given his mother the boot. But, apparently, the earl had enjoyed her too much in his bed to go to that extreme.

He'd grown up with all the privileges and benefits a rich, noble family could provide, never suspecting that he didn't actually belong there. He'd thought it natural that his brother, Justin, got all the lavish praise and affection from their father since he was the firstborn. But just recently his mother had divulged that the earl had done him a bad turn before he'd died: he'd made sure his legitimate son knew of his wife's indiscretion. And Justin's relationship with his brother had changed completely after that.

Still, Justin had never told him why his love had turned to contempt. At first, he'd thought it was just his gambling debts piling up—bloody rotten luck that—which Justin was furious about and refused to pay. Yet Justin had also ruined the young man's chances for two good marriages, letting the fathers of those young women know that his younger brother was penniless and without prospects, and if he married, he would no longer be welcome in his own home. That had been spiteful. That had been making sure the hole he'd fallen into just got deeper and deeper. It was a wonder Justin hadn't already kicked him out of his home—and only thanks to their mother that he didn't.

Now he hated this house he'd grown up in, overflowing with luxury, none of which would ever be his. He hated the brother he'd once worshipped. And he was beginning to hate his mother. If she hadn't told him the truth and pushed him to ingratiate himself with his real father, he would never have got his hopes up that wealth could still be his, only to have those hopes dashed by the man's scorn for him. He would never have got himself so deep in debt, sure that gambling was his only way to salvation. Would never have found out about yet another half brother whom his real father was so proud of he was going to leave his entire fortune *and* title all to him. Damned luck was going everywhere but in his own pocket.

His mother didn't know about this other bastard. She'd been so sure that all he had to do was appear at his father's door and everything would fall nicely into place for him. She should have realized that if the man had been jaded enough to have an illicit affair with her, of course he'd have bastards spread all over England. If there were others, he didn't know nor did it matter. *This* one that his father esteemed was standing in his way to the fortune Marianne had assured him would be his.

He thought he could just get away with ruining the bastard, so their father could scorn him, too, but that hadn't worked out a'tall. Killing him was not turning out to be so easy either. The man was bloody well blessed with luck—or *he* was cursed with incompetent thugs, which could be quite true. Hiring brutes off the street probably wasn't an ideal way to go about this business of getting rid of his competition.

His only other option was to kill Justin, but even though he hated his brother now, that hadn't always been the case, so he wasn't really serious when he said to his mother, "Why don't I just kill off your other son?"

She stood up abruptly, walked over to him, and left her handprint on his cheek. "And your nephews, too? *My* grandchildren? *This* title is not going to be yours, and don't you *ever* entertain that notion again."

"I didn't mean it," he mumbled. "I still have one ace up my sleeve."

"Then use it. You're running out of time. Your father could die any day now."

"But he doesn't even like me! I told you he had me investigated. He calls me a loser. He said he's not leaving me anything, that I'd just gamble it away."

Marianne tsked. "He's just disappointed in you, but he's got no one else to leave all that wealth to. He'll come around, as long as you dote on him."

He should tell her about his father's other heir. But he was afraid she'd cut him off, too, if she knew. Because she was depending on him to inherit his real father's fortune so he'd stop begging her for her precious jewels.

Chapter Thirty-Three

Amanda could have laughed at herself as she sat in the coach on her way to the Durrants' town house for a musical soiree. Just three weeks ago she had worried about how to fill her days to alleviate her boredom while in the city. The last few weeks had been a whirlwind for her not just because of the balls, parties, and new-gown fittings, but because of her riding lessons nearly every day and helping Ophelia with arrangements for the house party at Norford Hall. And Kendall did finally show up for tea!

That had been quite an exciting day last week. Kendall was every bit as handsome as she remembered, and she did think about him a lot, just not constantly, but that could simply be because she hadn't seen him for weeks and she'd been so busy. She hadn't even thought to warn Ophelia's butler to allow Lord Goswick past the door. Fortunately, he'd asked for Ophelia, since he was unaware that Amanda was staying at her brother's house now, so he was shown directly to the parlor, where she and Ophelia were having tea while they went over the current guest list.

After a charming smile in Amanda's direction, Kendall said, "You must forgive me, ladies, for not calling sooner. I've just returned from France."

"Yes, Devin mentioned your trip," Amanda said. "Was it successful?"

"Indeed! The Thoroughbred is on his way to my stable as we speak."

"Where is that?" Ophelia questioned politely.

"West of Kent."

"That sounds close to the town of Norford."

"Half a day, perhaps," he agreed.

"Ophelia has sent you an invitation to a house party we're having at Norford Hall next week," Amanda said.

"If you'll be there, I'll be delighted to attend," Kendall assured her. "I should be back by then."

"Back?"

"Yes, the trip to France proved quite exciting because I learned the stallion I purchased has a sibling, a mare from the same parents, though it was sold to a chap from Scotland. But I have his address!"

Amanda and Ophelia both laughed. Obviously, Kendall was hying off for yet another horse, but Scotland wasn't that far away. As long as he didn't delay leaving, he should be back with time to spare for the party. And at least this new trip didn't leave time for him to invite her for a ride in Hyde Park. She still wasn't quite prepared for that since Devin hadn't once suggested she was ready to try the sidesaddle again.

When Amanda stepped inside the Durrants' town house, she was surprised to see such a large gathering for a musical soiree. But a ballroom was at the back of the house, and the Durrants had even gone to the extravagance of filling it with several dozen tables for dinner, making it look almost like a restaurant! Only a few elderly guests were seated at the tables now. The glittering, well-dressed crowd was congregating near the refreshment tables at the back half of the room.

Amanda arrived right on time with her father. She'd learned her lesson about showing up late at the Hammonds' ball, not that the soiree was going to have dancing. And no young gentlemen raced to her side here. But that was solely because of who her chaperone was. Preston Locke was even more daunting to approach than his sister Julie!

She noticed immediately that Devin was present tonight, looking polished in his black jacket and loosely tied cravat. Because he was taller than all the other men in the room, it was impossible to miss him. And because he happened to be glancing her way when she saw him, she gave him a nod in greeting. Even if she didn't approve of his brash manner, they were on what could loosely be called friendly terms now, simply because he was her riding instructor. What wasn't appropriate was his amber eyes giving her the once-over. It almost made her glance down to make sure nothing was out of place. She resisted. She *knew* she looked fetching in the coral silk evening gown with her mother's rubies at her neck, and small, ruby-tipped pins holding her coiffure together.

The second thing she noticed was that Robert Brigston *wasn't* present, while many other eligible bachelors were. She couldn't help wondering why, but it would be inappropriate to ask their hosts when they'd invited such a wide assortment of people tonight, not just young people on the marriage mart. Besides, he might still show up.

"Let me introduce you to an old friend," Preston suggested soon after they arrived.

"Certainly."

He began weaving her through the crowd. But Amanda slowed her step when she saw whom he was leading her to, two of the more well-known matchmakers in the *ton*.

Understanding her hesitancy, he patted her hand on his arm. "It won't hurt to hear what they have to say about your options, will it?"

"But I actually have prospects this year."

"One is still a touchy subject, the other has only been able to call on you once due to his busy travel schedule. Do you actually know either of them well enough to be in love with one of them yet?"

She chuckled at the way he'd put that. "Very well, I see your point. By all means, let's hear what the old dames have to say. Maybe they do actually know some men I haven't already met."

That didn't turn out to be the case, though. Mabel Collicott, the more outspoken of the inseparable duo, expounded on three men as being perfect matches for Amanda. Oliver Norse and Carlton Webb she'd already discounted, but amazingly, Mabel's third choice was Farrell Exter.

Amanda was amused enough to say, "Lord Farrell? You can't really be serious. Doesn't he have a gambling problem? Loves it but isn't any good at it?"

"What young lord doesn't love to gamble? He's just bored, as most of these young men are. Once he's married, I know you'll make sure he toes the line."

She shouldn't have to do that and reminded the old dame,

"He's looking for a fortune to marry. He makes no bones about it."

Mabel raised a scoffing brow. "Everyone on the marriage mart hopes to marry deep pockets. You, m'girl, are the rare exception in not needing that criterion, so in point of fact, Farrell is perfect for you."

"Perhaps you should turn that around and say I'm perfect for *him*." To remain polite, Amanda added, "Thank you for your suggestions. I will duly keep them in mind."

But while Mabel had been praising those three young men, the more soft-spoken Gertrude was whispering to Preston. Amanda was curious enough to ask as they left the pair, "Did Gertrude Allen have another name for us she didn't want her friend to know about?"

"A surprising one that they apparently had a disagreement of opinion about because Mabel took an instant dislike to him. So perhaps it's not worth mentioning."

"But which of those two is *your* friend? Mabel didn't tell me a single thing I didn't already know about her three choices, which, by the by, I've already known for several years now and I'd already decided to give them another chance. But, to be honest, I just think of them as friends.

"Gertrude is who I am acquainted with."

"Then let's hear who she recommended."

"It wasn't so much a recommendation as a suggestion. She said I should pay attention to the sparks that fly when you and Devin Baldwin are near each other."

Amanda gasped.

Her father, hearing her, said, "My thoughts exactly. I can't quite figure out if Gertrude was saying I should keep you away from Baldwin because you two have taken a dislike to each other, or if she somehow relates sparks to—er—attraction."

Amanda was blushing. "I can't deny he's handsome, but he's far too arrogant and utterly lacking in simple manners for me."

Preston gave her a pointed look. "Then should you be taking riding lessons from him?"

She grinned sheepishly. "Yes, we've moved beyond the battleground to an unspoken truce. And I have to give credit where it's due. He does know horses. I've made quite a bit of progress in the past week. Even Alice and Becky, who take turns chaperoning me, have noticed. And Devin's the one who figured out how I could conquer my fear of riding. I'm grateful to him for that, so, well, I bite my tongue when he annoys me now."

Preston laughed. "You? Holding back? What exactly started that battle?"

She tsked. "He gave me unwanted advice that infuriated me. But he *is* Cupid, after all, and for some ornery reason has decided to make *me* one of his good deeds. Which is why he's willing to help me become a good horsewoman."

"Ah, I begin to understand. I suppose he recommends your horse enthusiast, Lord Goswick?"

"Indeed, but only if I actually end up with a love for riding, after I master it, of course."

Preston stopped abruptly. "You aren't serious? I wouldn't have taken him for a fool, but that is the most foolish notion for marriage I've ever heard. *He's* the one you got that silly idea from?"

"No, you misunderstand. He merely saw that I *like* Kendall Goswick. He just doesn't think it will be a good match if I *don't* like riding. I've told you before that horses are Kendall's passion. So it's sound reasoning, I suppose."

"What about this other boy you were interested in? Would you rather have Brigston? We can overlook his nervous first steps into society, if you favor him."

"It's too soon to say, Father. I've barely spoken with him. But I'm hoping both he and Kendall will come to Ophelia's party."

"Yes, I'm looking forward to speaking with them m'self."

She grinned and teased, "You're not going to scare them off, are you?"

"'Course not. Well, unless you say you'd like them scared off, then I'll be happy to oblige."

"I have high hopes for Ophelia's gathering at Norford. If they both come to it, I should know before the end of the house party which one I prefer. Imagine, I just might get myself married!"

"Yes, I've imagined it," he said with much less enthusiasm, but then he hugged her shoulder. "I'm going to miss you, m'dear. Do pick whichever of those two lives closer to Norford."

She laughed. "Don't worry, I'll visit so often you'll be saying, 'You're here *again*?!' Now let me chat with a few of my friends before dinner is served. I just noticed Phoebe Gibbs is here. I'll leave it to you to find which table is ours so I only have to look for you instead of reading all those name cards on each table. I'm surprised our hostess used name cards when this isn't a formal dinner."

"Aren't all these tables a novel idea as well?"

"Yes, but I suppose she just wanted to assure there would be at least one person at each table who is well-known for keeping the conversation lively, thereby assuring the evening is a success."

"You mean chatterboxes like you?"

Amanda giggled. "Exactly!"

Chapter Thirty-Four

AMANDA QUICKLY HEADED STRAIGHT for Phoebe before any of Amanda's beaus noticed she was briefly without her father in tow. She'd hoped Phoebe would have more to tell her about Lord Robert, but she only repeated what Larissa had already mentioned in her note, and nearly verbatim, so she'd probably got her information from Larissa, too. She did have one interesting new tidbit, though.

"Beware Jacinda Brown, Lady Anne's daughter, or have you already met her?"

"I don't think I've even met Anne Brown, much less her daughter."

"Then let me tell you, Jacinda is proving to be quite the minx. She's far too forward in her flirtations, dare I say, improperly so." Phoebe leaned close to whisper, "I wouldn't be surprised if she's—experienced."

Amanda frowned. "You shouldn't spread that around, Phoebe, not without proof."

"Of course I won't," Phoebe said in a wounded tone. "But

you're my best friend and I just wanted to warn you why you should stay clear of her. As bold as she is, she's bound to get into trouble. And she's being quite nasty to any of the young debs seen talking with Devin Baldwin."

Amanda stiffened. "Why?"

"She hasn't actually said so, but it's obvious she's set her cap for him. Yet she's not the only one hopeful in that direction, so tempers have been flaring, enemies are definitely being made, and there's bound to be an unpleasant scene sooner or later because of it."

So jealousy was running amok, over *Devin*? Did he even know? For that matter, was he looking for a wife this Season? If he was, wouldn't someone have mentioned it by now? He was still a hot topic for gossip.

Quite curious now, she asked Phoebe, "Is she here tonight? Jacinda?"

"Over there, already latched onto Baldwin. I wouldn't be surprised if she surreptitiously changed name cards around to make sure she sits with him tonight."

Amanda glanced in that direction. Had Phoebe got into the habit of exaggerating? Amanda had actually noticed Jacinda before in passing. She was one of the prettier debutantes this Season, blond, dark brown eyes, a little taller than normal, a lot more curvaceous than normal. They'd never actually met, but Amanda recalled she'd giggled to herself when she'd seen Carlton Webb ogling the girl's breasts one night. But the young debutante wasn't even talking to Devin as Phoebe had implied. She was chatting with his companion, Blythe Pace. No, actually, he *was* paying attention to their conversation. Was that a sultry look the girl just gave him?

Amanda didn't realize she was grinding her teeth and

burning a hole in Jacinda's forehead with a fulminating glare. But the heat in Amanda's eyes went away when Devin walked away from the two debutantes. Obviously thinking Blythe was well occupied for the moment conversing with Jacinda, he moved several groups away to talk to John Trask. Yet the moment he left, so did Jacinda, and poor Blythe was left standing alone and suddenly looking ill at ease because of it.

Amanda decided to rescue the girl, and telling Phoebe she'd see her at Norford soon, she crossed the room to stand with Blythe. Amanda only had to shake her head sternly at Farrell Exter who was quickly heading to intercept her, to discourage him from it.

"We meet again, Miss Pace," she said in a friendly manner. "How are you enjoying the Season?"

Blythe gave her a warm smile. "Wonderfully."

"It would appear your brother is still trusting you to Devin Baldwin's care?"

"Not by choice. William had an accident recently that will be keeping him in bed for a while."

"I'm sorry to hear that. But he'll be all right?"

Blythe grinned. "Oh, indeed, he's already complaining about it. He deplores idleness."

"Well, let's hope he recovers quickly, because your current chaperone is a little less attentive than he ought to be, isn't he, leaving you alone like this?"

"Actually he's very attentive," Blythe said in Devin's defense, then whispered, "I don't think he likes Jacinda Brown. She keeps joining us, pretending friendship with me, when she isn't the least bit friendly when we're alone. I don't doubt he'll be back in a moment, as soon as he notices she's gone elsewhere."

Amanda wished she could believe that, but it was probably just the impression he wanted to give Blythe. How could he not find Jacinda Brown attractive and her interest in him highly flattering? The chit was too pretty. Then it struck her. Good Lord, this was how she'd felt about Ophelia her first Season! Jealous? Just because Devin was *her* riding instructor? She did enjoy the give-and-take and the challenge he posed during their lessons, so was she feeling a little possessive over a man she was starting to view as a friend and confidant?

"You know him well, do you?" she asked Blythe.

"Oh, yes, since I was so high." Blythe raised a hand that didn't get any higher than their breasts. "My brother brought him home from school every year for a few weeks, and twice he spent the whole summer with us. I used to fancy I was in love with him," Blythe added with a blush.

Amanda pursed her lips. And still was, was her guess, but the girl obviously didn't want to admit it. But when Amanda heard herself say, "Used to?" she did some blushing herself. That was none of her business!

"Well, it's obvious he has no interest in getting married, while I do. And my brother would prefer I settle on someone immensely rich, which Devin isn't. The Baldwins aren't poor by any means, but you know how brothers can be."

And that satisfied Amanda's curiosity. He wasn't wife hunting himself. And she'd pried a little more than she ought to, so she steered the subject back to Blythe. "Making any head-way toward our collective goal this Season?"

"You mean toward marriage?" At Amanda's nod, Blythe confided, "I'm quite impressed with Oliver Norse."

Amanda smiled. "I believe you're both invited to Norford next week. A good time to get to know Oliver better. And it looks like Devin is on his way back to you, so I'll go find my father and our table. Enjoy the rest of the evening, Blythe."

Amanda couldn't leave fast enough. She didn't want to talk to Devin tonight. It still unnerved her to see him in genteel settings such as this, where he seemed so out of place, as big and muscular as he was. And after that silly bit of jealousy she'd just had, for whatever reason, she was afraid her temper was a bit too riled up, and he was the one man who could provoke it without even trying, so the less they spoke tonight the better.

She spotted her father already seated at their table and joined him. And in perfect time. The entertainment for the evening began, a young woman with a lovely voice, with piano accompaniment, who would be singing for the duration of the meal. That was the cue for all to find their seats. Most had already noted their name cards, but some hadn't bothered to, leading to a bit of a confusion for a while, and dinner wasn't going to be served until the last seat was filled.

Amanda wasn't really surprised that Lady Durrant would want the Duke of Norford at her table. But there were six chairs, and when Amanda turned to see who else was being honored to sit with their host and hostess, she met amber eyes she was all too familiar with.

Amanda quickly looked away. She should have guessed. The most lofty title in the room *and* the man whose name was still on everyone's lips were seated at their hosts' table. Quite a coup for the Durrants. And quite an annoyance for Amanda. She would ignore him, of course, and she didn't care how rude it would appear. It was easy to keep her eyes off him. But she couldn't ignore him, not when she was tingling with agitation because of him. She'd never been so *aware* of someone in proximity before. She could smell something spicy coming from him, and, good grief, she could even hear his breathing! But her wish that he'd ignore her and just talk to the others at their table *was* too much to hope for.

He seemed to wait until Lady Durrant had Preston's full attention on Amanda's other side before he said quietly to her, "Will you be coming to the farm at the usual time tomorrow? As long as you're not late, I should have time to make my appointment at the racetrack in the afternoon."

"Yes, I'll be there on time, and I'm always gone before noon," she reminded him without looking at him.

"I know, but I want you to bring your fishing pole along tomorrow."

"Excuse me?"

"We're going to find out if you still like to fish."

Her eyes snapped to his. "Are you still concerned with my interests? I could have sworn you said the only one I needed right now was riding. Which, I should point out, my father thinks is a ridiculous requirement for marriage."

"Yet you're still going to continue?"

"Yes," she mumbled. "But for myself. As for common ground, I'll have you know my brother is happily married and he doesn't share any of his wife's interests, nor she his. They simply love each other to distraction."

She caught his shrug before she glanced surreptitiously around the table to make sure no one was listening to them. Fortunately, two other conversations were progressing loudly enough that their low tones wouldn't be overheard.

"A rarity, that," Devin said. "More often, a marriage will deteriorate to complacency if the couple has nothing in common other than the first bloom."

" 'Deteriorate'?"

"The husband will start looking to greener pastures."

She blushed, as he so often made her do with his bluntness. "This isn't a proper topic of conversation for a dinner party," she reprimanded.

His grin was unrepentant. "Cupid's arrow can sometimes be rather pointed."

Much too blunt as usual, and now she was annoyed because she *would* like to go fishing again, but not with him! So she was going to spite herself and not bring a fishing pole along to her next lesson. She had to make Devin understand that she wouldn't tolerate being *his* good deed.

But before she could mention it, her father asked Devin how she was doing with her lessons, since he hadn't chaperoned her on her last few visits to the farm. Devin complimented her in his reply, and her father sighed, "I suppose we should start looking for her white mare then."

Amanda patted her father's hand. "My fear is completely gone." She grinned. "Of course I haven't gotten *near* a side-saddle again."

"And perhaps you shouldn't. Period."

She laughed. "Can you really picture me riding astride in Hyde Park?"

"No, but I can picture you confining your riding to private property such as our home in Norford, or if you're still doing it for your future husband's sake, on his estate. All points nicely satisfied, including my worry. What do you think, Devin?"

"I'm not a fan of those contraptions either, m'lord. I whole-heartedly agree with you."

But that would mean her lessons were pretty much at an end. The thought should have thrilled her, but it didn't, not at all.

Lady Durrant captured Devin's attention for most of the remainder of the meal, her questions a bit too pointed, but listening to the two without seeming to, Amanda wasn't hearing anything she didn't already know until the lady asked about his father. Her own curiosity was piqued, and she was disappointed to hear him bluntly change the subject without even acknowledging the question.

She passed on dessert and escaped for a few minutes to the terrace while her father lingered at the table, conversing with the Durrants. Quite a few other guests had had the same idea of catching a few breaths of night air, but she didn't join any of the groups and stopped by a tall, narrow statue of a mythical goddess and gazed up at the stars. She loved clear nights such as this when the full spectrum of stars twinkled in the sky, even if it was a bit chilly.

"So you like stargazing, too?"

She'd somehow known it was Devin approaching her, but she didn't take her eyes off the sky. "They're so beautiful."

"Reed and I used to lie out behind the stable when we were children and try to find all the constellations." She was surprised enough to laugh, which made him ask, "You find that amusing?"

She met his eyes, a twinkle in hers. "No, Becky and I used to do the same thing!"

He was standing close enough that she didn't feel quite as cold, yet she still shivered. He must have noticed. He immediately took off his coat and slipped it over her shoulders. His scent surrounded her, a nice scent that she took a deep breath of. The man did have his gallant moments.

"I'm surprised you're familiar with the constellations." He looked up at the sky as well. "Most women aren't."

"My education was a little more rounded."

"And you paid attention?" He grinned.

She chuckled. "Of course! With my father wanting full reports, I had to!"

"How many can you count?"

"I see three."

"There's a fourth."

He was pointing to his left, yet he was gazing down at her. She was arrested by the sudden intensity in his gaze, by how much brighter the amber in his eyes looked, and by his husky tone, which was almost like a caress when he said, "They're as beautiful as the stars."

"What is?" she heard herself whisper.

"Your eyes."

Amanda drew in her breath.

Devin abruptly took her arm, but it was to lead her back inside! He took her straight back to her father, who'd left their table, but was still having a few more words with their hosts. Devin thanked them for the evening, bid them good night, and Amanda was sure he wasn't going to say another word to her, he seemed so eager to collect Blythe and get out of there.

Yet he did, just two words: "Fishing pole." Which left her gritting her teeth. They'd actually shared—dare she say—a romantic moment? No, not romantic. That man wouldn't know *how* to be romantic. But it had been pleasant. Yet trust him to summon forth the rude brute to ruin it.

Chapter Thirty-Five

IT WASN'T DEVIN'S HABIT to do anything spontaneously. But he'd done just that last night when he'd told Amanda he was taking her fishing. What if she brought her father with her again? He couldn't exactly ask a duke to go fishing with them! This was a good example of why he never did anything spontaneously.

But he had to laugh at himself. A pond was near his farm, but he didn't even know if it had any fish in it. He'd never exactly had time to find out. He didn't have a fishing pole, either. His old one was at the Lancashire farm, but he was able to borrow his uncle's for the day, just in case Amanda took him up on his offer.

But he was going to be late getting to the farm today. Not because of traffic. The residential street was as empty as it usually was that early in the morning. But because the very last thing he ever expected to happen was to pass his father, who was just stepping out of his coach on that quiet street. He didn't recognize Wolseley at first. He'd never forget that coach, though, and the crest on it, or how many nights he'd stared at it from his window.

He harbored such a deep rage for this man who had taken his mother's love and had given so little in return—and had given Devin nothing of himself. The rage rose up, so overwhelming him he didn't even know how he got off his horse, didn't even realize he'd slammed his fist into Lawrence Wolseley's face—until he was looking down at him sprawled on the sidewalk, and Wolseley's driver leapt down from the coach to try to hold him back from hurting his employer any further.

But it was impossible to restrain him. Devin threw the man off. But some of the maddened haze was starting to clear as he snarled at Lawrence, "You cost me the last months of my mother's life!"

Lawrence looked confused and angry to have been attacked, he must have assumed, without provocation. He hadn't changed all that much in the nineteen years since Devin had last seen him. His hair was just as dark, he still dressed just as impeccably. If he was in his fifties yet, he didn't look it.

"Who are you and what the devil are you talking about?" Lawrence demanded.

"Elaine Baldwin?" Devin reminded the man. "My God, you don't even remember her?"

"Of course I—Devin? Is that you?"

Only then did it occur to him that Lawrence Wolseley wouldn't recognize him. Of course he wouldn't, Devin had been a child the last time they had seen each other. That realization did nothing to assuage his anger, but at least he was no longer blinded by it.

Lawrence waved his driver back from trying again to restrain Devin, but he obviously wished he hadn't when Devin said, "You can't imagine how many times I've thought about killing you."

The man paled. "Is that your intention?"

"I want to know why you've ignored me my whole life. Just tell me that. Give me a bloody excuse, anything, so I can understand how a man could—"

"I think you're under a misconception."

"Like hell I am!" Devin growled. "She sent me away because of you!"

"No, she sent you away because you were asking questions she felt you were too young to hear the answers to."

"That I'm a bastard? Did she really think I couldn't figure that out?"

"Yes, but not mine."

The mindless rage nearly returned. Devin didn't think the man would deny it at this point. He could feel the urge to beat the truth out of Wolseley rising within him.

Then, slowly getting to his feet, Wolseley added, "I do have a few, you're just not one of them. I actually wish you were. But I know your father. I was a friend of his for many years."

Devin didn't believe him. " 'Was'? I suppose you're going to tell me he's dead?"

"*Was* as in 'not any longer.' He confided in me and asked me to keep an eye on you and Elaine for him. I'd never met your mother before then. He asked that of me because he didn't want to do it himself. He thought it would encourage her and it probably would have. He hoped she'd get on with her life and forget about him. Believe it or not, he was fond of Elaine, in his fashion. And she didn't know he already had a wife when she was involved with him, or she might not have—"

"Had me?" Devin cut in icily.

Lawrence nodded sadly. "I'm not going to pretty him up for you, Devin. Your father was a lecher of the worst sort. Thathe was married, that he even had children from his marriage, he never volunteered any of that personal information until he was ready to move on to the next sexual conquest. Because he was so exceptionally handsome, women fell in love with him all over the country, and he took full advantage of it. But he wasn't really in the habit of ruining young girls from good families. Your mother was one of the few exceptions."

Lawrence might sound sincere, even look it, but Devin was still having trouble believing what he was hearing. His whole life he'd thought *this* man was his father.

"She claimed you were our landlord, yet I found out that was a lie when that damned house was left to me. How do you expect me to believe *this*?"

"Because deep down you know it is true. Good God, do you *really* think I could have ignored you if you were mine? Every time I saw you, I saw him, and I already hated him by then. You *do* look like him, you know. Well, obviously you don't know, but you do. You have his eyes, you have his height. You're not his spitting image, but I still see the resemblance from when he was a young man."

"It's very easy for you to say all this when the one person who could confirm it is dead, yet I *know* you were her lover."

"Ah, so that's it, yes, of course it is. No wonder you thought I was your father. Very well, I see I must confess a little more."

"The truth at this point would be welcome."

Wolseley actually sounded frustrated when he said, "I'm giving you the truth, as much of it as I can. I didn't mean to fall in love with your mother. I thought I could check on her and maintain my distance while doing so. But she was so gracious, so beautiful, and so obviously lonely, being estranged from her family because of her unfortunate situation. I stopped by more often than I should have. We became friends and . . ."

"Lovers."

"Not immediately. Not until a year later did she admit she'd come to love me. I'd loved her from the beginning, but I never once made any overture until that confession. He'd given her that house. It was the house he'd kept his mistresses in. He gave her nothing else. She was barely getting by that first year. I arranged for her to have a monthly stipend so she could live as she was accustomed to. I didn't tell her it was from me. For a while she thought it was from him. But she finally figured it out. It may have just been gratitude that turned her feelings for me to love, in the beginning. I don't know. But she eventually came to love me as much as I loved her. I'm sure of it."

"Who is he?"

"I can't tell you that. I am twice sworn not to. And beating me won't change that!" Lawrence added sharply when Devin started rubbing his fist.

"I'm not going to hit you again."

Looking relieved, Lawrence continued, "After your mother died, I stopped keeping an eye on you. I don't know if your father tasked anyone else to do so. I had come to despise him long before she died."

"Twice sworn to whom?"

"Both of your parents."

"One is dead and you say you hate the other, so who exactly are you protecting by not giving me his name?"

"I'm not protecting anyone. My word was given. My word

is my honor. But Elaine was going to tell you. She promised she was going to. Even when she knew she was dying, she said she would."

"How do you know?"

"I was with her those last days," Lawrence said. "I wouldn't leave her side."

Devin's urge to hit the man returned just for that. "I didn't see her again from the day she sent me away. She told me nothing!"

"I don't understand. She was determined that you be informed of his identity when you were old enough to understand why she did what she did. She didn't want you to know while you were still a child."

"And how was she supposed to tell me when I reached adulthood? From the grave?! If you know she wanted me to know at this time in my life, then tell me! I'm not a bloody child anymore!"

"I'm sorry, I can't. But I agree, you should know by now, it just can't be from me. I don't know what arrangements she made. She could have left the matter to a solicitor to handle when you reached a certain age. I just don't know."

"Is he still alive? You can at least tell me that."

"I haven't heard otherwise, but then I don't live near here. This is my first trip to town in ten years. Elaine was the only thing that kept me in London. I returned to my country estate after she died to devote myself to my own family. I haven't seen or spoken to your father in over twenty years. But to be honest, I hope he's dead. That's how much I hate him, for what he did to her."

Chapter Thirty-Six

IT WAS *NOT* A good time for Lord Robert to call. Amanda probably shouldn't have told the butler that she would receive him and Lord Kendall, if they did call. That could have waited until after the country gathering, where she expected to see them anyway. Besides, she was a bit peeved at him for having disappeared these last couple of weeks. Kendall's absence was understandable, he hadn't been in the country long enough to visit other than that once. But what excuse did Robert have for not even appearing at the recent social events?

But there he was, sitting in the parlor with her father when she entered it. While at any other time she might have been thrilled that he was calling on her, this morning she definitely wasn't.

She was dressed for her riding lesson, and no one other than her family and her riding instructor were supposed to see her wearing that odd skirt! So she was immediately embarrassed by it, which, no doubt, accounted for her not being very cordial to Robert.

But her father was. He'd recognized the name and had casually been grilling the young lord about himself and his family. *Grilling* was an apt way to describe Preston Locke's conversational style when he wanted information, yet he did it with such finesse, no one could possibly feel he was being interrogated!

Robert immediately leapt to his feet at her entrance, probably glad to be rescued from her father. His blond hair was a bit mussed—had he been nervously running his hand through it? But he was otherwise impeccably dressed in a dark gray suit and appeared just as handsome as she remembered him.

Still highly embarrassed over her own attire, she briskly crossed the room to him and extended a hand in greeting, but her tone was rather terse. "How nice to see you again, m'lord, but your timing isn't ideal. My father and I are going out this morning."

"If you must," Robert said with a grin, and bent to kiss her hand instead of giving it the bare touch of fingers that she'd expected. "Even a few moments in your presence has brightened my day."

"We aren't leaving quite yet," Preston told her. "Julie sent a note that she'd like to join us. So make yourself comfortable until she gets here."

That was unexpected, prompting Amanda to ask, "Does she know where we're going?"

"Indeed, and she's challenged me to a race," he said with a chuckle. "It's been quite a few years since she's done so, but nothing out of the ordinary. And she didn't want to miss this opportunity, access to—"

He was going to say *a racetrack*! She quickly shook her head, enough for her father to see that she'd rather not have Robert learn where they were going. She did *not* want it spread around that she was only just now learning to ride. All these years she'd found excuses of one sort or another to decline all suggestions and events that included riding. Not even her closer friends had known that she hadn't been on a horse since she was a child or why.

So she helped her father finish that thought by saying, "Access to you, since you so rarely come to London. I understand, Father."

She did, too. She knew that bit of family history quite well. All of her aunts, with the exception of Esmerelda, who was the oldest, used to race their brother on horseback. It was the only sport, hobby, or game at which they thought they had a chance of beating Preston, which they very much wanted to do to get back at him for his constant teasing of them. He still teased them, but she'd thought the racing was a thing of the past.

Robert was merely listening to them. He might be curious, but it wouldn't be polite to voice it. Amanda couldn't take her father's suggestion and sit, either. Robert might not notice she was wearing baggy britches while she was standing, but he would if she sat down because then the baggy britches would tighten about her legs. Color still on her cheeks because of her attire, she moved over to the window to watch for her aunt's arrival, actually giving Robert Brigston her back. She didn't even realize it might appear to him that she was snubbing him.

But he was persistent. "I wanted to apologize for the evening when we first met," Robert said, following her to the window. "I—wasn't m'self."

"Yes, we've heard. Unfortunate, but not a unique occurrence by any means."

"I was so worried that you, of all the ladies, would hold it against me. Thank you for understanding."

She shrugged lightly. "I didn't make as much of it as others did. But you may be even more relieved to know that my brother has decided he doesn't need to shoot you." Robert blushed. She allowed that was enough punishment for all the lectures she'd had to endure because of him, so she relented enough to add, "I was only teasing—well, not really, but it's nothing you need to worry about now."

"I'm relieved. I wish I could have found out sooner, but it was the worst timing, to hurt my foot later that week."

He extended the foot he was talking about. Amanda glanced down and could see nothing amiss, yet her natural sympathy shot to the fore. "How dreadful to be injured at the height of the Season! Did you break it?"

"No, nothing as serious as that. But the sprain was bad enough that I went home to convalesce rather than try to hobble around London. Couldn't fit in my shoes, anyway, while it was swollen, but as you can see, I've mended."

The smile she finally bestowed on him seemed to put him at ease. He began talking about some of the men he'd met at the ball and subtly asking what she thought of them. She knew the question he really wanted to ask was if she was interested in any of them in particular. But she recalled a piece of advice Julie had given her during her first Season—never let a man know he *doesn't* have any competition—so her answers were a bit evasive.

Aunt Julie finally arrived, and with hurried introductions *and* good-byes, they were finally in the Locke coach on their way out of town, with Julie's and Preston's mounts tied to the back of it.

Her father had only one thing to say about Robert's short visit. "Are you *sure* you like that boy? It didn't quite seem so."

Amanda sighed. "Yes, I do. I was just embarrassed to be seen in this outfit, hardly at my best."

She indicated the pale blue split skirt with matching jacket, then burst out laughing when Julie lifted the flap on her own skirt to show the same design, saying, "I confess I liked the idea so much, I had one done up for m'self."

"I'm surprised you didn't do that years ago," Preston put in. "Instead of wearing britches under your skirts."

"I know! You probably would never have won a race if I had!"

"As for Robert," Amanda added with a grin, "if I'm not at least a little cold to him because of his near scandal, he won't be repentant enough to make sure it never happens again."

"Sound reasoning, I suppose," Preston allowed.

"Perfect reasoning," Julie agreed, then changed the subject abruptly. "I'm looking forward to seeing Cupid's farm. It's hard to picture him as a serious horse breeder if he's as good at matchmaking as they say."

"And here I thought you just invited yourself along for our race." Preston laughed.

Julie snorted. "You and I can race anywhere, though the opportunity to beat you on an actual track *did* motivate me."

Preston laughed. "You could have just asked us about Devin. He's definitely a serious breeder. Remind me to show you Rafe's birthday present while we're there. It's not being delivered until the party next week. Magnificent animal."

Julie raised a brow. "This is a well-kept secret, I suppose?"

Amanda laughed. "Just from Rafe."

"Ah, well." Julie put her arm through Preston's, who was sitting next to her. "I'm still going to beat your father today, quite worth the trip."

Devin wasn't at the farm when they arrived. Reed Dutton had been sitting on the steps of the large house with his daughter, Amelia, and came over to inform them, "Devin isn't here yet. He's never this late, so he might not make it today."

Amanda immediately felt disappointed, though she assured herself it was just because she didn't think she would have time for any more lessons before she returned to Norford with her family this weekend. Disappointed because she couldn't ride? She nearly laughed at the thought. Yet that must have caused her crestfallen feeling. Or was it that she'd simply got used to spending time with Devin? She did feel at ease with him these days, possibly because he treated her so differently from other young men, not as a potential marital prize, but as a person.

Amelia must have noticed her disappointment because she offered, "You can ride my pony today if you like."

Amanda chuckled for the child's sake, saying, "That's all right. I think my feet would drag on the ground!"

As long as they were already there, Preston and Julie still took their mounts over to the little racetrack to have their race. Amanda followed them on foot, then leaned her elbows on the fence to watch them. She didn't doubt her father would win— though, come to think of it, he didn't always. She'd heard at least two of her aunts crow about beating him before, including Julie.

Amanda didn't turn when she heard the footsteps behind her, but her disappointment vanished. She guessed it was Devin and tensed in anticipation. She never knew what to expect from him anymore. That compliment from him last night had floored her, though she suspected his quick exit from the party meant he hadn't meant to show her that sweet side of himself. It must just have slipped out and he regretted it. Yet they had progressed to cordial talks—mostly. He could make her laugh without even trying. But she was just a client to him. That one kiss they'd shared had never been repeated. He'd probably already forgotten it while she couldn't—there! She was remembering it again!

"Did you leave your fishing pole in the coach?" was the first thing he said to her.

He had to bend a little to rest his arms on the fence, too. He was standing so close to her that their shoulders actually brushed, and for some odd reason it sent gooseflesh running down her arm. She hadn't even looked at him and wasn't going to, yet she still felt surrounded by his presence.

But what had he said? She huffed to herself as she calmed her flustered state and focused on his question.

"I don't need to test something I know I like doing. Having been reminded of that fact, I intend to do some fishing while I'm at home next week, which is where my pole is, tucked away in my closet, forgotten—until now."

"Was that a thank-you I just heard?"

She burst out laughing. "I suppose it was."

After a few moments he noticed her relatives. "What are they doing?"

"Having a race." She kept her eyes on Preston and Julie galloping around the track. "Most of my father's sisters challenge him to one from time to time."

"And he loses deliberately?"

She glanced at Devin now. "What do you mean?"

"He's holding back. His mount is clearly the faster of the two, yet he's keeping abreast of your aunt instead of leaving her in the dust."

She looked back at her father on his large gelding and

chuckled as she realized Devin was right. "So he is. I suppose he would let them win occasionally, just because he loves them. I have a feeling he's done that before."

Preston didn't do that today, though he had probably intended to. But with Devin there watching, at the last moment Preston shot ahead and won. Amanda guessed it was Devin's fault. Her father wouldn't want Devin mentioning that it had looked as if he was deliberately losing, which Devin might well have done as blunt as he usually was and not knowing the circumstances.

But this made Julie disgruntled, so her tone was about as gruff as it could get when she and Preston cantered over to the fence where Amanda waited, and Julie said to Devin, "I've a bone to pick with you, Cupid."

Devin burst out laughing. "Another bone picker?"

Julie ignored that. "You look like a sensible man, yet you *really* think the only way my niece can win that young buck she's interested in is by riding with him?"

"No, ma'am." Devin grinned at Julie. "I'm sure she can win him for any number of reasons. She's beautiful, she's courageous, and occasionally she's even amusing. My concern was for after they marry, because horses are his passion, but they definitely aren't hers. Consider his disappointment if she doesn't enjoy, at least occasionally, the one thing he loves to do most."

Julie snorted and said baldly, "I don't believe I just heard a *man* say that. Look at the gel. She'll make any man happy, even this horse lover, with barely any effort. But you got her back on a horse, which isn't a bad thing."

With a huff Julie rode toward the gate that a worker was opening. Preston said to Devin before he followed her, "That was my sister Julie Locke St. John, the most outspoken of my siblings."

"I've met the lady, so I'm already acquainted with her manner."

"Have you?" Preston said in surprise. "You'll have to tell me about that sometime. It probably won't surprise you to know I agree with Julie on the matter of winning a husband through his equestrian heart, but Mandy has assured me these lessons are for her, not for a future husband. Besides, for whatever reason they began, you've helped her conquer her fears, and for that I heartily thank you. I'm sure she'll excel at it before you're done."

Amanda was still stunned by the compliments she'd just heard from Devin, but she also bristled at the way he'd just changed his tune about her ability to win Kendall for her aunt's sake.

When Amanda turned away from the racetrack, she saw that Devin had brought his horse down to the track and that a groom was just then delivering Sarah to them, already saddled.

As Devin offered his cupped hands for her to step on, Amanda reminded him, "You said I'd lose Kendall if I don't ride with him."

"No, what I was getting at was he *could* shrug you off if he knows you won't ride."

"I've gone through this hell for a 'could have'?!"

"No, you proved something to yourself—that you can tackle anything, even your own fears, with the right incentive. You don't think that was worth discovering?" She started to answer, but he added, "Bloody hell, so now I have to make sure you *excel* at this?"

His obvious irritation at her father's order banished her own anger completely. "I'm sure you'll manage somehow," she said with a smirk.

"No, *you* better manage it. I was going to say you're ready for a ride with Kendall, but now I'm not so sure."

"You really thought I was ready?"

"With limitations, one being that you keep it slow. You can do that by using the excuse that you want to be able to talk with him while you ride. The other limitation is that—well, I do agree with your father, you should forget about the sidesaddle. If you'll be embarrassed to be seen in that skirt in Hyde Park, I suggest you ride with Kendall at Norford instead. You might even mention your dislike of the sidesaddle and why. Or we could resume your lessons at Norford."

Since he was apparently all business again, she told him, "I'm going for final fittings this afternoon, since I needed new gowns for the weeklong party, and we're going home this weekend to start preparations. The guests will start arriving early in the week, but I suppose we could get in a few more lessons at Norford Hall, if you'd like to come early." She grinned. "Not a bad idea, since that will guarantee you a room in the house. Those will go fast, once everyone starts arriving."

"I imagined a duke's home would be huge. It's not?"

"'Course it is, but Norford Hall has never had a party like this one, at least not after the last of my aunts moved out. The guest list is already approaching several hundred! We'll need to make arrangements with some of our neighbors to accommodate the overflow."

He mounted his horse, which had been eyeing Sarah from the moment she got there. "We're going to ride a circuit around the grounds today. Kendall's usual mount is a stallion. We need to see how you do riding next to one. It will be his duty to control his horse, and while I have absolutely no doubt that he will do so, the test is for you to see that all you need to do is not get nervous if the stallion comes too close."

That sounded easy enough, but it wasn't. Devin didn't control his own stallion today one little bit, and Amanda lost count of how many times both brutes got too close to her and Sarah. Odious man, he did it deliberately!

Chapter Thirty-Seven

She's beautiful, she's courageous, and occasionally she's even amusing. Amanda couldn't get that statement out of her thoughts. Compliments from Devin? It had almost sounded as if he liked her!

Even her father had remarked on what Devin had said about her on the ride back to town that day, saying with a grin, " 'Occasionally amusing'?"

Julie had burst out laughing and said to her brother, "You noticed that, too? Sounded as if he admitted that part grudgingly. 'Course *we* know you can be amusing and delightfully so, Amanda." Then Julie asked her pointedly, "Do you restrain yourself because you like him?"

Amanda had been blushing by then and mumbled, "I'm usually too infuriated with him to notice much else. He's a fine instructor. He's helped me to overcome my fears. But he's the most exasperating man I've ever met, brazen, too blunt, arrogant, provoking—"

Julie cut in, "Methinks she protests too much *and* forgets to mention how handsome he is."

"I *don't* like him," Amanda had insisted. "I merely tolerate him."

But she did find him fascinating, how could she not? He *was* like no man she'd ever before met. And she was having a deuced hard time getting him out of her mind ever since she'd returned to Norford with her family, even with Ophelia keeping her quite busy with her long list of tasks that had to be done prior to the guests' arrival.

But she'd known she was going to have some time to herself this afternoon and had planned ahead, arranging with one of the stable lads yesterday to find her some worms. The boy had been surprised that a lady would even want to go fishing. He didn't mention the time of year as a deterrent, but why would he, when he'd bragged he'd gone fishing just last week and stretched his arms to show her how big his catch had been.

And the weather did cooperate, splendidly so. The breeze was only slight, the sun had decided to shine, so it almost felt like an early-spring day rather than heading toward deeper winter. She found a dip in the creek with a slope at her back, which would keep the breeze away. It hadn't been cold enough at night yet for the creek to freeze along its edges. She was actually overdressed and a little too warm now with the sun shining directly down on her, enough that she was debating whether to take off her coat and gloves.

Well, maybe just the coat, which she shrugged out of. She stared at her little container of worms and wondered if she could bait her hook with her gloves on, or if they were too bulky for that. She should probably have invited the stableboy along to do it for her, but she realized she'd wanted to be able to brag to Devin that she'd been able to bait her own hook without even cringing about it. Now if she could just muster the nerve to do so.

"I confess, I didn't expect to find you here."

She gasped and glanced up behind her. She could only make out a silhouette of a man standing at the top of the little slope, with the sun behind him. But she'd recognize that deep voice anywhere.

"What are *you* doing here?"

Devin came down the slope and stood next to the thick wool blanket she'd brought along to sit on. Without the sun in her eyes, she saw that he carried a fishing pole himself and had already removed his jacket, which he held by a finger over his shoulder. "You said you fished as a child," he reminded her. "So I knew you had to have a good creek or pond nearby. I asked and was pointed in this direction."

"Yes, but you actually brought your pole to Norford? So you planned this ahead?" Then she scowled, wondering if he was reverting to his high-handedness. "Or were you intending to drag me out here?"

He chuckled. "No, I had just been looking forward to fishing with you the other day simply because I'd been reminded how much I used to enjoy it. Your declining to join me didn't change my wanting to fish again. And I figured I would have idle hours here that I usually don't have back home, so now would be an excellent time."

His sudden presence might have flustered her, but that was no excuse for jumping to wrong conclusions. She grinned to make amends. "In the winter?"

He chuckled. "I notice it didn't stop you—though it would appear the worms were going to."

She winced as he looked pointedly into the little container. "I was going to try it with my gloves on."

"And now you don't have to." He hunkered down to pull out a single worm and hold his other hand out for the hook she had in her lap. She handed it over with an exuberant "Thank you!" and quickly stood up so she didn't have to watch the gruesome process.

"There you go, Mandy. Now show me if you even know how to cast that thing."

"Of course I do. My brother was a good teacher." She whipped the line out into the water to prove it, then sat back down. "Help yourself to some of my worms, there are plenty."

He did, and after another moment his line was also in the water, but instead of holding his pole, he anchored it between some rocks close by, then asked, "Are you going to offer to share that blanket as well?"

Amanda wasn't expecting that. She hadn't exactly spread the blanket wide, having kept it folded for added thickness. But as long as he was being so cordial, she scooted over to the edge to make room for him. A mistake! As he sat down cross-legged next to her, one of his knees pretty much crossed her lap, and his arm rested firmly against hers. He made no effort to correct how close they were now, though she had to allow there probably wasn't any room to spare on his side of the blanket. But he didn't even seem to notice, so she held her tongue. It would be too prudish of her to ask for more room when the man had almost lain on top of her, as close as two people could be, to give her a lesson in kissing that *she* had provoked with a loose tongue. Darned whiskey.

Why did she have to remember that now? To put that lesson firmly from her mind, she said, "So you decided to be the first guest to arrive just so you could get in some fishing today? Or did you come early to give me more riding lessons so I'll be ready to ride with Lord Kendall while he's here?"

"Neither. You don't have to ride with Kendall here, either. It's a social gathering, so you can come up with any number of excuses why you need to remain in the house."

"So we're not going to have any more lessons while you're here?" She was appalled to hear the disappointment in her voice and hoped he didn't catch it.

But, apparently, he didn't notice it because he merely shrugged. "If you want to get up early for more lessons here, I'm sure we can keep it from his notice. The *ton* does tend to sleep inordinately late."

She grinned. "Indeed. And that's a splendid idea. But if not for fishing or extra lessons, why did you come early then?"

"I had to visit a breeder in the area, just a few hours from here. I also wanted to make sure your brother's present is on hand for tomorrow. The stallion is stabled in Norford Town, to assure the surprise."

"With as many horses as you have, you still buy from other breeders?"

"Only when I don't have what a customer wants."

He said that with some annoyance, leading her to guess, "It's important to you to satisfy all of your customers?"

"No, just this one in particular. The breeder I tracked down specializes in whites. I was worried they wouldn't meet all the requirements, but a few did. Your new mare is stabled at Norford Hall."

Her eyes rounded. "You found me a white?!"

He glanced to the side and grinned at her. "As gentle as you could ask for."

She squealed in delight and, without thinking, threw her arms around his neck, releasing her fishing pole. It slid into the water. Devin laughed, ran over to the creek, and retrieved the pole for her. After anchoring it in a pile of rocks close to where she sat, he resumed his seat. It gave her a moment to get rid of the blush from belatedly realizing she shouldn't have hugged him. But since he appeared to think nothing of it, had only been amused that it caused her to lose her pole, she put it from her mind.

Besides, she was so incredulous that he'd gone out of his way to do this for her, it left her all bubbly inside, and she had no one to share that with! She had so many mixed feelings about this man—and no one to talk to about it. It made her miss her mother all the more, the only person with whom she would have been able to share a special moment like this.

"You're sharing it with me."

She blinked. Surely she didn't say any of those thoughts aloud?!

"It's—it's just that I've missed her keenly since my come-out."

"What was she like?"

"Beautiful, soft-spoken. What I remember most often is she was always smiling. Always, as if she kept wonderful secrets."

"Did she?"

"No, she was just so happy, and so much in love with my father."

Devin smiled gently. "I see now why you'll settle for nothing less, nor should you."

"Yes, their happiness did leave quite an impression on me.

I just wish I could have had more time with her. I appreciate my aunts and Ophelia, but it's not the same as having a mother to advise me and give me more self-confidence. I could tell her anything and not be embarrassed by it. Do you know what I mean?"

"I know what it's like to miss a mother, yes." He looked away, picked up a small pebble, and seemed to angrily throw it at the water.

Hesitantly she asked, "Were you close to yours?"

"I was, until I started asking too many questions and she sent me away to live with her brother. And then she died."

That was definitely bitterness she was hearing, but she attributed it to his feeling abandoned by her death, the same way she'd felt when her mother died. "They say your father died when you were a baby. How much worse it must have been for you, to not have either parent growing up."

He turned a sharp look on her. "That was a lie to hide my mother's indiscretion. My real father isn't dead. The bastard wanted nothing to do with me. I don't even know who he is!"

Chapter Thirty-Eight

DEVIN WAS ILLEGITIMATE? AND bitter about it, by the sounds of it. But what struck Amanda's heart most deeply was that he'd grown up without a mother and a father's love. At least she'd had her father, and a brother who'd compensated in his way, and a huge extended family of aunts, uncles, and cousins. What had Devin had?

She suddenly felt like crying for him and had to fight back the tears. His rough-around-the-edges attitude wasn't from the lack of genteel upbringing as she'd thought, it was from losing what meant the most to him so early in his life. Did he want to let no one close to him because of it?

Staring at her, his expression turned confused. "Why do you look sorry for me? I didn't mean to blurt out my secret, but why aren't you disgusted by it?"

She gave him a tender smile without realizing it. "We can't arrange who we are born to, Devin. It's not *your* fault your mother had an indiscretion that resulted in you. There was nothing you could have done to prevent what she did, so why would you take the blame for it? It's got nothing to do with the man you are."

"Of course it does," he said harshly. "I am branded unacceptable by my peers. I am denied a lady of good birth for my wife because of it."

"Why? Your peers don't even know."

"Do you really think I could keep something like that from a woman I wanted to make my wife or her family?"

She gave him a slight grin. "Ah, I see, good conscience, an excellent quality. You're proving to be one surprise after another today."

"And you're proving to be as exasperating as always. I am a *bastard*. Why do you seem to be shrugging that off? No one else from your station of life would."

"I understand why you think that way. Yes, some fathers might deny you their daughters if they knew of this, yet some might not. You'd be surprised how many families of quality have that same secret hiding in their ancestral closets. I can count a few I know of where it's not even a secret. We've even had kings who've been born on the wrong side of the blanket!"

He snorted at her reference to the royals. "When an heir to the throne is needed, exceptions are made real quick. That's not the case—"

"Oh, stop. If you didn't know about this, it wouldn't be an issue for you, would it? Fie on whoever told you this secret."

"No one told me," he replied bitterly. "I figured it out for myself."

"So you aren't even sure?"

"I am now. My uncle knew and finally admitted it to me when I confronted him about it."

And Devin had let this govern his whole life, she guessed. It

was obvious he felt unworthy because of it. Again she felt like
crying for him. No one should feel like that based on something
that had happened before they were even born, but him—why
did she hurt for him? And she did. It was painful to see how
adversely he'd let this affect him.

Without thinking, her compassion impelled her to place a
soothing hand on his knee, which was still bent halfway across
her lap. But she immediately caught the mistake and gasped.
Touching a man's leg for any reason was so far beyond the pale.
She tried to cover the gasp with a cough, but he'd heard it. Her
touch didn't go unnoticed either. He actually took her hand in
his and brought it to his lips. Merely to thank her for understanding?

"Your empathy astounds me, Mandy," he said softly. "You
keep revealing the unexpected."

And he didn't? But she somehow felt closer to him after he'd
shared his secret with her. Perhaps they were even becoming
friends. . . .

"I'm glad you didn't soak the blanket with your tears," he
added.

She finally risked glancing at him, then chuckled to see
the teasing light in his eyes. "I only cry to good effect. Ask my
brother, he'll assure you of that."

"Little liar. The least I can do is remove your sadness on my
account."

He was suddenly looking at her so heatedly she thought she
might melt. Before he drew her closer with the hand he hadn't
yet let go of, she knew what he was going to do, and that *would*
definitely banish all of her sad thoughts. She had time to stop it.
She didn't. She probably couldn't have if she actually wanted to.
Instead she stared in fascination as he slowly drew her across his

lap until she was cradled there in his arms. Then he slowly bent to kiss one of her cheeks, then the other, then even her brow.

He drew back only slightly to say in husky tones, "That was to thank you for your understanding. This, however, is just for me."

This was the kiss she'd anticipated, the one she'd been waiting for since the last time his lips had touched hers. That had to be why passion sprang so quickly to life inside her. She'd thought about kissing Devin so often, had wondered if she'd ever experience it again, and now that she was, she held tight to his neck, reveling in the taste of him again.

His fingers gently touched her cheek, then her neck, but she truly caught fire when his hand moved lower and was suddenly resting lightly over one of her breasts. Although she barely felt his hand through the thickness of her clothes, simply the idea that he was touching her there inflamed her and brought forth a moan. Hearing it, he deepened the kiss, his tongue luring hers to dance with his, his hand moving more firmly over her breast. She moaned again, unable to help herself or contain her excitement. The feelings he was stirring in her were amazing! She trembled, could *feel* her blood racing to her core, could *hear* her heart pounding with excitement.

Then she was lying there on the blanket bereft, actually shocked, he got up so quickly. He stood above her running a hand through his hair. He was panting. His face was flushed. When he finally met her eyes, she saw the regret in his. He hadn't meant to arouse her like that, or himself.

That was even more apparent when he said, "We will forget that happened."

She was flustered, incredibly disappointed, but she somehow

managed to hide it by sitting up and pertly replying, "Of course, already forgotten." Yet she knew she'd *never* forget it.

He gave her a skeptical look. She gave him a smile. If it killed her, she wasn't going to let him know how deeply moved she was by what had just happened. So she added, "I'll just consider it another lesson from Cupid."

"Amanda, that's not why I . . ."

Whatever he was going to say, he changed his mind and fell silent. She was too disturbed to probe or say any more about it herself. But she suddenly had help in putting it from her mind—for now. Getting to her feet, she pointed out to him what was missing and was able to laugh.

"It would appear you've caught a fish—and it's run off with your pole."

Chapter Thirty-Nine

WHO WOULD HAVE THOUGHT anyone could be grateful to a fish, but Amanda certainly was today. First she couldn't help laughing at Devin's confounded expression when he realized his fishing pole was nowhere in sight, then at the sight of his running along the edge of the creek looking for it. He was almost out of view when he found it.

But that bit of humor helped her to compose herself and push away the last remnants of the amazingly passionate encounter she'd just shared with him. She'd had no idea she could want a man so much, and she could probably have gone on living indefinitely without knowing that if she didn't keep finding herself alone with such an earthy, virile man as Devin. She couldn't imagine Kendall losing restraint like that. Robert she could—no, actually not even him. His amorous behavior at the ball had been fueled by drink. Without it he would likely remain the gentleman to a fault, which would exclude stealing kisses or revealing any improper passion prior to marriage.

Aware now that *she* had passions—twice confirmed!—she felt some urgency again about getting married, and quickly, so she could experience more of those passions in the appropriate manner. Yet now she had still another worry, thanks to a few of her married friends who'd admitted their husbands wouldn't even sleep in the same bed with them and they made love with their bedclothes on! After today, she knew that she would *not* accept that sort of marriage, yet how the deuce could she find out ahead of time whether her choices would be that prudish after marriage? She certainly didn't have to guess about Devin in that regard. He'd want them as naked as the day they were born. He wouldn't mind her touching every inch of him. He'd probably encourage it!

She fanned herself for a moment, feeling quite steamy with the thought, then laughed at herself because she was feeling a little chilly now that the sun had gone behind a cloud.

She laughed again over Devin's expression when he returned. "After all that, the bloody fish got away."

"Well, I think I've had enough fishing for today." She stood and shook out the blanket in preparation for leaving. "And I confess, I'm eager to meet the mare you brought me, so I'm going to the stable."

He nodded and took the blanket from her to carry it and grabbed her pole. She paused only long enough to tip over the container of worms so they could crawl back to safety. She caught Devin rolling his eyes at her.

"And you actually thought you could bait your own hook?" he chuckled.

"I used to!"

"What a child will do isn't a reflection of what the adult

will do, because a child hasn't yet acquired all the qualities he or she will grow into or develop as an adult. *You* turned out too softhearted, minx."

She huffed, "That's not a bad thing."

"For a woman, no, it's not." He offered his arm to her.

She pretended not to notice and quickly moved off ahead of him. She was afraid to get too close to him right now because the passion they'd shared was still too fresh in her mind. He did catch up with her with his longer stride, but he didn't insist on guiding her through the woods, merely walked beside her, keeping a respectable distance between them.

It took about fifteen minutes to return to the manicured grounds. With the house in full view now, he remarked, "Two hundred guests would fit easily into that edifice."

She laughed. "Not really. The rooms are all oversize, and while many of the younger guests will be crowded together, many of the older ones will insist on private rooms. Did you get *your* room yet? Depending on how many people show up, you might be asked to share, too."

"I haven't been to the house yet. I stabled our horses and went off to fish."

She wished now that he hadn't. Some things were best left to the imagination. She'd known that she liked kissing Devin, but now she knew she liked it too much.

"Does she have a name?"

They'd gone straight to the stable and he'd just opened the stall so she could examine her new horse. The mare was beautiful, didn't have that albino look that some whites had. Her color was solid, her eyes were blue. It was love at first sight!

"You can call her anything you like," he said.

"I think I'll call her Sarahtoo."

"Another Sarah?"

"No, Sarahtoo." She spelled it for him.

"Lady Amanda, did you want your carriage hitched?" old Herbert asked, approaching them.

"Not today." She took a moment to introduce the old groom to Devin. "I came to visit my new mare."

"You're not happy with the old one?" Herbert asked curiously.

Amanda laughed. "No, I'm going to be riding this one." When Herbert's brows rose in surprise, she added, "Devin helped me to get over my fear. I've been riding for several weeks now."

Amazed, Herbert walked away, shaking his head, mumbling, "The man's a magician!"

She blushed while Devin chuckled. "Does everyone here know about your . . . reluctance to get back on a horse?"

"No, just my family and Herbert. He was my original instructor when I was a child."

Devin nodded, understanding, then glanced across the aisle. "Who does that fine-looking Thoroughbred mare belong to? I noticed her immediately when I got here."

Amanda didn't have to look to know which horse he was talking about. "Me. She won two races. Her owner retired her with that undefeated record so he could demand an exorbitant price for her! My aunt heard that she was going to be sold, and I talked my father into buying her for me. That was four years ago."

"But you were afraid to ride, so why would you want a horse like that?"

"For my carriage! I love racing it to Norford Town and back."

Devin gave her an incredulous look. "Your father doesn't object to that?"

She grinned. "Shh, he doesn't know."

"What else doesn't he—?"

He cut himself off abruptly and took his eyes off her. *She* blushed. His tone had been sensual! But he obviously hadn't meant it to be or hadn't meant to allude to their second kissing lesson, which she didn't doubt he'd been thinking of.

He cleared his throat and forced a casual tone. "So you never had her race again?"

"No, I liked owning an undefeated champion. While I was tempted a time or two to enter her, I resisted the urge because I didn't want to take the chance of her losing her title."

"Has she ever bred?"

"No."

"Would you like to have her bred?"

Amanda shrugged. "I never thought of it because that would have kept me from using her as my carriage horse, but I just might be riding to town henceforth on Sarahtoo, so that could be a possibility now. Are you recommending one of your stallions? A joint venture, as it were?"

"She could produce a champion. You wouldn't mind sharing a horse with me and having it entered in the races?"

What an exciting idea! A horse she actually owned racing *and* winning! Well, half-owned. But she liked the idea of sharing something like that with Devin even more. It would mean that she wouldn't lose contact with him after . . . she married. What the devil. She'd just been deflated at the thought of marriage?!

Thoroughly confused by her emotions, she merely said, "Definitely something to think about."

"In the meantime, are you ready for another lesson?"

Her stomach fluttered at those words! Because "lessons" with him had gone beyond riding. But he *only* meant on the mare, of course, and she left the stall, saying, "I'll need to change clothes first, and you need to get settled in the house. I'll meet you back here within the hour." And she hurried away before he noticed her blush.

Chapter Forty

AMANDA ENJOYED RIDING AROUND the estate grounds that afternoon with Devin. Sarahtoo proved to be as gentle as her namesake, and it occurred to Amanda that she was beginning to really like riding. Her father wanted her to give up the notion of rounding out her lessons with the sidesaddle, which she was happy to agree with, since she'd been dreading *those* lessons. So riding no longer had any worries associated with it.

She pointed out to Devin all the places she had played as a child with either Rafe or her friend Rebecca, reminding him, "You met Rebecca at the ball, and my cousin Rupert, whom she married recently. You'll see them tonight at dinner. Aunt Julie arrived this morning with her family."

"I won't intrude on a family dinner."

"Don't be silly. You're our guest. It would be rude to decline."

He gave her an amused look. "And how is it you think that would concern me?"

"Of course." She tsked. "I forgot rudeness is your forte."

He chuckled and said with a roguish grin, "I have a few, but that isn't one of them."

He was just teasing. She knew that. Yet the remark made her cheeks light up anyway because she didn't doubt he'd just made a reference to his kissing skill, which he'd demonstrated twice for her—or perhaps something even *more* intimate, which she dreamily imagined him demonstrating for her.

But he wiped away the titillating thought by reminding her that his skill with horses was also one of his fortes when he added, "I'm going to be training your mare while I'm here. I want to make sure she doesn't give you any difficulty."

"Thank you."

He did show up for dinner that night, when she'd almost been sure he wouldn't. Ophelia and Raphael were there, both greeting him when he entered the room, though Rafe's expression was a little less cordial than Ophelia's. Esmerelda, Preston's oldest sister, had shown up early, too, for Rafe's birthday. She'd brought a lap robe to dinner and was wearing a coat over her thick brocade gown, which she intended to keep on, causing a few grins from those already gathered when she shooed off the footman who tried to take it from her. Her presence was why the room was a trifle warm tonight. She complained of cold nearly as much as her mother, Agatha, did. Agatha Locke usually declined to leave her rooms for any reason these days because of it, and tonight was no exception, though tomorrow night Preston would insist she make an appearance.

Julie was delighted to see Devin again and gave him an effusive greeting. She found him to be a perfect foil to her gruffness because he didn't bat an eye over it, and she was in good form with that tonight, thanks to Rupert's attire. Rupert was too handsome. Women even called him beautiful when he put on effeminate airs, which he did deliberately whenever he wore his bright satins. He wore them just for his mother, to rile her. It always worked.

Julie had sacrificed her softer side so many years ago so she could take on the role of both parents for her sons while they were so young. In an extreme transformation that mostly amused the family, she turned herself into somewhat of a bully. Rupert simply gave his mother purpose when he donned such unfashionable clothes, giving her something to browbeat him about, so she would continue to think her boys needed her. He didn't actually wear those dandy clothes out in public, he only let her think he did. Besides, he rarely dressed outlandishly anymore because it was harder to get a reaction from his mother over it, when she was so pleased with him for finally settling down with a wife.

He was giving it a good attempt tonight, though, and his bright lemon satin coat with lace dripping from both cuffs immediately drew Julie's eyes and her caustic remark "One of these days I'm going to find where you hide those atrocious clothes and make pillows out of them."

Rupert gave her an angelic smile. "My tailor loves me."

Julie snorted. "Your tailor should be shot."

"Don't worry, Mother. I won't embarrass Uncle Preston once the guests start arriving."

Preston didn't even glance up from eating to say in one of his more authoritative tones, "I know you won't."

But Julie pointed directly at Devin to say, "We already have a guest."

Rupert glanced at Devin, too, grinned, then told his mother, "Cupids don't count because they favor flitting around bare-arsed naked shooting little bows." And to Devin: "Oh, I say, old man, we would make a pair, wouldn't we?"

Julie scowled. Everyone else followed Preston's lead and dug into his or her meal, except Devin, who was still watching the unusual one-sided bickering with interest.

"Using the proverbial *image* when the man does nothing of the sort?" Julie said to her son. "That doesn't let *you* off the hook, m'boy."

For some reason Julie wasn't letting the subject go tonight as she usually did after a few disgruntled remarks, probably because they *did* have a guest, so she was embarrassed more than usual by her oldest son's looking like a peacock. But Rebecca intervened, whispering something to her husband. He chuckled, but her expression turned stern, which made him stand up with a sigh.

He said with an aggrieved expression that most of them could tell was contrived, "You've finally won, Mother. You now have m'wife on your side."

"About bloody time," Julie mumbled as Rupert left the room to change into something reasonable.

Rebecca gave her mother-in-law a look that said, *Enough,* and Julie immediately turned her attention to Devin instead. Rarely mincing words, she posed a question that was bold even for her. "So, young man, we wonder, who is Cupid interested in?"

If Devin was surprised to become the center of attention with such a personal question directed at him, he hid it well, merely saying, "If such a lady existed, I wouldn't discuss her over dinner, madam."

"But I think more'n one of us are quite interested," Julie continued.

"Indeed? Why?"

"How will it look if the man who makes happy marriages for others doesn't have one himself?"

That was simply too personal even for Julie's bluntness, prompting Preston to intervene at last. "Julie, m'dear, if you don't give it a rest tonight, I'm going to hire Devin to find *you* a mate."

"That's not a bad idea," at least four relatives said in so many words, both of Julie's sons present included.

That did shut Julie up for the moment, and separate conversations started up after that. Raphael, sitting next to Devin, remarked on the pretty new mare he'd seen in the stable. Amanda didn't hear Devin's reply because she was reminded of her surprise just before dinner, when she'd asked her father what the mare had cost and found out that Devin had given the horse to her as a gift.

"He wouldn't take payment for her, although I insisted several times," Preston had answered. "Said she was a well-deserved gift for your courage and perseverance. You didn't know?"

"No, I—I suppose he was embarrassed by the gesture so didn't want to mention it to me" was all she could think to say about it.

He *should* have told her. The reason he gave her father was simple enough, so why couldn't he have told *her* that? But she wasn't sitting next to him tonight so she wasn't able to ask. She wished she were sitting next to him. Sitting across the table from him, she found it difficult to keep her eyes off him, and she lost count of the number of times their eyes met. She felt herself blushing every time she thought he might have noticed those covert glances. Rebecca noticed and kept grinning at her. Her brother noticed and frowned at her a few times.

Unfortunately, her father had noticed, too, and pulled her aside after dinner. "Should I speak to Devin about his intentions?"

She gasped. "No, of course not. His only intention is to turn me into an avid horsewoman."

Preston raised a brow. "Yet you have trouble keeping your eyes off the man."

She groaned inwardly. "Devin is very handsome. I can't help noticing that." She quickly added, "So are Lord Kendall and Lord Robert."

Preston gave her a skeptical look. "I saw you with Brigston, m'dear. You barely looked at him the entire time he was in the same room with you."

She sighed. "I'm confused is all. It's deuced difficult, deciding between them, and while I'd hoped and prayed to have this *very* difficulty to deal with, now that I do have it, I don't like it one bit!"

He chuckled over that complaint, but it suddenly dawned on her what his original question had implied. Amazed, she asked, "You actually wouldn't object to Devin as a husband for me?"

"Why would I?"

"When I first saw him, I thought he was a brute. He doesn't care if he gives that impression, you know. He is a gem in the rough, as it were, definitely not typical gentry. He'll insult you without blinking, won't even try to prevaricate to be polite as he ought to."

Preston laughed over her less than flattering description. "Yet he's still from good family, and I actually like his forthright manner. He's simply down-to-earth as many country lords are who prefer to avoid the frivolities of London. Besides, it's your happiness that concerns me. I don't think I'd object to any man you fell in love with, with the exception of someone mired in a scandal or an actual criminal. I would trust your heart in the matter."

Her heart. Which way *was* her heart leaning? Good Lord, shouldn't that be obvious by now?

Chapter Forty-One

"HE'S ARRIVED!"

Amanda hurried to her bedroom window to see whom Phoebe was talking about. Lord Robert was just stepping out of his coach. Not everyone would show up today, the first official day of the country gathering. But Robert's early arrival was a good sign that he was eager to see her again.

"He's so dashing and handsome," Phoebe continued, then with a sigh added, "Almost makes me wish I'd waited as you did, instead of settling on a husband last Season."

Amanda was shocked by her friend's statement. "I thought you loved your Archibald."

"I do, of course I do, but the bloom has definitely worn off. He's still as attentive as he's always been, but, he stays away from home more and more now and," she added in a whisper, "I'm glad he does."

"I'm so sorry, Phoebe!"

Phoebe gave a halfhearted smile. "Don't be silly, m'dear. It's still a solid marriage, I suppose. I don't really find fault with him. It's ironic, though, that I might not have ever noticed that we've grown apart if Cupid's philosophy hadn't turned up in the gossip mill, how he puts such stock in common ground."

Amanda scoffed, "You just have to look at my brother's marriage to know Cupid's approach isn't the *only* way to happiness."

"No, but definitely helpful. It just made me realize that my husband and I have no shared interests a'tall and never did—well, other than going to parties. We do both still enjoy that."

"Have you tried discussing this with Archibald? Perhaps there's something else you might enjoy doing together that you just haven't discovered yet?"

"Goodness no! We rarely talk about anything of a personal nature."

That was just—sad. Two people who shared a bed . . . Amanda winced at the thought, remembering that Phoebe was one of her friends who'd said she and her husband had separate bedrooms. It was still sad. Husband and wife should be able to discuss anything, not be wrapped up in "proper" so extensively they carried it into marriage.

Amanda tried to find a bright side for her friend. "It could be worse. He could be a philanderer and not even try to hide it. He could be a gambler and racing you to the poorhouse. And you know there was something there to begin with, or you never would have said yes to him. So don't give up yet! Rediscover that bloom you two had."

Phoebe hugged her. "Listen to you, the maiden giving the matron advice. I haven't given up hope, I've merely slipped into the comfortable part of marriage a little sooner than expected, I suppose. But you're right, there's no reason we can't ignite the spark again."

They were still standing at the window when the next coach

pulled up and Phoebe said, "Is that Lord Culley? I haven't seen him since I was a child. I thought he'd gotten too old to socialize."

Amanda chuckled. "Does anyone ever get too old for that? But Owen Culley is an old friend of my aunt Esmerelda. He married one of her school chums."

The party wasn't just for the younger set. Old friends of the family's had been invited, too, which was why the guest list had become so long. But the original idea was for the two men Amanda was most interested in to be in attendance, so she'd have access to them for a whole week to make up her mind which one she preferred.

That a third man was present whom she found even more fascinating now might just be a distraction from her goal. Especially now that she felt empathy for him, over his secret. He might not have meant to share that with her, but he did, and no matter how she looked at it, it had brought them closer, definitely friends at the very least.

Now *would* be a good time to go downstairs and make Robert feel welcome, perhaps even give him a tour of the house. She was about to say so when a knock came at the door.

Larissa poked her head around it. "So here you are." Unfortunately, Jacinda Brown was at her heels and followed Larissa into the room. "I don't suppose you're sharing *your* room?"

Amanda grinned. Obviously Larissa was annoyed that she would be separated from her husband for the duration. "Since I still live here, no, I claim the privilege being the daughter of the house. How many are you sharing with?"

"*Six* cots are in that room, but only three have been claimed so far."

"It will be fun," Phoebe put in. "It was fun when we all

went to Summer's Glade that first Season and were stuffed into a room together."

"We weren't married then," Larissa replied. "I miss my husband already!"

Phoebe teased, "Shh, you'll make Jacinda think there's something to like about marriage."

"Oh, I know what's to like about it," Jacinda purred as she walked about the room examining things.

Phoebe had been right about the chit, apparently. A remark like that couldn't have been made unless Jacinda had had "experience." And she didn't care who knew it?

The debutante shouldn't even be in Amanda's bedroom. Her friends might have met the girl, but Jacinda and Amanda had never even been introduced. Larissa took care of that belatedly, remembering her manners. "You've met Lady Brown's daughter, Jacinda, yes?"

Amanda didn't try to dress it up nicely, said simply, "No, I haven't," then regretted that when Larissa looked embarrassed by it.

"I'm sorry, I had no idea," Larissa said, and made the introductions.

Jacinda didn't even look at Amanda, didn't acknowledge the introduction, just said in a blatantly bored tone, "Nice house— I suppose."

It was a magnificent house! Amanda's bedroom was so large she had room for a full parlor set in it, the couch and chairs finely upholstered in cream-and-lavender silk brocade, the carpet so lush it was a pleasure to walk on.

But the lines were drawn with Jacinda's remark. Even Amanda's friends took offense, Larissa staring incredulously, Phoebe starting to frown. Why had Jacinda even tagged along with Larissa if she had no intention of being friendly? Then it became apparent why she had intruded. She'd let all the other young debutantes know whom she'd staked a claim on. She hadn't yet made that clear to Amanda.

"I saw Devin downstairs," Jacinda said casually. "I heard you're actually taking riding lessons from him. You naughty girl, to pretend not to know how to ride. I should have thought of that!"

Amanda blanched, but not for the reason anyone thought. Her friends actually assumed the same thing that Jacinda did, that she'd used riding lessons as an excuse to spend time with him, but unlike Jacinda, they were excited for her.

"Why didn't you say you liked him, Mandy?" Larissa said in delight.

"A brute, eh?" Phoebe laughed over the last thing Amanda had said about him.

Rather than admit the truth, Amanda replied evasively, "Lessons were an impulsive idea. I was simply curious about him at the start." But when she caught the glare Jacinda briefly revealed, she added, "But I confess, I do find him fascinating." Good grief, was that *really* jealousy sneaking up on her again?

"He does relieve the tedium, doesn't he?" Jacinda purred in such a way that she was implying they'd been intimate! "I certainly wouldn't waste a whole week of my time here if he weren't in attendance."

"I think your time is wasted no matter where you are, *and* everyone else's because of it," Phoebe said angrily, and marched out of the room.

Larissa, aghast over such rudeness, grabbed Jacinda's arm to drag her out of the room, saying on the way out, "I had *no* idea, Mandy. Forgive me for subjecting you to such a vicious cat."

"It's not your fault!" Amanda tried to assure her friend.

But the door had already closed and she whirled about to let out a hiss of exasperation. She wished she had actually had a look at Ophelia's guest list so she could have scratched that name off it. How the deuce did Jacinda Brown find out about her riding lessons? But she knew. The girl must have been at Devin's farm for a lovers' tryst and had to wait while he finished one of those riding lessons. Now she had to worry that it was making the rounds. Kendall might even hear of it!

Chapter Forty-Two

IT WASN'T A GOOD time for Jacinda Brown to be rubbing her voluptuous body against him. Under the pretext of bumping into him in the corridor? Devin set her away from him so fast her head jerked back. He did need a woman. Amanda had aroused his desire the other day, so much so that two days later he still couldn't stop thinking of how much he wanted to make love to her, even though that was impossible. She made him feel like a boy again with no control. And that made no sense. They'd merely kissed!

But while he definitely needed a woman right now, it wasn't going to be a promiscuous debutante who alluded to being more sophisticated than her age allowed. Unfortunately, he and Jacinda had been given rooms in the same wing of the house, and this wasn't the first time she'd appeared when he was on his way to his room. He was beginning to think she was lying in wait for him. Actually, he was sure of it.

He'd known from the day he'd met her when she and her mother had brought their dog to his aunt that Jacinda found him to her liking. She flirted too boldly, told him by look and the sensual movements of her body that she was available. But it wasn't until last night that she'd got verbal about it.

Passing him in the corridor then, too, she'd trailed her hand down his arm and whispered, "Country gatherings are made for trysts. There's all sorts of places here we could sneak off to and not be missed."

He'd walked on as if he hadn't heard her. Now here she was again, giving him a pretty pout for ending the contact she'd instigated so abruptly. He started to step around her, but she moved to block him again.

"You know you want me." She reached up to caress his cheek.

He caught her hand and moved it away from him before he let go. "You're looking for a husband, I'm not looking for a wife. Do us both a favor and set your sights elsewhere."

She turned on a sultry look. "That doesn't mean we can't have fun in the meantime, does it?"

He answered bluntly, "It means, back off, it's not happening between us."

A little angry, she said snippily, "What the devil is wrong with you? You're the first man I've ever met who wouldn't take what's being freely given."

"And you say that from experience?"

"I—"

He laughed derisively when she didn't finish. "Maybe that's the problem? Maybe I don't want what's given so easily? Or do you think I can't see the strings attached?"

She recovered and tried to laugh that off. "Don't be silly, Devin. If you don't want to marry me, fine, but I'd still like a taste—"

She was *still* persisting? He had no patience for spoiled chits who wanted to play with fire, but this one had picked the wrong time to throw herself at him when he was already a powder keg of unspent passions. Amazingly his voice was only cold when he cut in, "Stop making a nuisance of yourself. Or do I need to have a word with your mother about your loose morals?"

She stepped aside immediately and even raised her hands in surrender. "Don't do that! If you truly don't want to have a little fun with me, I'll—I'll look elsewhere."

He walked on, satisfied that he'd frightened her enough for her to stop pursuing him. As flattering as that was, he wasn't stupid. You did *not* make love to a debutante unless you were willing to marry her.

Ironically, though, when he returned downstairs after changing out of his riding clothes, the son of the house cornered him for nearly the same subject. Raphael joined him at the back of the music room, plate in hand. There would be no sit-down meals with this many guests. A few chairs were still empty in this less crowded room, but Devin was still in an explosive mood, so he ignored them. Damned passions. Racing his stallion to Norford Town and back several times this afternoon hadn't eased his turmoil, and that run-in with Jacinda had just made it worse.

At least Raphael didn't jump immediately into what was on his mind. He thanked Devin once more for his part in Ophelia's birthday gift, which had been presented yesterday, *then* got personal.

"What are your intentions toward my sister?"

"As I told you the last time you broached that subject, I don't have any."

"Why not?" Raphael asked curiously. "She's a prime catch, beautiful, talks a little too much, but that's easily fixed, and she seems to like you."

Devin laughed. "The last time we discussed her, I believe you were telling me to stay the hell away from her."

Raphael's look turned a little abashed. "That was then. We didn't know you yet. That was before you took it upon yourself to help her win another man, proving yourself selfless. You don't like her?"

Devin couldn't believe he was having this conversation with her brother. "It's not a matter of whether I like her. I think she can do better'n me."

"True or not, we just want her to be happy. You might keep that in mind."

Bloody hell, did her brother just give his permission for Devin to court Amanda?

Raphael walked away. Devin needed a drink. Actually, getting foxed wasn't a bad idea.

But on his way to find where the refreshment table had been set up for the evening, he saw his customer and friend Lord Culley and headed straight for him instead. After that run-in with Lawrence Wolseley in London, which had left him no outlet for his rage now that Wolseley had convinced him that he wasn't his father, it had sunk in that he might never know who his real father is—or was. But he was still unwilling to accept that he would never know his father's identity. And thanks to Lawrence, he might not have to.

Lawrence had given him a few clues about his father. Golden-brown eyes, more golden than brown, weren't all that common. Lawrence had also said his father had dark hair *and* was over six feet in height. He just had to ask around among the older set if anyone might remember someone of that description, which was why he'd spent all day at the racetrack on Saturday. But while a half dozen older lords had been there that day, only one had said he recalled another man with eyes like Devin's, but it had been so long ago, he couldn't remember the man's name.

Culley was probably too old to remember, too. The man had to be in his seventies. But Devin still had to give it a try. And the old lord had mentioned that he and his wife used to entertain in London in the early years of their marriage, right up until she died and he retired to the country.

When Devin joined the old fellow, they naturally spoke of horses first. "Is that new team working out for you?" Devin asked.

"Did you have any doubt? Nice steady ride. My bones appreciate it, and my driver is still in awe. He's not used to such well-trained horses."

They both laughed, but after a few more pleasantries, Devin broached what was on his mind, using the same excuse he'd used at the racetrack a few days ago. "My uncle was reminiscing about family recently and mentioned an old branch of ours that I didn't know about. I'm curious now as to whether some long-lost cousins from that branch are still alive."

"More Baldwins?" Owen asked. "Can't say that I know any others."

"No, and that's the problem. A Baldwin daughter married and moved away from London, then the family lost touch with her. The only piece of information that was passed down was that she had golden-brown eyes like mine and black hair. So little to go by, I know, and yet, it's not a common eye color."

Owen frowned and cautioned, "You might want to be

careful how you go about this search. If you say you're looking for distant family members, you might attract undesirables who could lie about a connection just to take advantage of you."

Devin almost winced. Since he'd just lied, he felt guilty now. Here was Owen expressing concern that Devin protect himself from unscrupulous individuals. But since there was no lost branch in the family, he didn't actually need to worry about that.

"A good point," Devin agreed, "but now that I've mentioned it, do you know of any other men with eyes like mine?"

Owen chuckled. "Frankly, the color of men's eyes isn't something I've ever paid much attention to. A woman's eyes, yes, and I can think of at least two who had light brown eyes, just not as bright as yours, but they could also trace their family trees back for centuries, so I highly doubt they can help you."

Devin nodded his agreement. As much as he hated the thought of even saying her name, he was going to have to modify his story and bring his mother into it and confine his inquiries to the year she came to London and met that womanizing bastard who seduced her. But it was too late to mention her to Lord Owen, after using that "family branch" story with him.

His mother had to have met many people the year she arrived in London for her come-out, people her age who would be middle-aged now. She would have needed a sponsor and a chaperone, and whoever they were, they were likely to have seen her with the golden-eyed man who'd been trying to seduce her.

Bloody hell, his uncle would have those names for him. He'd never asked because he'd been so sure all this time that Wolseley had been his father. But broaching the subject with Donald would have to wait until he returned to London. In the meantime, other middle-aged couples were visiting Norford Hall.

Chapter Forty-Three

AMANDA WAS LATE COMING downstairs for the first official night of the house party because Alice had been late returning with the gown they had decided on for the evening. "I expected there to be other maids in the pressing room, which is why I went early, but I had no idea there would be so many that a line had formed out into the hall!" Alice said the moment she rushed into Amanda's bedroom.

"It's all right," Amanda assured Alice. "I had a late lunch, so I'm not hungry yet for dinner. But I do want that gown to look perfect. How is it now?"

"Perfect indeed." Alice helped her into it.

The blue velvet complemented her eyes, and the gown was a bit daring because it was a shade darker than the pallid pastels she and all the other unmarried young women were restricted to. The gown was not dark enough to raise eyebrows, but so well suited to her coloring that she would have picked it out even if she were married and allowed any color she wanted. She was so looking forward to *that* benefit of marriage. Pale colors did *not* help her to shine, and she definitely wanted to shine to-night with Robert already in attendance, and hopefully Kendall arriving before the evening was over, if he hadn't already.

As she walked down the house's grand central staircase, she caught sight of Blythe Pace entering the parlor with her escort, who for once wasn't Devin! Amanda hurried to catch up to them.

"Welcome to Norford Hall, Blythe," Amanda said, then smiled at Blythe's brother. "And you must be William!"

He bowed over Amanda's offered hand. "We've met, Lady Amanda."

"Yes, of course, Devin mentioned that. It's just that I've met so many people over the last few years."

William sighed dramatically. "It's my bane to be forgotten by beautiful women!"

"Not a'tall." Amanda smiled. "I *do* remember you now. And I'm delighted to see that you have recovered from your accident in time to join us here."

He blushed slightly, evidently embarrassed that she knew about that, but Amanda quickly turned to Blythe and said with a grin, "Lord Oliver is here, if you haven't noticed yet."

"Where?" Blythe said excitedly.

Amanda glanced about the room and spotted Oliver chatting with John Trask and pointed Blythe in that direction. William chuckled. "I suppose it's time I met this chap who's turned my sister's head. She's done nothing but chew my ear off about him—"

Blythe poked her brother to silence, blushing, but was obviously so eager to greet Oliver that Amanda said, "I'm going to make my way to the buffet. I'll speak with you both later."

Blythe did indeed drag her brother straightaway to Oliver's

side, and Amanda even caught Oliver's look of pleasure when he spotted the younger girl heading his way, so Amanda had a feeling that eagerness went both ways. How nice for her friend!

But she wasn't interested in the buffet yet. She'd also spotted Devin conversing with Lord and Lady Dowling when she'd looked around for Oliver, and he had some explaining to do about her riding lessons becoming common knowledge. She headed in his direction.

"Goodness, Devin, I've met so many people over the years, names elude me. You might ask Lord Culley. He and his wife were living in London at the time."

Amanda was nearly tapping her foot, she was so impatient for Devin to finish his conversation with Lord and Lady Dowling and notice that she wanted a word with him. Should she intrude? Better than eavesdropping like this. How could he *not* see her standing to the side of him?

But he appeared to be in hot pursuit of information, and it was probably her fault, for reminding him about his mother the other day. He was trying to find friends of hers now, at least that's what it had sounded like. To find out more about her because he'd lost her when he was so young? But then a more likely reason occurred to her. He could be trying to find his father!

"Here you are, and alone? Dare I hope you've arranged that just for me?"

Amanda whirled around and met Robert's engaging grin. How the deuce could he call this "alone"? The parlor was so crowded right now you couldn't turn around without bumping into someone . . . what was wrong with her? Was that actually annoyance she was feeling over being bothered by Robert Brigston instead of delight that he'd found her in a crowded room? But he *was* keeping her from her current purpose, which was to find out how Jacinda knew about Amanda's riding lessons, so she would rather talk to Devin. . . .

She sighed to herself and put her arm through Robert's to lead him out to the foyer. Devin would just have to wait. She hadn't had a chance yet to speak to Robert since he'd arrived. When she'd gone downstairs earlier to look for him, he'd apparently already been shown to a room and was getting settled in, but then she hadn't waited around for him to appear, when she should have. Really, she needed to get her priorities straight, and Robert Brigston was one of them.

The foyer was crowded, too, of course it would be. Despite the size of the house and that probably a half dozen rooms were quite empty on the ground floor, people were still going to congregate near each other, and at the moment that meant near the parlor, where the bulk of the guests were gathered for the evening. Ophelia hadn't arranged any entertainment for tonight other than a splendid dinner. She should probably have opened the ballroom for that, when more than half the guests had already shown up.

Walking Robert slowly down the hall, glancing in each room to see if any were less crowded, she began, "Let me say how delighted I am you could join—"

"She wasn't 'alone,' as you put it, Brigston, and she's certainly not going to be left alone with you."

Amanda gasped, stopping in her tracks. Robert let go of her arm instantly, and she certainly couldn't blame him. Devin's words weren't just rude, his tone actually sounded threatening! So he *did* know she'd been standing there next to him in the parlor *and* he'd heard what Robert had said to her.

She turned and saw that Robert appeared offended, and

rightly so. Devin, of course, didn't care. Insulting people was a habit of his! But his tone hadn't been contrived. He *did* actually look angry.

Robert struggled to compose himself in the face of such obvious animosity and made an attempt to make light of it by saying, "You know, old chap, if I didn't know better, I'd think you were interested in her yourself."

"I'm interested in her happiness, but we've already had this conversation, haven't we? If you want to have it again, we can do so—right now."

Robert stiffened, but backed down immediately. He actually walked off without another word, leaving Amanda incredulous and outraged by Devin's rude behavior. She looked up at Devin, but he was staring after Robert and she had a feeling he was about to follow him. Not before she gave him a piece of her mind!

"My name isn't Blythe," she said vehemently. "You aren't my chaperone. I'm in my own home. What the devil d'you think you're doing, scaring Lord Brigston off like that? What was that about?"

He took her arm and continued with her down the main central hall. In a moment they were out of anyone else's hearing. Only then did he say, "I've told you he's not for you. Why can't you just trust me on that?"

"Why can't you trust me with your reason for saying it?"

Their eyes locked. For a moment she thought he was going to confide in her. But instead he put her on the spot.

"Do you love him?" he asked bluntly.

"No, not—"

"*No* was sufficient. So do yourself a favor and don't *try* to love him."

They'd reached the end of the long hall. He wasn't trying to find them an empty room to continue to speak privately in. He hadn't even glanced in those they'd walked past. He simply turned them about to head back toward the crowd, albeit slowly now.

Whatever he knew about Robert, he obviously wasn't going to share it with her. It could be no more than Robert wasn't *his* choice for her, Kendall was. No, that would be a petty reason, and Devin certainly wasn't like that. And it couldn't be jealousy, much as she might like *that* possibility, when everything he was doing for her was to prepare her to be Kendall Goswick's wife.

Reminded of Kendall, her earlier anger returned and she put him on the spot for a change. "My learning to ride at this late date in my life was confidential. I thought you knew that. So how is it possible that Jacinda Brown, whom I met for the first time today, knows about those lessons?"

He frowned. "She does?"

"You didn't tell her?"

"No. I only mentioned it to Blythe, when she wanted me to escort her to a morning event and I had to tell her why I couldn't. I was expecting you for another lesson. She must have mentioned it to Miss Brown, who's tried to become chummy with her recently."

No lovers' tryst? That took a little heat out of Amanda's reply, just not all of it. "Why would you tell even her?"

He raised a brow at her. "I wasn't aware you were keeping it a secret."

"Of course I was!" she whispered furiously. "It's embarrassing enough that I don't know how to ride at my age, but now Kendall might hear of it!"

He gave her a pointed look. "Why would that embarrass you when he will be highly flattered that you'd learn just for him?"

"I can't let him know *that*! That's something to tell him after we marry, not before."

"Why?"

She huffed, "Obviously because it will make him think he's already won me, so he'll stop trying."

He rolled his eyes at her. His good humor had apparently returned because she was aggrieved over what he would consider something silly. Her reaction *was* a bit overdone, she realized, yet she still felt as if she were going to explode with exasperation, or aggravation, or—oh, she didn't know *what* had her so highly charged that she was looking for things to rail about, but something did and it didn't want to go away. And being this close to *him* just seemed to make it worse.

Devin suddenly stopped. She followed his gaze and saw that Lord Kendall had just been let in the front door and was handing his coat over to the butler. She looked back at Devin to mention his arrival, only to see that Devin seemed to be wrestling with himself. Myriad emotions were crossing his features, all too fleeting to grasp, but he ended by dragging a hand through his hair and turning abruptly about, giving his back to the entry door.

Then he glanced down at her and with a sigh said, "Kendall is here."

"Yes, I noticed," she replied stiffly.

"I should take you over to him."

"I can do that well enough on my own, thank you very much. This is my house. I'm allowed to mingle *and* greet guests—or is there a reason I should cross Kendall off my list, too?"

She was being sarcastic, yet she actually held her breath, waiting for his answer. He didn't give it immediately. When he finally shook his head no, she walked away from him. She felt like crying. Did she really expect him to object to her pursuit of Kendall after that last kiss they'd shared? Well, she'd show him that she didn't care. She could look after her own marital prospects.

She approached Kendall with a gracious smile. "I was beginning to worry that you wouldn't be back in time from Scotland to join us. I'm so glad you've returned in good time. Was this trip successful, too?"

He bent to kiss her hand. "Indeed, in fact, after this party I may have to see about enlarging my stable, or building a new one!"

Not a word in greeting or even a compliment? No, that was her fault! She'd introduced the topic of his trip, which of course made him think of his crowded stable. She would have to get used to that, if she picked him. Perhaps she ought to find out what he thought about her riding—without a sidesaddle.

"I'm looking forward to riding with you tomorrow. Norford Hall isn't Hyde Park, but the grounds here are extensive."

He beamed at her. "What a splendid idea! I confess, I was going to suggest it m'self."

"Then let the butler get you situated. We'll have a chance to talk more when you return for dinner."

She ended that rather quickly, having spotted Mabel Collicott bearing down on her. . . .

Chapter Forty-Four

Amanda braced herself. The old dame, with her friend Gertrude in tow as usual, barely spared a greeting, simply latched onto Amanda's arm and dragged her straight across the parlor to stand before Farrell Exter. He didn't seem surprised that they were joining him, which made her wonder if Mabel had actually told Farrell he was now in the running for her simply because the old matchmaker had recommended him. She wouldn't dare! Would she?

Farrell looked a bit disheveled tonight as if he'd slept in his clothes. He did arrive yesterday, so it was possible. Had he not brought his valet with him? There was ample room in the servants' wing for maids and valets who came with the guests, but not everyone brought one along. Which was why Ophelia had made sure plenty of extra valets and maids would be on hand. She did think of everything, after all.

Amanda wondered if she should mention that, but dismissed the thought, since it would probably embarrass Farrell.

And he didn't seem to think anything was amiss with himself. He immediately took Amanda's hand to kiss it.

"Ah, the most beautiful lady in England, you take my breath as usual, Amanda."

Farrell did know how to turn a nice compliment, but that was about all he knew how to do well. But Mabel was beaming at him and said to her friend Gertrude, loud enough for everyone nearby to hear, "They do make a beautiful couple, don't they?"

Amanda was embarrassed enough to cough. That remark was out of line even for a matchmaker. Mabel's friend must have thought so, too.

"I believe that could be said no matter who Lady Amanda stands next to."

That salvaged the moment, but to change the subject, Amanda told Farrell, "I believe Ophelia is planning on setting up whist tables throughout the house tomorrow."

His eyes lit up as she'd guessed they would, so she was surprised to hear him say, "I'm giving up gambling."

"Even for fun?"

"Indeed, I've finally figured out there's no fun in losing."

It had taken five years for him to conclude that? A lousy gambler, he wasn't good at lying either. She didn't for a moment believe that he'd give up something he craved. Had Mabel convinced him that he had a chance with her? Was that why he was saying what he thought she would want to hear? She ought to be honest enough to tell him to look elsewhere for his "pot of gold." He might be amusing at times, but he certainly wasn't the man for her.

John Trask saved her from having to make that unpleasant confession right then and there—either from jealousy, since he hoped to win Amanda, too, or simply because he shared Farrell's love for gambling. Amanda didn't know and didn't care.

John grabbed Farrell, telling him excitedly, "A moment, old chap. You're the only one who can tip the scale on a wager we've got going," and he dragged Farrell away.

Amanda took that opportunity to tell Mabel, "I don't want to hurt his feelings but I will if you persist. Who is paying you to recommend someone so inappropriate for me? I assumed it was my father, but now I'm beginning to think you work for Exter's family instead."

Mabel gasped. But Julie had been close enough to hear that, and she, apparently, already knew what Mabel had been trying to do. Joining their little group, Julie said gruffly, "Good God, Mabel, have you gone batty in your old age? How dare you try to foist a ne'er-do-well on my niece?"

That left Mabel red-faced and speechless, but then Julie didn't expect or want a reply. Having made her contempt known, she added insult to injury by giving the old dames her back and leading Amanda away with her.

"Well, I never!" Mabel huffed as soon as Julie was out of earshot.

For once, Gertrude didn't hold her tongue. She didn't like to argue, which was why Mabel, with her more dominant nature, had got away with cowing her for so many years. But Mabel wasn't always this way. She used to be sensible. She'd just got too overblown with their successes, most of which could be credited to Gertrude's sound advice. But Mabel really had gone too far this time.

"I saw that coming," Gertrude said. "The Lockes aren't fools. That member of the family is simply more outspoken than the rest. And Julie was absolutely right. Even you know she's right.

If I can't recommend Exter in good conscience, neither can you. And don't think I don't know why you've done it. Just because his mother's a dear friend of yours whom you've known even longer than me."

Mabel was a little shocked that Gertrude was openly disagreeing with her. "But he *will* make a good husband—with the right wife."

"You mean someone who will overlook the fact that he'll never amount to anything other than a pile of debts? I warn you, Mabel, if you persist in ruining the reputation you and I have strived to achieve over the years, just to help out an old friend, then I think you and I are done."

"The boy *has* to marry, Gertrude. He's driving his mother to drink, she's so worried over him."

"I don't believe that's our problem, is it?"

"Since when don't we help friends—if we can?"

"When it would hurt *other* friends. But if you truly want to help them, then look for someone who would feel elevated to be a member of his family. I can think of at least one social climber who would be thrilled by that association, enough to overlook his gambling habits, and two others who would be thrilled, but only if he actually gave up those habits. *That* would be the sensible approach to helping out an old friend."

Mabel sighed. "I know you're right. It just would have been such an achievement for him to land a duke's daughter. I suppose I got carried away. I'll break the news to him." Then with a conciliatory smile she asked, "Which gel would overlook his nasty habit?"

Chapter Forty-Five

JULIE HAD LED AMANDA out of the parlor and into the dining room across the hall. The formal table had been removed for the duration of the house party, replaced by a half dozen long serving tables at which servants stood ready to assist guests and refill the platters and serving dishes as needed. Amanda still wasn't hungry enough to eat, but Julie was and began filling a plate. Unfortunately, Devin was also in the dining room, a drink in his hand, talking with yet another middle-aged couple. He noticed Amanda immediately, gave her a long look, but didn't break off his conversation.

After a few covert glances in his direction, Amanda tried to ignore his presence and kept pace with Julie as she made her way down the length of one table, taking a little food from each platter. Maybe she should eat, Amanda thought. Maybe she should get out of that room where her only urge was to glance behind her to see if Devin was still there. Maybe she should just cry and get it over with.

Aunt Julie, still concentrating on her plate and peeking

under assorted covers, questioned, "What's wrong, m'dear? I thought you'd be relieved after I rescued you from that addle-brained old bird."

"I am, thank you."

"You don't look relieved."

"I'm confused."

Julie glanced at her sharply. "Surely not over that bounder?!"

"No, really." Amanda gave her a half grin.

"Then what's troubling you?"

"It's just—I don't know. The only thing I can guess is that I thought I'd be happy with so many choices, but I'm not."

"Do you really have so many? Seems to me you only have one."

"Who?"

Julie snorted that Amanda would even ask that. "The one you can't keep your eyes off for more'n a minute."

Amanda winced to herself, having little doubt that her aunt was talking about Devin. Apparently her father wasn't the only one who'd noticed how often her eyes traveled to him. But she didn't want to acknowledge that guess or have to explain that he wasn't interested in getting married. So he really wasn't a choice—was he?

In an effort to get both their minds off Devin, she said, "You haven't even met Kendall yet. When you do, you'll see why—"

"I saw him. Handsome boy, quite dashing, can't deny that, no indeed. I suppose you *could* be happy with him."

Did her aunt have to sound so doubtful?

"Besides," Julie added, "if *you're* so sure about him, what are you confused about?"

"That's the problem, I'm not sure about him yet, when there's still Robert to consider, too. And with both of them in the same house, both wanting my attention at the same time, I really am going to have to decide which one I prefer."

"Thought you'd already figured on doing that by the time this party is over."

"That was the plan," Amanda agreed. "But that was before I realized that one of them might be offended and leave if I don't give him my undivided attention."

"Nonsense, you've had beaus competing over you for three Seasons now. They know how it's done."

She could almost feel Devin's eyes on her back. It was making it deuced hard for her to concentrate. Julie was staring at her, waiting for a reply.

She finally got out, "I—I'm afraid Kendall might be the exception, that he'll back off rather than compete. Unlike the others, Kendall didn't come to town to get married, hadn't even thought of marriage yet, *and* he doesn't actually socialize, so he's only here to see me."

Julie scoffed. "There's an easy solution. Just concentrate on the one you think will bolt. The other one will probably enjoy the competition as most of them do, giving you the time you expected to have to make your choice—or you could concentrate on the one you keep stealing glances at."

Amanda rolled her eyes. "I'm going to take your first bit of advice, which is the most logical, and give Kendall my undivided attention. Well, that's *if* he isn't scandalized tomorrow when we go riding, me astride."

Julie snorted. "If he is, I'll show him the door m'self. Now, if you're not going to eat, go enjoy your party. It *is* for you, you know."

With a grateful nod, Amanda hurried out of the room. Devin started to do the same, but Julie moved forward to intercept him. "She's not going anywhere you can't find her later," Julie said knowingly. "A moment, if you please."

"Of course, Lady Julie."

"I've come up with the perfect payment for your matchmaking efforts on Amanda's behalf."

"I told you that wasn't necessary. She's pretty much made her choice."

"Has she? I'm not so sure. And she mentioned to me your interest—"

"She did what?!" Devin said, alarmed.

Julie laughed. "Don't get ahead of me. Your interest in a champion stallion. A friend of mine has one for sale."

Devin blushed slightly before he said, "We're probably talking about the same horse, but your friend keeps raising his price on me."

"Yes, Mandy mentioned that, too, which is why I got him down to a firm, reasonable price for you. My payment, as it were, for Cupid's assistance. The question is, when are *you* going to get in the running?"

Devin burst out laughing. Lady Ophelia had cornered him an hour ago to tell him how pleased she was with his work as Cupid, and if the happiness Amanda had been displaying continued to the altar, he would earn a big bonus. The Lockes didn't need a matchmaker, they had a house full of them!

Chapter Forty-Six

IT WAS A HECTIC two days for Amanda, riding with Kendall, still taking early-morning lessons with Devin, and helping Ophelia organize activities to keep the guests amused during the day. Aside from the usual parlor games, the ladies were offered tapestry sewing, which was typically a chance to gossip without men around. But Ophelia had had a special tapestry drawn for the occasion, though the ladies weren't aware of that. If they had been, they would no doubt have asked why they were putting their needles to a finely sketched image of Scottish bagpipes. The Highland musicians hadn't arrived yet—and were still Ophelia's closely held secret for her husband's birthday ball!

But the highlight of the party thus far was indoor croquet! Trust Ophelia to come up with something novel. The game was set up in the ballroom, with specially crafted wickets that would stand upright despite the absence of grass. But the very absence of grass threw a new wrinkle into a game everyone loved, since the balls went flying across the wooden floor with nothing to stop them other than strategically placed rugs that might or might not slow them down a little. So everyone had to adjust his or her mallet swing and soon figured out how to aim toward those rugs first, then the wickets. Laughter poured out of the ballroom, Amanda's included.

Ophelia had, realizing belatedly, said, "I probably should have had pillowy balls made up that wouldn't travel so far."

Amanda had disagreed. "This is more fun! As long as nothing gets broken, including people's ankles!" Quite a few guests had to hop out of the way of the speeding wooden balls.

Kendall enjoyed himself and was even heard to remark, "Didn't know parties could be so entertaining."

Nervous about her first ride with Kendall, Amanda had been amazed that his only comment about her riding astride with him had been "Wouldn't have suggested this if you were on your usual saddle, but would you care to race?"

Amanda had laughed and politely declined, telling him, "I'm not used to this mare yet, she's new."

She should have been more pleased by Kendall's acceptance of how she chose to ride. She'd worked so hard for this, and she *did* like him. Everything about him was right, but—but what? Was it just that Devin now excited her more? It probably was, but *that* wasn't going anywhere. He was even back to being strictly professional and rather abrupt with her during their lessons, as if he was trying to distance himself from her—or push her toward Kendall, *his* choice for her.

Tonight she wore a pale lavender gown with front closures because she knew the servants were going to be invited to join the festivities tonight as soon as the Highland musicians arrived, but rather than spoil the surprise for Alice, she just told her to take the night off.

Amanda's father was waiting for her at the bottom of the stairs and gave her his arm to escort her to the ballroom, but paused on the way. "I also want to give you a well-deserved gift, for the same reasons Devin did." He showed her the bracelet dangling from his finger. It had a single charm on it, a white opal horse.

"How thoughtful!" she exclaimed, hugging her father, then holding out her wrist so he could put the bracelet on her. "It's beautiful, Father. Thank you."

"You deserve it for what you accomplished. Now, may I have the first dance?"

Amanda laughed. The Scotsmen were already playing, and no waltzes tonight! The music was lively and the dancing much more exuberant because of it. It took the servants to show the nobles how!

"Are you sure you want to try that?" Amanda asked her father.

"I've been to Scotland a few times in my day. This does bring back memories."

They took to the floor. Amanda spotted Duncan MacTavish and his wife, Sabrina, standing with Ophelia. Inviting Rafe's old friend to the party had been Ophelia's other surprise for her husband. To go by the surprise and pleasure on Rafe's face when he joined them, Amanda could see that Ophelia had succeeded in keeping that a secret, too. Rafe swept his wife into an amorous embrace that ended with an even more amorous kiss. Quite a few people cheered, guessing correctly that he'd just got another birthday gift.

After the dance, Amanda started toward her brother's group to greet his friends, but was surprised to see her eldest aunt, Esmerelda, in the ballroom without a coat on and couldn't resist stopping to tease her about it. But Esmerelda was talking to her sister Julie, and Amanda caught the tail end of their conversation before they noticed her.

"Those two never could keep their hands off each other," Esmerelda said with a chuckle, gazing at Raphael and Ophelia. "I knew what kind of hanky-panky was going on in my house when they stayed with me before they married."

Amanda decided not to interrupt them after all. She wasn't sure if her aunt meant Rafe and Ophelia had actually been intimate before marriage, but obviously Phelia had been bold enough to share something with Rafe prior to marriage, which could well have opened their eyes to how much they were in love with each other. What if she was a little more forward, even seductive, with Devin? It was worth a try when she wasn't sure she could go forward with marriage to someone else without at least knowing what Devin's feelings for her really were.

She went off to find him. The bracelet from her father reminded her that she'd never thanked Devin properly for his gift of Sarahtoo. She found him standing alone, his friend William just leaving his side.

She gave him a warm smile. "Sarahtoo was one of the nicest gifts I've ever received. I know I thanked you for finding her for me, but I didn't know you'd—"

"You deserved it," he cut in, obviously uncomfortable with her gratitude. "You accomplished what you set out to do. In fact, if you're not going to tackle the sidesaddle, you don't need any more lessons."

"I still might," she said quickly, alarmed at the thought of not seeing him after the party was over. "Haven't made up my mind about it yet."

He raised a black brow. "I could have sworn your father

made up your mind for you on that subject. And Kendall didn't mind your riding style at all, did he?"

She didn't want to discuss Kendall, sidesaddles, or that she'd gone to a lot of trouble to win a man she was no longer thrilled with. Making an effort to be a little more assertive, she asked, "Would you like to dance one of these Scottish reels with me?"

"Too rambunctious for me, I'll pass."

She was going to suggest a moment of stargazing on the terrace instead, but he looked directly into her eyes, and the warmth she saw in his amber gaze stole her breath away.

"But you go ahead and enjoy the dancing," he said, then actually walked away from her! She glanced down and away to hide her acute disappointment.

William approached Amanda and, apparently, noticing her hurt expression, said, "Devin's abruptness can sometimes seem insulting, but it's not intentional. He's a fine man, he just had a hard time as a child growing up with no parents. He resists getting close to people. I used to wonder if it was because he thinks they'll leave him as his parents did."

She was amazed by William's insight. She'd felt sorry that Devin had grown up without parents and had felt closer to *him* when he'd told her about it. But it hadn't occurred to her that his unusual childhood would make him afraid to risk loving someone.

Wanting to assure William that she wasn't as hurt as she must have appeared, she said with a smile, "Thank you. Would *you* like to dance?"

He grinned widely. "It would be my honor."

Robert found her for the next dance, then Kendall after that, though he seemed quite uncomfortable dancing a reel. John Trask gave it a whirl, though she could tell by the fumes coming off him that he'd been drinking a bit heavily with his gambling cronies tonight, so it was a wonder he didn't trip them up. But she did spend the rest of the evening trying not to think about Devin and managed to have a fun if exhausting time. She even danced with the butler!

But by the time the Highlanders proved they could play a waltz, Amanda didn't feel like dancing anymore. Despite the early hour, she decided to slip away, letting her father know that the Scots had worn her out and she needed a little extra rest tonight.

The lamp that had been left on in her room had burned out, and the fire in the fireplace was down to just embers, but the moonlight streaming in was bright enough that she didn't need more light simply to prepare for bed.

She stood in front of the fireplace, and after removing her gown, she tossed it onto the nearest chair. She was reaching for the ties on her chemise when she felt the draft on her bare shoulders and thought Alice had followed her upstairs to help her. She swung around to scold her maid and send her back to the party, but sucked in her breath instead. It wasn't Alice who'd opened her door. . . .

Chapter Forty-Seven

"THEY'VE JUST TOLD ME you won't have me. I'd been willing to wait, to win you fairly. But now they want to push drabs on me instead. I won't have it!"

Farrell Exter stood just inside the door. He sounded so foxed, he probably didn't realize the door was still open. If she screamed now, it would carry down the hallway, but none of the family's personal servants were in their wing tonight, they were all at the party! And her screams weren't likely to be heard downstairs over the noise of a hundred conversations. The realization made her blanch.

She was paralyzed with indecision. Would screaming spur Farrell to action or frighten him away? If he didn't sound furious, too, she could probably talk sense into him. But inebriation and anger were a lethal combination. It had given him the foolish courage to show up in her room. For what? Just to complain because she wouldn't have him? Yet the fear that was upon her warned her he wanted something she'd never willingly give him. She opened her mouth to scream, but he laughed.

"Go ahead, and find out how quickly we get rushed to the altar."

Oh, God, *that* was his plan? She began to tremble, so terrified now that her voice cracked. "Get out."

"No, I don't think so," he said in a smug slur. "It occurs to me I can't lose here. We get discovered, you're compromised. I bed you, you're compromised. Either way, I win. So I might as well have a taste of what it's going to be like having you for a wife."

"My father won't give me to you no matter what!"

"No? Then he'll have to pay me off, won't he? To keep my mouth shut that you've been ruined. Sounds to me like I still win, with you or without—"

Farrell didn't get a chance to finish. Someone whipped him around and Amanda heard the crack of bone before Farrell hit the floor. But with him down, she now had a clear view of who had come to her rescue. Relief washed over her so quickly, she sank to her knees.

"Sounds to me like you just lost," Devin snarled as he bent to one knee to smash his fist into Farrell's face twice more. "Come near her again and I'll kill you." Then Devin yanked Farrell to his feet and tossed him out into the corridor. "Get out of this house now while you still can. Tonight! Tomorrow will be too late!"

Devin stood at the door, apparently making sure Farrell left the wing. He was facing the servants' stairs, which was probably the way Farrell had snuck up here.

"Sounds like he's tumbled down the stairs, he's in such a hurry. Good. Hope he broke his bloody neck!" Devin turned back into the room, drew in his breath sharply at the sight of her in her underclothes, and didn't move another inch. He seemed as transfixed as she was.

Then Devin pushed the door closed behind him and quickly strode over to her. He gently took her by the arms and lifted her to her feet.

Amanda clung to him, trembling. "Hold me, please, Devin. Don't let me go."

His arms immediately encircled her tightly. "I won't leave you, Mandy. I'm here. I won't let anything hurt you."

He held her like that for a long while. Her fear was fading, yet she didn't want him to let go of her, didn't want him to leave either, now that she was safe. So she squeaked in protest when she thought he was stepping back from her, but it was only to lift her in his arms and carry her to the bed. He tossed back the cover before he sat down with her in his lap, then pulled the cover over her. A blush showed up. She had been completely unmindful of her scanty attire, but he wasn't. But at least he was still too concerned over what had just happened and its effect on her to leave her yet.

Cradled in his arms, he began slowly picking the pins from her coiffure. Such an odd thing to do for her under the circumstances.

"You saved me," she said in a small voice.

"I think you could have done that on your own, he was so foxed. I doubt he'll remember this in the morning."

She would, but what she would also remember was that she was in Devin's arms again and it was the only place she wanted to be. But his gentle touch was making her feel a little too—oh, God, were those passionate feelings showing up again? She'd soon be squirming, and he'd think he was making her uncomfortable and try to leave!

"What were you doing in the family wing of the house?" she asked.

He was massaging her scalp with his fingers, now that her hair was tumbled back over his arm. "I saw you leave, but then I noticed Farrell leave right after you. I had a feeling he might be up to no good, so I came up here just to make sure it was all quiet—and found that it wasn't."

That's when his eyes met hers. A moment of exquisite combustion. She knew he'd wanted to soothe her and comfort her, which was why he'd covered her. But his desire to be chivalrous seemed to be overpowered by his real desire—ignited by hers.

The kiss was explosive. Her arm slipped from under the cover and went around his neck. She wasn't going to let him back off this time as he'd done twice before. My God, this is what had been driving her crazy, she'd been waiting for this again, to touch him, to taste him, to feel his passion.

He laid her back on the bed. Slowly and carefully, he removed the little she was still wearing. The cover that had shielded her no longer covered anything, she was lying on top of it now, watching him literally fight with his own clothes, he was removing them so fast. She held her breath, avid in her scrutiny, fascinated as he revealed more and more of that magnificent body to her. First, the thick muscles in his arms she'd seen before, then the wide chest, skin so taut it had no give. When he started to unbutton his pants, her maidenly senses reared and she turned her eyes away, looking quickly back up at his handsome face. Her breath caught yet again. It was there in his eyes, how much he wanted her. No, he wouldn't leave her this time. Whatever scruples had stopped him before were gone, and the very thought made her want to cry out with joy.

But she didn't dare make a sound until he was back in her arms. She didn't want him to know just how much she wanted him, too. He could still come to his senses. . . .

But then he was kissing her again, and lying so close to her that she could curl around him and did, placing one leg over his hips, locking it there, putting both arms around his neck, locking those, too. She couldn't hold back at that point, feeling so much of his skin against her, his heat, that a moan of pleasure escaped her, but it didn't scare him away, it urged him to greater boldness.

He didn't share her hesitancy or the deep shyness that couldn't be conquered quite yet, much as she wished it would go away. A desperate need made her hold so tight to him when she wanted to do so much more. But she was aware of everything he did, when his hands began moving all over her and stirring her to even greater heights of sensual pleasure.

Everywhere he touched, she tingled. Her neck, her shoulder, down her back, and slowly over her derriere before continuing along the thigh she had wrapped around him. But when his mouth began to take that same path, he seemed to want her to let go of his neck to give him more access. She whimpered, held him tighter, and heard him laugh just before he won that battle by leaning up and immediately lowering his head to capture one of her breasts in his mouth. Suckled with heat, her body was no longer in her control and arched into him, played to his tune, and it was galvanizing, her breaths coming in small pants now.

It was too much, what he was evoking, such a constant swirl inside, so many primal emotions that were almost frightening her, they were so unfamiliar, but deepest and most primitive was the urge to surrender to the torrent.

Then he was holding her eyes captive again. He wanted to watch her when the pleasure washed over her, and that's what happened the second his fingers slid inside her. Her eyes flared, then closed in that delicious abandon, her breath held, her amazement complete—no, not complete at all. He entered her while she was still in the throes of climax, drove deep to claim his own prize, and took her up to new heights. It was a different pleasure, so profound she felt it to her core, to the tips of her toes . . . to the recesses of her heart.

He was kissing her again, languorously, tenderly. Amanda was only vaguely aware of it, floating in a haze of happy contentment, until his brief laugh shook her. But she didn't even wonder about it since he lay back and drew her leg across him again. He pulled her arm across his chest, too, and wrapped his around her shoulder, holding her firmly to his side. She smiled to herself as she snuggled even closer.

His humor was directed at himself, she realized, when he said, "It's usually not so quick."

She didn't want to concentrate, she wanted to just savor the cocoon of happiness she was wrapped in, but she managed to at least say, "So it was special for us?"

"*Special* doesn't begin to describe something that beautiful."

She was going to say she agreed, but she floated into sleep instead, now that she could, now that the turmoil was gone.

Chapter Forty-Eight

AMANDA HID HER FACE under the blanket when she heard Alice enter the room with her morning tray. Or was it Devin leaving—no, she vaguely recalled waking in the middle of the night to find herself alone. She'd merely gone back to sleep, still smiling. She couldn't get back to sleep now, not as early as she'd—they'd—gone to bed.

But she continued to hide her face simply because she was smiling again, couldn't seem to stop it, and she didn't want Alice to see and ask why. Good Lord, how was she going to get through the day feeling like this, so happy she felt like shouting?

"Come on then," Alice said from the other side of the bed. "You don't think I wanted to get up this early, do you?"

Early? Amanda pushed the blanket back to see that the room was still dark, with no light around the edges of the drapes to indicate it was morning yet.

"Why are you waking me?"

"Because you told me to. A riding lesson at dawn, before the guests arise. You don't remember?"

Amanda laughed and leapt out of bed. Devin might have said last night that she didn't need any more lessons, and she didn't—now. Her choice had been made for her, which might be quite illogical, but there it was, and she wasn't about to fight it when it felt so right. But after what they'd shared last night, she had no doubt that he'd still be waiting for her at the stables.

"And don't you look perky this morning," Alice remarked as she helped Amanda into her robe. "So tired you didn't even put your nightclothes on? That must have been a good sleep."

"Indeed, it feels like the best I've ever had." Amanda walked over to examine the tray of pastries.

"You've made your decision, haven't you?" Alice guessed.

Amanda kept her back to the maid. She was smiling again! But she didn't want to tell anyone why, not even Alice. At least, not until she'd spoken with Devin and shared her feelings with him first. Would he be surprised? No, he'd probably known that she was in love with him before she'd figured it out! No wonder he'd given in last night.

"Well?"

Amanda peeked back at Alice with a grin. "I'm not going to say until after he declares himself—which just might be today!"

Alice laughed, drawing her own conclusions. But she was moving toward the bed to change the bedding as she did every morning. Amanda's eyes widened, appalled by the realization that Alice was about to find some very noticeable evidence of last night's activity. How could Amanda have forgotten about that?

She quickly said, "The bedding can wait. I ate so early last night, I think I need something a little more substantial from the kitchen. But do hurry, I don't want to be late for my lesson."

Alice nodded and headed for the door. "I don't think you

need to worry about being late. There was a stir in the kitchen when I arrived, something about one of the guests blocking the back stairs. He must have gotten lost and was too foxed to go any farther, so he slept right there! But he got nasty when the butler tried to wake him. Then your Cupid came in for a bite, heard the fuss, and said he'd take care of it. So he's helping the young lord to bed."

Alice didn't wait for a reply, not that Amanda could think of one. Devin was going to help Farrell? Off the property would be her guess. But while she had a few moments alone, she rushed to the washstand for a quick rinse, then changed the bedding herself and hid the old sheets. But with the evidence gone, her smile didn't return.

Exter had got off too easy last night. She hoped Devin would trounce him again. Actually, she should tell her father about Farrell's nasty plan, but realized she couldn't, not without talking to Devin about it first. Preston would want to know why Devin was keeping such a close eye on her that he'd actually come to her room last night to check on her and be on hand to rescue her. While she didn't doubt that Devin would propose marriage to her now, she wanted to actually hear him do so, before she shared that wonderful news with her father.

Outside, Devin was walking Farrell Exter to the stable. Forcing was more like it. Arm around the other man's shoulders as if they were friends, Farrell didn't know how close he was to another beating. The bounder was wisely holding his tongue. No apologies, no excuses. Did he even remember? But Farrell finally noticed where they were headed and tried to stop.

Devin kept them walking. "You're leaving."

"No, I'm—"

"Leaving now. And let me refresh your memory, just in case your sodden state deluded you into forgetting. If you ever come near Amanda Locke again, I'll kill you."

Farrell paled. "I was drunk, man. I didn't know what I was doing."

"Doesn't matter. My promise stands." Devin shoved Farrell the last few feet toward the stable door.

Farrell dropped all pretense and swung about to snarl at him, "I have belongings in that house!"

"I'll have one of the servants leave your things outside the back door. Get your horse saddled, pick up your belongings, and be gone. And I would advise you to avoid me in the future. You don't know how close I came to killing you last night."

Fear on his face, yet impotent fury in his blue eyes, Farrell turned and disappeared into the stable. Pathetic man, as bad as John Trask, both chained to their weaknesses. Trask had begged Devin not to mention to anyone that he'd gone even deeper into debt with that unsavory lender. Yet Devin had seen Trask since then gambling again! Unlike William, whose parents had left him in debt, those two gamblers had no excuse. They looked for a free ride in the turn of a card when they could have done what most second sons did, join the military to distinguish themselves with honor, instead of shaming their families with debtors' prison, which is where those two were headed.

Devin returned to the house to have Exter's things fetched, then moved to the corner of the house where he could watch to make sure Farrell left the property—and stop Amanda if she came outside before that happened. He wasn't going to let her have words with the man again if he could prevent it.

But he didn't really think she'd show up this morning. He wasn't sure what he was going to say to her if she did. His conscience was prompting him to take off with his tail between his legs just as Farrell was. She deserved so much better.

He'd lost every bit of common sense he had last night. He hated Farrell Exter for setting that in motion, for what Farrell had attempted to do to Amanda, for what the man had caused *him* to do to Amanda. Devin had been so scared by what could have happened to her that he'd lost all control and just let his feelings take over.

It was an amazing night. He was so tempted to believe that she could love him and he could have a life with her. But he knew better. Now he was wallowing in guilt for not having had the will to resist Amanda Locke.

Chapter Forty-Nine

AMANDA MISSED CATCHING THE sunrise, but only by minutes. That early in the morning, there was no doubting winter
had arrived, as cold as it was. But Alice had dressed her accord-
ingly in her longest and thickest coat. It had the added benefit
of covering her riding skirt, at least it would until she was actually on her horse. The ride would warm her. It always did, considering who rode beside her.

She hurried to the stable, was nearly running in her eagerness to see Devin again, bubbly with excitement. The door was
open. Devin was just inside with his horse, already saddled,
tightening the straps. Herbert had been getting her mare ready
for her for these early-dawn rides, ever since she'd told him
about her lessons, but the groom was probably late this morning because of the party last night.

Devin heard her arrive, glanced her way, but his expression was more solemn than she'd ever seen it, and that wiped
the smile from her lips. She thought for a moment that the
light of day behind her might be preventing him from seeing

who she was, until he said, "I didn't expect you to show up this morning."

She moved forward slowly, confused. "You were going riding without me?"

"No, I'm leaving."

She was crushed, pain welling up in her chest, but she fought to push it back. Now would not be the time to jump to conclusions. Something could have happened that she didn't know about to make him have to leave for a while—and look so serious about it.

"Why?" she asked hesitantly.

"Last night shouldn't have happened. I was supposed to help you made a good match, not get in the way of you making one. I don't belong here, Mandy, and I certainly don't belong in your life. The most I could ever be for you was a riding instructor, and now those lessons are over."

She was too shocked and hurt by his rejection of her to say a word. She was about to run for the house when she saw old Herbert coming up the aisle with her mare, and she ran past Devin to reach Sarahtoo instead. Herbert started to give her a boost up, but with her split skirt, she didn't need it. She nudged the mare toward the door, would have raced out of there if Devin weren't blocking the way.

"Move!" she cried when she reached him. "I'm riding with or without you."

"Mandy—"

The anger had arrived, but unfortunately her tears did, too. But she embraced the anger. "Don't worry, I'll consider last night just another of those lessons you want me to forget!"

"Don't cry!"

She didn't wait for him to move but pushed past him and

bolted out of the yard, heading straight toward the woods and one of the riding paths her brother had cut through them. She spurred the mare to the fastest pace she could get out of her, as if she might be able to race away from the pain in her breaking heart. She was in the woods before she knew it, but Rafe's trails were wide. Not that she could see much of it through the tears. Not that she cared.

But Devin followed her! He was shouting at her, *and* gaining on her. His stallion was faster. Much as she wanted to, she wasn't going to escape him out here in the woods. She needed to return to the house to do that. She just had that thought when she saw his stallion next to her and felt his arm about her waist. He was going to yank her off the horse! She started to tell him that wasn't necessary, but the crack of gunfire was too close, drowning out her words.

He pulled her toward him, but didn't stop there. He actually fell off his horse, taking her with him! No, he landed on his feet, holding her to his side, and immediately lowered both of them behind the brush beside the trail.

"Stay down," he hissed at her.

"That was a—"

"Quiet."

Having cautioned that, he let out a loud whistle, more noise than she would have made. Both horses had raced on without them, but his came trotting back after a moment. Devin leapt up to grab the rifle she hadn't even noticed was attached to his saddle, then he whacked the horse to run off again and rejoined Amanda on the ground.

She was staring at him wide-eyed, her heartache forgotten for the moment as she frantically looked for the blood that would account for his losing all the color in his face. But all she could see was a tear on his jacket high on his upper arm that looked to be no more than a nick. Yet, realizing which arm it was, and that if he hadn't bent to the side to grab her off her mount, the bullet would have entered his chest, it was no wonder she was shaking like a leaf in the wind.

She kept quiet as ordered, since he was obviously listening for sounds of movement. Yet whoever had fired that shot was apparently doing the same thing, unless it hadn't been as close as it sounded and the person had already slunk away.

A good ten minutes later, with still no other sounds around them, she whispered, "You carry a rifle with you? Why?"

"Since I started getting shot at, yes, it seemed like a good idea."

"Who's been shooting at you?"

"If I knew that, then I wouldn't be the one dodging bullets."

"Farrell?"

Devin snorted softly. "I actually wish it was that bounder, but, no, this has been going on long before Exter showed what an arse he is."

"You have enemies?!"

"At least one."

"Then that's who it is, so who is it?"

"I repeat, I don't know."

"You just said—"

He put a finger to her lips. "This isn't the time to discuss it. That bullet could have hit you, Mandy. I only took precautions before, now I want blood. I *will* find out who just risked your life to get at me, but right now, I need to get you to safety."

So that's why he'd paled? Because he was frightened for her? And well he ought to be, she thought as her anger returned.

She wasn't going to take risks for him when he wanted no part of her.

He whistled again. Once more his horse trotted back to him. If she wasn't filled with painful, angry emotion, she might have asked him to teach her how to do that. But there would be no more lessons from him, of any sort.

He still wasn't taking any chances. He tossed her up on his mount and leapt up behind her. But he even forced her to lean down against the stallion's neck for added cover as he raced them out of the woods. No more shots were fired though. His enemy was either hiding, thinking he'd missed, or long gone, thinking he'd succeeded.

He didn't take her to the stable, but to her front door, dismounting before he helped her down. He started to touch her cheek, but she jerked her head back.

"You can leave now," she said stiffly.

"Do you think it's not killing me, to keep you on the proper path? You deserve better'n me. No one has to know what we did. Kendall's too innocent to figure it out. He probably doesn't even know what a maidenhead is, so he won't know it's missing on your wedding night."

She slapped him for that. "I'll know! But you're right, I can do better than a bastard who takes what he wants and doesn't give a damn about the consequences. Sounds like your father, doesn't it?"

"Mandy—"

She'd already entered the house, slamming the door shut behind her, so she didn't see the effect her words had on Devin.

Chapter Fifty

H<small>IS FATHER. SUDDENLY IT</small> all made sense. The man who didn't want him, didn't want to even lay eyes on him, wouldn't want to be confronted with a *mistake*. He probably hadn't liked it when Devin moved to London where they might cross paths. That run of bad luck with the animals? That could have been his father trying to ruin him so he'd leave town again. When that didn't work, he'd arranged that shot at the farm, not a poacher after all but a warning—or he'd already decided the easier way to make sure they never met was to kill him. Good God, even the attack on William could have been meant for him, since Will had been using the same coach that night that Devin used when he needed one in town. And now Devin was asking questions, which could have alerted his father that he was actually looking for him now.

Was the man panicking? Afraid Devin would show up at his home and his family would know about his youthful indiscretions? Devin couldn't begin to guess the workings of a mind like that. Hating his father as much as he did, he'd never once thought of killing him. All he'd ever wanted was answers, to know why he'd been denied a father so completely.

He mounted his horse, but stared at the closed door for a moment more. He was glad Amanda was angry, better than that hurt he'd seen in her eyes, when there wasn't a bloody thing he could say to take it away. She didn't understand and he didn't know how to fix it, short of letting her be stuck with him, which she wouldn't thank him for. But he couldn't think of that now. He had to protect her first. Talking to his uncle could no longer wait. He rode straight for London and his answers.

Arriving at his uncle's home, he was directed to Donald's study, which was no longer a study. Furniture removed, easels filled the room now with canvases mostly finished, but some works still in progress. Donald spent his mornings here with the hobby he was surprisingly good at. Though he preferred park scenes, he'd tried his hand at a few portraits, and the one he'd done of Lydia now hung above the mantel in the parlor.

Donald's two hounds were lying outside the door, waiting for him to come out. They both sat up at Devin's approach, probably hoping he'd let them in to be with their master. He didn't, but it wasn't easy slipping inside with both of them trying to follow him in.

"Why do you keep your dogs out?" he asked as he closed the door again.

Across the room, Donald laughed. "Because I'm tired of picking their hair off of my paintings, especially whichever one I'm working on that isn't dry yet. I thought you were in Norford for the week?"

"I came home for some information." Devin wound his way

around the easels to reach Donald. One distracted him though, a portrait of Devin himself. "When did you paint *that*?"

Donald came over to stand next to him and gave his work a critical look. "Recently."

"Do I really look that unhappy?"

"No, of course not, you're just—always preoccupied with the business. And—" Donald paused to chuckle. "I was just never able to sketch you in a more lighthearted mood. The fault was mine. I should have just asked you to pose for me, instead of sneaking about to sketch you when you weren't aware of it so I could present the painting as a surprise."

"It looks finished. Why did you never present it?"

"For the very reason you just mentioned, you look too serious in it. I was going to try again."

"Remind me to sit for you then sometime soon, or maybe not soon. Actually, I have a feeling you won't be seeing me lighthearted for a while."

"Has something happened?"

"Much more than expected." Devin briefly explained about the attempts on his life, ending with "This can't be shrugged off with 'better left unknown' anymore. I need to find my father to put a stop to his nefarious madness."

"But you're only guessing it's him!"

"Can you honestly think of a more likely culprit?"

"*Anyone* other than your actual father, Devin. Truly, he would have to have the darkest heart imaginable—"

"Who says he doesn't?"

"But he paid for your schooling! That's not something a blackhearted bastard would do."

"You said that missive came to you anonymously. You only

assumed it was from him. But I have since learned that Wolseley was the one supporting my mother. He loved her all those years in London, and he was a generous man. It's much more likely that Wolseley paid for my schooling, as a final gift for my mother." Devin wished he'd asked the man about it when he'd had the chance. "We don't know a bloody thing about my real father. It's time we did. I need a name, Uncle. Who was my mother's solicitor? Her sponsor that first year in London? The name of her maid. Give me something to work with."

"We were ten years apart in age, Devin. I never involved myself with her come-out. Our mother arranged it before she died."

"You don't have *any* name you can give me?"

"No, I'm sorry. But I kept all of her personal belongings. They are stored in the attic in Lancashire, even that last missive from her. You *do* still have that figurine she sent with it? There was something else in the note, that wasn't appropriate to tell you at the time, something about that figurine."

"What?"

Donald rubbed his brow for a moment, then sighed. "Damned memory, I can't recall the words. But I do remember thinking, 'Why would she be so concerned about a damned figurine when she was dying?'"

"Why do you say 'concerned'?"

"It's all that missive, written from her deathbed, was about, that porcelain horse. You do still have it?"

Devin looked down at the floor, remembering the night he'd buried it next to her grave. "Yes, it's in Lancashire, too. And if I leave now, I can probably get there before midnight."

Donald snorted. "You know that's not possible. I'll go with you, to make sure you break the trip with some sleep."

Devin grinned. "I was joking, but I'm still going to be riding hard. I'll let you know what I find out as soon as I get back."

Devin left immediately. It was a long trip, but the fastest he'd ever traveled the route—and Amanda wouldn't stay out of his mind. He'd never thought he'd want a woman this much, so much he wanted to spend every day of his life with her. But that was impossible. He recalled his mother's words to him so long ago: *You don't know what it's like to love like this. I hope you never find out.* But he'd done exactly what his mother had warned him against doing, he'd fallen in love with a woman and it was breaking his heart that he couldn't have her.

He wasn't racing to Lancashire, he was racing away from his thoughts, and exhaustion kept them away. Sleep didn't want to find him anyway. Between two nights of trying, he maybe got a total of ten hours of sleep. And he was too close to the farm to stop a third night, so he did actually arrive around midnight after all. Ironic. Hadn't he buried that figurine around the same time?

He still didn't know what it was supposed to tell him, but he dug it up and took it up to his old room. He set it on the mantel, then got a fire going. He doubted he'd ever live in this house again, yet the servants still kept it at the ready for him, logs beside the fireplace, fresh towels on the washstand, clean bedding, which he was definitely going to appreciate tonight. But first things first.

He lit the lamps and took one with him up to the attic. Elaine's things were all in one corner of the huge room, five trunks of clothes, two small chests. He wasn't about to go through all of that tonight, but he did open the two little chests. One was filled with her jewelry, the other contained her correspondence. Quite a few letters and notes were stuffed in it. That ought to put him to sleep, reading through those, so he took the chest back to his room and dumped it out on his bed, then lay back and started reading.

Most of the letters were from old childhood friends from Lancashire. Two were from Donald, but he decided not to read those, written at the time of their estrangement. Donald had already told Devin he wasn't proud of the things he'd said to his sister back then. Countless notes were from Lawrence Wolseley, mostly silly love notes. The man hadn't lied, he had really loved Devin's mother. Nothing yet from a man whose name he didn't recognize. Then he finally found the note written by Elaine that Donald had added to the pile.

> Give the figurine to Devin. It's very important that he not lose it. He's too young to understand now, but when he's older, he will, and will realize how much I loved him. When he's a man, remind him of the horse.

That was it? How the devil were cryptic words like that supposed to lead him to his father? He stared hard at the figurine, still covered in dirt. Could a name have been etched into the porcelain or painted on it, too tiny for him to have noticed when he was a child? Had he even examined the horse before he buried it? He couldn't remember, but doubted it.

He got up and grabbed a towel to wipe the horse clean. He got all the dirt off it except for what had lodged in a thin seam on the underbelly where the porcelain halves had been joined. The seam on the upper horse had been polished to smoothness, but less care had been taken with the underside, which wouldn't be in view while the horse stood on display. But no hidden words were written in the fancy trappings painted on the horse.

He was too tired to figure out Elaine's cryptic words. Even if he did find a name etched on the figurine, it would probably be the name of the artist who made it. My God, still no answer? Angrily, he started to throw the horse at the fireplace, what he should have done years ago. He wasn't sure what stopped him this time, but he went downstairs to the kitchen instead to find a knife to dig the dirt out of the seam. He had to examine every single inch of the figurine first, *then* he'd break it for good.

Back in his room, he grabbed the horse and sat on his bed with it, next to the lamp. But as soon as he picked at the dirt with the tip of the knife, it was pushed inside the figurine and the blade slid in with it. An open crack and wider than it should have been, as if it were intended that way. So something could be slipped inside?

Excited now, he inserted the blade as far as it would go and twisted it. It didn't pry the horse apart, merely broke off a piece of the porcelain. To hell with trying to preserve the thing. He wrapped the horse in the towel, went to the fireplace, and hit it against the granite mantel, then opened the towel and picked out a folded piece of paper from the broken pieces.

My dearest Devin,

I hope you have found this when you are old enough to understand. I couldn't tell you the truth when you were a child, though I always intended to when you were grown. I'm sorry you must read it instead of hearing it from me, but fate decreed it so. I make no excuse for myself. I loved your father, even after I found out he wasn't worth loving. The heart is so foolish that way. But Lord Garth was charming, handsome, and he professed to love me, too. I was young enough to believe him without question. It was a lie. He told all his women that, it's how he seduced them. Don't ever be that way, Devin. Don't ever say those words unless you mean them.

I thought he would marry me, even though he stopped pursuing me after he got what he wanted from me. I didn't know he was already married, that he even had children. He didn't confess that until I found him and told him about you. I was devastated. His true nature was revealed. He was no more than a heartless rake, not a father for you to be proud of. He didn't even apologize for what he'd done to me. He thought giving me a house to live in was ample payment for ruining me. He even suggested that I leave you at an orphanage, the easy solution. This is the man who sired you. I kept you, of course. You weren't even born yet, but I already loved you.

You may ask why I am telling you this now. I should also confess that I continued to love Garth Culley despite his callous treatment of me, though I was miserable because of it. Yet there was that foolish hope that someday he would forsake his family and come to us. His curiosity about you after you were born gave me hope. He didn't actually want to meet you himself, but he sent his friend Lord Wolseley to check on you. That was the only nice thing he ever did for me. Lord Wolseley was a man whose love I could depend on. But this letter isn't about Lawrence.

Eventually I came to feel nothing for your father other than the contempt he deserved. That is all I feel for him today. You are a man now. You have a right to know who he is and form your own opinion. He may even have found you before now. He may have changed and now regrets the man he used to be. Anything is possible, I suppose, and if this is so, then I'm sorry for telling you this.

Lastly, please know that it broke my heart to send you away with my brother, but it was getting harder and harder to lie to you. You were such a smart boy. You were figuring things out for yourself much too soon. And I was afraid I would give in and tell you the truth before you were old enough to really understand. My worst fear was that you would want to meet Garth and would be impressed by him, might even want to be like him. He could be so charismatic when it suited his purpose. I couldn't bear the thought of that happening. But I wouldn't have left you in the country indefinitely. I missed you too much. And now, I've waited too long to bring you home to me.

The knot in Devin's chest formed before he read the last words. His anger at his mother, which had been so painful to live with all these years, slowly faded away as the tears ran down his cheeks. She hadn't abandoned him. She'd tried to protect him from a man she despised, a man who now wanted him dead. It was ironic, though, that for his sake she had hoped Garth Culley might have changed for the better, when instead, he'd changed for the worse. But at least now Devin knew who his enemy was.

Chapter Fifty-One

"I NEED A WORD with you, Raphael, if you have a moment," Devin said.

Amanda's brother stepped outside and closed the front door behind him. Understandably, Devin's having sent the butler to find him, Rafe looked a bit confused, particularly since Devin was holding the reins of his mount.

"You don't want to come inside, I take it?"

"No, I don't want to see Amanda yet."

"And why is that? She's been acting deuced strange these last couple days since you disappeared." Then Raphael grinned. "Pining for you?"

Considering Raphael's complete turnabout where Devin was concerned—he'd even implied that Devin should be courting his sister!—Devin was about to deal a double blow to him. The easiest way to do that was to say, "I'm on my way to London to confront my father."

"Thought your father was dead."

"My real father."

Raphael's eyes widened, then abruptly narrowed. "I see. Well, bloody hell. You couldn't have mentioned this the other day when I was shoving you in Mandy's direction?"

"I did tell you she could do better'n me."

"So you did, but that meant absolutely nothing in the scheme of things. That you're a bastard bloody well does."

Devin winced. "Until this week, I didn't even know who my father was."

"Who is he?"

"I'd rather not say."

Frustrated, Raphael demanded, "Why are we even having this conversation?"

"Because while I know I'm not good enough for her, and that I'd only be an embarrassment to your family, that didn't stop me from falling in love with her."

Raphael snorted. "You and half of London. And your point is?"

"I've compromised her. I'll marry her if you see fit, but I'm in agreement with you that—"

Raphael's blow landed on Devin's jaw. It merely snapped his head to the side. The next blow to his middle doubled him over and cost him his breath. Raphael grabbed a handful of Devin's hair, lifting his head for the third blow, which cracked against the side of his cheek.

But after that one he snarled, "Why aren't you fighting back?"

It took a moment for Devin to straighten and start breathing again. "Because this is what I came here for. You can't imagine the guilt I'm dealing with."

Raphael backed away. "So I'm giving you what you want? To hell with that!"

"It wasn't supposed to happen! I found Exter in her room, terrifying her with his threats to marry her by force. I got rid of him, but our emotions were heightened from the incident—it just happened, Rafe."

"I didn't need to hear the bloody details! Good God, I can't believe I haven't killed you already. Go away, Baldwin, and don't come back."

"I can't oblige you in that. I've hurt her. I have to make that right before I bow out of the picture."

"Don't bother. I'll let her know you're a bastard."

"I already told her that. It sparked her compassion, which is why she might think she's in love with me, too. I need to help her to see the difference."

"The only thing that's going to happen if you come back here is I'm going to shoot you. Don't ever get within sight of Amanda again!"

Raphael wound his way through the guests looking for his sister. Again, she wasn't among them. He spotted his wife and headed to her side instead.

"Is she still hiding in her room?"

"If you mean Mandy, yes, I do believe so. And why do you appear so . . . angry about it?"

He sighed. "I thought I was hiding it quite well."

Ophelia patted his cheek. "You are, just not from me. So—why?"

"She's not going to get herself married if she doesn't get her arse down here. Did you find out why she's barricaded herself?"

"She doesn't want to talk about it, whatever *it* is. But you're closer to her than the rest of us are. Why haven't you asked her?"

He mumbled, "Because she bit my head off when I tried yesterday. She's not upset, she's furious."

"Well, I have to disagree with that conclusion, since I found her crying."

Raphael groaned. "A bundle of emotions? Well, now that I know why—"

"Wait just a moment. What do you mean that you know why? You were just asking me why! What just rang your bell?"

"Baldwin did. Mandy thinks she's in love—with the wrong man. I need to go tell her why she's not. Relieve her mind, et cetera."

"Good luck with that!" Ophelia called after him.

Did she have to sound so amused? Raphael gritted his teeth and went straight upstairs to pound on Mandy's door, but all he heard from inside was exactly what she'd said the last three times he'd knocked: "Go away."

"Not this time, m'dear. Open the door now, or I'll have to go to Father with what Baldwin just told me."

The door swung open wide. "Devin's come back?"

She tried to get past him, to go find the man. Raphael held her back and closed the door behind him. "A dozen men are downstairs hounding us with 'Where is she? Where is she? Where is she?' and I mention Cupid and you want to fly downstairs? Why is that?"

Her chin jutted out mulishly. "I don't want to discuss *him*. Now let me out of here."

"So you can go discuss him with—him? Sorry, but he didn't stay, he's—good God, don't cry!

"I am *not* crying!" Amanda said furiously, but she swung around to hide it.

Raphael winced. He couldn't abide tears, they quite undid him, but Amanda's were usually fake. These weren't. He started to put his hands on her shoulders but winced again when he heard the sniffle and stepped back with a sigh.

"Blister it, if you love him, then—"

"I don't, I hate him."

Raphael raised a brow, recognizing a whopper when he heard one. "He told me that he compromised you." He heard her gasp. "Tell me he has some different definition for that than I do."

She quickly wiped her eyes before she glanced back at him. "You mean he was just seen in my room and nothing else?"

"Yes!"

"No." She turned around to stare at him. "It was something that just got out of hand. It was a mistake. It won't be repeated. No one else has to know about it. I will *not* marry a man who doesn't want me."

"Are you sure about that?"

"I could shoot him right now. Yes, I'm quite sure."

"No, I meant that he doesn't want you? Seems to me that he does."

She drew in her breath. "What exactly did he tell you to give you that impression?"

"He thinks you're mistaking compassion for something else. He said he'd return to help you figure that out. He only stopped by on his way to London, something about going to meet his father."

"He found out who the man is?"

"Apparently. Wouldn't say who, not that it matters. Whether his father is a pauper or a lord, he's still a bastard."

"So? Don't you dare think that would matter to me *if* I loved him."

"But it does make you feel sorry for him, doesn't it? Admit it, you've let pity—"

"Don't be absurd. I merely understand him better now that I know about this secret of his. He's let it affect his entire life. He's let it make him feel unworthy. I think it's ridiculous for a person to shoulder the blame for something that was done before he was even born. And you know very well Father wouldn't turn him away because of that *if* I loved him."

Raphael grinned. "You're stressing that *if* an awful lot, m'dear. But buck up. He'll probably return tomorrow and you can shoot him or tell him you love him. You might want to figure out which course of action you'll take before then."

She stabbed a finger toward the door.

"I'm going." Yet he still paused to add, "If you want him, you can have him. You do know that, right? Wouldn't be the first time the groom arrives at the altar with a gun at his back."

She glared at him. "Wouldn't be the first time a bride runs like hell in the opposite direction, either. I won't have a man who doesn't love me, Rafe. I won't."

"He said this is killing him. Doesn't sound like a man who's not in love."

Raphael closed the door behind him. She yanked it back open and shouted down the corridor at him, "He said that?!"

He didn't stop, just started whistling a happy tune. He wasn't going to say what she needed to hear. He wouldn't have wanted to hear from someone else that Ophelia was in love with him. Amanda needed to hear it from the man himself. It was her feelings about Baldwin that had concerned him, and he had his answer to that.

She was still standing just outside her door waiting for him to answer her though. He stopped at the top of the stairs and yelled back at her, "I'll have my pistol sent up to you, just in case."

She didn't appreciate his teasing. "Careful I don't use it on you instead!"

Chapter Fifty-Two

Iᴛ ᴡᴀs ᴀ ᴍᴀɴsɪᴏɴ, the Caswell town house in the fashion-able upper end of town. It took Devin half the day to find it, so it was nearing dusk when he knocked on the door. He was delayed because the house didn't actually belong to the Culley family but was an inheritance from the Caswell side, left specifi-cally to their last descendant, Garth Culley.

Rich, obviously, even a marble floor in the foyer and a silk-upholstered bench for visitors who didn't get any farther than that. The butler, impeccably dressed, was gracious when he in-formed Devin that Lord Garth wasn't receiving. So Devin felt bad to tell the man, "I'm not leaving until I see him. Inform him that Elaine Baldwin's son demands his presence." Rather harsh, but it made his point.

The butler was surprisingly not perturbed, though, and merely nodded. "Very well, m'lord, you can wait here while I deliver your message." The man moved off down the hall to mount the grand stairs in the center of it.

Now that Devin was actually here and about to meet his

father for the first time, he would have thought some nervousness might show up. It didn't. The anger was there, just
barely under the surface. Eagerness was there, to have what had
haunted him his whole life finally resolved. But he felt an odd
calmness, too, despite knowing he was probably going to have
to kill the man, or maybe because of it. He had a pistol in his
pocket to do so. It would be like cutting out a cankerous sore—
or putting down a mad dog.

The anger took precedence when the butler appeared at the
top of the stairs instead of Garth. So he'd refused to see him?
Or was he loading his own pistol? Devin braced himself. But
the butler actually beckoned him forward and, when Devin
reached him, led him down the corridor to open a door for him
at the end of it.

He still braced himself. The man could be insane enough
to shoot him in his own house. And Devin couldn't stop him
immediately. The bedroom was well lit and lavishly furnished
in early-century French extravagance more suited to a woman's tastes. As if his mind had been read, he heard, "I've never
changed anything in this house. This was my maternal grandmother's room."

Devin's eyes were drawn to the bed, the last place he expected to find his father. He felt at a disadvantage now because
he stood there in plain view, giving Garth time to take his mea-
sure, while he had to approach the large four-poster bed to do
the same.

The first thing obvious to Devin was that Garth Culley
looked so much older than his fifties. His hair was prematurely
gray and thinning. If his eyes had ever been amber, they were
just a dull light brown now, bloodshot, sunken. His face was
gaunt, the skin loose as if he'd lost a lot of weight. There wasn't

much left of the man under the covers, certainly not one healthy enough to be running around the woods taking shots at Devin. But he was rich. He could afford to hire as many killers as he needed.

Garth was still taking in every inch of his son avidly. Devin went straight for the jugular with his question. "Why are you trying to kill me, Father?"

The question shocked the man, it was unmistakable. The confusion wasn't just in his expression but in his voice, surprisingly still strong for a man who looked so sickly. "Why would I kill my heir?"

Now Devin was shocked, but he recovered more quickly. "You really are crazy, aren't you? Your heir? When you don't even know me, never wanted to know me?!"

"You're wrong. I've had people spying on you all of your life. I even visited your school, talked to your teachers, watched you from afar. You fascinated me. You faced life with such courage."

"Liar," Devin snarled. "You would have introduced yourself if that were so!"

"No, the time for that was long gone. I'd made the decision early. I didn't want you to know what sort of man had sired you. I understand your mother didn't want you to know either. How is it you know now, when she's been dead all these years?"

Devin's anger was so strong now it was choking him. He couldn't believe what he was hearing. It made no sense. If the man really was as interested in Devin as he was claiming, he would have met him at some point, even if under pretense, without revealing who he really was. But he'd never done that.

Devin wasn't sure how he managed to produce an even tone to say, "She left me a letter. I only just found it."

"Sweet Elaine, what did she think to accomplish by that?" Garth said, truly perplexed.

"She entertained the thought that someday you might change and be worth knowing."

"Foolish girl, she should have known better. I don't remember most of the women I've wronged, but I never forgot Elaine. I was fond of her in my own way, which is why I was interested in you, I suppose. More'n my legitimate children, if truth be known."

It actually hurt to hear that. What the hell, did he *want* to believe it? He needed to sit down to get control of the emotions flaying him, but there was no chair beside the bed. Did no one ever visit the man? He did appear to be bedridden.

"What's wrong with you?" he asked bluntly. "With your health?"

"The better question would be, what isn't wrong with me," Garth said wryly. "You can't lead a life like I have and not pay the price."

"You're dying?"

"Indeed. They wonder why I haven't drawn my last breath yet. I wonder the same thing. Too many whores, too many diseases, have taken their toll. But I'm told it's consumption that's actually killing me."

Oh, God, where was the satisfaction in hating a dying man? This—meeting—was not going as expected. Not as hoped for. Not as ever imagined. Devin could at least say the words.

"I've hated you my whole life, even when I thought you were someone else."

"Why?"

"Because you denied me. Because you weren't there for me.

Because you wanted no part of me. And because you ruined my mother!"

Garth nodded. That might even have been something of a smile that twisted his lips. "Good reasons to hate, I suppose. But you would have hated me much much more if I had let you know me. Your mother, however, could have salvaged her life, could have still married well, even with a child. She was that beautiful. What did she do instead?"

Devin's fists clenched. "Went from loving one married man to another, yes, I know. Her taste in men was abhorrent."

"Nonsense. Wolseley worshipped her. He would have left his family for her, you know." At Devin's indrawn breath, Garth added, "You didn't know? It's true. But she wouldn't let him create a scandal for her. She was protecting you. Just as I was protecting you, in not giving in to the urge to be part of your life."

"I don't believe you."

"It doesn't matter. It was only a brief moment of madness, to entertain the notion of divorce and living a normal life with you and Elaine. It was a selfish notion. Nothing good would have come of it. Believe me, I'm not trying to make you see me in a better light. None exists."

"Good." Devin hit his chest. "Because I've lived with this hate so long, nothing you can do or say will remove it."

"Then you should be pleased to know that I've lost everyone in my life, everyone that I had the slightest care for. My wife died long ago, though she meant nothing to me. The son she gave me died in an accident, though he was as worthless of character as I was, exactly what I tried to keep you from becoming by denying *myself* access to you. The daughter she gave me died in childbirth, my only grandchild with her. My mother died before I reached adulthood. My father long ago disowned me and rightly so. Even the few friends I had have long since washed their hands of me."

"As you deserve?"

That twist of the lips that resembled a smile came again. "Why make that a question? Of course I deserve no better. And yet I have all this wealth, left to me by my maternal grandmother. She died when I was still a child, or she probably would have disowned me, too. Instead I get the immense wealth from her side of the family, to do with as I please. Didn't find that out, though, until after my father kicked me out of his life. I'm not sure he even knew. Probably stuck in his craw, to learn that his disowning me wasn't going to hurt as much as he'd thought, that I ended up richer than he is."

"He was petty that way?"

"No. It's a weakness of mine, to think everyone is as despicable as I am when I know they aren't, my father least of all. He's a good man. I am his greatest disappointment."

"He still lives?" But Devin answered his own question. "Owen Culley is your father, isn't he? A man I actually like?"

"I'm not surprised you'd like him. And, yes, he's your grandfather."

Devin felt an odd gladness, the very last thing he expected to feel in this house. "Then why didn't he tell me about you when I asked him?"

"What exactly did you ask him?"

"I told him I was looking for distant cousins with eyes like mine."

"Of course he wouldn't think of me."

"Then he doesn't know I'm his grandson?"

"He might suspect, if his eyesight is still good. You do

resemble the younger me somewhat, after all. And I'm sure he assumes I have bastards all over England. But he hasn't spoken to me or seen me in over thirty years."

"Why didn't you tell him I am your son? At least *he* could have been part of my life!"

"That would have been a decent thing to do, wouldn't it?" Garth said drily.

"And you've never done a single decent thing in your life?"

"Just one—I made sure you never met me. Fie on your mother for ruining that. But I do actually have a letter prepared for him, to be delivered upon my death, that mentions you. It wouldn't matter if he knows, after I'm gone. I wouldn't tell him sooner. It would have led you to me, and we were never supposed to meet. But now that we have, I suppose I can have the letter dispatched tonight. No need for you to be burdened with the task of telling him you two are related."

"He'll probably prefer it coming from me."

"So? I have never taken the opinion of others into account, why would I start now?"

"Fine. Do as you please!"

"This is how I've led this wretched life, Devin, doing whatever takes my fancy—no matter who it hurts. Did we not agree, you have every reason to hate me, and none to forgive? That you're my heir is only a matter of default."

Devin frowned. Why did that suddenly not have the ring of truth? Was his father making sure Devin continued to hate him? Not wanting him or anyone else to know that he might be trying to redeem himself in the last days of his life? Oh, God, he would be the biggest fool alive if he tried to see anything decent in this man.

Garth continued, "I thought it was ironic, that I would be

doing something to please my father after I'm gone, and never doubt, he will be pleased with you. You've turned out to be everything that I wasn't. You've tried to be hard, to remain aloof, and now I understand why, but—"

"You *don't* know me!"

"On the contrary, I have trunks filled with reports on you, from your servants, your mother's servants—no, don't look stricken, your friends and family would never betray you. It's so obvious that you care about everyone in your life. You're a good man, Devin. By making sure I didn't tarnish your life, you've grown into a man any father would be proud of. And this is why you're my heir. My only other choice isn't worth mentioning."

"Someone is trying to kill me. If not you—is it because of you? Because you've named me your heir?"

Garth looked stricken. "He wouldn't dare!"

"Who?"

"This needs investigat—"

"Who?"

"You can't intimidate a dead man, Devin. I will see to this for you, my last act of kindness."

"I want nothing from you, no inheritance, no favors. Just give me his bloody name! He's not waiting until I'm alone to shoot at me from the shadows. He could have hurt Amanda!"

"So you love her? I wasn't sure—there you go, looking surprised again. My spies are very good, they just can't read your mind."

"Then you know *why* I need to kill him!"

"No, if I've learned anything in my wretched life, it's that you don't need that on your conscience. If it's who I think it is, be satisfied he won't survive my retribution."

Devin walked away before he did something right then that

LET LOVE FIND YOU

he'd regret. He was still as furious as when he'd arrived. How unsatisfying that meeting had gone. He should be pleased the bastard was dying, but he hadn't expected that. What did he expect—before he thought the man was trying to kill him? What had he hoped for, prior to that? Some noble reason for his father's staying out of his life? His father *did* think he'd done the noble thing, to keep them apart. Was it? Would Devin be any different now if he'd grown up knowing the man? Wouldn't he have hated him either way?

He went home to Jermyn Street. He had so much filling his mind, his aunt had to yell at him to get his attention. She handed him a note with a worried frown. "This wasn't sealed, care to explain?"

He read, *She hates your guts, but she's going to shoot me if I shoot you. Come back to Norford, we need to talk. Rafe.*

Devin burst out laughing. Raphael Locke certainly had a way with words, but these words washed away Devin's guilt and every other nasty emotion that had been bedeviling him.

"I do believe the lady loves me," Devin said with a grin.

"You gather that from her hating your guts?" Lydia huffed. "Amazing."

Chapter Fifty-Three

"YOU KEEP HAVING MY chair removed from your bedside."
The whiny tone was so typical. Garth was disgusted as usual.
At least he didn't hold himself accountable for how this pathetic
excuse for a man had turned out. The boy's mother had spoiled
him beyond redemption, paying his way out of every scrape,
never letting him face up to the consequences of his actions.
It's too bad her husband didn't show them both the door when
she cheated on him. But Garth wasn't her first indiscretion, and
Marianne's husband would have been a hypocrite to divorce her
when he'd never been faithful either.

"Possibly because I don't want your company?" Garth said
as the boy came to stop by his bed. "But you are too stupid to
take the hint."

Farrell pretended not to hear that, reminding him, "You
sent for me."

"This once, yes, I did. But you won't be here long enough
to get comfortable, so the arrangement of my furniture is of no
consequence."

"Actually, I thought I might stay here with you for a spell, if you don't mind. Got a damned duke's son after my hide. Thinks I tried to force m'self on his sister. He showed up at my brother's house. I just barely managed to slip away."

"Yes, I know."

"You know? How—?"

"I've had a letter from your mother this morning. The Locke heir is the least of your problems. Your family has now officially washed their hands of you."

Farrell paled. "Mother won't forsake me!"

"Of course she will. Why do you think she sent you to ingratiate yourself with me in the first place? Because she was fed up having to pay for your weaknesses. But you've outdone yourself this time, haven't you? Your stupidity at the Locke estate gave your mother what she finally needed, an excuse to be done with you for good. But I've assured her I will take care of you."

Farrell laughed in relief. "I've grown on you, haven't I? A chip off of the old tree, eh?"

"That was your first mistake, to compare yourself to me. To live a life with nothing to be proud of? Did you really aspire to that?"

"Isn't that what you've done?"

"Indeed, but as you see, I can and always have been able to afford to sin. A debauched luxury, as it were. You, on the other hand, have done nothing but hold your hand out to your mother, expecting *her* to pay for your sins. It's fortunate for you that she didn't know just how deeply in debt you really are or she would have turned her back on you long ago."

"But you're going to pay off my debts now? It's a trifle amount to you. I would have asked you sooner . . . but . . ."

"Yes, we know why you didn't. You didn't want to appear

to have your hand out, when you had it out the moment you walked in my door."

"I'm your son, damnit! Just because you didn't raise me doesn't make me any less your responsibility. You can't leave everything to that other bastard of yours. I deserve at least half—"

"You didn't want half, you wanted it all. Did you think I wouldn't find out what you've done, what you've attempted? How dare you try to kill my heir!"

"Because you're an old bastard making the wrong choice!" Farrell snarled at him. "He's no better than I am. With him gone, you'll have no choice but to leave it all to me."

"The minds of fools still manage to amaze me. That would never have come to pass, boy. Reward a pathetic imitation of myself? Not bloody likely. But you're too stupid to recognize the truth when you hear it. You would still try to kill him, wouldn't you? Even when it would net you nothing."

"I hate him because you favor him! Just as the earl favored Justin over me!"

"Envy, jealousy, sloth—if I had a shred of regret for what I'm going to do, you've put it to rest. I suppose I should be glad you bragged to that moneylender that I was your father. It expedites this nicely, that he came to me quite some time ago. If you don't know what that means, it means I'm already in possession of your debts."

Farrell started laughing. "Ha! I knew you couldn't forsake your own flesh and blood. Thank you, Father. But you should know, that blighter still takes payment on my debt from me. I'll have to get that back from him."

"Truly, you didn't inherit this stupidity from me. He accepts your mother's trinkets because I told him to. You weren't to know that your freedom rests in my hands until I was done being amused by you. That day has arrived. Can you pay off your debt today, Farrell Exter?"

"You know I can't."

"Did you hear that, magistrate?"

"Every word, m'lord."

Farrell gasped and swung around to see the large men blocking the doorway. There was a scuffle as he tried to escape. Garth closed his eyes, too tired to be interested any longer. But a fragrance warned him he couldn't sleep just yet, a scent he hadn't smelled in over thirty years. It surrounded him, took him back to a time of innocence. . . .

"Like me, he won't be missed," Garth said without opening his eyes. "But I'm sorry you had to witness that, Father."

"Cleaning up your mistakes this late in life?" Owen responded.

"One of them." Garth opened his eyes to feast them on his father. The old man had aged well. Garth had resisted the urge, all these years, to find that out sooner. "How much did you overhear?"

"Enough to hope his debt warrants a long term."

"He will end his days in prison," Garth said cryptically. "I take it you got my letter?"

Owen nodded as he came forward. "It was eloquent. It actually sounded as if you were dead, until I got to the postscript that you were still alive."

"I was too tired last night to rewrite it. It wasn't supposed to be sent until I was gone, but Devin found me, so I suspect you'll be hearing from him soon now that he knows the truth. Figured you might appreciate prior warning."

"I never thought I would have reason to thank you for anything, but thank you for Devin. I wish I could have known sooner, but you explained why you kept him a secret, and even I agree with your reasoning. You never cared about your legitimate children, much less your bastards."

"I don't have as many as you assumed. I wish I could have known this one sooner, too, but, don't worry, I made sure he won't remember me with fondness. You two can hate me together."

"I never hated you, Son. I hated what you did to yourself, and to others. I hated that you never felt remorse for those you wronged."

"It takes death to want atonement—when it's too late," Garth said tiredly.

"It's never too late to ask for forgiveness."

Incredibly, tears filled Garth's eyes. He shouldn't ask. He knew the answer. Too late was too late. "Could you forgive me, Father?"

"I already have."

Chapter Fifty-Four

HER EYES WERE SO red from crying, Amanda wasn't letting anyone other than Alice into her room. She felt bad, though, to use the same excuse with her father that Ophelia was giving the guests who asked after her, that she wasn't feeling well. Preston didn't insist on seeing for himself, as Rafe did. All he'd said was "When you're ready to talk, I'm here," which made it pretty clear that he knew she wasn't really sick.

Rafe must have blabbed—before or after he got back from calling out Farrell Exter? Ophelia had told her about that, and how angry Rafe was that he didn't get his hands on the would-be rapist. But at least Exter's family had assured Rafe that Farrell would have no more help from them ever again, and because his debts were so high, they expected him to be in debtors' prison soon. His brother Justin had even confided that would be less embarrassing to them than a scandal over what he'd attempted to do and hoped Rafe would be satisfied that he'd be in prison for a long time.

Most of the guests had already gone home. Only a few

stragglers were left. Having decided that she was going to be an old maid after all, Amanda knew it was time to stop hiding. The thought of marrying one of her previous choices just for the sake of getting married was now abhorrent to her when her heart was already taken. She'd have to let her family know and went downstairs to find her father. She'd let her beaus know, too, if any of them were still there.

Reaching the bottom of the grand stairs, she was shocked to see the butler opening the front door—with Devin on the other side of it. Panicking, she swung about before he noticed her and came face-to-face with Kendall Goswick blocking a quick escape. Not now!

"I trust your appearance means you are feeling better?" Kendall's tone seemed a bit stiff, but that wasn't surprising. He'd come here just to see her, but she'd been absent the last few days of the party!

"Yes, I—"

"I saw you riding with Devin the other morning. I confess I was struck with jealousy that you prefer to spend time with him instead of me."

It sounded as if he was still jealous. She ought to leave it at that, but couldn't. He deserved to know why she was going to be an old maid.

"He was teaching me to ride so I could ride with you, at least that's how it started."

"Good God, the truth would have been preferable!"

"That was the truth, but—you're right, I did fall in love with him. I'm sorry, Kendall. You really were my first choice before that happened."

"I will take my leave now." He bowed stiffly. "I'm sure you two will be very happy."

"Kendall—"

He didn't stop. He quickly ran up the stairs to collect his belongings. She didn't try again to stop him. She felt so bad for dashing *his* hopes.

Then she heard the voice behind her that could make her heart quicken. Usually. It just made her want to cry now.

"Who was he wishing happy?" Devin asked.

She took a deep breath. She blinked back the tears in her eyes. She wouldn't turn to face him, though. "You and I. He didn't give me a chance to tell him I've decided to never marry."

"Never is a long time, Mandy."

She heard the amusement in his tone, she just doubted her hearing. He wouldn't dare find this amusing!

"What choice do I have?" she said bleakly. "You've ruined me for any other man."

He shook his head. "You aren't ruined, not in the least."

"I didn't mean because of what we did. I mean—oh, never mind. If you've come to give me the reasons why you won't marry me, save your breath. That you simply don't love me would have sufficed. *Nothing* else is worth this—"

"In here, you two."

Amanda winced at her father's stern tone and expression when she saw him standing by his study door. She followed him into the room. She hoped Devin wouldn't, that he'd just leave. But he came in behind her and closed the door. Preston took the seat at his desk and indicated the chairs in front of it. Amanda shook her head. She felt she was going to burst into tears at any moment and run out before anything was said.

"I have given you both more leeway than I ever should have, because I was informed by a reliable source that you've fallen in love with each other and just hadn't realized it yet," Preston said. "My own observations support that fact. So what, pray tell, are you both waiting for? Why haven't you asked for her hand, Devin?"

Amanda gasped. "Father!"

"Quiet, m'dear. I cornered your maid. I know exactly how much you've been crying your heart out over this man since he disappeared. I demand to know why, when it's clear to everyone else that he loves you."

She bolted in embarrassment. But Devin didn't let her get to the door, wrapping his arms around her, ignoring her struggle to get loose.

Over the top of her head he told Preston. "There is nothing I want more than to marry your daughter. But I knew when you learned the truth about me, you wouldn't allow it. So I couldn't tell her how much I love her. As impulsive and brave as she is, she would have defied you and married me anyway. I couldn't do that to her. She would have come to regret hurting you."

Amanda had stopped struggling and put her arms around Devin. He felt it and looked down at her, let go to cup her cheeks in his hands. "I told your brother the whole truth, about myself, about what we did. I was pretty much leaving my heart in his hands. If he could say that my illegitimacy didn't matter, then nothing on this earth would have stopped me from marrying you—other than you. But I've changed my mind about leaving the decision to him, or to your father, for that matter. Mandy, I want you no matter what, and if you'll have me, I *will* marry you, even if we don't have your family's blessing. I'll make you so happy, there will be no regrets, and once your family sees that, maybe they'll come around and forgive me—"

Preston coughed. "I could have done without hearing that.

But I will say in your defense that you simply don't know this family well enough yet."

"What he means by that, *and* what I tried to tell you before, is we don't judge a man on something *he* didn't do," Amanda said. "You haven't done anything except make me not want to live without you. Yes, I'll marry you. I love you! If I were strong enough, I'd drag *you* to the altar."

Devin was looking a little bit amazed. But he wanted to hear it confirmed by her father. "My illegitimacy really wouldn't have had you turn me away?"

"No, it wouldn't have. Mandy's happiness means more to me than any trifle like that. But—I better never hear of her crying again because of you."

Devin laughed and got a groan out of her, he hugged her so tightly. "I assure you, m'lord, she will never find fault with me again." Then he bent his head to whisper by her ear, "If you weren't sure, that promise was for you. I hurt us both by trying to do what I thought was right for you, instead of just trusting that we could overcome any obstacle. I'll never make that mistake again. I love you too much."

Preston cleared his throat and stood up. "Well, that went much quicker than I figured. I'll go make Ophelia deliriously happy now by telling her she has a wedding to plan." He headed to the door to give them some time alone, but before closing it behind him, he added, "And stay out of my daughter's bedroom—until after the wedding."

Amanda hid her face against Devin's chest with the realization that her father knew *too* much. She was going to kill her brother!

"I can honor that, if you can," Devin said to her.

She peeked up at him. "This passion you make me feel is a bit overwhelming. I'm not sure I can."

He groaned. "There are other rooms." He began kissing her. "Including this one."

She took a moment to savor his taste, his tender touch, before it sank in what he meant, and she broke away. "Not in my father's study!"

He laughed. "I was teasing. I will respect your father's wishes. That's the very least I can do for the man who has lifted this guilt from my shoulders. I would have married you anyway, Mandy, but to not have your father's blessing would have kept our happiness from being complete. You do understand that, don't you?"

"I understand it worried you. It never even occurred to me. But you!" She wagged a finger at him. "You still tried to foist Kendall on me when you and I share more interests than I ever would with him—fishing, horse racing, and, believe it or not, I've even come to enjoy riding."

"If I wasn't sure I didn't stand a chance with you, I would have pointed that out sooner."

She grinned. "So Cupid would have recommended himself?"

"Imagine my amazement, to be struck by my own arrow." He put a hand to her cheek. "I'm sorry for not presenting my misgivings to you, but to your brother instead. Leaving it to your family to decide, when I was so sure they wouldn't decide in my favor, was the hardest thing I've ever done. But on the way back here, I knew I couldn't do it. I couldn't leave *our* happiness to chance like that."

"I wish you had come to your senses sooner, before I soaked my bed with tears." She'd only been teasing. Her happiness had already wiped away that heartache. But he winced. She threw her arms around his neck. "It's all right, I forgive you! I cried because I love you so much and didn't understand. Now I do. But never hold back your feelings again, Devin, please."

"Never. I will share anything and everything from this day forward."

"I promise to as well. Now come." She took his hand to lead him out of the room. "I want to share this happiness with my family. I think some of my aunts are still here. Oh! How could I forget." She stopped, turned to ask, "What happened with your father?"

"He's really not worth mentioning, Mandy."

"Stop it. You *just* promised me no more secrets."

He gave her a wry smile. "I didn't want to tarnish the moment. I will say I'm glad I got to meet him at least once before he dies, if only to understand that it was an act of kindness, probably the only one he ever did, to stay out of my life. So I have my answers, which is all I ever wanted from him."

"It was deliberate? For your own good?"

"Yes, but he's not worth a single one of your thoughts."

"I'm just sorry he wasn't what you'd hoped for."

He chucked her chin and tried to lighten the mood. "That's because you're too sympathetic! We're going to have to work on that flaw."

She understood what he was doing and went along with it, snorting. "It's not a flaw. And I'll be grateful to your father, thank you very much, for giving me you."

"The irony is, I have reason to be grateful to him, too, for one unexpected gift—a grandfather who is still alive and is already a friend. I will be proud to introduce you to Owen Culley."

"Owen?" She smiled. "My family has known him for years.

368 ᒐ JOHANNA LINDSEY

Oh, and wait until you meet *my* grandmother! She can't remember a thing anymore, she'll even call you by every name but your own, but you'll adore her."

"Your family will soon be mine. I expect my feelings will mirror yours where they are concerned." Then he pushed her up against the wall, a teasing light in his amber eyes. "Were you really going to be an old maid? Really?"

"Weren't you going to be the male version?"

He laughed. "No, I was just determined to never let love into my life because I knew how much it could hurt. I had no idea how wonderful it could be instead—until I met you."

Such a wealth of emotions filled her heart as she gazed into his eyes. It hadn't happened overnight. It had taken much longer than anyone expected. But love had finally found her and it was *so* worth the wait.

Epilogue

THE ENTIRE LOCKE FAMILY had wanted a spring wedding. Devin had been willing, wanting to please his new in-laws. But Amanda had put her foot down. With her father's edict ringing in her ears and Devin determined to respect Preston's wishes, the most she would delay was a month, so her wedding reception would be one last party, as it were, to finish off the current Season. It was amazing how many other engagements were announced in that month, though most of them were from her flock of beaus, so they'd obviously had second choices lined up all along. Amanda thought that was funny. Even John Trask found an heiress.

Robert Brigston's congratulations had been the most hearty the day she became Devin's wife, surprising Amanda at how genuinely pleased Robert was for her. But Devin had been by her side when they received it, and seeing her brow knit in confusion after Robert walked away, he asked, "Something wrong?"

She whispered, "He wasn't invited to the wedding. He crashed it just to say he was happy for us?"

Devin laughed. "Told you to trust me, that he wasn't for you. In fact, he's probably the most happy, next to us, that you're marrying me instead of him."

She raised a brow at him. "Do you realize how odd that sounds?"

"That's all I'm going to say about it," he teased.

"Say about what?" William asked as he and Blythe came up to offer their own good wishes.

"About her ex-beaus," Devin said.

"Ah, those poor sods, and, no, I don't feel as if I'm in that group anymore." William chuckled. "You were right about the Honorable Margery Jenkin, Devin. I swear I'm in love already, least it feels like it. She's wonderful!"

"Sounds like he's in love to me!" Blythe added, grinning, then leaned closer to show Amanda her own engagement ring.

"Lord Oliver?" Amanda guessed.

"Yes!"

Amanda had already known that secret, though she didn't let on that Oliver, considering her a friend, had told her at the house party that he was going to ask for Blythe's hand. It had been their secret, but she was glad to know that Blythe had accepted his proposal. Love was definitely in the air, and it wasn't even close to springtime yet!

It had been a private wedding at Norford, just family and friends, but still quite a crowd for the reception, with most of their neighbors invited for that. Amelia Dutton was there with her father and mother. Amanda had delighted the child when she'd asked her to be her flower girl. Owen Culley was present, sitting at a table with Devin's aunt and uncle. Owen had cried the day Devin took Amanda to meet him and introduced him as his grandfather. She didn't want her husband anxious about anything, ever again, and that could have been a difficult meeting if Devin and Owen hadn't already been friends before they learned they were closely related, too.

The newlyweds were taking ship to the south of France for their honeymoon, for some warmer weather and fishing! They hadn't yet decided where they were going to live afterward, although Amanda was surprised by more options than she'd counted on. Devin even owned a town house in London! Although he'd also mentioned the farm in Lancashire, he said if she picked the new farm instead, it would give him an excuse to finally remodel the house there. She rather liked that idea the best, since some of the remodeling decisions could be hers.

Approaching the hour to leave, Amanda slipped upstairs to change out of her wedding dress. Devin, watching her go, didn't even want to be parted from her that long and started to follow her. But then Ophelia and Julie both converged on him. They didn't come together, just happened to both arrive in the same moment, and they both had coin purses in their hands.

He rolled his eyes at them. "You weren't *really* thinking of paying Cupid for arranging his own wedding, were you?"

They both blushed, though Julie snorted, "'Course not."

Ophelia said, "Just a little wedding gift," and slapped her purse against his chest the same way she'd done the day she hired him.

And just as he'd done that day, he shoved it back into her hands. "Just so we're clear, you can lavish whatever you want on my wife, but you are *not* paying me for making her mine, when today is the happiest day of my life."

He left them to follow his wife upstairs. Julie stared at Ophelia. "So you had a hand in this?"

Ophelia grinned. "Just a little nudge in the right direction is all. I'd noticed the night she first clapped eyes on him how many glowers she sent his way."

"Humph. That should have warned you to keep her away from him."

"When she hadn't so much as raised a brow at her other beaus?"

Upstairs, Devin smiled as he realized he didn't need to knock on Amanda's door anymore and opened it. But she wasn't alone. He stared at her maid and said, "You can go. I'll help my wife out of her dress."

As he closed the door on Alice and turned a heated look on Amanda, she grinned. "Is that so?" she teased.

He started to slowly cross the room to her. "I have a feeling I'm going to be doing this a lot—now that I can."

She laughed when he tumbled them onto the bed, giving her a preview of what married life was going to be like with him. He hadn't kept his hands off her before the wedding. They'd been caught in amorous embraces a number of times. He'd dragged her into empty rooms every chance he got. But he always stopped short of making love to her, honoring her father's wishes. So it was quite a frustrating time, for them both. Until today.

She didn't think they would be leaving the room anytime soon, he was kissing her so passionately. He did get her dress off, and she was right, they didn't leave the bed.

She couldn't stop smiling, but it was hard to smile and kiss at the same time.

He noticed. "Pleasant thoughts?"

"More'n that. Do you even know how happy I am today?"

He started to tease, "After three Seasons—"

She poked him to silence with a laugh. "This has nothing to

do with anything other than you. Love really does make all the difference, doesn't it? I'm so glad I waited for you!"

He kissed her deeply, but he wasn't done teasing. "So am I. Old maids are more my style."

"Oh!"

He rolled her over before she could sputter anything else and, in one fluid movement, entered her, filled her, and put every other thought from her mind. Oh, God, he was every bit as virile as she'd thought the day she first saw him. She'd just had no idea at the time that would be *just* what she wanted!

She'd barely caught her breath, was still holding Devin tight to her, when they heard Rafe yell from the other side of the door, "You're going to miss your ship!"

Devin grinned and snuggled his face between Amanda's breasts a moment before he leaned up to yell back, "We'll catch another ship!"

Rafe, as he walked away, mumbled something about starting honeymoons too soon. Amanda was blushing.

Devin raised a brow at her. "It bothers you that he knows what we're doing in here?" he asked curiously.

"No, I almost told him what we did the night of his birthday ball, before you did! I think it would have shocked him, coming from me."

"He'll get used to the idea that you aren't just his baby sister anymore. You're mine now, to have and to hold—" He paused, his expression turning serious. "Make one more vow for me, Mandy. Promise me you'll never leave me."

She knew he was thinking about his mother. She was almost moved to tears—for him. Holding him tight, she whispered, "I promise! But I'll have one from you now."

"Anything."

"Swear we'll never sleep in separate bedrooms!"

He leaned back, incredulous. "Are you out of your mind? My bed is your bed and I'll break down any doors that say otherwise."

She had a feeling he would, too. After all, she did marry a wonderful brute. The thought made her laugh!